D1492440

RED TRAITOR

www.penguin.co.uk

ALSO BY OWEN MATTHEWS

Fiction

Black Sun

Non-fiction

An Impeccable Spy

Glorious Misadventures

Stalin's Children

RED TRAITOR

OWEN MATTHEWS

BANTAM PRESS

TRANSWORLD PUBLISHERS
Penguin Random House, One Embassy Gardens,
8 Viaduct Gardens, London SW11 7BW
www.penguin.co.uk

Transworld is part of the Penguin Random House group of companies
whose addresses can be found at global.penguinrandomhouse.com

First published in Great Britain in 2021 by Bantam Press,
an imprint of Transworld Publishers

This edition published by arrangement with Doubleday,
an imprint of Knopf Doubleday Publishing Group,
a division of Penguin Random House LLC

Copyright © Owen Matthews 2021

Owen Matthews has asserted his right under the Copyright,
Designs and Patents Act 1988 to be identified as the author of this work.

This is a work of fiction. All incidents and dialogue, and all characters with
the exception of some well-known historical and public figures, are products of the
author's imagination and are not to be construed as real. Where real-life
historical figures and public figures appear, the situations, incidents, and dialogues concerning
those persons are entirely fictional and are not intended to depict actual events or to
change the entirely fictional nature of the work. In all other respects, any resemblance
to persons living or dead is entirely coincidental.

Every effort has been made to obtain the necessary permissions with
reference to copyright material, both illustrative and quoted. We apologize
for any omissions in this respect and will be pleased to make the
appropriate acknowledgements in any future edition.

A CIP catalogue record for this book
is available from the British Library.

ISBNs
9781787634961 (hb)
9781787634978 (tpb)

Printed and bound in Great Britain by Clays Ltd, Elcograf S.p.A.

The authorized representative in the EEA is Penguin Random House Ireland,
Morrison Chambers, 32 Nassau Street, Dublin D02 YH68.

Penguin Random House is committed to a sustainable
future for our business, our readers and our planet. This book
is made from Forest Stewardship Council® certified paper.

For Xenia, Nikita, and Teddy

CONTENTS

CONTENTS

PROLOGUE

ARKHIPOV

Severomorsk Naval Base, Headquarters of the Red Banner
Northern Fleet of the USSR
Dawn, 4 July 1962

Breathe. Breathe, Vasily. Captain First Class Vasily Arkhipov fought his way out of his nightmare like a drowning swimmer struggling for the surface. Gasping down air, he forced his eyes open. Pale Arctic summer sunlight streamed through the thin curtains. He flexed his hands, cramped from clutching the damp sheets tangled around his body.

He inhaled, slowly. No submarine stink here. No smell of unwashed men and strong tobacco, no taste of sweet Navy tea in his mouth. No tang of molten solder, polymer sealant, hot oil, battery and reactor-coolant fumes choking your nose. No invisible poison in this air.

Arkhipov leaned over, fumbled for his watch, squinted to focus on the luminous dial. He followed the second hand as it ticked toward 0515. One year and one hour, precisely, since the reactor accident.

Eons had passed since that distant and only half-remembered horror. But there were times—more or less every night that Arkhipov refused to take the knockout pills the docs had given him—when he was still in the middle of it, time snagging back on itself and entangling him like seaweed.

It never felt like a nightmare. Not really. Rather, Arkhipov had the sensation of waking in a parallel and absolutely real world, located somewhere on the other side of sleep. A clamoring place of panic and screams. A familiar place of mayhem, steam heat, and fear, stuck on an endless loop like a scratched record. In Arkhipov's waking world the dead were invisible. But he knew they were not absent. His restless dead were always present, always busily locked in their agonies, always ready to come and assert their claims.

The clock in the control room of Northern Fleet submarine K-19 had been electronic. It purred rather than ticked, the hands sliding over the minutes and hours smoothly, watch after watch. Arkhipov's dream always began in that last moment of calm. The eerie silence of K-19, its futuristic smell. The metallic odor of the new instruments in their smooth, green-painted steel cabinets full of dials, glowing like a thousand eyes. And the quiet of the ship. Instead of the continuous, headache-making thud of a diesel engine, K-19's brand-new nuclear reactor emitted a low thrum, deep and powerful. The Soviet Navy's newest missile submarine cruised ninety meters below the surface of the North Atlantic as smoothly and quietly as a spaceship.

He would try to will that sliding second hand to stop. Arkhipov always knew what was coming but was powerless to speak, to warn the comrades as they settled sleepily into their stations at the beginning of the fateful morning watch of 4 July 1961.

A blankly dreaming instrument panel spread before the commander's station. Arkhipov had just taken his post in the skipper's leatherette chair. Officer of the watch, commander of the ship while his superiors slumbered. An awesome honor and responsibility, as the Political Officer never tired of telling him. In front of him, Postev, the lieutenant in charge of propulsion, was slumped at his station in his spotless engineer's overalls, fighting sleep.

Pay attention, Postev, Arkhipov wanted to shout. Wake up! But his dream self remained relentlessly mute.

Within hours, Arkhipov knew, Postev's young face would be scorched scarlet, the skin peeling as if scalded. The lieutenant would be screaming, and Arkhipov would be trying to hold him down while the medics struggled to cut through the thick rubber of his thermal suit to get a morphine syringe into him.

Wake up!

The dream would always fall into a familiar groove. The intercom light from the reactor control room blinks on. Red. Something urgent.

Arkhipov snatches up the telephone in the communications panel and presses a switch.

"Sir? You'd better come. Quickly."

A rising edge of panic in the duty sergeant's voice.

Arkhipov and Postev sprint toward the reactor control center. The companionway is lit scarlet by red emergency lights spilling through the doorway. Yury Postev crouches forward, his face just inches from a dial labeled Reactor Coolant Pressure. The needle is vibrating violently, almost at zero. As Arkhipov watches, the needle settles on its restraining peg and goes still.

A klaxon sounds. Arkhipov feels a sickening tightness in his bowels.

"Shit," says Postev, glancing over to another panel. Swearing on board is strictly forbidden. For officers, especially. Postev looks over his shoulder and hisses to Arkhipov. "Sir—we've lost coolant pressure. Both coolant pumps are out of action."

Before Arkhipov can reply, the whole control panel blossoms with scarlet warning lights. A large panel over the controls blinks on, illuminating the words Safety Control Rods Activation Mechanism—SCRAM. The reactor is shutting itself down automatically. One by one, a few of the indicators go green.

"Did it work?" Arkhipov asks. The lieutenant doesn't immediately respond as he swings from one instrument to the other, cursing as he goes.

"Postev! Is the reactor shut down?"

In reply the young officer simply straightens, white-faced, and points at a large dial marked Core Temperature.

"Control rods are down. Reactor successfully SCRAMed, sir. But look."

The reactor's temperature is climbing perceptibly.

"Residual heat, sir. The core will keep cooking at low power for about a hundred hours till it's finally burned out. Without coolant, it's going to melt down. Burn through the hull."

"How long?"

In the four minutes since Arkhipov has been in the reactor control room, the dial has moved from 250 to 325 degrees Celsius, and is rising fast.

"Don't know, sir. A few hours."

Arkhipov hurries forward to the command deck. He struggles to keep his voice loud and steady. He sees his own fear reflected in the eyes of the men as they turn to him, the senior officer on the bridge.

Eyes that will remain on him, always.

Back in fitful sleep, Arkhipov turned restlessly in his bed. Under closed lids his eyes flickered, and his fists clawed at the sheets as though he were desperately seeking to escape. But the bedding only wound itself closer around him, tight as a shroud.

MOROZOV

Pioneers' Ponds, Central Moscow
Dawn, 4 July 1962

Under the windows of Colonel Oleg Morozov's apartment, the surface of Pioneers' Ponds spread like a black mirror. Up above the rooftops a pearly gray was beginning to light the eastern sky. But down at water level darkness lingered, disturbed only by the single Cyclopean head-light of the first tram of the day as it rumbled down Malaya Bronnaya Street. In the apartment buildings that surrounded the park one or two lights flicked on.

Morozov's uniform tunic hung over the back of a chair. On the desk that faced the window were a metal table lamp embossed with Soviet hammers and sickles, a copy of *Novy Mir* magazine, a stack of official reports carrying the stamp of the Soviet Ministry of Defense. Next to them stood a sawn-off brass artillery shell case full of cigarette butts and a Wehrmacht pressed-steel gasoline lighter. On a silver tray under the lamp lay a tiny curl of paper no bigger than a cigarette paper covered in tiny, almost undecipherable, typed script.

On the sofa, under a cocked lamp, Morozov hunched over, scribbling notes from a book held in his lap. His concentration was intense, inter-rupted only by the occasional whir of the building's elevator and a faint stirring from the bedroom which made him freeze, listening. At length he snapped the book shut and reread the notes he had been making.

Morozov swore softly before crossing the room and crunching the paper into a ball and placing it in the ashtray. He flicked the German lighter and set fire to his notes and to the tiny strip of paper.

Once both were burned to ash, he leaned across the desk to open the window, flooding the room with chilly early-morning air. Morozov wore only a shirt with uniform breeches, and the dawn breeze bit fresh and clean through the smoke-filled study. But he sat on, oblivious to the draft that stirred the papers on his desk, holding a lit cigarette in his hand and watching the smoke stream out into the breaking day. At length he shrugged into his uniform tunic. The jacket was still snug on his muscular shoulders, but Morozov had to breathe in to button it down the belly. He moved into the hall and pulled on a pair of boots and a raincoat. Taking care not to wake his sleeping family, he closed the front door silently behind him.

Morozov was alone as he crossed the Ponds. Or almost alone. A street sweeper with a threadbare birch-twig brush worked his way down the sidewalk. On the corner of Yermolayevsky Lane, an elderly man paraded a wiry terrier. The pay phone on the corner was deserted.

The Colonel picked up the heavy Bakelite telephone receiver, deposited his two-kopeck piece in the slot, and dialed. He waited as the phone rang on and on.

"Yes?" A woman's voice, thick with sleep, answered. "I am listening."

Morozov hesitated before speaking, listening to the soft breathing on the other end of the line.

"Daria Vladimirovna? Forgive me for calling so early. I wanted to catch you before you left for work."

"There is no Daria Vladimirovna here. You have the wrong number."

"My apologies, citizen."

Morozov replaced the receiver and hurried back home before his wife and daughter awoke.

The dog walker kept up his trudging pace. But instead of making yet another circle of the pond, he continued straight toward the Garden Ring. As he approached a parked Volga sedan, a heavyset man got out of the passenger seat to make room. The dog's lead was taken from the old man's hand. As he settled into the car, the driver deferentially held out the receiver of a radiotelephone.

"Sir—the Ears. They're standing by."

The man grunted in acknowledgment and spoke into the receiver.

"Hear me there, boy? Need a recording of the pay phone on the corner of Malaya Bronnaya and Yermolayevsky. Call made today at 0548. Bring it to my office. Half an hour."

Half a mile across town, in the basement of the Central Telegraph office on Gorky Street, a young KGB lieutenant tore off a sheet of notepaper and set off at a trot down a subterranean corridor. He entered a low room filled with ranks of reel-to-reel signal-activated tape recorders, some turning, most not. Finding the right machine, he flicked the stop switch and marked the place with a white wax pencil. Then he pressed rewind and waited until the magnetic reel ran all the way back and its flapping end spun free. Cradling the reel to his chest, the officer sprinted from the room.

KUZNETSOV
Sagua la Grande Air Base, Cuba
Dawn, 4 July 1962

A dawn breeze off the sea woke KGB major Vadim Kuznetsov, bringing with it the corrupt, sweet smell of clear-cut undergrowth. Stirring jungle trees hissed like surf, and a cacophony of birds and insects started up a clamoring morning chorus. Kuznetsov kicked off his sweat-soaked cotton sheet, groped under the bed for his thermos, and thirstily swigged cold lemon tea.

In Cuba for nearly nine months and he still couldn't get used to the cloying heat of the place, its indecent fecundity. And he still couldn't get used to the rum. Unlike vodka, it didn't taste like it was bad for you. Just a warm, sweet buzz as it went down with no warning of the revenge it would take in the morning. Sweet but dangerous. Just like Cuba itself, he heard himself quipping. More or less nightly.

Kuznetsov reached up to switch on the squeaking ceiling fan and flopped back down on his cot. The State Security apartment building was newly built of prefabricated concrete panels, as haphazardly fitted together as any structure in the Moscow suburbs. The furniture was Romanian, apparently a gift from the fraternal Securitate secret police to their Socialist brethren in the Caribbean. The red pine was already splitting from the damp. There was only one air-conditioning unit in the whole military base, a hulking Carrier unit in the villa of a Batista-era plantation owner which now served as the officers' mess and bar.

The bar. Kuznetsov ran a sweaty hand down his face and beard. Last night. Whose idea had the goodbye party been? Not his. One of the Cuban Air Force colonels, doubtless. Kuznetsov remembered guitars, scratchy Cuban Revolutionary songs on the record player, a fog of cigar smoke, a new batch of suspiciously pretty waitresses. Did he even . . . dance? Local girls were off-limits for Kuznetsov and his fellow KGB officers. So he'd drunk too much instead. As usual. And maybe danced. Just a little. But only to show fraternal solidarity.

Kuznetsov's suitcase stood, packed, by the door. A day's ride in a bouncing Volga sedan would bring him to Havana in time to catch the evening flight. This time tomorrow, after stopovers in Madrid and maybe Frankfurt, he'd be in Moscow. Kuznetsov had been surprised, when he first came to Cuba, by how much he missed his hometown. Missed Moscow's solidity, the city's trundling pace, the dour lack of color and of histrionics. Now he was surprised by how much he didn't want to return, even for a couple of weeks of consultations with his bosses in the Lubyanka. Kuznetsov remembered some foolish song he'd heard the Soviet air crews singing: "It's good there, where we're not at."

He reached for his watch—a chunky Raketa chronograph he'd won in some bet from a drunken MiG pilot. The commander's office would soon be open. It was time to retrieve the progress reports he'd spent the last week diligently typing up for his bosses in Moscow from the fire-proof safe in his chief's office.

Giving up any hope of getting back to sleep, Kuznetsov rose and dressed. He was particularly proud of the beige cotton tropical suit he'd bought in a commission shop in Havana, made by Haspel in New Orleans. It made him look like a capitalist exploiter, his fellow KGB men had joked. Hardly suitable for the corridors of the Committee for State Security in Moscow. Fuck them. Kuznetsov liked the look of himself in his suave suit. He *enjoyed* looking like a foreigner. As he buttoned his shirt, Kuznetsov looked out over the newly built base. When he had arrived the previous winter, the place had been a sea of uprooted tree trunks, mud, and ruts that harbored angry, homeless snakes. Now the ground was raked flat, crisscrossed with asphalt roads and rows of prefabricated huts and hangars.

In the middle distance, rising slightly above the tree line, was the camouflage-painted outline of a radar station, the antenna pointed like a cupped ear toward the northern Caribbean—and, just ninety miles away, the United States of America.

VASIN

Frunze Embankment, Moscow
Dawn, 4 July 1962

Vasin woke hungover, his neck smarting from sunburn and his face rubbed raw by the sofa cushion. His wife, Vera, had chosen the garish East German sofa bed, the newest and most expensive one available. But the bristly nylon plush tortured Vasin nightly.

Vera's voice—pitched to the note of high sarcasm she reserved for waking him up—called from the kitchen.

"Sashaaaaa? Phone for you. The *kontora*."

The *kontora*—literally, the office. Also, a not-so-respectful nickname for the KGB. Vera followed her husband with her eyes as he staggered down the corridor, stumbling into the walls as he came.

"One moment," she said into the receiver. "The Comrade Colonel is on his way. He has been *very busy* this morning."

Instead of handing Vasin the receiver, she put it down on the counter just as he reached for it. Then she pushed past him toward the bathroom, primly hugging her silk Chinese dressing gown closed as she went.

"Vasin speaking."

It was his boss General Orlov's most venomous secretary, summoning Vasin for an unscheduled meeting at the Lubyanka in tones of icy formality. Vasin stammered his acknowledgments, glanced at the kitchen clock, and swore under his breath. Forty minutes. On the smart new stove an unappetizing breakfast of burned buckwheat porridge smoldered in the pan. No time. He urgently needed a shave and a shower. At the instant the thought entered his mind, he heard Vera noisily bolting the bathroom door and turning on the water as if commanded by his brain waves.

"Vera? Can I get in there for a second?"

Silence. Vasin knocked on the door irritably.

"I need to get ready for work."

The water stopped running and Vera slid back the bolt. She gave her husband an indignant look before flouncing past him into the bedroom and slamming the door.

The Vasins' smart new apartment, three whole rooms on the Frunze Embankment, looked out onto an apple tree–lined boulevard and the Moscow River. It was the stage on which the tragicomedy of Vasin's family life played out, with pathetic variations, every morning and evening. Nine months before, he'd returned from his previous assignment covered in glory. The *kontora* had rearranged his life to reflect Vasin's new status as General Orlov's favored pet. A new apartment, a new car, a promotion—and, in a voodoo flourish, a new wife. Of sorts. Somehow, since his return, Vera had become another person. Or to be more accurate, she treated her husband as though *he* had become another person. Someone important. Someone dangerous to her. Lieutenant Colonel Alexander Ilyich Vasin of the Committee for State Security—a man to be respected. And kept at a distance.

Vasin and Vera had quickly slipped into a stilted, unforced domestic theatricality. They spoke as if in front of an audience of unseen listeners. When they did speak, that is. Vera's initial respectful wariness had soon worn away to be replaced by a brooding, injured insolence. Their life had become a relentless mime play of unspoken reproach.

Vasin's fourteen-year-old son, Nikita, also had found himself pulled into the orbit of his father's mysterious new eminence. He was signed up for the elite Young Pioneer camp, Artek, and his schoolmates viewed him with new respect. Nikita treated his father differently, too, his habitual shyness shifting into a nervous awe. And the new respect with which his schoolmates and teachers treated the boy had only increased the poor kid's bashfulness.

There was not a moment of Vasin's waking or sleeping days—neither at home, nor in the clunky little car that he acquired with his promotion, nor in the newly built wooden dacha in the village of Vnukovo—where Vasin was not surrounded by reminders of the power of Lieutenant General Yury Orlov. He felt as trapped as a dragonfly in glass.

PART ONE

THE RESTLESS DEAD

Whether you like it or not, history is on our side.

SOVIET PREMIER NIKITA KHRUSHCHEV, 1956

1

The summer sunlight slanted through the heavy net curtains of General Orlov's office. The room was uncomfortably hot and smelled oppressively of floor polish. Vasin glanced around the table at the colleagues who had, like him, been abruptly summoned. Pushkov, the veteran KGB *rezident* who had won notoriety in the service by organizing the poisoning of Ukrainian nationalists and other collaborators after the war in Paris and Berlin. Ignatenko, the pudgy communications man with permanent dents in his flabby temples from his hours spent in headphones. Vasin's team of crack spy catchers, all melting in their chairs like ice cream on a hot sidewalk.

Nobody spoke.

Pushkov took a slim file marked TOP SECRET from a neat pile in front of him and used it, irreverently, to fan his face. There was a thumping clamor as the boss bustled in, flushed and irritable, as though it were they who had kept him waiting, not the other way around. Orlov took his place at the head of the table.

"Schultz has something for us," grunted Orlov without preamble. Ignoring the men in the room, he fixed his attention on the papers he had brought with him and began reading them with aggressive attention.

Vasin might have guessed. Boris Ignatyevich Schultz, the chief watcher on Vasin's surveillance team. Also—Vasin's instructor at the KGB school. Also—the best surveillance man in the business. Typical of Schultz, after all these fruitless months, to catch some kind of breakthrough on his night shift. And bloody typical of Schultz to call the head of the Special Cases Department—Orlov—rather than report to Vasin, his immediate superior.

Schultz was a skinny, stooped man with a cadaverous face and a dapper clipped mustache. He entered the conference room and winced at the sight of his colleagues as if at a roomful of particularly unpromising student spies. A young sergeant followed in his wake, lugging a bulky reel-to-reel tape recorder in both arms. As the kid busied himself with plugging in the machine, Schultz settled his lanky body into a chair next to Orlov's, folding into himself like a telescope.

"Telephone box on the corner of Malaya Bronnaya Street." Schultz's voice was reedy but commanding. "This morning. Just before six. Listen."

Schultz turned the dial that set the machine in motion. An electronic purr, then the rattling clicks of the number being dialed and connected.

"Yes? . . . I am listening."

"Daria Vladimirovna? Forgive me for calling so early. I wanted to catch you before you left for work."

Colonel Oleg Morozov's voice was unmistakable.

"There is no Daria Vladimirovna here. You have the wrong number."

"My apologies, citizen."

Schultz switched off the machine and made a grimace that might have been a smile. Vasin felt his pulse quickening.

"Morozov made no follow-up call, Boris Ignatyevich? To another number?"

"No follow-up call, Colonel Vasin." Schultz eyed his former pupil down the table with the tiniest nod of approval. Vasin, perhaps you are not such a total idiot, the old man's look said. Vasin pressed on.

"Our target gets up at dawn to make a single call to a wrong number from a phone box. A number he has never called from home, I presume? A number . . ."

"So who picked up?" Orlov spoke over Vasin. "Do we have an address? Have we got her in custody yet?"

Schultz made a small moue before answering.

"Comrade General. The number is listed to Dmitry Ulyanov Street Forty-Two. The Hotel Ulaanbataar. That line is installed in the loading bay of the kitchens, in fact. But . . ." Schultz, with the invincible confidence of the elderly, raised a hand before Orlov could interrupt him. "At six in the morning the place is full of deliverymen. At least eight trucks came in between five thirty and six thirty, according to the watchman, each with one driver and at least one loader. Many kitchen staff and members of the hotel administration passed the area. We have not been able to find any witnesses who saw anyone using the phone."

"An untraceable contact. A cutout." Orlov clasped his hands together and flexed his shoulders as though limbering for a boxing match. "Which means what, Schultz? Tell us, please."

"We have him, General. Morozov has contacted his controllers at the CIA. Activated himself. Or is acknowledging a contact. Over the past nine months of surveillance in Moscow, he has not put a foot wrong. We assume that Morozov has been under orders not to break cover till he has something important to report. So now . . ."

"Now we must do *what*? Colonel?" Orlov's head snapped toward Vasin. The other team members followed the General's lead, obediently looking to him for an answer.

"Now we arrest him, sir." Vasin straightened in his chair.

"No, Vasin."

Of course. Vasin should have known better. There was never a correct answer to the boss's rhetorical questions.

"Sorry, sir. First we must find out who he is working with."

"That is correct, Colonel Vasin. When you pull a weed, you do it by the root, not the leaves."

In the security forces of the glorious Soviet Motherland, everything must be connected to something else. Inside one spy must be the lead to another spy lurking inside him, like an endless set of matryoshka dolls.

Alone with Vasin after his colleagues shuffled out, Orlov made no move to rise. The General instead sat like a malevolent fungus, glaring down the conference table at his protégé. His small eyes danced with barely suppressed glee.

"Thank and praise the Lord God Almighty." Orlov's voice was a deep, emphatic hiss. The General had once studied for the priesthood, Vasin remembered, and kept his face blank. "The *Director* has been asking about PLUTO."

PLUTO—the suspected traitor in the heart of the Soviet security establishment. Orlov's obsession, and Vasin's daily nightmare. At the end of his last assignment, in the secret nuclear city of Arzamas-16, Vasin had invented an American spy. The case had been a mess, and Vasin had to bend—break—many rules to stop a misguided zealot obsessed with a nuclear holocaust. He regretted nothing. But to get out with his skin intact, Vasin had made the lunatic an American spy. It had seemed so neat, back then, to pin an invented sin on a dead man. More, Vasin had emerged with glory. Special Cases' new top spy catcher.

But now that Vasin's spy report had been duly logged, his fantasy had become official fact. And spies, real or not, need a handler. Which was why General Orlov had chosen Vasin to track down PLUTO. Connect your imaginary spy to a real one: the insoluble puzzle that Orlov had handed to his new favorite. Go on, Vasin, join the damn dots. Good luck. So for the last nine months Vasin had been chasing this ghost, chasing rumors, watching for the slightest hint that Colonel Oleg Morozov was in fact the fabled PLUTO.

"So now, finally, I can tell the Director that we have a breakthrough. Uncovering PLUTO will lead us to the next link. We find out what information he is passing to the Yankees. We find out who is supplying him that information. But most important, we find out who Morozov's *krysha* is. You understand me, Vasin?"

Krysha—literally, a roof. Criminal slang for protector. Vasin felt the world swim before his eyes. Yes. He understood exactly what Orlov meant. Or rather, *who*. The next link of the chain of treachery that Orlov imagined led ever upward, right into the very highest reaches of Soviet power.

"Morozov's *protector*, sir?" Vasin's mouth had gone dry. "A senior officer with whom he may be personally associated?"

"Precisely, Vasin. Perhaps Morozov is somebody's family friend. Perhaps he goes to barbecues at the dacha of some big pine cone. Goes on hunting parties with the top brass. Have you come across anyone like that, Vasin, since Morozov has been under your expert eye?"

He felt Orlov's eyes drilling into him. Oh yes—both men knew precisely who Orlov had in mind. Colonel Morozov's old pal, his dacha and hunting-party host. His personal friend and mentor, his boss and protector. None other than General Ivan Serov, head of the Main Intelligence Directorate of the General Staff of the Workers' and Peasants' Red Army. Better known as the GRU, the KGB's chief institutional rival. Serov—Orlov's great bureaucratic adversary. And, for reasons Vasin could not begin to understand, Orlov's personal enemy.

Vasin saw his boss's logic clearly enough. Use Morozov to get some dirt on the man's protector, Serov. Maybe some fatal dirt. What a thing it would be for Orlov to have the head of the rival service on the hook.

A few months before, Vasin had watched a new American film—part of a closed session for the exclusive benefit of *kontora* officers only, rather than for the general public—about a mad nineteenth-century sea captain who chased a phantom white whale around the seas of the world. Orlov was that captain, Special Cases was his ship—and his unfortunate first mate, destined to pursue the skipper's obsession to the ends of the earth, was Vasin.

"We *have* observed such an association, sir. As you know." Vasin's voice had become a whisper. "You believe that Comrade General Serov may be involved in the activities of the traitor Morozov?"

"If not involved, then perhaps Serov has been misguidedly covering for his friend? Either could be plausible. Our business admits no loose ends. You find a guilty man, Vasin."

Vasin summoned the courage to speak into Orlov's scorching gaze.

"You mean—find *Serov* guilty, sir?"

For a moment Vasin feared that his chief would swell and burst like an overripe puffball. But no. Orlov, always unpredictable, instead leaned back in his chair and raised his palms to the heavens with something like a chuckle.

"We follow the evidence, of course. The evidence of our own eyes and ears. The evidence in Morozov's eventual confession. Vasin. You have two loose ends to tie, one at the beginning of the Morozov story and another at the end. This began with your story about the traitor in Arzamas . . ."

Something in Vasin tightened whenever Orlov referred to the Arzamas spy being "his" story, "his" case. There were moments when Vasin wondered if the old reptile suspected that the espionage charge had been a figment of his imagination. But his boss continued smoothly, counting off the points on his hand.

"In turn, that led to a quest to find your spy's controller. As soon as we catch Morozov, prove that he is PLUTO, then we find who is next. Who he is linked to. Upward, downward, sideways."

Orlov stood, walked down the length of the table, and put a confiding hand on Vasin's shoulder. The General's voice was low and soft in Vasin's ear.

"My Sasha. Two loose threads, one man. God's sake, Vasin. I gave you good people. Time to bring this the damn case home. Quickly."

2

Defense Ministry, Moscow
12 July 1962

Captain Vasily Arkhipov sat alone at an empty table in the corner of the Defense Ministry cafeteria. His briefcase was squared in front of him, alongside a cooling cup of Cuban coffee. He rested his hands on the case. Barely a tremor. He exhaled deeply.

Across the room he spotted the old comrade he'd been waiting for. Like Arkhipov, he wore the uniform of a naval captain, first class. But unlike the sunburned Arkhipov, Timofey Zviagin was deathly pale, his head and face entirely hairless. Arkhipov stood, and the two men embraced tightly.

"Brother! How the devil are you, Tima?"

"Been better."

"Docs say what?"

Zviagin shrugged, held his friend's eye for a long moment.

"It's in remission, they promise. But they keep pumping me full of poison just to make sure."

In his dreams, Arkhipov saw his friend nightly. Timofey standing at his station outside the boiling steam heat of K-19's melting reactor compartment, his engineer's overalls stained with grease and his face lurid in the red emergency light. The reek of welding, a choking miasma of escaped reactor coolant. Zviagin's voice, raised in command to shut up the panicked squabbling in the line of men waiting in line for their turn to seal the welds on the emergency cooling system. Steady, Comrades, steady.

"You're looking well, Tima."

"Vasily, you never were a good liar. I'm looking like shit. So what brings you to our bureaucrats' bordello?"

"Assessment board."

"Here in Moscow, not up at Northern Fleet Headquarters. Must be top level. How'd it go?"

"Admirals. Glotov. Komarov. Some Defense Ministry bigwigs. A general from Strategic Missile Forces."

"Sounds like you're up for a big command, my friend. Something secret. My congratulations."

"Spit three times."

Zviagin turned and made a triple spitting noise with his lips over his left shoulder. Protection against the evil eye. Even senior Soviet naval officers remained sailors—as superstitious as peasant women.

"But you must be happy, right, Vasily? A fancy new command could be a new start. Nothing less than a hero veteran of the K-19 disaster deserves, right?"

"You're the hero of K-19, Tima. You should have got the new command."

"Don't mock an invalid. But you're keen to go back out to sea, right?"

Arkhipov shrugged and looked down at his hands in silence as his old shipmate gave him a searching look.

"Vasily—I hear things, at my desk upstairs. Read things. Your cruise won't be on a nuke, if that's what you're sweating over. I can promise you that. After the accident . . . after K-19, they're overhauling every nuclear submarine in the fleet. Every one, confined to base. Even the newest Project 658–class boats are having their reactors rebuilt. They tell me even our old K-19 will be fit for sea again one day. But not soon. So relax. It's still just the old diesel-electric subs allowed out on long-range patrols till next year at least. Take that from someone who knows. So no need to worry about . . . Remember what that crazy Uzbek cook called the reactor? 'Satan in a tin can.'"

Arkhipov smiled crookedly. Of course he remembered the cook. K-19's doctor had jammed a massive dose of diazepam into his arm to shut the man up when he wouldn't stop screaming during the accident. Panic in a drowning submarine a thousand kilometers out in the North Atlantic could be as fatal as sinking to crush depth.

"Don't mind either way. Satan or no Satan, a boat's a boat."

Arkhipov's friend nodded sarcastically.

"Like I said. You're a bad liar, Vasily. You said a general from Strategic Missile Forces was at your board?"

19

"Yeah. What was that?"

"They say anything about a special weapon, deployed on your new mission?"

"Special weapon?"

Timofey puffed air.

"Maybe just a rumor. Nothing to tell you as yet. How about a cognac? Doc says I shouldn't—but fuck it, right?"

Arkhipov watched Zviagin's bald head weave its way across the cafeteria counter. He looked down at his hands once more. Steadier.

3

Pioneers' Ponds, Moscow
12 July 1962

Morozov walked out of his apartment building at half past ten into the rising heat of the Moscow summer morning. He carried his jacket slung over one shoulder and a canvas shopping bag in the other hand. Ignoring an elderly man feeding ducks by the pond, Morozov hurried toward the Mayakovskaya metro station. A young woman who had been checking her makeup in the window of a bakery spotted him, made a final adjustment to her hat, and set off in front of Morozov. Thirty yards behind, a lanky student also kept pace.

At Belorusskaya Station, Morozov trotted up the steps that led to the wide corridor that connected to the Circle Line platforms. In approved *kontora*-style, his two watchers bracketed their mark as he walked. He boarded a westbound train and exited at Kievskaya Station, making for the interchange with the Arbatsko–Pokrovskaya line. KGB junior lieutenant Mikhail Lyubimov, new out of the Dzerzhinsky academy and with Boris Schultz's training seared freshly into his mind, was growing nervous. This second change of trains made close surveillance risky—the mark was more likely to notice familiar faces on two successive trains. Lyubimov risked glancing down the carriage at his female partner, Tatiana Dulatova, who had taken up position in the far corner. He was too far away to catch Tanya's eye. A mistake, putting a pretty girl in the lead. Too conspicuous. The whole team knew by now that the old goat Morozov had a keen eye for the ladies.

The doors opened at Arbatskaya Station and Morozov was out ahead of both of them. Tanya, desperate to keep ahead of their mark, broke into a run, pushing past the commuters in a flurry of apologies. Again, a blunder. Lyubimov cursed his partner, struggling to keep his eye on Morozov's balding head thirty yards in front as the crowd slowed to a slow shuffle in front of the escalators.

"Keep your eye on the people on the escalator as they come up into your eye line," old Schultz had taught him. "You won't see through the backs of people's heads right in front of you, however hard you stare. Eyes only on the . . . ?"

"Only on the escalator, Comrade Colonel," the class had repeated.

But Lyubimov's eyes weren't on the escalator. They were on the steel barrier that separated the streams of passengers, looking for a place to duck under and jump the line. That was how he found himself face-to-face with his target, heading back toward the platforms. Morozov had ducked the barrier himself, donned his uniform cap and tunic, and switched direction. A primitive dry-cleaning trick, but an effective one.

Tanya would be near the top of the escalator by now. Lyubimov was on his own. Lose the mark, or get spotted? A calculated risk, and a dangerous one. He had to wait before Morozov was well out of sight before swinging athletically over the steel barrier and hurrying after him. But the kid was lucky. Morozov had just missed a train. His young shadow squeezed in almost alongside him on the next one. Lyubimov stuck with his target back to Kievskaya, and on to Oktyabrskaya. Four train changes now. By now Lyubimov had taken off his own jacket and pulled a summer cap low on his face, praying that the Colonel still hadn't noticed him. The young agent felt a heady, nauseous thrill. His first real chase.

"Press kiosks are your friend," Schultz had once intoned in his thin, whining voice. If you were checking for tails, that is. The ubiquitous kiosks often stood directly opposite the street entrances of metro stations, their row of angled vertical windows giving a helpful panorama of everyone who emerged. And sure enough, on exiting the Oktyabrskaya metro station, Morozov did indeed linger. He pretended to browse a selection of magazines for a full five minutes, forcing Lyubimov to take up a risky position in plain sight at a nearby trolleybus stop. That wily bastard Morozov knew every trick in the KGB countersurveillance book. But then again, Lyubimov remembered, it was his own teacher, Schultz, who had literally written the book.

The young watcher followed at a cautious distance as Morozov made his way to the Shokoladnitsa café on the corner of Kaluzhskaya Square. The place was crowded to capacity as usual, with a line of hopeful customers snaking out the door. Morozov walked blithely past the queue, scanned the large, table-filled space, and squeezed between the diners to join a young, dark-haired, strikingly beautiful woman at a corner table. She wore the olive-green uniform of an Army lieutenant and stood as Morozov approached. They did not salute, embrace, or shake hands. Their body language seemed formal. As Morozov began the long process of attracting a waiter's attention, Lyubimov slipped outside to a public phone booth. A flip of his red KGB ID card was enough to cut short the conversation of the occupant and send the frightened man scurrying away. Lyubimov's call to Special Cases' emergency number connected on the first ring.

"PLUTO has made contact. Requesting a reinforced team of watchers. Photographer. Two cars. Crash. Repeat, crash urgency."

4

KGB Headquarters, Moscow
12 July 1962

The surveillance report was on Vasin's desk within two hours. Schultz had trained the kid Lyubimov well, Vasin had to admit. And the old man had personally arrived on the scene in a radio car within eight minutes of his pupil's call. By the time Morozov and his coffee companion had emerged—separately, Vasin noted—into the polluted air of the busy intersection, a *kontora* team as big as an opera chorus was ready for them.

Vasin pulled out a grainy, blown-up headshot of the woman, skimmed through Lyubimov's notes, and looked up at the kid for explanation.

"She works at Gogolevsky Boulevard Thirteen, building three? What's that?"

"Defense Ministry building, sir. Part of the General Staff headquarters. Newly repurposed, we think. Used to be a department of the Army

Procurement Bureau. But the old institutional nameplate by the door has been taken down, sir."

"An *Aquarium* office?" Vasin used the latest slang for the GRU, named for Soviet military intelligence's newly built glass-fronted head-quarters in Yasenevo in suburban Moscow, which resembled a vast fish tank.

"Not sure, sir."

"Leave that to me. We'll get someone on the inside to check it out. Meanwhile . . ." Vasin checked his watch. "You have a team to follow this woman home?"

Lyubimov nodded. They both knew the *kontora* would have no problem identifying Morozov's woman the moment she put her key in any front door in Moscow.

Vasin dismissed the young officer and picked up the phone to make an urgent appointment with Orlov. For once, a piece of luck. After months of behaving like an ideal Soviet citizen, Morozov was finally acting like a spy.

5

Defense Ministry, Moscow
15 July 1962

The Ministry of Defense, like the Lubyanka, housed a myriad of cafe-terias, each a signifier of complex codes of status and access. Orlov's man on the inside of the Aquarium had chosen the largest, lowliest one, located in the basement.

"How will I know this Major Tokarev?" Vasin had asked Orlov.

"Unmistakable. Old cavalry man. Mustache. No hands."

As lunchtime approached, the cavernous dining room filled with groups of uniformed young men and a few preening women secretaries, their handbags and scarves colorful splashes in a uniformly khaki, mas-culine world. Vasin nursed a cup of weak coffee. A wiry, mustachioed officer in breeches and high boots peered about the room. He was in late middle age, sporting an old-fashioned cavalry mustache. Vasin ges-tured discreetly with his cup and the old officer raised a black-gloved hand in salute. Vasin stood to shake the man's outstretched hand—

which turned out to be a hard plastic prosthesis set to a half-open grip. Tokarev's other hand was plastic also.

No hands.

"Smolensk, 1943. Tried to toss a German hand grenade out of a trench. Wasn't fast enough. Everyone wants to ask, so I save them the embarrassment. You don't have to say anything."

Tokarev sat, tucking his plastic hands under the table. His face was spattered with old pale-brown shrapnel scars, like splashed clay.

"General Orlov sends his greetings."

"Bet he does. Send 'em back, with bells on."

"You're old friends?"

"One way to put it. Saved my backside, in his time. Got captured outside Mozhaisk in 'forty-one, escaped, ended up in the hands of SMERSH. The 'Death to Spies' outfit of the NKVD? Tasked with rooting out Fascist agents. Orlov decided I wasn't one. Long story. Sent me back to the front. Helped me lend a hand to the war effort. Both of them, in fact. Good work, Colonel. One minute in, and you already know everything there is to know about me."

Vasin ignored the old man's sarcasm and nodded. Orlov sent you back, with his hook deep in your throat. Vasin knew how that felt.

"You must have been grateful."

"Must have been innocent. Orlov said you needed help."

Vasin glanced around.

"We're going to talk here?"

"Neutral ground. You would stand out at the Aquarium. I would stand out at the *kontora*."

"I need to find a woman."

"Cherchez la femme."

"Very funny. Colleague of yours. Spanish girl. Details are here."

Vasin slid a thin file across the table, which Tokarev didn't pick up. It took Vasin a moment to realize he couldn't, with his hard prosthetic hands. Vasin opened the file and spread out the two typewritten pages. Tokarev leaned forward and scanned the document.

Sofia Rafaelovna Guzman, born 16 March 1932, in Barcelona, Spain. Resident of the USSR since February 1938. Unmarried. Current home address: a complex of Defense Ministry communal apartments for single officers on Malaya Gruzinskaya Street. That was as far as an evening rooting through the municipal housing registry and the *kontora*'s files had got Vasin's team.

"So tell me—why do you need to know about this Spaniard, Sofia Rafaelovna?"

"Counter-intelligence operation."

Tokarev raised an eyebrow—which Vasin took to mean, Keep talking.

"Got our eye on a possible enemy agent. He's been talking to this girl. Need to find out why. Where she works. What she does. What she has access to."

Tokarev seemed to mull asking for more particulars, but thought better of it.

"*That's* the favor Orlov needs? I'll see what I can do. Write."

Vasin fished out a notebook and Tokarev dictated a series of telephone numbers.

"None of them secure. Now write yours for me. My notebook. Top right pocket."

Vasin gingerly reached across the table and pulled a black book from Tokarev's tunic pocket, dutifully wrote down his own contacts, and tucked it back in, along with the sheet with Sofia's details.

"How do you . . ."

"Use a phone? Dress? Write? Piss? With a little help from my friends. Looking forward to getting to know you better. Maybe I'll even play the piano for you."

Vasin stood quickly, embarrassed. He chose an awkward half salute rather than attempting to shake hands, and headed for the exit.

Three days after his meeting with Tokarev, Vasin received a letter marked "personal" at the office. It was one of those prestamped folding letters sold to tourists, decorated with views of the medieval cathedrals of Suzdal. On the inside were just three lines.

"Dearest Comrade—heartfelt Communist greetings to you and to our mutual friend! Will be in our Socialist capital this week and will wait for you between 1800 and 1830 on Wednesday at the back entrance of the Ministry of Defense building at Frunzenskaya. My firmest comradely handshake to you, VT."

6

Frunze Embankment, Moscow
19 July 1962

Tokarev limped over to Vasin's Moskvich car, pushed down the door handle with a practiced movement of his hip, and clambered inside.

"Here."

The battered leather briefcase that Tokarev held cradled in his plastic arms had tooth marks on its straps. Vasin opened it and slipped out a slim file. The cardboard cover also had the imprint of human teeth on it. Quite delicate, just on one corner, but unmistakable. Tokarev's equivalent of a fingerprint.

"You're just going to stare at it?"

A summary of Sofia Guzman's personnel file, evidently written by Tokarev in an outlandish, oversize scrawl. Parents—Rafael and Maria Guzman, both Spanish Communist Party members. Raised in an orphanage outside Moscow after arriving in the USSR in 1938, aged six. Graduated from the Military Institute of Foreign Languages in Moscow—the GRU's finishing school for its foreign service operatives—in 1953 with a Red Star diploma. Worked as a translator at the Ministry of Defense ever since. Fluent in Spanish, French, and Russian, commended for exemplary service in 1960.

"She came to the USSR on her own, as an orphan? What happened to her parents?"

"Spanish Communists sent their kids to the USSR to keep them safe from the civil war, at the invitation of Comrade Stalin. Thousands of them came over. Most went back after Stalin died."

"So she wasn't an orphan?"

Tokarev just shrugged. "One way or another, I guess she is now."

Vasin turned the page. A list of Sofia Guzman's assignments to various departments dealing with Spanish-speaking countries. The last entry was dated nearly three months earlier. "Twenty-second of April 1962: Assigned to Operation Anadyr following Grade III security clearance."

"What's . . ."

"Operation Anadyr? Good question. In a word, it's Cuba. In two words: big and secret. Should have seen their faces when I asked around. Why are you asking, Major? Who's been talking about Anadyr, Major? I got the message: Stay the fuck out of it. All I can tell you is that Operation Anadyr was assigned a building of its own back in March, near the General Staff on Gogolevsky Boulevard. Kicked out a whole department to house them. And I can tell you they've been drafting in people like it's harvest time at the collective farm. Several hundred officers, at least. Every Spanish speaker in the Aquarium's got their marching orders. And it's all Cuba, Cuba, Cuba. Doing exactly *what* in fraternal Socialist Cuba—don't ask. But if your spook is sniffing around Sofia, it's because he's interested in Anadyr. Or maybe he just fancies some Spanish ass."

Vasin folded the notes and handed back Tokarev's briefcase. The old major nodded and used his elbow to open the car door.

"Tokarev . . ."

"If I hear anything more about Anadyr, or about Cuba, or about Sofia, I'm to let you know? Yes, repeat, no."

The door slammed shut.

7

Maurice Thorez Embankment, Moscow
21 July 1962

The riverboat terminal by the Estrada Theater was crowded with out-of-town tourists. Vasin pressed through a crowd of sunburned men in identical open-weave porkpie hats and women in gaudy printed-cotton summer dresses. He spotted Vadim Kuznetsov sitting on a granite embankment, fanning himself irritably with a wide-brimmed Panama and looking like a cartoon capitalist in his luxurious foreign suit.

"Vadim! Fancy an ice cream?"

Kuznetsov hopped down from the low wall, brushed the seat of his trousers, and fixed Vasin with a dark stare.

"Ah. My old, high-flying comrade Alexander Vasin. Just when I was thinking that I don't have enough excitement in my life—there you are, on the phone! Somehow, you knew I was in Moscow and where to find me. Only true comrades go to such lengths to ferret out their old friends. I'm flattered."

"I've missed you, Kuznetsov. I was lucky to catch you here in our glorious Socialist Motherland, apparently. How are the tropics?"

"The tropics are . . . tropical. I suppose you'll be wanting me to thank you for my assignment to fraternal Cuba?"

"My friend—you *earned* that posting."

Kuznetsov rolled his eyes.

"Vasin, did I ever mention that you're trouble?"

"Can't recall that you ever did, no. Come on—our boat leaves in five minutes."

"Our *boat*?"

"We're going on a river cruise. I have tickets."

"You're putting me on a damn *barge* so I can't run away from whatever heinous favor you're about to ask me to do for you? Did I guess right?"

The steam horn of the sleek white cruiser blew. Vasin, grinning, pulled his comrade into a trot toward the gangplank.

The two men settled into seats on the upper deck. A party of Central Asian workers, all women in headscarves, gossiped excitedly beside them as the craft pulled out into the stream of the Moscow River and nosed eastward, toward the Kremlin.

"You going to tell me about your exotic new assignment? Can't wait to hear all about your glamorous Caribbean life."

Kuznetsov ran a hand through his thinning hair and groaned.

"Here we go again. The Who, What, Why, When and Where Show, hosted tonight by Major Alexander Vasin."

"Lieutenant Colonel to you, chum."

"Even better. Now you even outrank me. Can you just move over and let me jump in the river right now?"

"Don't do that. We need to save the Motherland."

"Again. Why is it that I think I'm going to regret coming here today?"

"You won't. I promise. So you don't want to tell me about Cuba. I get it. But let me tell you why I'm asking."

"Answering only yes or yes? Remember I've been on this show before."

"Very funny. So listen. I'm running a counterintelligence operation. We think a senior Aquarium officer is spying for the Yanks. And he's been nosing around Operation Anadyr. In fact, we think he has recruited an agent *inside* Operation Anadyr."

Kuznetsov turned away as if to block the words spoken by Vasin with his own bulky body.

"Mother of *Christ*." When he finally turned back to Vasin, the levity had vanished from Kuznetsov's voice, which had fallen to an urgent hiss. "Why aren't you sounding the alarm, then? Official channels? What does this have . . ."

"To do with you? Simple. We can't risk tipping off our man. I can't tell you exactly why—except to say that we suspect he may be protected. By an even more senior colleague in the Aquarium. So no alarm. Yet."

"No. No, no, no. Just stop talking. I'm going."

Vasin put a firm arm on his old handler's arm, pressing him down on the white-painted bench.

"Listen. I need to know from someone I trust, a friend, what exactly is going on with Anadyr. With Cuba."

"Well bloody well find a friend who can tell you. I'm not your friend."

Kuznetsov's glare was hostile.

"Listen. Vadim. If I don't catch this man, I'm destined for some uranium mine in Magadan. And yes—you *are* my friend. You trusted me. You helped me before. And right now I need to know what our spy is after. What information he's trying to get to the Americans. Because I need to bait a trap. And I can't do that while I'm flying blind. Please. This isn't some maverick mission of my own. It's national security. Official."

Kuznetsov raised an eyebrow and raised a hand to the soaring wedding cake of a skyscraper on Kotelnicheskaya Embankment as it drifted by.

"Aha. So this is an *official* meeting, is it? At your new mobile office?"

Vasin looked away at the passing rows of newly built apartment blocks on the opposite bank.

"Vadim. I beg you. Don't make me . . ."

"Do this the hard way? That what you were going to say?"

Kuznetsov's complexion had darkened, anger brewing in his face.

"Yes, old friend. Exactly. Don't forget that I work for Special Cases. The outfit that got you your assignment in Cuba? It's headed by a monster. A fucking monster, Vadim. General Orlov will shred me. He'll shred you, if I tell him you didn't cooperate. So please. Help me. Help yourself. Make Orlov a friend."

"By telling you top-secret information?"

"We're on the same side, Vadim."

"So you keep telling me. Last time it was right before you shot dead a Soviet colonel of aviation."

"Who was an American spy. This one is worse."

Vasin's hand had been clutching Kuznetsov's shoulder, hard. He released it now. Kuznetsov exhaled heavily.

"I can see why they promoted you, Vasin. I'd forgotten what a ruthless asshole you can be."

"I *work* for a ruthless asshole, Kuznetsov. I'm asking you as a friend . . ."

"Enough of the 'friend' bullshit. Fine. Want to know the deal with Cuba? The Soviet government is preparing to station nuclear missiles in Cuba. Covertly. There. Happy?"

"When? Now?"

"We have already sent thousands of specialists to prepare the rocket launch sites. Our leadership is in talks with the Cubans to obtain their permission to send the missiles. That's why Raúl Castro is coming to Moscow this week. Brother of Fidel?"

"I've heard of Raúl Castro. But why are we doing this? Sending nukes to Cuba?"

"Why? Above my pay grade, Vasin. Your guess is as good as mine."

"To protect Castro?"

"Maybe. The Yankees tried to invade Cuba once already, if you recall. Didn't end well for them. Sent a bunch of hothead Cuban exiles who got themselves massacred."

"And what do you reckon the Americans will do if they find out about these missiles? Invade again? Something worse?"

Kuznetsov's voice became heavy with sarcasm.

"Well—I guess young President Kennedy wouldn't be very happy. With us. With Fidel. Might even get angry, finally. Why? You planning to tell him?"

"What if . . . my spy tells the Americans? Before we arrest him?"

Kuznetsov settled back in his seat and shook his head.

"Vasin? Stop talking. Don't tell me anything else. Just—stop."

The two men sat in silence for a while. The crowd of Uzbek women had become bored of throwing crumbs of bread to the wheeling seagulls at the ship's rail and began to stroll around the deck in small chattering groups. At the set of locks that marked the beginning of the Moscow-Volga Canal, the boat turned in midchannel and headed for the North River Terminal to dock. Kuznetsov stood, adjusting his smart Panama hat.

"I'm getting off here. But I'll tell you one thing for free, Vasin. If you really have a spy in your sights, reel him in. Now. Whatever the reasons you have for delaying—and I *don't* want to know them—aren't bigger than Anadyr. Just fucking catch him."

"Just one more favor, Vadim."

"That's a bad habit of yours, Sasha. One favor, another favor . . ."

"I need to meet a woman. Someone who works in Operation Anadyr. Socially."

"But not for social purposes."

"No, Vadim, not for social purposes. I need to put her on the hook. And fast. Her name is Sofia Guzman."

8

The Kremlin, Moscow
24 July 1962

The Kremlin Palace of Congresses was packed with a who's who of the Soviet military and political elite. The brand-new modernist interior was lit with crystal chandeliers two stories high, and the reception hall was lined with white-covered tables piled with imported luxuries— bananas, pineapples, and tropical fruits. A line of barmen mixed an endless stream of rum cocktails, and the air was pungent with the smoke of Cuban Upmann cigars.

Vasin had had a new uniform made specially at the exclusive military tailor's near Orlov's home on Kutuzovsky Prospekt. He examined himself in one of the floor-to-ceiling mirrors. He looked like shit. It was the new, modern-pattern shirt and clip-on tie in place of the old high-collared tunic, trousers instead of breeches and boots, a jacket with unfashionably pointed lapels. He looked like a pathetic desk jockey. And unlike almost everybody else in the room, Vasin had no row of medals arrayed over his heart.

He spotted Kuznetsov, stuffed into a too-tight uniform, but when he waved, his old friend merely glared and nodded significantly in the direction of the buffet.

Sofia Guzman was surrounded by a group of young Cuban men. Vasin had never seen people looking so healthy and vital. Their skin was bronzed and they wore crisply pressed field fatigues and red neck scarves. Many sported beards in imitation of their leader, Fidel Castro, and his brother Raúl—who was evidently being entertained separately by Khrushchev himself. The Cubans in civilian dress looked even more impossibly glamorous in fine cotton suits with wide shoulders and lapels sporting scarlet spots of Revolutionary badges. By comparison, the Soviets, even in their array of splendid dress uniforms, looked over-dressed, overweight, and pale. God, thought Vasin, we all really need to get more sun.

Sofia was chatting five directions at once in guttural Spanish. Her admirers pressed drinks and food on her. One Cuban Revolutionary Armed Forces colonel cheekily stole an orchid from a table decoration and tucked it flirtatiously behind her ear. Even the drab green Soviet army uniform looked glamorous on Sofia's shapely figure.

Nothing for it. Fortifying himself with a shot of rum grabbed from a passing waiter's tray, Vasin pushed his way through the crowd and edged toward the circle around Sofia. Squeezing between two young Cuban officers, he caught Sofia's eye for a split second before a brawny arm encircled him.

"Compadre! To the friendship of nations!" A drunk Cuban planted a hairy kiss on his cheeks. Sofia's gaze slid across Vasin and she resumed her animated chatting.

Vasin finally caught up with Sofia again in the queue for the exit, where pretty Cuban girls in military blouses and black berets were handing out souvenir boxes of cigars to the men, bunches of carnations to the women.

"Lieutenant! Been trying to catch you all night. It's Sofia Rafaelovna, isn't it?"

Sofia's dark, hard eyes took in Vasin's lieutenant colonel's stars and the KGB sword-and-shield badges on his lapels.

"That's correct, sir."

"Mine's Vasin. Alexander. Can I walk you out?"

She stiffened, as though drawing herself to attention.

"What do you want from me, Colonel? And how do you know my name?"

"I'd just like to chat, Lieutenant. Ask you a couple of questions."

Sofia appeared to catch someone's eye, over Vasin's shoulder, and she raised an arm in greeting.

"I'm always ready to help the state security forces of our great Soviet Motherland, Colonel . . . Vasin? I'm sure you know where to find me. Through official channels."

An imposing, muscular older man in the uniform of a special forces major-general appeared at Sofia's side. He wore an open-necked battle dress tunic over a striped undershirt, and a beret rather than an officer's cap. Just like an asshole from the GRU's Special Designation Forces— better known as the Spetznaz—to show up at a Kremlin reception dressed for a commando raid.

"Ready to go, Comrade Lieutenant?"

The General threw Vasin a brief, contemptuous look before steering Sofia to the table where they were handing out carnations. Vasin swore under his breath as Sofia sashayed to the open double doors, head held high, her companion courteously holding the door open for her.

She would be a tough one to recruit; Vasin could feel it. Haughty. Steel in her gaze. Well-established career in the GRU, the one institution in the Soviet Union where the KGB couldn't reach in to mess with her career. No family, therefore hard to threaten. And Vasin would be asking her to work against one of her own—on behalf of the *kontora*. Even more difficult.

To put this one on the hook, he would need leverage. Good leverage.

9

Severomorsk Naval Base
25 July 1962

Even the stench of welding could not quite erase that deep, human submarine stink. Arkhipov emerged from the forward hatch from the darkness and confusion of the interior onto the narrow foredeck of his new boat—or to be precise, the flagship of the small flotilla that Arkhipov now commanded. B-59, one of the USSR's newest class of diesel-electric hunter-killer subs, fast and reliable. And no nuclear reactor to leak its poison on him.

Beyond the crowded dockside, the low hills that surround Severomorsk were covered with the brief-blooming wildflowers of the Arctic summer. Arkhipov wore engineer's overalls, unbuttoned to the waist, and the back of his neck stung with sunburn. Around him on the narrow deck were a group of weapons engineers, poring over papers and shouting orders to the sailors below.

They were taking new torpedoes on board through the loading hatches in the bow and stern of the submarine. The hatches were shorter than the torpedoes, so the weapons had to be lowered into the ship at an angle in order to slide them obliquely into their racks. A nerve-racking process—like threading sausages back into a mincer, his old mate Timofey had once joked. A dockside crane hauled another T-5 torpedo into the air—the biggest firecrackers in the entire Soviet arsenal. The weapon was half a meter wide and nearly six meters long, a drab black tube. Only the twin brass-alloy propellers glinted brightly as the torpedo swung free for the brief few minutes of its existence that the weapon would ever spend in sun and air.

"Captain!"

Arkhipov squinted into the lowering sun. An older man, in the undress uniform of a rear admiral, waved from the dockside.

"Comrade Admiral Smirnov! To what do we owe the honor?"

Arkhipov jogged down the steel gangplank and shook his old superior warmly by the hand.

"Vasily. You're looking well. I haven't seen you since that business . . ."

"And am I okay? Seems so, the docs say. For the moment."

"Born lucky. I told them, you know, that they should have run extreme corrosion tests on those reactor units before sending men out to sea."

"How is K-19?"

"Clean. They say. Rebuilt the whole plant. She'll be back out and at 'em soon."

"I'm guessing this isn't a social call?"

"No. I wanted to give you your orders personally. A four-day torpedo test-firing cruise next week. Just a run around the backyard here. Your whole flotilla, all four boats."

"Torpedo tests? Testing us, or testing the torpedoes?"

Smirnov flicked his junior on the chest with a single finger.

"You always were a smart one. See, the Admiralty needs to be sure that your flotilla comms are up to speed. Group maneuvers. Long-range torpedo firing drills. Don't want to take any chances."

"Chances with what?"

"A new weapon, Vasily. Science eggheads want you and the other senior officers for a full briefing. Tomorrow, at Northern Fleet Head-quarters." Smirnov leaned forward confidentially. "I told them you were the best man for the job, Vasily. There were naysayers, I don't mind telling you. But I said, 'Arkhipov's your man. Backbone. Brains. Experience.' You'll do great."

"Sir!"

Arkhipov stood to attention and saluted his old chief, who returned the salute with a flourish. As he followed Smirnov up the companion-way, Arkhipov could feel his bowels tightening.

New torpedo. Long-range. Powerful. That could mean only one thing. One of those new *nuclear* torpedoes.

He was going to sea with Satan on board after all.

PART TWO

SATAN IN A CAN

He should feel his superiority over the enemy,
know the enemy better than he knows himself. That is
the guarantee of victory.

Essential Instructions for Intelligence Officers,
SECOND EDITION, 1958

1

Severomorsk Naval Base
29 July 1962

The screening room was uncomfortably warm from the heat thrown off by the hulking projector. There were twenty men in the auditorium, half of them in dark blue Navy uniforms, the rest in civilian suits. Vasily Arkhipov looked around the tired faces of his comrades—the commanders of his new flotilla and their first officers, plus two spares.

Savitsky and Manuilov of B-59. Shumkov and Krivitsky of B-130. Dubivko and Gendin of B-36. And the youngest pair, Ketov and Rilsky of B-4. He'd been to sea with Dubivko. The rest, other than the youngsters, he knew from fleet exercises, staff college, the naval academy. The world of submarine commanders was a big village.

"And so, comrade officers, we come to our fifth and final set of estimates of blast patterns, based on the underwater tests of the Korall prototype—what is now known as the Type 53-58 torpedo."

The lecturer was a skinny, bespectacled technician who glanced up nervously from his notes to check that he had everybody's attention.

"Can we just see the damn film please, Prof? It's baking in here."

Captain Savitsky's voice was the irritable growl of a man used to command. Their instructor—a functionary from the Soviet Ministry of Medium Machine Building—yielded the floor to his superior in a flurry of dropped papers. The new man had arrived earlier that afternoon, his cases carried by four military policemen. He was tall and broad-shouldered, with a soldier's bearing under his civilian clothes. He did not bother to introduce himself.

"Comrade Captains. I see you are fatigued. Bored, even."

The officers straightened in their chairs to the stern tone of the man's voice.

"The last three days you have been lectured on flotilla formation.

How to keep track of each other's position when preparing to deploy the Special Weapon. On minimum safe ranges, on target tracking at long distances. What you have not been shown, Comrades, is the capacity of the Special Weapon itself."

The speaker examined his audience, one by one.

"You have all fired torpedoes. The T-5 in particular, of course. And what is the payload of a conventional T-5 torpedo, Comrades? Four hundred kilos of high explosive. The explosive yield of a nuclear-armed Type 53-58? Four point five kilotons. Four and a half thousand kilos, in other words. Just a number. An impossible number to imagine. But tonight you will see how this explosive force looks in practice."

The pair of military policemen who had been loading film reels into the projector signaled that they were ready.

"So, Comrades. October tenth, 1957, off the coast of Novaya Zemlya. Submarine S-144 is tasked with test-firing a nuclear-armed T-5 from a depth of twenty meters and a range to target of ten kilometers."

An image flashed onto a screen, filmed from a slowly circling aircraft. A wide bay, dotted with small ice floes, with three surfaced submarines clearly visible in a staggered line.

"These vessels are S-20, S-34, and S-19. Decommissioned submarines, the designated targets of the test."

"Old S-20! I trained on her!" Krivitsky's loud whisper was indignant. "Bastards. Using her for target practice."

"The firing boat is out of the picture," continued the lecturer. "She is submerged, obviously, at a safe distance from the targets. In order not to compromise the test, the torpedo's range and the target's position were known to the firing party in advance—"

"Wouldn't want them to send that kind of firework off in the wrong direction," Savitsky interjected, and the more junior naval men laughed nervously. The speaker again ignored the interruption as the film whirred on.

"In combat conditions, Comrades, you will obviously not have the luxury of a preset course and range. Watch, please. At twenty meters' submersion the torpedo is running too deep for us to see it from the surface. But wait. Wait . . ."

The blast came entirely unexpectedly, a sudden white circle that spread with infernal speed through the water, quickly engulfing all three boats. The sea seemed to be rising, erupting like a volcano that eventually burst into a plume of water. A massive wave crashed on the sides of the bay and rebounded with unbroken force back to where the submarines once were. But two of them were gone, and the third lay capsized and half-sunk.

"*Figa'se . . .*" hissed Ketov under his breath. "Goddamn."

Arkhipov glanced around at the faces of his fellow officers. Most had clapped their hands to their faces, their eyes riveted to the screen. Only Savitsky seemed excited, a grim smile on his face.

"*Nu chto? Kruto, ryabyata! Ura!*" Savitsky's voice boomed around the room. "Cool, right lads? Hurrah!"

From the vantage point of the aircraft circling two thousand meters in the air, the broad sweep of Mityushikha Bay looked like a child's bathtub roiled with furious waves, the subs that had once been on its surface swallowed like paper boats.

"The sensors recovered from the hull of S-20 were too badly crushed to yield any readings," continued the lecturer. "But those on S-34 show a pressure wave of four hundred atmospheres. I do not need to remind you that the crush depth of that class of vessel is thirty atmospheres. S-19, as you see, was the furthest from the blast, and bow-on to the wave. She was critically damaged. Six of her nine compartments were ruptured, but she retained enough buoyancy in her tanks to remain afloat."

The aerial footage flickered to an end, to be replaced with a steadier view of the familiar dry dock at Severomorsk, floodlit. In it was the wreck of a submarine literally stamped flat, as though by a colossal boot. The roof of her sail had popped open like the lid of a can, and most of the plating had been ripped away from the ribs of her hull, exposing an intestine-like tangle of piping and wires.

"Here, the wreck of S-34. You observe the catastrophic damage that she has sustained. And here, the remains of S-20."

Ketov had covered his eyes. The steadiness of the lecturer's voice seemed to insult the sum of every submariner's fear—a vessel crushed. As the lights went up, Arkhipov was the first to break the tense silence.

"Comrade Professor. Tell me—what happens to the sailors who survive the first blast wave? Men in the water? Is the sea . . . contaminated with radiation, after such a detonation?"

Their instructor looked down at his notes, though he was not reading them.

"Captain . . . Arkhipov?"

"Correct."

"First officer of K-19."

"Correct."

"My respects for your sacrifice. And to answer your question—yes. Yes, the water is radioactive. Highly radioactive."

Arkhipov felt his sweat suddenly grow cold under his uniform.

2

Marx Prospekt, Moscow
30 July 1962

On the broad boulevard in front of the Hotel National, Vasin eased his little Moskvich to a halt among a crowd of cars. A scattering of bread and produce trucks filled the five-lane road, as well as a few official limousines and a tricolor sea of private cars in the only colors Soviet automobile factories produced: cream, blue, and black. Winding down the window, Vasin called across to a taxi driver at the wheel of his rumbling Volga-21.

"What's the problem?"

"Probka," the driver replied without removing the *papiros* cigarette from the corner of his mouth. Literally, a cork. Figuratively, a traffic jam. Vasin had never heard the word before, let alone experienced one in a city where only one family in a hundred owned a car. But it described the stalled mass of traffic ahead of him well enough. He cut the engine and got out of his car to get a better look.

Overhead, strings of twinned Soviet and Cuban flags fluttered in a summer breeze. Further down Marx Prospekt, the side of a ministry building was decorated with a freshly painted mural depicting a swarthy Cuban comrade arm in arm with a blond Russian worker in overalls, marching together toward a common Socialist future.

A wail of police sirens rose over the crest of the hill, and a cortege of official Chaika limousines appeared on Gorky Street, accompanied by a phalanx of motorcycle outriders. A crowd of schoolgirls on the corner, all wearing white nylon lace bows in their hair, waved flowers. The motorcade swung left toward the Bolshoi Theater and disappeared in the direction of the Kremlin. A pair of traffic policemen lowered their raised striped batons and began twirling them in circles to unblock the cork.

At the Lubyanka—late for work, for once—Vasin leafed through a stack of the day's newspapers. *Sovietskaya Rossiya* had a double-page photo spread on Comrade Raúl Castro's gala visit to the capital of international Socialism. One of the photos showed Castro speaking animatedly with a collection of generals. Standing behind the distinguished visitor, speaking into his ear, was a beautiful woman in military uniform. Sofia Guzman.

Once, the catacombs of memory below the Lubyanka had been a place of revelation and horror for Vasin. The collective memory of injustice and terror on which the entire edifice of the KGB quite literally stood. But now, Vasin realized as the elevator rattled him down to the third basement level, he was entering the archives with keen purpose. Not as a shocked outsider, but as an insider with a mission. The power of secrets had become his own power. And now he must find something in these rows of tombstone files that could give him the key to Sofia Guzman.

Except that the records he needed weren't there. "Spanish Civil War. Listed as nonessential," the archivist told him blandly, and turned away. The blood and passion of a fraternal nation's revolutionary struggle had been relegated to a footnote of failure in the history of the Soviet Union's fight to liberate the world's masses. The files on the Spanish Republicans who fought and died for Stalin—and their children— had been relegated to a distant depository on the outskirts of Moscow. Where? Nobody seemed to know.

"Remind me—why exactly are we messing about in the historical records, Vasin?" Orlov's tone was deadpan, and no more than usually menacing.

"Because I want to put Sofia Guzman on the hook, sir. She is Morozov's agent. If we have her, we have Morozov."

"Not unreasonable."

"She's GRU, sir. If we try to threaten her, she could go to her bosses."

"To Serov."

"Exactly. We need something to catch her. Intrigue her. Compromise her. Maybe from her past. I won't know . . ."

"Until you see it? Vasin—here's a better plan. Save us all some time. Find out enough about her past to put together some convincing lie. Something good enough to get her 'intrigued,' as you so coyly put it."

Orlov pinched the bridge of his nose, as he did when trying to remember something.

"Yes. Talk to Borovitsky. He was in Spain with the NKVD." The People's Commissariat of Internal Affairs—the prewar name for the KGB. "Not many of them survived. But Borovitsky managed to dodge a *kontora* bullet at the end of it all, somehow. Must have betrayed enough of his colleagues to keep his own skin whole. When you see him, ask him from me: How are you still alive, Borovitsky?"

3

Saltykovka, Moscow Region
31 July 1962

The Borovitskys' sagging wooden house was so nondescript and buried in undergrowth that even the locals in the suburb of Saltykovka didn't recognize the address. But eventually Vasin found the place, half-hidden behind a thicket of jasmine at the end of a garden run wild. An elderly woman, her hair scraped back into a tight bun, opened the door a crack. Nina Alexeyevna Borovitskaya seemed to nurture some grudge against the world, and at first took Vasin as the personal representative of every species of officialdom that had wronged and overlooked her.

"So where is our building's renovation on the list, Comrade? We have been told for five years that we are a priority, and all that time we have to contend with this."

She gestured irritably around the crumbling windows and subsiding walls of the house, once a respectable pre-Revolutionary dacha which now resembled a beached shipwreck. What was it about the endless legion of Soviet babushkas that gave them the ability to stop senior KGB officers in their tracks, force ministers to sheepishly wipe their boots, and send police packing?

Delicately, as though imparting a secret, Vasin unfolded his red KGB ID card.

"Comrade Borovitskaya, I need some information. About a girl who was brought here from Spain in 1938."

Naum Abramovich Borovitsky was a lopsided old warhorse in a sagging cardigan and worn woolen tracksuit bottoms. His eyes were red-rimmed, and his hand trembled as he studied an old magazine. The man was visibly shaken to have a visitor from the *kontora* bearing greetings from General Orlov.

"Whatever it is . . . just keep my name out of this, Comrade. Please."

"Comrade Borovitsky. Or should I say, Major Borovitsky? I need to talk to you about the Spanish children's transports."

"Spain?" Borovitsky spoke the word as though Vasin had said "the moon."

"You were in Barcelona, Major, with the NKVD, in 'thirty-eight. Tell me about the children."

"What children?"

Vasin began to wonder if the man was in his second childhood himself. Nina Alexeyevna struggled for a moment, evidently torn between caution and an impulse to scold Vasin for his ignorance, then spoke up.

"In 1937, after the Fascist bombardment of the city of Guernica, the Spanish Republican government arranged a mass transport of children to places of safety," she recited as though from a guidebook. "The Soviet government offered to provide shelter to three thousand children of Spanish Republicans for the duration of the civil war. They were embarked in Bilbao on boats chartered by the Basque Republican government, as well as from Barcelona, and brought to the USSR. They were housed and educated by the Soviet state."

"In orphanages?"

"Correct."

"And then they went home?"

"A few did. In 'fifty-six. Most stayed. Why would they return? There was nothing for them in Spain. Which remains—as you will be aware—a Fascist country."

"And the parents?"

Nina Alexeyevna shrugged.

"Dead, most of them. Martyrs to the Revolution. Or else they would have tried to find their children, no?"

"And the records?"

"If they were PCE, they're here in the Soviet Union somewhere. If POUM, obviously not." She registered Vasin's blank look. "PCE. The Communist Party of Spain. Loyal to the Communist International. The POUM were Trotskyite traitors."

"In Barcelona, did you know a man called Rafael Guzman? Either of you?"

Borovitsky stirred in his ancient armchair, struggling as though trapped in the collapsed upholstery. He squinted at Vasin. Special Cases records had told Vasin that Borovitsky was born in 1901, but he looked twenty years older than his sixty-one years.

"Guzman?" Borovitsky wheezed. "One of the most common surnames in Spain."

"Nonetheless."

"And why should I know this man?"

Vasin remembered that defensive tone from his days as a police detective. An obstructer, a witness determined not to give anything away—not necessarily for any good reason.

"Because you were in the same Spanish city, working on the same side, at the same time? Borovitsky, I'm not interested in you or any of that ancient history. But I need to find out what happened to Guzman."

"Can tell you that without knowing the man. Killed. Like all of them. During the final fighting in 'thirty-nine. Or rounded up and shot. They are all gone. All our old Spanish comrades. Apart from the ones who survived and became collaborators."

Borovitsky began sniffing as though overcome with emotion. A blubberer, too. For God's sake.

"So which one was it?" Vasin made no effort to conceal his irritation. "Martyr or collaborator? Dead or alive? Think, man."

Borovitsky went still, rummaging in his memories, then suddenly remembered.

"Rafael Guzman. Deputy political commissar of the Barcelona section of the Catalan Front. Wife . . . Maria?"

"Sounds right. What happened to him? To his family? His daughter?"

"They took all my photographs. Took all my papers, when I got back to the Soviet Union. Can't remember the details now. All gone."

Vasin raised his eyes to the stained ceiling. Borovitsky's wife stepped forward and sat on the arm of the sofa as though her husband were not there.

"I remember them, Colonel. Rafael and Maria? Rafael worked with Naum's boss. Maria came to me asking what life in the USSR would be like. Lots of the wives did, while the children's transports were being prepared. They wanted to be reassured. I told them—better than here. The bombing was getting bad. The Socialists were losing. There was no future for them in Spain. They all assumed it would be just a few months, like sending the kids to Young Pioneer camp. I promised them that Comrade Stalin loved children and would give them a better life."

"And?"

The woman shrugged indifferently.

"Guess they must have sent their kids, like so many others did. As for the parents—maybe they escaped to France. Or changed their identity. Shot by Franco. Killed in the bombing of Barcelona."

"Was anyone keeping records?"

"After the war, the Spanish Communist Party was banned. The Fascists had lists of members to arrest, after the government fell. So you could ask the Fascists."

There was no sarcasm in her voice, only numbness. A dead end, then. In the Borovitskys' collapsing house deadened indifference seemed to hang in the air like stale cigarette smoke. Vasin stood to take his leave. Borovitsky's wife seemed suddenly pained to see him go.

"Wait . . . maybe you could ask Marfa. Marfa Scherbak. She was a nurse, married to a Spaniard. Traveled on the transports with the kids. She tried to run some kind of club for them. Organized some reunions, after the war."

Nina Alexeyevna lumbered off to find Marfa's address: the Red October collective farm near Odintsovo. An hour's drive west of Moscow. Vasin hesitated. The choice was Odintsovo or heading back home. Or the office. At the Red October collective farm there was at least the ghost of a chance that someone might be pleased to see him.

4

Red October Collective Farm, Odintsovo, Moscow Region
31 July 1962

Marfa Scherbak had lank gray hair and a ravaged alcoholic's face. Vasin found her perched on a stool outside a dilapidated workers' barrack behind the collective farm's bathhouse, nursing a jam jar full of murky *kvass* bread beer in the dying rays of the day's sunshine. But her lined face lit up when Vasin asked about the orphans.

"Mis niños!" she said. "Haven't forgotten my Spanish, see. My children!"

She led him inside a long, low building that stank of cabbage and unwashed humanity to her room, which she had turned into a shrine to hundreds of bygone childhoods. Photos of young children covered the walls, many of them sitting in the lap of a young, strikingly pretty nurse in a crisp white uniform. It took Vasin a moment to realize that this was Marfa herself.

"I'm looking for a girl called Sofia Guzman. Her personnel file says only that Sofia arrived in the USSR in February 1938."

Vasin knew it wasn't much. But Stalin used to say, "Give me a name and I will give you the crime." Surely a name and a date must be sufficient to pry open a life, if you looked in the right place? To Vasin's surprise, Marfa immediately began pulling boxes from under her bed and pulled down more from on top of her wardrobe. They were full of letters, postcards, a jumble of correspondence going back years.

"I still used to see them for holidays, when they were grown up, after the war. Not Easter or the Día de los Reyes Magos. They'd forgotten about those religious holidays. But Revolution Day. May Day. Ah, the fun we had!" Marfa produced a wad of photographs of a group of young people gathered under a banner with a Spanish inscription, herself in the center. "That was before so many of them went back home. Then we lost touch. They were afraid to have a pen pal in the USSR. You know . . . Franco."

The jumble of letters was useless to Vasin, unless Marfa remembered Sofia Guzman personally. But her face registered a blank.

Marfa narrowed her eyes, judging whether she could trust Vasin.

"They did give me some of the card indexes. When I wrote to the Children's Distribution Center in Odessa after the war. They were going to throw them out."

From a wooden trunk at the foot of her incongruously neatly made bed, Marfa hauled out two long box files, each filled with cardboard registration cards and folded papers. They were arranged, to Vasin's delight, by date.

The identity document that had accompanied little Sofia Guzman on her journey from Spain to the USSR was a badly mimeographed form produced by a wartime Spanish government stationery office. It had evidently been filled out by her parents. Marfa translated. Father: Rafael Pablo Fernández de Guzmán Calderón García Iglesias, PCE member since March 1930. Served as deputy political commissar of the Barcelona section of the Catalan Front, just as Borovitsky had remembered. Mother: María Dolores Martínez Ruiz, non-Party member. Address: Ronda de Sant Pere 39, Barcelona, Spain. Daughter: Sofía María Caterina Guzmán—Russified to Sofia Rafaelovna Guzman by the addition of a patronymic. The child had been duly signed over by her parents to the care of International Red Aid for the duration of hostilities.

But there was another name on the paper, another child who was on the same transport. Vladimir Lenin Guzmán, born 24 May 1934, in Barcelona. Sofia's younger brother, just four yours old when he was sent away to a place of greater safety. On the back of the form, scribbled in looping handwriting on different dates, were the names of the orphanages where the children were assigned. Sofia's was in Solikamsk, in the Urals. Vladimir's was in Donetsk, Ukraine.

The siblings had been separated on arrival.

"What are you going to do with this information, Comrade Colonel?" Marfa's haggard face was creased in protective concern. "Is she all right? Is she in trouble?"

Vasin didn't answer immediately as he looked down once more at the flimsy paper. The scribbled writing on the back resembled a row of tiny fish hooks.

5

KGB Headquarters, Moscow
1 August 1962

Vasin was just about to head out of his stuffy Lubyanka office when the telephone began to ring insistently. An outside line. But nobody beyond the *kontora* administration knew the number. Nobody except . . .

"Sasha. It's me."

The smoky voice of Katya, General Orlov's wife. Vasin's onetime mistress. The seductress who had first slipped her husband's hook deep into Vasin's throat.

"We need to meet. This afternoon?"

"Do I have a choice?"

Ignoring Vasin's petulance, Katya named the time and place.

Winding her way through the tables at the crowded Café Praga, Katya looked every inch the Party aristocrat. Her corseted figure was squeezed into a loud blue tweed suit, and she wore a fashionably enormous straw hat that a much younger woman would struggle to carry off. She was in full war paint, her lips glistening bright scarlet.

"Sasha. You look well. We haven't seen each other for so long. Tell me—has Orlov made you happy? He promised to make you happy."

Orlov, the dispenser of happiness. The sun of their universe, around which all must rotate—though at different distances and speeds. Vasin thought of his new apartment, his new car—the juddering little Moskvich. Nikita's upcoming Young Pioneer trip to Artek, the Crimean paradise for exceptionally worthy, or more usually just well-connected, children. The chilly truce with Vera that had held since his return from Arzamas, underpinned by some secret undertakings, or maybe warnings, from the *kontora*. Or maybe, for all Vasin knew, from Katya herself.

"I'm happy, Katya. Thanks. We're all very happy."

She gave him a long look and squeezed his clenched hands across the marble table.

"He likes you. He trusts you. Trust him."

"Did Orlov send you to say that?"

Katya was unfazed by the defiance in his voice.

"No, Sasha. He likes you because I liked you."

"You chose me, like a dress? Tried me on for size?"

Vasin knew he was being rude, but could not help himself.

"Dearest. Just letting you know who your friends are."

Without glancing backward, Katya waved a hand to summon the headwaiter, who appeared instantly at her side.

"You, Sasha, have to try the bird's milk cake."

She said it like an order. Vasin remained silent as waiters bustled about them bearing coffeepots and plates of sticky desserts.

"You're my friend, Katya?"

"Of course I am, Sasha."

"Then I need you to do me a favor."

Katya shot Vasin a sidelong glance.

"Thought you might, darling."

"I need you to keep your ears open. When Orlov's bigwig friends come to dinner. When you're chatting with their wives. I need you to find out everything you can about Cuba."

"Cuba? What about it?"

"Like what the hell we're up to there. And why."

"Oh dear. And what do *you* think we're up to, Sasha?"

"Something . . . reckless. And there's another thing."

"Two favors. Go on."

"What's the story between your husband and Ivan Serov?"

"They hate each other. I imagine you knew that already. And there probably is a story, as you put it. But I don't know it."

"Could you find out?"

Katya straightened in her chair and took a sip of her coffee.

"My dear Sasha. You ignore me for months. And when I invite you out, you deluge me with requests. And you don't even say please. You used to be such a gentleman. So obliging to a lady's needs."

As Katya spoke the last phrase, she bent coquettishly forward over the table. Vasin had to stop himself from recoiling reflexively as she leaned close, the smell of her sweet perfume strong in his nostrils.

"Forgive me, Katya. Please."

6

KGB Headquarters, Moscow
3 August 1962

Sometimes the truth hid in plain sight. Vladimir Lenin Guzman, Spanish orphan, was nowhere to be found in the KGB's capacious registry—no denunciations, reports, arrests. But the humble archive of the ZAGS— the Registry of Acts of Citizen Status, the bureau which regulated the births, marriages, and deaths of all Soviet citizens—yielded a slim collection of cards. The issue of an internal passport to the sixteen-year-old Guzman, pupil of the General Technical Institute in Dnipropetrovsk, in the Ukrainian Soviet Socialist Republic. And then, six years later in 1956, the issue of a foreign travel passport. Highly unusual. Foreign travel was a luxury usually reserved for approved Party cadres.

A trip to the Foreign Ministry registry on Smolenskaya Embankment yielded Guzman's applications for a Soviet exit visa. The sponsor of his trip was listed as the Embassy of the Kingdom of Spain. The document was duly issued and used to leave the USSR. As Nina Alexeyevna had said, some Spanish children returned to their homeland after Stalin's death. The records showed that Vladimir Guzman departed on a passenger vessel from the port of Leningrad on 2 September 1956, bound for Bilbao. And never returned.

There was a final document in the Foreign Ministry files. An application to renew Guzman's Soviet passport in 1959. Vasin's eyes widened as he read. It had been filed at the Soviet Consulate-General in New York City. Guzman listed his address as 2571 SW Eighth Street, Miami, Florida.

Sofia Guzman—security-cleared Soviet military officer, trusted translator of secret documents, occasional interpreter to Raúl Castro— had a brother living in America.

"*Vladimir Lenin* Guzman? Really?" Orlov looked up from Vasin's report, flashing a rare smile. "Does she know?"

"Almost certainly not, sir. Nor does the Defense Ministry. She would never have passed security vetting if the Soviet authorities were aware of her brother's emigration to the United States. It seems to be a common surname. They seem to have been separated soon after arrival in Odessa in 'thirty-eight. So nobody ever connected brother and sister."

"Until you connected them. We have her, Vasin. Good work." Orlov was gloating like a schoolboy as he examined the blowup of Guzman's passport application photograph. "And what is our Spanish Vladimir Lenin up to, under the Florida sun?"

"We would have to put an official request in to the First Chief Directorate, sir."

Orlov's grin faded. The First Directorate—the powerful *kontora* department with exclusive authority over all the KGB's foreign intelligence operations. The General's brow furrowed momentarily as he calculated the cost of asking for favors from another branch of the service.

"Or . . ." Vasin continued after a carefully calibrated pause. Was he starting to learn how to play Orlov's game at last? "I could use my own private channels. Ask an old comrade from Arzamas-16. *Kontora* man, of course. Owes us a good turn."

Orlov nodded slowly.

"Do that. But in the meantime, bring her in. You have enough to put her on the hook. Get her working against Morozov. Now."

7

KGB Headquarters, Moscow
3 August 1962

The old bruiser Pushkov sat to Vasin's right, a hulking presence in his crumpled suit. Nadezhdin sat opposite, sweating profusely in the heat of Vasin's stuffy Lubyanka office. On the table were a mess of brimming ashtrays, surveillance photographs, telephone transcripts, watchers' reports.

"I say we bring her in hard." Pushkov spoke with authority. Every man in the room knew he'd spent years hunting down renegade Soviet agents. Turning them. Killing them. "Yank her off the street now. Don't let her go till she breaks. Bring her here, to the cells. Downstairs."

"Not the Lubyanka. She'll push back. Clam up. She's proud." In truth, Vasin was dreading the moment that he would have to face Sofia, angry and defiant, and somehow bend her will to his own. Orlov had authorized him to use the full, terrifying might of the Soviet secret police to break her. Some men—like Pushkov—gloried in their power and wielded it as casually as a butcher might his bolt gun. But Vasin knew the machine well, and feared it.

"A *kontora* safe house, at least. A nice one."

Pushkov grunted dismissively.

"You want flowers in it? Nice tea service?"

"Both those things. We're not brutes, Pushkov. She's a Soviet officer and a patriot."

"Saw quite a few Soviet patriots down in the Lubyanka cells in my day. Sir."

"Happily, we're not in the old days anymore, Major Pushkov. I'm interested in results, not fulfilling some death-list quota. We do this nicely. I'm helping Sofia Rafaelovna to see that her duty to the Motherland obliges her to work for us. But it's going to be her choice. Understood?"

The old thug sighed, nodded dismissively, and stood.

"Flowers and teacups. Coming up, boss."

The August morning promised heat. There would no mistaking Sofia in a crowd. Tall, proud as a high-stepping dressage horse, the Spanish girl had coal-black hair and the scything regard of a woman who knows her own power. Vasin had seen such women on the cinema screen, but he had never seen such a creature in the flesh on a Moscow street. And this woman was not a man's ornamental plaything. She wore her uniform skirt short, her *pilotka* uniform cap at a defiant angle. On her shoulder, the new-model lieutenant's epaulettes; in her stride, the confidence of a Soviet career woman. A confidence that Vasin had been ordered to destroy.

Vasin hovered uncertainly in the street behind the General Staff headquarters on Gogolevsky Boulevard watching a stream of personnel heading toward the metro. He kept glancing up at the giant stucco star on the side of the building's central tower as if for inspiration, practicing his introductions out loud like a nervous teenager.

Vasin turned back toward the building and spotted Sofia Guzman walking briskly with a small group of colleagues. He stumbled to intercept her, raising a hand in greeting. Sofia looked at Vasin as though he were a madman. She attempted to step into the road to pass him but Vasin blocked her path.

"Comrade Lieutenant! Good day to you." Vasin winced inwardly at his awkwardness but plowed on. "We met at the Cuban reception, remember?"

Sofia stopped, unsmiling. Her companions hesitated, then walked on. Some glanced back, intrigued at the unfolding scene.

"You. So you tracked me down after all."

"I wanted to ask if you have time to have a cup of tea. With me, I mean."

"My thanks, Colonel. But no, thanks. If you want to see me officially, go through the proper channels. And now I have to get home. Please excuse me."

Sofia's tone was icy cold, but there was a spark of angry fire in her eyes.

"Wait. Please." Vasin was grateful that his waiting *kontora* team could not hear his stuttering performance. "It's about your brother."

Sofia had pushed halfway past him, but stopped in her tracks and turned back to face him. She inhaled sharply, as though she had touched a live wire.

"My brother?"

Ah. There it was. Vasin felt the old, guilty thrill of power. In a second, the roles of the stuttering, balding man and the haughty, beautiful woman had snapped into something different. The man now holding the power of secret knowledge, the woman suddenly humbled, anxious.

"Your little brother, Vladimir. You came to the USSR together. Do you remember him?"

Sofia's fine face struggled to maintain composure for a few moments before crumpling.

"Yes. Yes, I remember him. What's happened?"

"I have good news for you. We have found Vladimir. But you need to come with me."

Vasin took Sofia by the elbow and steered her, unresisting, toward the Volga with Nadezhdin at the wheel. Pushkov courteously opened the door for Sofia and Vasin before settling into the front passenger seat. They drove in silence, Sofia staring resolutely out the window all the way.

The *kontora* apartment was not much less sterile than one of the Lubyanka's basement interview rooms. Standard-issue government furniture, flimsy nylon net curtains, and a carpet of institutional brown. But, Vasin noted, Pushkov had indeed brought flowers, which leaned crookedly from a too-big vase on the coffee table. The place was wired, and looked it. Beyond the windows, there was a low grumble of traffic from Novinsky Boulevard. Sofia shrugged off her jacket on her own, refusing Vasin's gesture of help. When she turned back from the coat-rack, she had composed her face into a mask.

"So how much will I have to pay in order to hear Vladimir's story?"

"Nothing at all, Sofia. This isn't a bazaar. But there are some things that I think you need to know."

Sofia stood ramrod straight, her eyes flashing in defiance. He gestured to her to sit, and she hesitated for a long, insolent moment before obeying. She was not going to make this easy for him.

One by one, Vasin produced his papers. The embarkation form from Marfa Scherbak; Vladimir's orphanage documents that he'd ordered up from Dnipropetrovsk; his passport applications from ZAGS; the Foreign Ministry passport applications. As Vasin talked Sofia through them she remained impassive. He felt like a conjurer attempting a trick for an audience resolutely determined not to be impressed.

"And so you see, Sofia Rafaelovna—you have a brother living in the West. A brother of whose existence your superiors are not aware."

Sofia merely blinked hard and kept her eyes on the meager crop of documents.

"You have a photograph of him?"

"Maybe."

"And what does Vladimir do, in Miami?"

"I cannot tell you that, Lieutenant."

Sofia's eyes snapped upward to meet Vasin's.

"You are bluffing," she said simply.

Vasin straightened in his chair, summoning his stoniest face.

"Sofia Rafaelovna. I need to ask you about Oleg Morozov."

"Morozov?"

The question had evidently taken her by surprise.

"You had coffee in the Shokoladnitsa café."

"We did. We met at a May Day reception. He's been inviting me out ever since. Coffee. Theater."

"Why do you agree to meet him?"

Sofia's mascaraed eyes glared, resentful.

"Why does any woman meet a man? He's intelligent. Amusing."

"Married."

"Not for much longer, he says. Not that it's your business."

"And does he ask you anything about your work?"

Sofia stiffened.

"Perhaps. He tells me about his. I talk about mine. What is this about, Colonel? What does this have to do with my brother? If this man you are taking about is my brother."

"Morozov never asked you to pass him any documents?"

"No."

"And Operation Anadyr?

At the word *Anadyr* Sofia's face firmed into a sneer of outright defiance. She raised an eyebrow in place of an answer as if to say: Above your pay grade, Colonel. Vasin felt the interview slipping out of his hands. Time to land the blow.

"Sofia. Listen to me very carefully. We believe that Morozov is an American spy. We need you to help us catch him. Do you understand? We are asking you to perform a secret task for the security of the Motherland."

She blinked, rapidly, but did not answer.

"Sofia, I need to know what you have told him. Does Morozov know what Operation Anadyr is?"

"He does." Her voice had become deadpan. "But not from me."

"Tell me what he knows about Anadyr. The outline."

"Colonel. I don't think you know what you are doing." Sofia's composure had become adamantine. "Allow me to put you straight. Indeed, Colonel Morozov recruited me for a special mission. Someone to keep an eye on Operation Anadyr, from the inside."

"Morozov asked you to work as a spy? For him?"

"Not for him. For his boss, naturally."

"His boss?"

"Don't play games with me, Colonel Vasin. We both know."

Control your face, Vasin. He studiously maintained a moment of silence. When Vasin spoke, he made his voice deliberately flat.

"Speak his name, please. For the record."

Sofia glanced around, as if looking for hidden listeners.

"Colonel General Serov."

Involuntarily Vasin shot a look at Pushkov, who stood invisibly concealed behind a large mirror that hung over the sofa.

"Ivan Alexandrovich Serov?"

Sofia sensed the surprise in Vasin's voice and drew strength from it. She straightened her back, smoothing her skirt.

"Yes, Colonel. You didn't know? Morozov is working for Serov. Personally. And so, I suppose, am I."

8

Frunze Embankment, Moscow
4 August 1962

"Ivan fucking *Serov?*"

Tokarev and Vasin sat out a summer shower in Vasin's Moskvich car, watching sheets of rain ripple across the surface of the Moscow River. Tokarev turned to look at Vasin as though he were a village idiot.

"You're seriously asking me, what if your alleged spy works personally for Ivan Serov?

"You heard me right."

"Then I say, you're very fucked, kid."

"Why?"

"Oh—only because Serov is the most powerful man in the Soviet security apparat. Start with that. You know he used to head the *kontora,* right? Director of the KGB for eight years. Now—director of the GRU."

"I'm not a fool, Tokarev. I know the history."

"Right. Good to know. Well, think about this. Serov personally sent tens of thousands to their graves during the Stalin years. And yet he's still here. What does that tell you about him? How many of his own colleagues and bosses did he have to sink to remain alive? He's ruthless. Follows no principle but his own survival."

"I know a few people like that in the *kontora.*"

Meaning one in particular. General Orlov.

"Glad you do. Hope this ruthless person is on your side."

"Why wouldn't he be?"

"Because you said that your suspected spy is a close personal associate of General Serov's. So—if this man is indeed an American spy, then Serov himself is in for the high jump. If he's not, then what? You're taking a potshot at Serov's man. Which means you're attacking Serov, too. And he won't take kindly to that. You take a shot at the boss, make sure you don't miss."

"I have no intention of taking shots at anyone, Tokarev. I don't care about Serov, I care about my spy. But I need to know something. I need to know . . ."

As Vasin searched for the right words, Tokarev finished his sentence for him.

"You need to know, might your guy actually be pulling this spy shit on Serov's orders? Is he actually being *run* by Serov? Is your man—what do you spooks call it—a dangle? Trailing his coat in front of the Yankees to feed them disinformation? That your question?"

Tokarev was smart. Alarmingly smart. Vasin wondered how much he really knew.

"That's my question, precisely, Major."

"Well. You can start by telling me your supposed spy's name. Guessing Orlov has authorized you to."

Again a moment of disquiet for Vasin. That morning Orlov had just authorized that very thing.

"Fine. Oleg Morozov. Colonel in the GRU."

Tokarev let out a long, low whistle.

"Morozov?"

"Know him?"

"Seen him. Know of him. Chose a tough one, there, chum."

"Tough, why?"

"Because—yes. He is a protégé of Serov's. Morozov gets invited to jolly lunches at his boss's dacha, goes on hunting trips with top Army brass."

Which would make Morozov the most dangerous kind of spy, Vasin had long ago realized. To learn the USSR's deepest secrets, Morozov simply needed to pour the drinks for his superiors and listen to their loose talk.

"Anything else I need to know, Tokarev?"

"Maybe. But I don't trust you. Yet."

"So how can you help me?"

Tokarev held up his plastic hands in a gesture of powerlessness.

"Please, Tokarev. Morozov is guilty. I know it. I just need to prove it."

The old cavalryman crooked his head with a look of deep skepticism. "You *know* it?"

"Okay. Put it this way: Morozov has to be guilty. Orlov has ordered me to nail him. Therefore I have to nail him. You know how it works."

The older man nodded curtly. The shower was abating. Tokarev fumbled with the stiff door latch and levered himself out of the tiny car, gesturing Vasin to follow. They walked a few yards from the car to a bus stop, where Tokarev stopped and looked about him conspiratorially.

"You know Orlov and Serov have a history, right?"

"What history?"

"Long story. But you're caught between two big beasts who despise each other. Ever considered that you might be our friend Orlov's pawn? A sacrificial pawn?"

"What makes you say that?"

"Consider this. Whatever else he might be, Morozov is the great man's friend. You think of that as your main problem in investigating him, right? But what if it's not the problem but the point?"

"Orlov wants to bring down Morozov just to embarrass his old enemy?"

"Embarrass? To *destroy* his old enemy, more like. Get him fired. Get him jailed. Get him shot, maybe. That's the game. Those are the stakes. Still want me to go ahead and join you as you jump into the meat grinder?"

9

KGB Headquarters, Moscow
4 August 1962

Kuznetsov marched down the fourth-floor corridor of the Lubyanka, chatting loudly with a group of colleagues. All four men wore new-pattern uniforms and sported deep tans—ineradicable evidence of their membership in the *kontora's* elite Cuban detail. Kuznetsov was in mid-anecdote when he spotted Vasin heading down the corridor toward him. He stopped abruptly, muttered an excuse, and turned on his heel to scuttle back into the meeting room from which the group had just emerged.

"Kuznetsov—you can't escape. I spotted you."

Vasin leaned on the door frame, blocking Kuznetsov's exit from the now-empty room.

"Fuck off. Leave me alone."

"That's not very friendly."

Vasin closed the door behind him.

"I need another . . ."

"Favor? You always do. That's why I said fuck off, in advance."

"Know anyone working Miami for the First Chief Directorate?"

"What part of 'fuck off' didn't you understand, Vasin?"

"I'll take that as a yes. We need some information. On a Soviet citizen of Spanish origin, living in Miami, Florida. Vladimir Lenin Guzman. Here's his address. We need background. Photos. Dirt, ideally. And we need it very fast. And before you say it again—yes, I will fuck off. After you do this for me. But right now, I need that info. That guy is the brother of someone working inside Anadyr, right here in Moscow. We need to know what he's up to."

"Vasin . . ." Kuznetsov gestured desperately around him at the high-ceilinged room with its heavy net curtains. "You know you actually work for the Committee for State Security, right? As in, we are actually *in* the fucking Lubyanka? If you want this info from the First Chief Directorate, why not ask them yourself? Why do you always have to brush your teeth through your asshole, Vasin?"

"Like I told you last time. We don't want our guy tipped off."

"Bullshit. This is some private thing you've got going. Or your evil boss has got going, more like. My advice—get yourself out of it. And . . ."

"Fuck off?"

"Exactly."

"I've already promised you I will do just that. Like I said—right after you do this last thing for me. Here are his details. Oh—and here's something I picked up for you. Special Cases had a few going spare."

Vasin reached inside his tunic and pulled out a postcard. It bore the scarlet trident logo of the AZLK car factory, a stamped number, and a set of printed instructions.

"Looks like your number in the *kontora*'s car queue has come up early. Not 1971, as scheduled, but 1962. Next month, in fact. You need to pay your deposit of eleven hundred and thirteen rubles by the fifteenth of August. You should have the cash, with your overseas pay, right?"

Kuznetsov snatched the card from Vasin's hand, peering suspiciously at his own name and date of birth written across the top.

"A Moskvich?"

"Only astronauts get a Volga sedan, pal."

"No . . . I mean, this is a bribe."

"Not a bribe. You're paying for the car with your own money. We just moved you up the list a bit. Because we think you deserve it."

Kuznetsov screwed up his face in a grimace of distaste.

" 'We' being . . . ?"

"Special Cases. Welcome to the family."

10

KGB Headquarters, Moscow
6 August 1962

The surveillance photos Kuznetsov rustled up from the First Chief Directorate two days later were grainy but clear. They showed a fine-boned young man, indecently handsome, with a lick of greased-back hair and a fashionably baggy suit. There was something unmistakably familiar about the high arch of his brows, the long, noble Spanish nose. Sofia's brother, Vladimir, photographed on a Miami street corner by a KGB goon team a month before.

In the picture Vladimir leaned forward, snapped in the act of handing a flyer to a passerby. The next photo was an image of the flyer itself, and on the back a helpfully typewritten translation. "Cubans for Peace and Justice," read the top line. "Responsible citizens of America! Join us to rid our continent of the scourge of Communist dictatorship." At the bottom was a grotesque cartoon of Fidel Castro and Che Guevara as wild animals feasting on the carcass of Cuba. Then more surveillance photos of Vladimir entering the headquarters of Cubans for Liberty— apparently an anti-Castro émigré group. Vladimir carrying bales of freshly printed newspapers with a lanky young American by his side. Vasin turned the photo to examine the caption. "Subject with Cubans for Liberty fellow member identified as LEE H OSVALD—State Security Person of Interest: See Case File KZ1862-78-TS."

Whoever the hell this Osvald was, Vasin didn't need to know the full story—he had more than enough. He picked up the phone and dialed an internal number.

"Pushkov? Bring Guzman in. Here, to the Lubyanka. Right now."

Vasin glanced at his watch. Half past nine in the evening. Forty minutes had passed since Pushkov called up to say that Sofia was in the building. She'd been waiting long enough. He gathered up his papers and took the elevator to the Lubyanka's ground floor. The "soft" interview rooms—not the cellars, as Pushkov had wanted.

The interrogation room had a single, narrow window that looked out over the central courtyard through a sturdy steel grille. As he walked in, Vasin could almost smell the tension in the air of the dusty, airless space. Sofia sat, hunched forward, on a plain wooden chair. Opposite her sat Pushkov, his face grim. It was clear that he had smothered the woman into quiet with his own menacing silence.

"Sofia Rafaelovna. I am so sorry to keep you waiting."

Pushkov looked up, contemptuous of his boss's politeness. Vasin dismissed the man from the room with a nod.

"Forgive me for the location. I didn't mean to alarm you."

By which he meant, I brought you here to alarm you. Just a little. Please Sofia, Vasin wanted to say. Make this easy for both of us.

Sofia straightened and raised her head defiantly.

"Colonel, I'm expected. At a friend's house. They'll be missing me."

"Would you like me to get someone to telephone your friends?"

Sofia's lip curled in a sarcastic smile.

"Tell them I'm detained in the Lubyanka?"

"Sofia Rafaelovna, you are not in any trouble. On the contrary. We need your help."

"So you said."

"You need to know that he's lying. Morozov isn't working for Serov. He's working for the Americans. He's a spy and a traitor."

Sofia looked sullen.

"You said that, too. But if he's a traitor, why not let us deal with it, Colonel?"

"Us"—meaning the GRU. The tribal instinct of every intelligence service: keep your secrets close, wash your dirty laundry in private.

"Comrade Lieutenant. I do not wish to make this difficult for you. This is not a betrayal of your service. You are just sharing information with another of the Motherland's very secret services. It will go no further. And we are all on the same side."

The glibness of his own lies made Vasin's mouth go dry. Sofia unclenched her hands and sat straighter. She seemed to come to a private decision.

"No."

"No?"

"I will say no more. Do your worst, Colonel. So, I have a brother I last saw when he was a tiny child. Now you claim that he is in the West, without showing me any proof. And even if what you say is true, he made a bad choice. This has nothing to do with me. What will you do, Colonel? Tell my superiors? *What* will you tell them? That I am responsible for the actions of my lost brother? I made a mistake not calling my bosses immediately."

She stood, and Vasin with her. Sofia was nearly as tall as Vasin, and looked him straight in the eye. She seemed to be drawing strength from her own righteousness.

"Lieutenant. Not so fast." Vasin heard the harshness in his own voice. "You need to see these. Sit. You asked for proof. Here it is."

After a moment's hesitation, Sofia obeyed. She took the photos that Vasin handed her, one by one, and examined them minutely before putting them gently on the table. The family resemblance in the two siblings' haughty, handsome faces was undeniable. She said nothing. The joy of seeing her brother for the first time in her adult life crossed her face first, followed by cold shock as another realization crystallized, photo by photo. Vladimir was a counterrevolutionary, an anti-Communist, a traitor. A fatal threat to her and the life she had made for herself in the USSR. This, at least, Sofia understood without being told. Her face was suddenly haggard, her eyes puffy with welling tears.

"There is more." Vasin forced himself to be merciless. "As you see, he is working for a counterrevolutionary group dedicated to the downfall of our Socialist brothers in Cuba. But I have not told you that he has been targeted. He is on a list, Sofia. Our list. A *kontora* list. For liquidation."

Vasin tried to make his eyes hard enough to resist Sofia's penetrating gaze. He winced inwardly at the pitiless lie that had just come from his own mouth. But he said nothing more. They sat in silence in the gathering gloom of the interview room, listening to the ticking of an ugly wall clock, letting time do its work.

"Is that true?"

Her voice had cracked. Vasin sensed that Sofia was finally close to breaking.

"Yes, Sofia. It was confirmed to me yesterday. A *kontora* team is in place in Miami, waiting for orders. The gunmen are armed and briefed. Only you can save him. But to do that you must agree to show us all the documents that you pass to Morozov concerning Operation Anadyr. You will bring every paper to me for vetting, first. Work with us, Sofia, to keep our country safe. And to keep Vladimir alive."

Was there a better way to do this? Vasin glanced in the wall mirror, from behind which Lukyanov was filming the scene. He saw himself, shabby in his sweaty uniform. A blank notepad squared on the table. A scattering of photographs. Microphones on the underside of the table. Opposite him, a weeping woman caressing the images of a sibling she had not seen since early childhood. But what neither the mirror nor the camera could see was Vasin's profound sensation of absence, of not recognizing himself as he sat impassively before the storm of human emotion he had conjured up from the dead paper of the files and photographs. Sofia's tearstained face as Vasin laid out his cards, one by one. A visible sag in her body as she realized that her life was being taken away from her and gathered into alien hands.

Christ, Vasin thought. What have I become? Was he becoming a native of Orlov's shadowlands where lies and secrets were just weapons in a war to break human will? Vasin felt the power of the lie inhabiting him like an evil spirit, curling around his conscience and his reason and infecting his life.

11

Smolensky Boulevard, Moscow
11 August 1962

A hot Moscow summer afternoon, the sidewalks baking and the court-yards full of citizens escaping from the stuffiness of their apartments under the shade of the poplar trees and the angular shadows of build-ings. Vasin wore a short-sleeved cotton shirt, a straw porkpie hat that was a souvenir from a holiday in Gagra, and a pair of German gold-framed sunglasses he'd bought in the commission store. He caught sight of himself in a shop window and saw a man he half recognized—only this simulacrum was fatter, older, slower. A midranking apparatchik in too-tight trousers. Vasin hurried along Smolensky Boulevard and turned down the hill toward the trolleybus stop.

Sofia waited among a crowd of bickering families on Saturday after-noon expeditions to the park. Her cotton sarafan dress was the simplest and most unflattering kind, a droopy bag of cheap printed cotton. She wore no makeup and her hair, under a plain cotton worker's cap, was tangled and lank. Despite Vasin's instructions that they should ignore each other, Sofia fixed him with a glare as soon as she spotted him.

They stood, a few meters from each other, not speaking until the trol-ley arrived two minutes later. They both boarded, Vasin waiting until the last second to check out the other passengers. No watchers. They rode one stop down the Garden Ring and both alighted, as agreed, at the Neopolimovsky Lane stop. As they stood alone, Vasin could feel Sofia's contempt and anger as perceptibly as the heat radiating off the sun-scorched expanse of sidewalk.

The *kontora* apartment felt even gloomier than it had at the first meeting. There was a clammy smell of unaired rooms, and of stale ciga-rette smoke, and of an unemptied bin. Vasin trotted over solicitously to open the windows, but found them painted shut except for the small window-in-a-window in the top corners, which he succeeded in prying open after a struggle. The noise of traffic spilled in from the boulevard.

"Sorry. They left it in a mess." Vasin gestured around, though the place was in fact the opposite of messy. The institutional armchairs were precisely arranged, and the crockery was stacked impeccably in a glass-fronted cabinet. The place was as impersonal as a hotel room. "Tea?"

Sofia said nothing, standing in the exact middle of the room as though to keep maximum distance from anything owned or touched by the *kontora*. Vasin took that as a yes and went to the kitchen.

"You can relax, Sofia Rafaelovna," he called as he filled the kettle. "There's nobody else here."

She moved to a place where she could see him through the open kitchen door. Her stare was wary.

"Which means what?"

Vasin paused in his search of the almost-empty cupboards for tea, a teapot, cups, and saucers. *It means I'm breaking the rules.* Say it or not say it? He met Sofia's eye.

"It means I'm breaking the rules, Sofia. We're not supposed to have any unrecorded contact."

Her eyebrow crept up a fraction in contempt.

"You would like to put me at ease?" Sofia's voice was thick with scorn. "First, flowers. Then, photographs of Vladimir. Now—tea and privacy. So we can get to know each other better? Become friends?"

Sofia had moved closer to the kitchen door. A bead of sweat had broken out from under her cap and ran down her forehead, but she made no move to wipe it away. There were dark stains under her armpits, and her jaw was set hard.

"Lieutenant Guzman. Sofia. I'd like . . . I'd like to explain, at least. I want you to understand. I want you to know why it's so important for you to help us. And I want to help you, too."

Sofia slowly tugged the sweat-stained cap from her head, wiped her face on the short sleeve of her dress in a shrugging motion, and made a grunt of acknowledgment.

"Sure you do. Bathroom?"

Vasin nodded down the corridor. By the time she returned he had set the tea things on the table. Sofia's face and hair were wet.

"Oh, I'm so sorry. Let me find you a towel."

"Don't bother. Say what you have to say. I am listening respectfully for your further instructions, Comrade Colonel."

She stood, arms folded across her chest and feet planted apart, immovable as a statue. Her pose reminded Vasin of his mother, squaring up to some petty bureaucrat or shop manager. The ground I stand on is what I am, the stance said. I will not yield it.

Vasin had rehearsed his lines beforehand, of course. But now all his prepared sweet-talk crumbled into a tangle of deceitful dross. With a case of this delicacy, Sofia's mere acquiescence would not be sufficient. Breaking her resistance had been easy enough—especially with the sledgehammer of a lie that Vasin had used to crush her will. But he needed more. He needed Sofia to lie for him—and lie convincingly. She had to be able to look Morozov in the eye and not betray the fact that she had been turned. In short, Vasin needed Sofia not just to take his orders but to be on his side. To actually believe.

Yet the woman who stood before him was, in spirit, as far away as Kamchatka.

Vasin hung his head, sat, and poured two cups of tea. He ran two hands through his thinning hair and gestured for Sofia to join him. She ignored him.

"I used to be a policeman, once, you know. Before I joined the *kontora*."

Silence. Vasin didn't bother to look up. He knew that Sofia's face would be a snarl of contempt. But he continued nonetheless.

"I miss it. A lot. The certainty of it. You knew where you were with Moscow criminals. Murderers—that was my area. Homicide. Saw a lot of sad, stupid, lost people. Interrogated them. Most of them were just violent drunks. Nothing to interest Holmes and Watson. I thought, when I started, that evil would be something dark and fascinating. Glinting in the dark like coal, if you dug hard enough for it. But it wasn't like coal. It was like digging through a trash can. Foul, stinking waste, worse and worse the deeper you got. Till you got to the bottom, and there it was. The truth. The solution. The guilty man. With nothing fascinating to say at all. Just banality. But . . . he was guilty. And so I punished him. Or, occasionally, her. But I brought justice. It felt good. Even though a detective was, I realized, pretty much identical to a sewage worker. Nonetheless, there we were, every day, the good guys hunting down the evil guys. Two teams. Two sides, in their different-colored jerseys. You know. Clear."

Still not a word or movement from Sofia. If anything, her still defiance seemed to have grown more deeply rooted.

"Then the *kontora* found me. Picked me out. Offered me a new apartment, privileges, all the rest. You know the story. We're both intelligence professionals. We move in the same world. In some ways I liked that world. I liked the power the *kontora* gave me. The superiority. Being above the rules. The Party's invisible avengers. All kinds of top people, professors, apparatchiks, dancing attendance at the snap of your fingers. Or of your boss's fingers. The power that wielding secrets— wielding fear—gives you. Yes, Sofia. I tell you honestly that I liked that. And . . ."

Vasin swiveled around in his armchair to finally face Sofia, but her eyes were still resolutely fixed on the wall.

"And I know you think that I am telling you all this just to gain your confidence, to get you to lower your defenses. And you would be right. That is precisely what I am doing, Sofia. But also I am telling you the truth. And the truth is this—at the *kontora*, I discovered that there is no justice. That the guilty are not punished. Or at least they are not punished solely because they are guilty. There is only expedience. And power games. Bureaucratic plays. A huge horse fair that trades secrets for power. Information to be hoarded like ammunition and used later in some gunfight between top apparatchiks. It stinks. But . . . and this is what I really want to say to you, Sofia . . . for the first time in all my years at the *kontora* I have come across a case where I know what I am doing is right. That finally I am pursuing someone who is actually guilty. Someone who is an urgent threat to the Motherland. A man who is bad. Genuinely dangerous. A man who truly deserves his bullet. Unlike the millions that the *kontora* has felled with their bullets over the years."

Sofia was looking at him at last, an expression of disbelief on her face. Her jaw throbbed as she fought against her evident resolve to remain silent, but after a moment she spoke.

"You mean Morozov?"

"Morozov. Yes."

She nodded slowly, casting her eyes around the room.

"Liberal comrades, your bosses. They really do allow you to say anything to get your way. But are you quite sure they will approve when they hear the tape of your little speech?"

"There's no tape, Sofia."

"We're in a *kontora* apartment. I did notice that much."

Vasin stood and walked down the corridor, past the kitchen, to a doorway adjacent to the sitting room. It stood ajar. He pushed it open and flicked a light switch. Sofia, doubtless against her better judgment, had followed him and peered into the listening station. The lounge was clearly visible through a two-way mirror, in front of which a bulky camera was positioned on a tripod. Along the opposite wall were banks of reel-to-reel tape recorders, labeled with their various listening circuits. A long, narrow table covered in notepads, spare tape reels, and full ashtrays ran under the recording machines.

"See? Nobody here. We're alone. Nobody listening."

Vasin walked to the far end of the observation station and picked up a magazine from a pile. It was an old copy of *Ogonek,* a popular picture magazine. Underneath it was a copy of *Evening Moscow,* a crossword puzzle album, and below that a Spartak football club fan magazine.

"What a fucking boring job. Sad bunch of losers."

Sofia, despite herself, cracked a smile.

"I'm starting to believe that the *kontora* really isn't listening. Unless they're hiding in the trash can."

Vasin smiled back, wryly. She'd cracked a dry joke. *Musor*—"trash"— was the universal slang for cops. He settled on the arm of a chair that was pushed against the back wall. Sofia leaned on the long table, her fingers sliding across the glossy plastic switches of one of the recording machines. He let the silence thicken between them.

"How can you be so sure that he's a traitor, Colonel?"

"You're not supposed to know. But I will tell you anyway. Story began in France, last year. Morozov was at the Paris Air Show. Part of an official delegation. Of course, the *kontora* was keeping tabs on them. But it's hard to know where everyone is all the time. Or so they tell me. I've never been to the capitalist countries, so I don't know. But the point is, Morozov went missing for some hours. I mean, deliberately missing. Dry-cleaned himself, if you know what I mean?"

Sofia raised her eyes to the ceiling to say, Obviously I know.

"And the *kontora* has also known for a while—don't ask me how, because I honestly don't know myself—that there's a high-level American mole somewhere inside the Soviet security establishment. So after his disappearing act in Paris, the *kontora* naturally began to suspect

Morozov. The higher-ups decided not to reel him in straightaway. Decided to watch him, here in Moscow. And again, right after he arrived back and before they . . . I mean before we . . . had put a proper net round him, he likely met with someone from the US Embassy. Nobody saw it. But there was Morozov, there was an American diplomat, both evading their asses off, similar time, similar place. Not enough, again, to catch him. But enough for the *kontora* to put him under close surveillance. Which was when I came on the team. Last November."

Sofia made a moue of acknowledgment. At least she was listening. And apparently taking Vasin's words seriously.

"Since when does the *kontora* act with such delicacy? Toward an espionage suspect?"

Now it was Vasin's turn to evade her eye.

"Well. Good question."

"It's not a question. The answer's obvious. Because Morozov works for the Aquarium. And you KGB guys wanted to reel him in yourselves, rather than hand him over to the Army's own counterintelligence people. Am I right?"

Vasin had no choice but to shrug in affirmation. Sofia pressed on.

"But so far you have nothing concrete against Morozov."

"Until we spoke to you."

"What does that mean? What did *I* give you that made you think he was an American spy?" Sofia's voice rose in indignation.

"Excuse me—Sofia, you told us that he was asking for information on Operation Anadyr."

"So he was. On General Serov's orders. As I also told you."

"False flag operation. Recruited you on false pretenses . . ."

"Thanks, Colonel. I know what a false flag operation is."

"Of course you do. But did it not occur to you to ask why a Soviet colonel general—Ivan bloody Serov, head of the GRU—would be recruiting spies inside his own service?"

"You're wrong, Vasin. It did occur to me. That's exactly what I asked Morozov, when he first spoke to me about Anadyr. I said, 'But surely the Director already knows everything that goes on here.' And you know what he said to me? He said, 'Kid, believe me when I tell you that General Serov didn't survive as long as he has, where he has, by taking his subordinates at their word. All over our service, in every department, he needs his little birds. His little foot soldiers, his loyal whisperers, to tell him what's really happening. And you will be his little bird inside Anadyr.' Now, does that make sense to you, Colonel?"

Sofia was leaning forward, hissing her words, her hand gripping the edge of the desk.

"And you believed that he was some secret emissary of the boss?"

"Yes. Why would I not?"

"Took him at his word?"

A pause, in which Vasin sensed Sofia's patience with him stretching thinner and thinner. But eventually she turned her head back to him and answered.

"He showed me some photos. Of him and Serov. At the boss's home, arm in arm. Hunting together. He said they were good friends. That the boss trusted him to run his personal network. And . . . yes, I believed him. Believe him."

The last phrase came with an emphatic gesture of her hand—a chopping motion.

"After what I have told you?"

"What did you tell me, Colonel? That you have suspicions? Suspicions that you don't even quite believe yourselves? Where is your evidence?"

Vasin felt his control leap like a frog from his cupped hands. Now the conversation was spinning into disastrous territory.

"Morozov was recently observed taking deliberate evasive action to shake off our surveillance."

"In order to do what?"

"In order to meet *you*, Sofia."

"Which makes him a spy? Maybe it just makes him a *married man*."

Vasin felt himself exhale involuntarily. He was falling into himself. He knew exactly where this was going, sensed the precise parameters of his coming failure.

"Yes, Colonel," Sofia pressed on. "Oleg Vladimirovich is a professional. You think he doesn't notice when a *kontora* team is on his tail? When he wants to meet a woman in private, maybe he doesn't want an audience."

"You mean he . . ."

"Was interested in me? As a woman? Yes, he is. Which is not to say that I am interested in him. I am a decent Soviet woman. I will be no man's mistress. But that is Colonel Morozov's nature. A ladies' man. Or used to be. But I am not here to slander him. I put this to you—that he ran from your watchers not because he was a spy but because he was a man in love. Or in lust."

Oh Christ, thought Vasin. I had this woman on the hook. The biggest and most terrifying hook imaginable. And now she was twisting away from it, effortlessly, back into the depths.

"So, Sofia. You say Morozov is innocent."

"I didn't say that. I said, nothing you have told me proves that he is guilty."

"Let's suppose that he is innocent. Let's say the *kontora* has made a terrible, embarrassing mistake. It's possible. Morozov isn't a spy, he's a confidential agent of his boss. The *kontora* is barking up the wrong tree, and because we are so keen to take a scalp on the GRU side of the tracks we are blinded to the absence of evidence against him."

Sofia nodded, warily.

"Therefore, how can you help this man whom you seem to respect and trust? You can prove him innocent."

"By doing what you say."

"Exactly. By doing what I ask."

"You know that I will do that anyway. You have my brother, Vladimir, in your pocket. You have my assent already. So I don't know why we are here."

"Because, Sofia, I don't just need your hands and eyes in this operation. I need your heart. You have agreed to tell me about all the documents, all the information that Morozov asks for. And we will tell you what we think you should actually give him. But you must do all of this in such a way that he will never know that you are working with us."

"And that will save him—how?"

"If he is truly innocent, we will never catch him passing this information to the Americans. Because he has no contact with them, or so you insist. If your Morozov is really working for Serov, then Serov himself will ultimately confirm all the information was passed at his request. But, Sofia . . ."

Vasin crossed the narrow space between them and put a hand firmly on Sofia's shoulder. She tried to shrug it away immediately, but Vasin held her.

"Understand that I cannot stop the machine for which I am work-

73

ing. That is an impossibility. The investigation is under way. It is a juggernaut. I know that we have given you no choice but to comply. But believe me in this. If what you say is right—if Morozov is not an American spy—then the only way to save him is to help me know everything I can about him. If he has nothing to hide . . ."

"Then he has nothing to fear? Is that what you are about to tell me, Colonel Vasin?"

Their eyes locked. Vasin slowly released his grip on Sofia's shoulder and straightened.

"Yes, Sofia. That is exactly what I am telling you. If you want to protect him, cooperate. Wholeheartedly."

PART THREE

NOBODY WAS PUNISHED

You will hear thunder and remember me,

And think: she longed for storms . . .

ANNA AKHMATOVA

1

Serebryany Bor, Moscow
12 August 1962

The riverbank at the dacha settlement of Serebryany Bor was crowded with Sunday-afternoon sunbathers, a pale tribe of bloated white figures in unflattering floral swimsuits. Arkhipov edged his spluttering little UAZ jeep past the clusters of pedestrians, drawing up by a gate in a tall, green-painted wooden fence. He beeped his feeble horn, summoning an elderly, uniformed naval retainer who hauled the gates of the private compound open and made an approximation of a salute.

Unlike the packed public beach, the Navy Staff dacha was a picture postcard of idyllic Russian rural life. The house itself was a sprawling pre-Revolutionary manor, painted white and blue and set in birch woods. A freshly cut lawn stretched down to a pristine private river beach where a handful of officers' families were sunbathing or setting out food.

Captain First Class Valentin Savitsky spotted Arkhipov and stood, waving.

"Over here. Welcome!"

Arkhipov's comrades occupied a large wooden picnic table in a small grove overlooking the river. It was laid with an assortment of bottles and jars, a bowl of cucumbers and tomatoes, a great platter of cold cuts.

Half a dozen men sat around the table, all in civilian shirtsleeves and baggy summer trousers or shorts. Most had identical patches of sunburn on their chests and necks from working in the sun in their uniform undershirts. They all stood as Arkhipov approached—except for an older man who remained seated at the head of the table.

"Comrade Admiral—a wonderful surprise." Arkhipov saluted smartly.

Vice Admiral Leonid Leontyev, deputy commander of the Northern Fleet, waved down his salute with an open palm.

"No formality today, Vasily. We're all comrades together. Come, sit by me. You know everyone here . . ." Arkhipov nodded to the skippers and first officers of his new flotilla. "Except maybe young Maslennikov here? My sister's boy. Commander Ivan Semyonovich Maslennikov, naval intelligence. He'll be shipping with you and Savitsky on B-59. Your *politruk*."

Politruk—the boat's political officer. The Party's man on board, second only to the skipper in authority and his equal when it came to fire control. On ballistic-missile boats, only the commander and the *Politruk* carried the arming keys necessary to fire the nukes.

Maslennikov made to salute, stopped himself, then did it anyway. "It's an honor to serve under you, Captain."

The group shifted along the two wooden benches to make space for Arkhipov. Plates were passed and loaded with food, glasses filled. Toasts were drunk to the Soviet Navy, to their respective boats, to wives and sweethearts—may they never meet. The oldest joke in the fleet. Arkhipov wasn't really a drinking man—and after K-19, the docs had kept him off the booze for most of the last year. He could feel the summer heat and the chilled Kristall vodka going to his head.

"Let us drink to Captain Arkhipov's Order of the Red Banner!" The old admiral was by now also unsteady with drink. "Vasily Alexandrovich—to your decoration. To your heroism, sir."

There was something in Leontyev's hearty tone that caught on Arkhipov's ear. He raised his glass and stood, a little unsteadily.

"With your permission, sir? We all know why I got that medal. So let's not drink to my heroism. We'll drink to our lost comrades." The husky seriousness in Arkhipov's voice brought all the men to their feet, composing their faces into appropriate solemnity. "For them."

They did not clink glasses, as was customary when drinking for the dead, and drank off the toast in silence. When they resumed their seats, the jovial mood of the lunch party had evaporated. Leontyev was the first to break the silence.

"I'll say it, because nobody else will. What really happened on K-19, son? Tell us the war story. We all want to hear it."

Arkhipov looked down the table at the men who would be commanding his flotilla, at the eager young face of Maslennikov, at the weatherbeaten face of the Admiral.

"Out with it, man. All we ever heard was official guff and outlandish rumors. Do us good to hear it from the horse's mouth. Do you good to tell it. To fellow submariners. Shipmates."

"Maybe you're right."

Arkhipov poured himself another shot and downed it grimly, without waiting for a toast. He paused, then came to a private decision.

"Very well. Just between us. As you know, it was K-19's maiden voyage. Brand-new boat, pride of our fleet. Our first nuclear-powered ballistic-missile sub. First of her class. The whole crew were veterans, proud to serve on her. No wet-behind-the-ears new recruits. Best food in the whole Navy. The cook was seconded from the Navy Staff headquarters. Anyway. We had some teething troubles getting her up and running. A reactor screw-up before her sea trials meant that the whole kettle had to be taken apart and rebuilt. Then, when we finally got her out to sea to stretch her legs, a faulty gasket nearly flooded her. The old lags from the engineering section started to say she was unlucky."

"I was at her launch," interrupted the Admiral. "Some old Politburo dinosaur did the honors. Should have been launched by a woman, not a man, and when the damn fool swung the champagne bottle against her in the dry dock, it hadn't broken. Whole hull was covered in heavy rubberized paint, remember? Bottle just bounced off. Superstitious bunch, we sailors."

Maslennikov looked shocked. Mocking a member of the Politburo in front of junior officers was pushing the boundaries even of old Leontyev's seniority.

"We put to sea in June last year," continued Arkhipov. "On our way to our first war games. Our orders were to sneak into the North Atlantic undetected by the Yankees. Everything was going well. We celebrated the Captain's birthday with double rations of ice cream and red wine. Zateyev, Nikolai Vladimirovich—that was the skipper. You served under him, didn't you, Savitsky?"

"I did." Savitsky's booming voice contrasted with Arkhipov's confiding tone. "Fine fighting officer. Old-school, that man. Zateyev was a war veteran, like the respected Comrade Admiral here. No time for pussyfooting about. Would rather go to the bottom than stain the reputation of the fleet."

Arkhipov weighed his words for a long moment before resuming.

"You're correct, Savitsky. The Captain cared a lot about the honor of the service. More, maybe, than he did for his sailors. Anyway, he certainly kept a tight ship, made sure the men were happy. We got orders to proceed north along the west coast of Greenland and then cruise under the Arctic ice. Test how good the boat was at generating her own oxygen, see. She was built to stay under for weeks. In theory. Sneak all the way up to the Yankee coast without being detected."

"Amazing machine," breathed Leontyev, shaking his head.

"Indeed, sir. On the morning of July fourth I'd just started my watch, taken command of the boat. We were cruising at about ninety meters' depth, all systems normal. Then I had a call from the reactor control room. Me and Yura—Yury Postev, the lieutenant in charge of propulsion—ran to see what was wrong. The Captain would fine you for swearing. But Yura started saying, 'Shit, shit, shit.' Vibration in the coolant pressure. Needle went all the way down to zero. Then an alarm went off. The reactor SCRAM system kicked in, shut the reactor down automatically."

"And it did shut down, immediately?" It was Captain Rurik Ketov of B-4 who spoke—a former reactor officer himself.

"Sure. Control rods went in fine, under their own weight, just like they were designed to. So, yeah, the reactor shut down okay. But that wasn't the problem. The core was no longer producing power—but it had so much residual heat that we still needed to pump coolant in for days afterward. But the cooling piping was bust. The reactor compartment was full of radioactive steam from the breached coolant circuit. Temperature up to a hundred forty degrees in there. And the core itself was pushing eight hundred degrees and rising. Thing got so hot that it started a fire as the insulation of the coolant system caught light. Filin—the reactor officer—took a crew in there and put out the fire himself. Bloody hero, that man . . ."

Arkhipov's voice trailed into nothing until Leontyev prompted him.

"Didn't Zateyev order an evacuation?"

"Evacuate? We were still submerged, Admiral. For nearly two hours after the accident. Wasn't until after six a.m. that the skipper ordered us to surface. Guess he was worried about giving away our position until he was absolutely sure the reactor was screwed. Thing is, without the reactor we were more or less immobilized. A sitting duck. But it was not like we had a choice. We hoisted up the long-range radio mast to signal Moscow for orders, but the damn antenna had been damaged. So we put out a distress call on our short-range set and raised one of our diesel subs, S-270. She was about half a day's sailing to the south of us. Then we got a signal from another boat, much closer. But she was an American warship. Offered to come to our assistance. Captain Zateyev refused. Didn't want the boat falling into the hands of the imperialists. He was more concerned with what the *kontora* guys would do to him when he got back than with saving the lives of his crew . . ."

"Damn right," Savitsky chimed in. "You don't surrender a fighting ship to the enemy just because of some technical fault. Or maybe you disagree, Captain?"

Arkhipov pointedly ignored the interruption.

"So we were on our own till S-270 reached us. The skipper called all the officers into the mess. We were ventilating the reactor spaces to the outside air as hard as the air-con pumps would run. But even aft of the bridge it was still hot as a sauna. The runaway reactor was cooking up the whole boat. Filin said that unless we got the coolant running once again, the core was going to melt right through the hull and send us all to the bottom. Laid the reactor schematics out on the table. Said, 'We have one chance. Connect the ship's fresh water supply to the coolant system, and pump it full of cold fresh water.' But that meant welding inside the reactor compartment, which was hotter than hell, and radioactive to boot. Radiation gauges showing lethal levels. And there wasn't any kind of protective gear aboard, apart from gas capes. The skipper knew he would be sending the lads to their deaths, so he asked for volunteers."

Something, a kind of smile of pain, crossed Arkhipov's face as he paused, weighing the memory in his mind's eye.

"Filin's whole engineering team stepped forward. Every one. Eight men. That's heroism. Filin organized a system where the men went in in pairs, for no longer than ten minutes at a time. In their foul-weather capes and rubber thermal suits. That's all the protection they had. Doctor mixed them up some dried milk to drink. Milk, can you imagine! But the lads drank it down like it was a magic potion. First one in was an engineer sergeant, with a hacksaw. Boris Korchalov. Came out ten minutes later, red in the face like he'd been too long in the *banya*. Puked his guts out and collapsed when they pulled him through the hatch. Couple of the others lined up to go in started to weep, so Filin slapped them in the face, one by one, told them to pull themselves together. So in they went, one after another, sawing, sawing, resting for a while, then back again when their turn came. Took them two hours to saw through the steel piping and cut new threads. The steam had spread through the whole sub by now. Everyone knew we were breathing poison. In the galley the cook had a panic attack, started screaming to be let out of this floating coffin, scrambling for the escape hatch. Maybe that's why the Captain didn't want to surface at first. Nowhere to go when you're underwater. On the surface, you've got to fight the urge to run up that ladder into God's fresh air."

"The skipper didn't want to let the crew out on the deck?" Captain Alexei Dubivko of B-36 this time, his face creased with strain as he imagined the unfolding disaster. "Away from the poison?"

"It's the North Atlantic, Comrade. You know it as well as I do. Swell breaking over the hull would have swept the men away. And in any case, how would he ever get the men back down? No. The skipper felt the panic flickering like a flame up and down the ship. I went from compartment to compartment telling everyone reassuring lies. I got back to the control room and the Captain had ordered the sergeant-at-arms to gather all the small arms from the lockers and throw them overboard."

"He thought the crew would mutiny?" Leontyev was shaking his head. "That wasn't in the official report."

"Somehow word got out from the radio operators that the skipper had turned down the offer of help from the Yanks. Crew were muttering that the boss preferred them all to die heroes than surrender the boat. So yeah, the Captain was probably right. He even ordered the rocket flares from the inflatable lifeboats tossed. He kept one pistol for himself and issued four more to his most trusted officers. That included me—just in case you were wondering, Savitsky."

The two men exchanged a hard look down the table.

"But then the word came forward that Filin had done it. Rigged up a pipe to the cooling system and started running water through. The Captain got on the intercom and asked for three cheers for the engineering crew. Not that the poor bastards could hear much. Horrible sight. Skin peeling off them, hair falling out. Looked like they'd been boiled alive. But the reactor core temperature was coming down. For an hour or so. Then the seal they'd made burst. Filin had to get his men off their stretchers and in there again to fit a new one. With superheated steam pouring out of the cooling system. It was hell. They were all scalded."

Arkhipov ran his hand down his face as though to erase the image from his eyes.

"You were heroes, Vasily. Real heroes." The old admiral put his hand on Arkhipov's shoulder.

"No, sir. Those men who went into the reactor were heroes. The rest of us? Sweated out that infernal steam and thanked God it wasn't us."

"But you got the boat home. And the crew."

"We did. S-270 finally showed up more than thirteen hours after the accident. When I finally got on deck, that first breath of sea air was like being born again. The evening sky, those stars, were the most beautiful thing I'd ever seen. We extended the stabilizer fins till they touched to make a bridge to carry the stretchers with casualties over to S-270. We got all the crew into the relief sub, by some miracle. We all know how cramped a sub is, even with its normal complement. Once we were all on board, S-270 was like a crowded trolleybus at rush hour. Every man double or triple bunking, even the Captain. We were in there like sardines in a can. Crew didn't want to touch us. I mean physically. They made us share berths with each other rather than bunk up with one of us. It was like we were contagious. Even after they'd tossed the clothes of the engineering crew overboard, their bodies still emitted radiation. Their actual *bodies* had become radioactive.

"They turned the petty officers' quarters into a field hospital. The first man from the engineering crew died a day later, another seven within a week. The worst-injured men started to sweat blood. Medic ran out of painkillers. The guys could barely whisper, they were in such pain. They begged the doc to kill them, put them out of their misery.

"We towed K-19 nearly a thousand kilometers home. First few days we had to stop every watch to check that the coolant pumps that Filin had rigged were still working, till the reactor core had cooled down. I volunteered to go back nearly ten times. Suppose that's why I got my medal. But Christ. It was the most difficult thing I've ever done, open that hatch and go down into the boat. Like diving into a well of poison. And so we crawled home. They didn't send a faster boat to evacuate us. Political department wanted it kept a secret."

Arkhipov's eyes locked on Maslennikov, down at the foot of the table.

"Isn't that right, Comrade Political Officer? We'd become the shame of the fleet. An embarrassment to be covered up."

Maslennikov blushed, and launched into a stammering answer.

"Not an embarrassment, sir. Never that. But I guess they were thinking of the effect on the morale of the fleet. Seeing the men like that. Seeing K-19—the pride of the Red Banner Northern Fleet—limping home under tow? Think about how that would look."

Arkhipov furrowed his brows. He was working hard to keep bitterness out of his voice.

"They even made us wait until dark in order to creep back into the nuclear boat base at Polyarniy, like thieves. That's the pride of the Soviet Navy for you."

Maslennikov lowered his eyes to the table. Despite his struggle to remain upbeat, Arkhipov felt his composure crumbling as his eyes bored into the political officer.

"Commander Maslennikov, look at me. And tell me something— whose fault do you think it was? The reactor accident?"

"Whose *fault?*" Maslennikov raised his head and peered at Arkhipov quizzically, as though the question had been asked in Chinese.

"Someone must have screwed up, Commander. Whose negligence caused the accident?"

"Captain—we all saw the official report. The inquiry established that the accident was caused by faulty welding during the boat's construction. Some welder failed to cover the exposed pipe surfaces with asbestos cloths while he was working. A drop of hot steel fell on an unprotected surface. Produced an invisible crack. The pressure in that primary cooling system is more than two hundred atmospheres, so the pipe eventually burst."

"You have a good memory for detail, Comrade Maslennikov. But were the engineers punished? The quality control people? The welder himself?"

Maslennikov looked baffled, then offended.

"They removed some people from their posts, sir. Reviewed the quality control protocols, took steps . . ."

Arkhipov realized that his tone had become aggressive, but plowed on regardless.

"Nobody was punished. How many of our comrades died? Seventeen. Seventeen dead Soviet heroes. All decorated posthumously. But their murderers got off scot-free. That's how our glorious Soviet Motherland works. Punish the innocent, leave the guilty at their posts."

Maslennikov's face had clouded with something close to horror. The Admiral raised his hands in an emphatic gesture, as though he were stopping traffic.

"Enough! Vasily, dear man. What the devil's got into you? It was an accident."

Arkhipov glanced around at his comrades, suddenly ashamed at his anger. He had no right to take away his colleagues' sincere beliefs in his service and country. More, Arkhipov realized that maybe something in him even envied their faith. Sensing that he had gone too far, he made his tone lighter.

"Forgive me, Admiral. You're right. Good news is that most of us survived. Out of our complement of a hundred thirty-nine, only seventeen dead. They made us all have full blood transfusions. Even tried bone marrow transplants on some of us. The latest thing. No expense spared to save us. The medics have worked wonders."

The Admiral put a consoling hand on Arkhipov's shoulder.

"Some time at sea will do you good, Comrade. In the company of solid, simple lads. Put your mind straight. Remember what they used to teach us, back at the Academy? 'There's nothing in the world more concrete than a warship'? Everyone and everything in its place. I always liked that idea. Being part of a beautifully efficient machine. *Davai*. Let's drink. To the Motherland. To the Service."

Leontyev sloshed some vodka into their glasses. He linked his arm through Arkhipov's and they drank together. Arkhipov found his vision cloudy with tears.

"And you have a new mission, Captain. A whole flotilla, commanded by these good men here. And in good, old-fashioned diesel boats."

Simultaneously, they knocked back the vodka. As Savitsky drained his glass, he watched his tearful new flotilla commander through narrowed eyes.

"Comrades!" The Admiral had clearly had too much to drink, and his voice was growing hoarse and reedy. "We must thank Captain Arkhipov for his frankness. And be glad that thanks to the actions of all the officers of K-19 we have all been able to learn hard lessons. Valuable lessons, which mean that such a misfortune will never again occur in our glorious Soviet Navy. Never again!"

2

Bolshoi Theater, Moscow
13 August 1962

The sight of himself in the gold-framed mirror in the sumptuous lobby of the Bolshoi Theater brought Vasin to a halt. He could barely recognize himself. Too much greasy Lubyanka cafeteria food, too little sunlight and air. The bureaucrat's pallor they called a Kremlin tan. A sag to his face he'd never noticed before, with dark rings under his eyes. Even in the warm golden light of the Bolshoi's grand staircase, he looked haggard. Three bells rang in rapid succession, and the last stragglers hurried to take their seats.

From his place in the dress circle, Vasin scanned the audience, trying to catch a glimpse of Sofia before the house lights went down. He failed to spot her before the curtain rose, revealing a sumptuous set of medieval Russia, populated by brightly dressed extras. The swelling overture of Mussorgsky's *Boris Godunov* filled the auditorium.

Vasin found his spy at the place he had appointed for their first clandestine meeting—on the landing above the ladies' toilets. Sofia wore her everyday uniform and her usual dark scowl. Her hair was untidily pinned under her fore-and-aft cap. Refusing to dress up for him was apparently the only way she could think of to defy the system that had her clamped tight in its jaws.

"Good evening, Sofia Rafaelovna."

She said nothing and nodded curtly. First things first—always set the next rendezvous before doing anything else. One of the pieces of basic tradecraft that he had tried to explain to his reluctant agent in her initial operational briefing.

"For our next meeting, I will again send you a ticket to the theater at your office in plain cover. If you cannot attend, make a call to my office number and ask for Valery Samuilovich. If it's an emergency and you need to speak to me urgently, ask for Samuil Valeryevich. Like we talked about."

She nodded perfunctorily.

"You have something for me, Sofia?"

Sofia glanced furtively left and right before answering in a stage whisper. She really made a terrible spy.

"How is he?" she hissed. "Have you heard anything?"

"*He* is who?"

The Spanish girl shot Vasin a look of pure hatred. Some dark, nasty part of him liked it. But her dislike was better than her usual contemptuous dismissal.

"My brother."

"Vladimir is safe. From us at least. Your material?"

Sofia pouted, rummaged in her handbag, and slapped a crumpled packet of Yava cigarettes on the sill of the large mirror that filled the landing. Vasin felt for the small film canister that was inside.

"Nice to talk to you, Comrade," Vasin called after her retreating back. As he followed her with his eyes as she mounted the stairs, Vasin noticed a man in a dark suit who was hovering on the next landing, also watching Sofia. There was something about his studied nonchalance that marked him as a watcher. Or was he just another middle-aged man with an eye for a shapely girl?

The suspicion that pervaded the corridors of the Lubyanka was infectious.

Vasin waited until the progression of intermission bells herded the last audience member back for the second act, leaving him alone in the theater lobby. Only then, sure that he was not being tailed, did he collect his coat and step into the rainy night.

It was just a short walk from the Bolshoi to the Lubyanka, past the soaring mosaic-covered facade of the Hotel Metropol and the bulk of the Children's World department store. The giant, square mass of the KGB headquarters loomed in the drifting late-summer drizzle like an ocean liner, lights still burning in more than half the windows. Vasin took the elevator to his ninth-floor office, locked the door behind him, took out the cigarette packet, and slipped out the canister. He picked up the internal telephone to summon a messenger from the photographic department—which, along with the rest of the *kontora,* worked around the clock. There was no rest for the guardians of State Security.

3

Orlov spent nearly ten minutes reading through the stack of photographic prints in silence as Vasin waited, standing, in front of his desk. Tucking his reading glasses into his tunic pocket, he showed no sign of alarm or surprise.

"So, Vasin?"

"It's a briefing paper for the Cuban delegation, sir. Prepared for Comrade Raúl Castro's visit last month."

"So I read."

"It says . . . we have asked Castro for permission to deploy intermediate-range nuclear missiles to Cuba, sir. Covertly. We have already sent specialists to prepare the launch sites. Our leadership has been in talks with the Cubans to obtain their permission for this démarche since May."

"I read that, too. Fascinating. And?"

Vasin could not read his boss's expression—except to know that he was playing another of his infuriating, blank-faced games. *Your move, Vasin.*

"And . . . Sofia Rafaelovna is waiting to hear from us whether she should pass this information to Colonel Morozov."

"Indeed. And?"

"And if we allow her to pass it on, Morozov will undoubtedly attempt to give this sensational information to his American handlers."

"I would agree. But?"

Vasin, standing like a schoolboy in front of a teacher, felt a flush of fury at Orlov's teasing tone.

"But . . . sir . . . this is explosive. This is a covert operation of extreme strategic sensitivity. Can we just use it as bait to catch Morozov? What if he finds a secret way to communicate this to the Americans before we have caught him? If he just picks up a public phone and dials the Embassy? Then we will have let slip a secret of such value—"

"*Can* we?" interrupted Orlov. "My dear Sasha. Did you say, *can* we?

We can do anything we choose, in the interests of our Motherland's security."

Vasin resisted the urge to retort, and held the silence between them. When Vasin finally spoke, he kept his voice dry.

"So you authorize the passing of this information to the traitor Morozov, General?"

"I do, Vasin. I do. The risk is justified. Just make sure that you catch him before he can pass it on. As he will surely attempt to."

"Of course, sir."

Vasin stared at a place beyond Orlov's head but felt his boss's eyes scanning him for signs of defiance. He emptied his face. Orlov nodded curtly and handed back the report.

4

Frunze Embankment, Moscow
14 August 1962

"So your girl is on the hook?" Tokarev eyed Vasin with a grudging respect. "That was quick. What's it been—four weeks? And is she ready to nail your man yet?"

Vasin shifted in the driver's seat to face his contact.

"Yes. Yes. None of your business and . . . not yet."

Tokarev snorted.

"No need to get touchy. So I guess I'm over and out. I'll take your thanks as read."

"No. You're not out, Tokarev. I need some more information first."

"What information? And why?"

Vasin turned back to the steering wheel, staring ahead. Why, indeed? He had his orders from Orlov—instruct Sofia to pass on the secret report. So why was he here with Tokarev?

"About Cuba. Look."

Vasin slipped a packet of photographs out of his briefcase and propped the first one on the dashboard for Tokarev to read.

"You're just going to stare at it, Major?"

The old cavalryman grunted and leaned forward to read. The documents were on crested Defense Ministry notepaper. Every page was stamped TOP SECRET.

"Who's this report for?"

"Our Cuban comrade Raúl Castro. This paper was prepared for him. Prior to discussions with our Politburo."

Tokarev read on. At the end of every page he flicked his head, and Vasin set a new sheet down. When Tokarev was done, he leaned back on the flimsy car seat and tipped his head backward with a deep whistle.

"Thanks for that, Comrade. My curiosity satisfied. My head—on the block for reading classified material."

"You're welcome, Tokarev. But what does it really mean? What is this Cuban adventure about?"

"*About?*"

"I mean—why are we doing this? Proposing sending missiles to Cuba?"

Tokarev sighed.

"I guess you don't know the worst-kept secret in the Soviet Union. Worst kept in military circles, anyway."

"And what might that be? Everyone always has a secret I don't know."

The old cavalryman turned and glowered. Vasin, in a silent gesture, pointed with an index finger to the roof of the car. As in, the higher-ups need to know. Orlov needs to know.

"Spit it out, Tokarev."

"We don't have enough long-range missiles. The kind that can hit America. That's the secret. Know how many long-range intercontinental ballistic missiles the glorious Soviet Army has in its arsenal? Take a guess."

"No idea. Didn't Khrushchev say we're producing long-range missiles like sausages? Five hundred?"

"Close. Four. Not four hundred. Four. Just four."

"Wait . . ." Vasin struggled to recall a conversation at the officers' mess at Arzamas, many months before. "Didn't I read somewhere that we could launch them from submarines these days? Did a test last year, no?"

Tokarev nodded in grudging acknowledgment.

"Correct. Yes. We do have subs that can fire nuclear missiles. But since the K-19 accident last summer, all our long-range nuclear subs have been confined to base while the nuts-and-bolts boys figure out how to prevent them from going up in smoke halfway across the Atlantic. Another badly kept secret. Anyway, the Project 658 class—the one K-19 belongs to—is the only one capable of firing missiles at sea. And they're all in port. So the Motherland is down to four intercontinental strategic rockets. And our strategic nuclear bombers. But if we can shoot down one of the Yankees' U-2s, then the Yankees can definitely shoot down a Tu-95 bomber."

"U-2? You mean American spy planes?"

"Right, like the one we shot down over Sverdlovsk in 'sixty. The point is that nuclear bombers are obsolete. Easy to pick off as a fat goose. Especially those that can deliver really big bombs like the fifty-megaton one we popped off last October up on Novaya Zemlya. Nice big bang. But no realistic way to get that sucker over Washington. Our missile subs are grounded. The eggheads can't get our strategic missiles to work. So . . ."

"So we're actually defenseless?"

"We are unable to respond to an American nuclear attack, to be precise."

"So why Cuba?"

"We have four long-range rockets—but hundreds of intermediate- and medium-range ones. Which means, to people hearing about this shit for the *first time,* a range of two to four thousand kilometers."

Tokarev's swipe was not meant kindly.

"We want the Cubans to agree to have the rockets on their island because that's the only place we can hit America from."

"Correct, Comrade Colonel. I see the makings of a strategic expert in you. We put our rockets there because we have to. Otherwise we are, as you put it, defenseless."

"And what if the Americans find out?"

"About which part—the missile gap, or our little Cuban proposal?"

"Either."

Tokarev shrugged, settled back in his seat, and shook his head in place of an answer. They sat side by side in silence for a long moment before Tokarev moved to open the door. He leaned back into the car for a final word. "I'll tell you one thing for free, Vasin. Whatever the fuck this is all really about, Orlov is in over his head. And as for you . . . you're so deep over your head that whale shit is going to look like Sputnik."

He slammed the door in Vasin's face.

5

Revolution Square Metro Station, Moscow
15 August 1962

"You really want me to give Morozov the report?"

Vasin and Sofia stood side by side in the wide vestibule in the center of the Revolution Square metro station. Rush hour crowds flowed around them in a steady stream. Like Orlov once said, sometimes the safest place to hide is in plain sight. There had been no time to organize another meeting at the Bolshoi, so Vasin had simply followed Sofia from the office.

"You heard me right."

An arriving train spilled jostling passengers, forcing Vasin and Sofia into the lee of a larger than life-size bronze statue of a border guard with an Alsatian dog.

"I don't understand. That report is confidential."

Vasin had a sudden, mad urge to laugh at Sofia's understatement. *Confidential?* Just a little. The press of passengers ebbed, and the train's door closed with a violent clack. Sofia glanced around them and lowered her voice to a loud hiss.

"How does this track with your . . . theory? You say our friend is an enemy spy. Yet you want me to give him government secrets?"

A swelling crowd of passengers gathering for the next train began to press in around them once more. Vasin put his mouth close to Sofia's ear.

"Trust me, Sofia. We know what we are doing."

She shot Vasin a dubious glance.

"When?"

Vasin paused for a moment. He badly needed a few days more to work out the real reason why Orlov had approved handing the report to Morozov—in defiance of all caution and reason.

"Soon. Wait for my signal."

"And news on Vladimir?"

"What kind of news are you expecting? That he's changed his mind and decided to come home to the USSR?"

Sofia looked down at the ground, her lips pursed. Vasin realized he'd make a mistake with his ironic tone.

"Listen to me, Sofia. We can't stop Vladimir from making his own mistakes. But know this. Your cooperation is keeping him as safe as the *kontora* can make him. I promise. We're all in this together."

Vasin knew, even as he spoke the words, that neither of them really believed that.

6

3rd Frunze Street, Moscow
16 August 1962

Vasin's home phone rang on and on. On his makeshift bed on the living room couch, Vasin pulled a pillow over his head. It was Vera who eventually answered. She shook her husband awake.

"For you. Someone called Ekaterina Orlova."

Vera kept her voice pointedly neutral. Only the bedroom door that slammed behind her as she returned to bed betrayed anything of what she was feeling. Vasin stumbled to the phone. It was well past one in the morning.

Katya's familiar, husky voice was slurred with drink.

"I must see you, darling."

"Now?"

Vasin struggled to keep the tension out of his voice. To be a late-night gigolo on call to the boss's wife was more than he could bear.

"Now, darling. Right now. Come over to mine."

The Orlovs' apartment on Kutuzovsky Prospekt was indecently opulent. A row of tall windows faced onto the broad avenue to one side. Pompous portraits of Soviet and Russian military heroes lined the walls. Katya, swaying with booze, wore a frilly pink negligee. Her makeup was smeared across her face. Vasin saw that she had been crying.

"Don't worry. He's away. Out at someone's dacha. Drink?"

Vasin shook his head. Katya did not insist, but sloshed cognac from a decanter into her own large glass.

"You wanted to see me?"

Vasin knew that he was failing to control his face. Orlov's wife, her pendulous breasts swinging loose under the nylon of her slip and her hair in disarray, disgusted him.

"I can see that you hate me, Sasha. I would, if I were you."

"I don't hate you, Katya."

So it was going to be one of those talks. At least she wouldn't be demanding sex. She lurched toward him, grabbing Vasin's lapel.

"Listen to me. We have to talk about something important. And no, it's not about you and me. Or Orlov."

"Katya. Everything's always about Orlov, sooner or later."

She smiled lopsidedly.

"You may be right. He talks about you a lot, you know that? You're important to him. And yesterday he said that you were going to help him bring down the warmongers. I asked, 'What warmongers?' And he said, 'The fools that think we are invincible now that we have our great bomb. The fools that think Kennedy is a frightened boy to be bullied. The fools that are going to push us into a war. Over Cuba.'"

Katya released her hold on Vasin's coat. He said nothing, waiting for her to continue.

"You know what he's talking about, don't you, Sasha? Tell me you know."

Again Vasin remained silent, his brain spinning. He could not wrap his tired mind around this latest piece of Orlov mystification. Katya slumped against a sturdy ornamental table, sending a mirror that rested upon it shuddering dangerously.

"I'm not trying to test you, Sasha. This isn't one of Orlov's games."

"Of course it's not, Katya. Why would I think that? But since you ask, no, I have no damn clue what you're talking about. What warmongers? Why would they want to provoke America?"

Vasin examined Katya's mascara-stained eyes, the need and vulnerability in them.

"Orlov thinks I'm his slave, his little puppet. He thinks everyone around him is. I let him think that. But I have a mind of my own. And eyes and ears, too."

"Your eyes and ears are just what I need, Katya. But I don't understand what you are telling me. I need you to find out more. Help me to see. You want to help me, right?"

Katya smiled crookedly.

"I do want to help you. But do you know why? Because I like you, Sasha. And I don't want my husband to own everything in my life. Maybe I want part of you just for myself."

7

Kutuzovsky Prospekt, Moscow
16 August 1962

It was nearly two in the morning, and the twelve-lane-wide Kutuzovsky Prospekt was deserted except for a pair of traffic cops vainly waiting for cars to stop. Vasin walked toward where his Moskvich was parked, a hundred yards from the compound where Orlov lived. Only a single Party limo, its engine running, waited at the curb. Doubtless waiting for some bigwig to finish a late-night boozy dinner in Orlov's elite building.

The men were out of the car before Vasin had time to turn at the sound of opening doors. The limousine's headlights flicked on to high beam, dazzling him. Strong hands grabbed his upper arms and almost lifted him from the ground as they marched him toward the Chaika. A hand pushed his head down and another hauled him into the car. The last thing Vasin saw before a bag was expertly tugged over his head were the tips of several pairs of polished officers' boots. As the vehicle accelerated, Vasin was thoroughly frisked by the men pinning him to the bench seat.

A lurching turn to the left, then a moment later, left again. They must have been making a U-turn under the Kalinin Bridge. The car gathered speed and the streetlights flickered by like strobes through his blindfold. Vasin guessed they were now speeding down the central lane of Kutuzovsky Prospekt that was reserved for government cars. The highway ran toward the government dacha compounds of the USSR's top elite. He considered kicking and demanding explanations, but thought better of it. He already had an idea what this was about.

After half an hour on the highway, the limo made another abrupt turn off the main road, gravel crunching under its tires. A metal gate creaked open and a dog barked. A wash of wet, pine-scented air came through the open driver's-side window. The hood was whipped off his head and Vasin found himself face-to-face with a dapper Army lieuten-ant with slicked-back hair who sat with his back to the driver on the limo's jump seat.

"Colonel Vasin." The man seemed to be sizing up whether his pris-oner would try to run. Vasin remained motionless. "Please follow me."

The house was a pompous baroque redbrick pile, three stories of pre-Revolutionary splendor set deep in pinewoods. It was more a manor house than a dacha. The place seemed to be deserted except for some lights burning on the ground floor. The two goons who had been sit-ting by Vasin's side fell back and allowed him to follow the young sub-altern unescorted.

A grave, elderly man in an old-pattern sergeant's uniform greeted them at the carved wooden front door. The interior was a mixture of bourgeois luxury and standard government-issue fittings—a long red carpet, a pair of portraits of heavily bemedaled generals. Vasin was shown into a barren reception room lined with oak chairs. The door closed behind him, and Vasin heard the key turn in the lock. He could guess how this game worked. Vasin checked his watch but found it gone, slipped off his wrist in the car by expert hands. He settled down for a long wait.

Vasin was woken from a slumber by the noise of a car on the gravel outside the window. There was a commotion of footsteps and voices, the sound of the heavy front door opening and closing. A muttered conversation outside the door of the reception room that he could not make out. Eventually the key turned once more and the sleek young lieutenant peered in, gesturing with a nod of his head for Vasin to follow.

The grand old house was fully illuminated now, the light of the chan-deliers reflecting off the foxed floor-to-ceiling mirrors. A wide oak stair-case led to an upper hallway lined with doors. The subaltern knocked gently on one of them, received a muffled command, and opened the door wide for Vasin with exaggerated formality.

A muscular man in his midfifties stood by a large marble fireplace, reading a handwritten paper. Vasin immediately recognized him as the Special Forces major-general who had swept Sofia away from the Krem-lin Palace reception for the Cubans. He wore a gray cardigan over his striped undershirt and combat pants, and his hair was cut high and tight, grunt-style.

"Sit down, Alexander Ilyich."

"General. We've met."

The man smiled quickly, like a camera shutter snapping across the frame of his handsome sadist's face.

"Indeed."

Vasin took a seat in an ornate armchair by the empty fireplace.

"How may I address you, Comrade?"

"Comrade General will do fine. General Zimin."

Zimin continued to read the long memorandum to the end, flicked back a couple of pages, and settled into a chair opposite Vasin's.

"You are nosy. Thorough. Ruthless. We see why Orlov chose you."

"*We*, sir?"

The General ignored the question and flipped through the notes again.

"You have threatened Lieutenant Sofia Guzman with some information you claim to know about her past. Does it exist, or did you invent it in order to put her on your hook?"

Had Sofia talked—risking her brother's life? Almost certainly not. Vasin silently cursed Tokarev.

"Sir, with the greatest respect, I must tell you that only General Orlov can answer . . ."

"Let Orlov go to his mother. Our bosses have their own accounts. They're no concern of yours. You're here because you have your nose deep into something that does not concern you. Or Orlov. You're investigating Colonel Morozov."

Vasin straightened in his chair. Denial would be pointless.

"You know my orders, then, General."

Vasin felt Zimin's hard gaze sizing him up, weighing him with his eyes like a boxer before a bout.

"Morozov is one of ours. He's on our side. And you need to remove your nose from his business. Immediately."

"One of us—meaning an officer of Soviet military intelligence? I am aware."

"I'm telling you that he's working for the good of the country. He's working for us."

"Is he working for you when he passes information to the Americans?"

Zimin's eyes narrowed, but he showed no other sign of surprise.

"You have observed him passing information to the Yankees?"

Now it was Vasin's turn to hesitate. To bluff or not to bluff?

"No, sir. Not directly. But he has been seeking information from Sofia Guzman on Operation Anadyr. Why would he be gathering this information covertly?"

"I thought you would have discovered that for yourself, Vasin."

The conversation was turning into a duel. Could it be that Zimin didn't know Morozov's cock-and-bull story about being a personal envoy of Serov's? That was interesting.

"But you haven't answered my question, General."

"Don't play games."

"Morozov claimed to be a special envoy for your boss, sir. For General Serov. He told Guzman that Serov needed his own source inside Anadyr."

There was a pause as Zimin digested this information. The pause was long, and telling. So Zimin hadn't known. Which confirmed that he hadn't interrogated Sofia. So his source, as Vasin had suspected, had to be Tokarev.

"What Lieutenant Guzman told you is correct, Vasin. Morozov is working personally for General Serov. The information he is gathering is on the General's behalf."

"May I ask for what purpose?"

"You may not. This is an internal military affair."

"And yet, we at State Security have good reason to suppose that your Morozov has had contact with the enemy. Both here and abroad. Which makes this a counterintelligence case, and consequently—"

"There is no *consequently.*" Zimin interrupted him with a stab of an outstretched finger. "Everything that Morozov does, he does at our command."

Vasin met the man's eyes for a long, appraising look.

"Including meeting foreign agents."

Again, a pause.

"Even that. Do not be fooled by appearances."

"You are telling me that you have been ordering Morozov to contact the Americans . . ."

"*Not* what I said."

"Which would mean that you are running Morozov as a double

agent? A decoy to feed the Americans false information? Is that what I am to infer from this conversation, General? Forgive me if I have misunderstood."

Zimin crumpled his notes in his fist, anger boiling up into his face. Vasin had caught his words and pinned them down. To the General's fury.

"*Not* your damn business. Or Orlov's."

Zimin turned on his heel, walked to a table littered with papers, tossed the crumpled notes onto it, and ran a hand through his hair, his back to Vasin. A nerve touched, clearly.

"Orlov knows what you know? You know what Guzman has passed to Morozov, concerning Anadyr?"

There was something unsettling in the man's tone. Almost as if he was . . . alarmed?

"Of course, sir. Briefed Orlov fully, immediately. And yes," Vasin bluffed. "Morozov has been given the material."

"*Bylad,*" the man breathed, almost to himself. "Fucking hell."

Vasin remained silent as his interrogator paced up and down the end of the study. His mind raced. Did the notion that the GRU was running Morozov as a double agent make any sense? Or was Serov's man just covering his boss's back, buying time while Serov came up with his own private way to silence his treacherous protégé forever? Vasin decided to break the silence.

"Comrade General. You've told me to leave Morozov alone. But I am an officer under orders—and my orders are to track him. If you wish me to desist, you will have to talk to my chief. I'm under his command, not yours."

Zimin had turned back toward the fireplace, his meaty fists planted on the desk in front of him. Vasin felt his confidence quake and falter under the man's furious gaze.

"Very well, Alexander Ilyich. No orders. If you prefer, we will call it advice. Officer to officer. You will discover nothing. You will go blind and deaf. You will report to Orlov that Morozov is clean. Is that clear? And you will walk away. While you still can."

8

Zhukovka, Moscow Region
18 August 1962

Orlov, surrounded by nature—an oddly disquieting sight. The boss, shirtless and clad in a pair of antique cotton shorts, lounged in a rattan chair beside Vasin. The last days of Moscow summer were at their humid height. The foliage around Orlov's dacha was abundant, the branches of a lilac bush indecently thick with heavy flowers. Vasin's linen shirt and trousers were soaked in sweat. The unmowed lawn behind Orlov's sprawling wooden summer house buzzed with mosquitoes. Katya, in a loose cotton dress covered in flouncy ribbons that revealed too much, emerged onto the veranda.

"Lunch is ready, boys!"

A couple of serving girls hurried to lay out plates on a broad wooden table on a terrace that was shaded by the house. Orlov and Vasin joined a dozen senior *kontora* officers at the table. Separately, a gaggle of chunky wives, clones of Katya, gossiped in low voices. The chauffeurs were in charge of grilling the kebabs around the back of the dacha, generating a low hum of male voices and wafts of charring meat smoke and cheap tobacco. At Katya's word, the company obediently shuffled into their appointed places around the table. Orlov insisted that Vasin take the seat on his right as Khrustalev, the boss's veteran driver, went round the table with a plate of steaming lamb and chicken skewers.

"Eat! Eat, Comrades! My wife made this pepper sauce herself."

Vasin, in an agony of embarrassment as he took the place of honor, stole a glance at the rest of the faces around the table as they tucked into their lunch. All were senior in rank to Vasin. They all seemed to know something he did not. They had, Vasin guessed, seen their fair share of young hotshots in the seat by the boss.

A Saturday afternoon of small talk with these veteran KGB sharks, interspersed with endless vodka toasts, had rendered Vasin almost speechless with drink and exhaustion. When Vasin finally got away from the table and into the cooling foliage of the garden, the shadows had grown long. The last of the guests tossed their cigarettes onto the lawn and lined up to bear-hug the boss's sweaty torso.

Orlov came lumbering down the steps, walked past Vasin, and chose a frothy stand of mimosa in which to noisily relieve himself.

"Enjoy yourself, Sasha?"

"Yes, sir. Very much. Honored."

Orlov tucked himself in and turned toward Vasin.

"This Aquarium business. Zimin, that his name? Warning you off. I reckon they're shitting themselves."

"Sir?"

"Serov knows his favorite boy's guilty. And he knows that when Morozov blows up, he's going to end up spattered in shit."

Vasin bowed his head in reverent silence—not least because he didn't trust his vodka-addled tongue to talk straight.

"This bullshit about Morozov working for them. They're inventing stories because they're covering their own asses. And the deeper Morozov goes, the deeper in the shit they are themselves. Let's see how far down he drags them."

Orlov gave a throaty chuckle. Vasin finally found his voice.

"But this material that you have authorized Sofia to pass to Morozov. Shouldn't we . . ."

Vasin's mouth dried under the lowering scrutiny of Orlov's stare.

"Hold off? In case he evades our trap and succeeds in sharing our secrets with the Yankees? Your old song, Vasin?"

"My old song. Sir."

"And let Morozov off the hook? Continue buggering about with your fruitless surveillance? Perhaps-maybe-possibly General Serov's dear friend and protégé is a traitor, but we will never know because we never dared to flush him out? Screw that, Vasin. We've got to catch him attempting to sell the whole bazaar to his American friends. We wait. And we watch. And then we pounce."

"And if he does sell the whole bazaar? Right under our noses, even as we watch him?"

"You will make sure that doesn't happen."

"But if Serov knows we are onto his man—surely Morozov knows it, too?"

Orlov swayed slightly. Vasin saw just how drunk his boss was. But his lowering face suddenly split into a wide smile, and the General spread his hands to the blue summer sky.

"Maybe. Maybe not. You say Zimin asked you if Morozov already had the Anadyr papers? Sounds like they don't know. And therefore, Morozov hasn't been tipped off. Why? The devil knows. But I know this. We shoot the geese in our own skies, Sasha."

"Sir?"

"We shoot the geese we can shoot. The ones that come over our guns. With the ammunition we have."

Vasin's drink-sodden brain struggled to comprehend. It sounded a lot like Orlov cared more about his private feud than the security of his country.

"Sir—the goose is . . . Morozov, or Serov?"

"My boy. You haven't been listening. They are the same. By the way—when is Guzman handing over the report?"

Vasin hesitated. It was always dangerous to lie to Orlov. There was no more time to buy.

"Monday, sir. They have a meeting planned for Monday evening."

Orlov, his chin raised to the lowering rays of the sun, closed his eyes in a private moment of triumph.

"Come here. Dear boy." Orlov opened his arms. Awkwardly, Vasin allowed himself to be embraced. Orlov smelled strongly of sour vodka sweat and woodsmoke. The General patted his back—hard, more like a slap—and released him. "Good work."

"It's been a wonderful afternoon. General, thanks so much for—"

Orlov raised a hand to still Vasin's thanks and smiled beatifically. But as Vasin was about to turn to leave, Orlov closed his hand into a single, raised finger.

"One more thing. It must have been Tokarev who blabbed to Zimin, correct?"

"So it seems, sir. Couldn't have been anyone else. Sofia would never—"

"Understood," Orlov cut him off. "Consider it dealt with. You know I look out for my people, Sasha. I won't let those box-headed Army bullet-stoppers get away with insulting us. Insulting *me*. 'It is mine to avenge; I will repay. In due time their foot will slip; their day of disaster is near and their doom rushes upon them.' The book of Deuteronomy, Sasha. You see—my Bible studies weren't entirely wasted."

The General said the words as though he were imparting a social pleasantry. Vasin groped for words that might stay Orlov's wrath against

Tokarev. The man might be a snitch, but he was also Vasin's only pair of eyes inside the Aquarium. And could it be that some mistake of Vasin's had given away his connection to Tokarev to his ruthless Army bosses? He almost felt responsible for what was about to happen to the poor handless bastard.

But before Vasin could say anything more, Orlov raised both hands in a gesture that was half-hieratic, half-comic, waved goodbye to Vasin, and disappeared inside the house.

9

3rd Frunze Street, Moscow
20 August 1962

The morning was breezy, with a hint of autumnal freshness. The courtyard of Vasin's apartment building was scented with the fragrance of the sour green Antonovka apples ripening on the boulevard outside the archways. A competing cacophony of upbeat radio music sounded from open kitchen windows. Vasin strode out his front door and looked up at the cloudless blue sky. For the first time in months, he felt confident and almost happy. Morozov would soon be caught red-handed. Vasin's personal nightmare would soon be over. As for the rest . . . Vasin felt, frankly, that he didn't give a damn. He could forget about missiles, forget Cuba. As long as he got the Morozov case closed.

The second he spotted Tokarev, Vasin knew that something was terribly wrong. The man was leaning by the large archway that led from the courtyard onto the street, his uniform tunic unbuttoned. His body hung limp, like a marionette with cut strings. Vasin flinched. Orlov's vengeance had come swiftly.

"Tokarev! What's happened?"

The old cavalryman's look was wild.

"Vasin. I beg you. Get Saida back. Please."

"Get *who* back?"

Vasin steered the older man under the shelter of the archway, out of earshot of the curious babushkas who inhabited the courtyard.

"My wife. They came for her last night."

"The *kontora*? What was the charge?"

"Not the *kontora*. The nuthouse ambulance. Took her to the Serbsky Institute."

The words hit Vasin like a punch to the stomach. The Serbsky State Scientific Center for Social and Forensic Psychiatry was Moscow's most secure, and most notorious, psychiatric hospital. Vasin closed his eyes for a long moment. "Consider Tokarev dealt with," Orlov had said. But . . . the man's *wife*? To the Serbsky? The picture was already horribly clear in Vasin's mind. Tokarev's wife, struggling and screaming, the burly orderlies holding her down and jamming needles into her arm until they found a vein. And then—slackness and silence. Terror locked in her eyes only, her body paralyzed. Vasin had seen it done in the madhouses where his poor, crazy sister Klara had ended her short life.

"Vasin, I can explain. It's true. I talked to Zimin. He made it sound like he knew everything already . . ."

"That can wait. Just tell me why."

"*Why?* You're saying you had nothing to do with this? Orlov didn't?" Tokarev was so desperate that he could barely speak. Anger flashed in his eyes.

"I meant, why your wife. Saida? Why did they take her?"

"Because Saida had . . ." Tokarev flailed to find words. "Something wrong with her head. When she was young, she saw some things during the war that drove her mad. Under Fascist occupation in Kharkov. She was a slave laborer. They made her do . . . terrible things. Things that broke her mind. Execution pits. Witnessing mass murder. Things you and I can't imagine. She had a breakdown. Ended up in the *durka*."

Durka—slang for *durdom,* literally the crazy house.

"And so you asked Orlov to help get her out?"

"Don't pretend you didn't know, you piece of *shit*."

Vasin stepped back, afraid that the powerful old soldier was about to swing at him with his clublike hands.

"I didn't. Tokarev, I had no idea. I swear."

Tokarev wiped the spittle from his mouth on his sleeve, visibly willing himself to calm down.

"She was my fiancée then, Vasin. And yes. Back when Orlov first recruited me, I asked him that favor. And he did it. He got her out and gave her back to me."

"The favor that put you on the hook."

"Whatever you Chekists call it. But right now we have to get her out. Now."

"Before they tie her to a cot and pump her full of drugs."

Vasin was speaking half to himself. The image of his sister Klara, skeletal and delirious on her psychiatric hospital bed, rose from the darkest place in his memory. The indifferent doctors, the rancid stink of the patients' urine-soaked bedding, the naked fear in Klara's eyes in the moments when she was not sedated.

"What do you know about the nuthouse?" Tokarev peered at Vasin narrowly, suspecting some trick.

A young woman shepherding a group of boisterous children appeared in the archway, passing between the two men and forcing them into silence as they made their way into the courtyard. Once they had gone, Vasin closed the space between himself and the older man. He drew close enough to breathe Tokarev's sour breath. The man was unshaved—was it Saida who shaved him?—and his shirt and even breeches were unbuttoned. This smartly turned-out officer, just days before so stiff and proud, had been undone in every way.

"Let's say family history."

Tokarev's taut and furious face sagged, against his own will, into something more tragic and desperate.

"Vasin. You have to understand . . ."

"No. *You* have to understand. You fucked with Orlov. What did you expect, for God's sake?" Vasin felt his anger rising. He had never met Saida Tokareva, but his heart ached for what she must be going through. "Don't you know Orlov? Did you have no fucking idea of what he does to people who cross him?"

"We were seen together, Vasin. Don't ask me when or where. But Zimin came to me. He knew all about you. He asked me, 'We know you've been talking to Orlov's man. This Vasin—who the fuck is he?' And what could I say? This is *your* fault."

Vasin took half a step back and turned to face the sunlit courtyard. It was possible that he had inadvertently exposed Tokarev to danger. And Vasin could think of no earthly reason why Tokarev would go to his bosses voluntarily. Because Tokarev must have known precisely what Orlov was capable of. *Shit*. Even at one degree of separation from Orlov, Vasin poisoned everything he touched.

"I beg you, Vasin. Get her out. Help me get her out. Do anything.

I will do anything. But . . . I can't live without her. I can't." Abruptly, Tokarev burst into tears. The sight was so terrible that Vasin involuntarily turned away from it. He struggled to find words of comfort, but could think of none. Except for one thing.

"Tokarev. I can't help you right now. Nothing I can say to Orlov will change his mind. You know him. Or you knew him. He may be an avenger. He's cold—but he's logical. Cross him, and he'll destroy you. Help him, and he'll reward you. So please. For Saida's sake, find out something that Orlov can use. Something secret. Something powerful. That's the only thing you can do to save Saida."

With another man—a less proud and less valiant man—Vasin might have put a comforting hand on the shoulder. But Tokarev stood almost to attention before him, infinitely pathetic and at the same time dignified in his unbuttoned clothes. He fixed Vasin with bloodshot eyes and nodded, slightly, in acknowledgment of Vasin's cold, brutal logic. Then he turned on his heel and marched—not walked—out into the sunlit street.

10

VDNKh, Moscow
20 August 1962

There was a chill in the air of the sunny afternoon that made Vasin shiver in his thin raincoat. The Exhibition of the Achievements of the People's Economy was crowded with groups of schoolchildren and shuffling busloads of workers up from the provinces. A group of janitors in blue overalls, wielding mops and rags, was giving the gold leaf—covered fountain a cleaning before it was enfolded in its burlap winter coverings.

"Are you going to buy me a soda?"

Despite being married to a KGB general, Katya Orlova was terrible at conspiracy. Her idea of being inconspicuous was to wear a foreign-looking bright yellow coat and electric-blue headscarf. Vasin stood wearily to greet her. A sleepless night had drained the strength from his body and the color from his face.

"Sasha. You look terrible. What's happened?"

"Orlov happened. Serov happened."

Katya's face clouded over. She took Vasin by the arm and began walking away from an approaching crowd of tourists.

"Tell me."

"Serov threatened me. His man did, at least. Told me to lay off Morozov. Claimed that he's being run as a double agent by the military. Suggested it, anyway. But he's not."

"They threatened you with what?"

"With being crushed, like wheat in a mill. Between the *kontora* and the Aquarium. Your husband already bulldozed the Army man who informed on me. Old cavalryman, war veteran, lost his hands to a grenade. Your husband had his wife committed to a mental asylum. So Christ knows what they'll do to *me*."

"So you're nervous because you think you're expendable? A pawn in my husband's game? Sasha—that's exactly what you are."

Vasin stopped in his tracks.

"He said something more to you?"

"Orlov never says much to me. But I promised you to keep my eyes and ears open. And he speaks to his cronies, at dinner. Last night they talked about Cuba again."

"Operation Anadyr?"

"Be quiet and listen. They said the Cubans have agreed. Castro's brother finalized the details when he was in Moscow. So it's now on. That's the news. Something about our military coming up with a plan for a missile base close to America? Well. The Cubans are convinced. They think it will make their island safe from Yankee attack."

"And Orlov? His *kontora* friends . . . ?"

"Think it's madness. Especially if the Americans find out about it. It will provoke a war, unless it's stopped. That's what Voznesensky said. Deputy head of the First Chief Directorate."

"Stopped how? If the operation is under way it means that the Politburo has already signed off. It's happening, right?"

Katya shrugged in reply.

"I didn't ask any questions. I just fetched the cognac."

"Did they say anything else?"

"That's not enough for you? I promised to give you the table talk of generals. Sounded important to me."

"Yes. Katya, it's very important. But . . ."

"Sasha. You don't get to ask the questions. You take what you are given, by those who do. Does that seem brutal? I don't mean to be brutal. But we live in the world where we live. You take the freedom that you are given. I can give you knowledge, which is also a kind of freedom. Because it is power. Just do me a favor—use it to stay alive. For us."

So Anadyr was a go. Not even Orlov and the *kontora*—or at least, his friends in the *kontora*—had been able to do anything to stop it. Sofia was waiting for Vasin's coded call, a wrong number from a public telephone to her office line. The signal to pass on the Anadyr file that evening. Vasin could stall no more.

He parted from Katya with as much warmth as he could summon. Then Vasin stared, unseeing, at the soaring golden spire of the Moldavian Soviet Socialist Republic pavilion.

Could it be that Orlov *wanted* Morozov to tell the Yankees about the Soviets' catastrophic lack of long-range missiles? About Anadyr?

11

Pioneers' Ponds, Moscow
23 August 1962

The surface of Pioneers' Ponds was absolutely still. Even the ducks on their floating islands in the middle of the small lake slept, motionless as decoys. A few citizens hurried home through the late-summer dusk.

Vasin crept across the darkened *kontora* surveillance apartment and crouched beside Pushkov's bulk as he sat at his post by the window. In front of Pushkov, a pair of artillery binoculars mounted on a tripod pointed straight at Morozov's windows on the opposite side of the Ponds. The veteran watcher moved aside, allowing Vasin to peer through into Morozov's dining room, where the Colonel was stolidly slurping soup with his wife and daughter. The family's halting conversation about the weather came over a hissing loudspeaker attached to an ever-spinning reel-to-reel tape deck.

"Anything?"

But Vasin could see from Pushkov's face that their man had not broken cover. He retreated into the lit kitchen of the apartment with Pushkov to pore over the surveillance reports. Office. Metro. Home. Office. Three days since Sofia had passed him the crucial Anadyr file, and still no sign of any variation in Morozov's daily routine. No sudden disappearances, no attempts to dodge surveillance. And yet there remained huge spaces of blank time when their target was beyond their sight. Whenever he was at work in the Aquarium headquarters, for instance. Or inside the Ministry of Defense. And all the time in between he was moving, moving, brushing past dozens of strangers every day in the office, in the metro.

"A handoff can be a dropped matchbox, Colonel." Pushkov's voice was hoarse from smoking, his tone gruffly comforting. The old thug knew the stakes—some of them, at least—for Vasin's career if he failed to nail Morozov. The tired team had been briefed to be on high alert from the moment that Sofia had handed Morozov the file on Monday night. "A signal can be a raised curtain. A flowerpot in a window, moved about. A bag carried in the left hand or the right. Could be anything."

Vasin felt the older man straightening to receive an earful of recrimination from a frustrated boss. It would bounce off the old bruiser like dry peas off a wall. But Vasin could feel himself starting to panic and plowed on. "Not *your* fault if you miss a traitor meeting with his American controllers, correct, Pushkov?"

"No unusual activity reported among any American diplomats, despite reinforced observation. We continue to fulfill our duties to the maximum, Comrade Colonel."

The older man's voice had gone very flat. Pushkov's unspoken message to Vasin was clear. Whatever shit we're going to be eating if we fuck this up, boss? You get a wagonful. And me? Just a spadeful.

12

Kursky Station, Moscow
23 August 1962

The crowded concourse of Kursky Station was an outpost of southern Russia in the heart of Moscow. The platforms were full of Ukrainian peasant women in bright cotton sarafan wraparound summer dresses. Some hauled suitcases stuffed with dried apricots and raisins while others swigged cloudy homemade fruit juice from bottles. A group of swarthy men were arguing in guttural Armenian over a spilled sack of sunflower seeds whose oil gave off a sweet scent as the kernels were crushed under the feet of the passing crowds. The travelers' faces were red-brown, scorched by the hot sun of the south.

Vasin kept a hand on Nikita's shoulder as he steered the boy through the throng. The lanky fourteen-year-old was nearly as tall as his father. He wore a spotless white shirt, black shorts, and a carefully ironed Young Pioneer scarlet tie. His black fore-and-aft pilot's cap was decorated with good-conduct badges.

The train for the elite Young Pioneer camp at Artek in the Crimea stood in pride of place on platform 1, usually reserved for official delegations and bigwig visitors. A sea of white-and-scarlet-uniformed boys milled about a series of numbered flags held by older boys as they slowly separated themselves into groups.

"You're in Four Company, right, Nikita?"

"Dad. I know. I'll be okay from here."

"Got your documents? Ticket?"

"Dad."

Nikita took the heavy Army knapsack from his father and hoisted it over his own shoulder. He smiled quickly and gave Vasin a private, belly-height wave as though waving goodbye might be seen as babyish. The kid turned and was quickly lost in the crowd of identical Soviet boys.

Vasin joined a group of parents and chauffeurs who were waiting to see the train off. A well-heeled crowd had gathered for this, the most prestigious of the camp's end-of-August vacation slots. The housewives of the Party elite were in their summery finery, accompanied by the occasional bodyguard. Vasin had put on his KGB uniform for the occasion—not that it made Nikita any less embarrassed to be seen with his dad. Looking around, Vasin realized that he was probably the only father present. In this exalted company, being a mere lieutenant colonel was positively humble.

A barked order echoed down the platform and the boys' excited chatter died down as they hurriedly shuffled into rows, standing at an approximation of attention with their right arms raised in the Young Pioneers' salute. On the next command they broke formation and boarded their respective carriages in obedient silence. Vasin prayed that Nikita would enjoy the camp. According to the lavish brochure, Artek boasted three swimming pools, a stadium, and even its own film studio, Artekfilm. But maybe it had been a mistake to send the boy off with so many *mazhory*—the not-so-respectful slang for the spoiled kids of the elite.

"You don't want him to become a *mazhor*?" Vera had asked sarcastically when Vasin voiced his doubts. "What do you want him to be? A simple Soviet person?"

She had said it like an insult.

Once the throng of children had boarded, a row of smartly uniformed conductresses, one to each carriage, took their positions along the length of the train. Each carried a triangular red flag under her arm. In a charmingly choreographed move, the women all swung left, then right, then raised their flags in unison to signal the all-clear. The guard's whistle blew, answered by a blast from the locomotive. As the train began to slowly move out, the conductresses stepped on board. Some lingered, riding on the steel-mesh steps for a few moments until the train exceeded walking pace before climbing inside and hauling the doors shut behind them. Some of the mothers politely applauded the girls' performance and waved their children off south, to the sea and sun.

As Vasin turned to go he froze. A group of soldiers in camouflage battle dress and the maroon berets of the Spetznaz stood on the concourse. All carried sidearms and new-model folding-stock Kalashnikovs. At their head, standing squarely with his hands on his hips and staring directly at Vasin, was General Zimin.

Involuntarily, Vasin looked from side to side for escape routes. But no—a voice of reason in his head told him that even the GRU would never dare to try to arrest him in the middle of Moscow's busiest rail terminal. Steeling himself, he forced his body into a slow and steady walk, right up to the glowering Zimin.

"What are you doing here, General?"

"Kid get off okay to Artek, Colonel?"

Vasin struggled to suppress a blinding wave of rage and fear that swept over him like nausea.

"God damn it, Zimin. If you even think . . ."

"What's that, Vasin? You going to tell me that women and children are off-limits? After what your *motherfucking* boss did to poor Tokarev's wife?"

Zimin's barked profanity caused heads to turn in disapproval. Surrounding passengers waiting for trains began to watch the growing confrontation with interest. Vasin's anger burst like a popping balloon.

"That's between your chief and mine. Nothing to do with me. Or you." Vasin had moved closer to Zimin, his voice a furious whisper. He was half a head shorter than the General, but transported by his rage, Vasin stuck a finger in Zimin's broad chest and held it there as he spoke. "And you are right. *My* man Orlov is an evil motherfucker. But he's *my* man. Do you have any conception of how utterly and completely the KGB can fuck you and your family up if you touch me? Or my kid? So listen to me very carefully. I was there when Orlov decided to destroy Tokarev. He didn't think about it more than he would swatting a mosquito. Orlov has files full of dirt on every Politburo member and Army bigwig. He's picking some kind of death match with your boss. You and I are merely under orders. You think our chiefs give a shit about either of us? Our kids? I can speak for Orlov: he really doesn't, I promise you. Both of them will toss us to the dogs if they need to. We'll just be collateral damage. But just think about this, Zimin—you don't fight dirty with the guys who *invented* dirty fighting. We listen in on half the country as they screw their wives at night. We know every person you call and every movie you see. Your kids' teachers, your doctor, your wife's friends? They're ours. The *kontora* runs over two thousand gulags. We have torture chambers. We have nuthouses. And we have a whole army of very expert, very experienced sadists at our command. Believe me when I say that I've seen what they can do to a man. Or a woman."

Zimin had retreated a step before Vasin's rage. His eyes had widened, as though a puny kid he'd being expecting to bully easily had suddenly waved a switchblade in his face. Vasin pressed on, relentless.

"So here's what's going to happen, General. We're both going to walk away from here. We're going to do our jobs as honorable Soviet officers, and nothing more. That way everyone stays alive. And maybe one day both of us get to work for normal human beings instead of a pair of hate-fueled maniacs. Have I made myself clear?"

Both men looked around at the crowd of spectators who had gathered in a circle, at a wary distance, to observe the scandal. Zimin's men shifted nervously at their commander's obvious discomfiture. Vasin's and Zimin's eyes connected once more for a moment of what could have been mutual understanding. The General gave a barely perceptible nod and turned on his heel.

As Zimin and his men retreated across the concourse, Vasin found that he could barely move. Every part of his body was trembling with exhilaration at his own audacity. And with fear.

PART FOUR

THE MAIN ADVERSARY

And remember: you must never, under any circumstances, despair. To hope and to act, these are our duties in misfortune.

BORIS PASTERNAK

1

CIA Station, US Embassy, Moscow
3 October 1962

The view from the CIA Moscow station chief's office was even more depressing than the October weather. Wallace Baker's barred windows faced the Embassy courtyard and looked directly onto a boxy accommodation block and a row of jerry-built garages. The afternoon was overcast and gray, and Baker's lights were already on as gloom crept up the building. Even the Stars and Stripes that hung on a pole at the rear of the Embassy compound seemed to have given up on active duty and hung, sodden and limp, in the steady drizzle.

"Sir?" The young officer who hovered in Baker's doorway was a relatively new boy. Dick Jacob, pale beanpole of a guy. One of the new intake, less than six months on station. But the kid was keen and, as far as Baker could tell, decently competent.

"All good?"

Picking up the dead-letter drops of Agent HERO was the most nerve-racking part of Baker's week. Especially now that Langley was taking such a keen interest in what their star spy in Moscow had to say.

"We collected the drop just now, sir, via the usual cutouts."

Baker swiveled his banker's chair upright and snatched the envelope Jacob was holding out. He peered in to inspect a tiny steel microfilm canister that nestled inside. It appeared intact. Baker opened a desk drawer and removed a normal-sized thirty-five-millimeter film canister filled with cotton wool. He picked out half the padding, carefully placed the microfilm inside, replaced the cotton, and screwed the canister's aluminum lid tight. HERO film had to be delivered to CIA headquarters undeveloped—and undamaged.

"Good work. Is it Walters who's up for the diplomatic bag run?"

"On his way up now, sir. Car's waiting."

"He's heading out when?"

Jacob checked his watch.

"With this traffic he won't make the Aeroflot flight to Paris. But there's a Royal Dutch Airlines flight to Amsterdam just before eight p.m., sir."

"Fine. Get the connections worked out and have someone meet Walters at Dulles."

With the advantage of time difference, the message might just be in Washington in time for the President's morning briefing. As Jacob darted down the corridor, Baker busied himself filling in codes on the canister's label, duplicating them on the cover of a padded cardboard box into which he carefully placed the film. For good measure he added, in underlined capitals, RUSH—EYES ONLY, DIRECTOR OF OPERATIONS. Baker remembered Wild Bill Donovan, the crazy old bastard who had been his first chief at the old Office of Strategic Services. "Never underestimate the capacity for screwups" was Donovan's First Law, coined when they'd been running agents into occupied France during the war. Over the years Baker had seen its wisdom. Comms fail. Parachutes fail. People fail. Always play for the miss.

Once the package had been safely handed over to the courier, Baker stood and flexed his shoulders, stiff around the scar tissue from a Chinese shell fragment picked up at Inchon. His waistcoat sat tight across his belly. It had been, what, six months since he'd been on a tennis court? A year and a half in Moscow, and the place was getting to him. Especially with the added headache of kid-gloving HERO product.

HERO. The legendary asset that Baker had been briefed about but whose identity he didn't know. Except he could guess that HERO was pretty damn senior—enough for his intel to go straight to Langley in a rush pouch, unopened and always by hand.

Of Baker's CIA staff, only he and his deputy station chief had been cleared to even know about the existence of HERO, and of the agent's importance. And Baker knew from his old boss Ambassador Llewellyn Thompson, now temporarily assigned to the President's personal advisory team in Washington for the duration of the Cuban crisis, that Kennedy relied heavily on HERO's reports.

Baker knew he wouldn't sleep until he'd had confirmation that his package had safely touched down in Amsterdam. He crossed the office and peered upward into the lowering Moscow sky. The wind was picking up. A rainstorm was coming in.

2

Vnukovo Airport, Moscow
3 October 1962

Moscow's Vnukovo Airport in the autumn rain, the sky hanging low and oppressive. Vasin stood on the windswept open terrace that adjoined the rooftop cafeteria, sucking on a cigarette and scanning the horizon for signs of an incoming aircraft. A white dot appeared in the sky, then three—the nose and wing lights of a plane swinging wildly like a child's spinning top teetering off-balance. The outline of the aircraft grew clearer through a shifting curtain of mist as it squared up to the runway. The pilot was fighting a strong crosswind and the plane fishtailed as it came in to land, the tail snapping from side to side with alarming violence.

Would the wind flip the fragile thing into a fireball, cartwheeling down the asphalt trailing a shroud of flames? These days Vasin found himself shocked by the things that went through his mind. It had been more than six weeks since Sofia had handed over the first set of Anadyr documents to Morozov. More had followed. And yet the infuriating bastard had shown no sign of breaking his routine. The stress of the fruitless surveillance of Morozov was getting to him. But at least Zimin had had the good sense to stay out of Vasin's business. So far.

Vasin shook his head and forced himself to look away from the aircraft's bouncing progress. He lit another cigarette from the butt of the previous one.

By the time he had turned back, the Royal Dutch Airlines Douglas DC-8 was bunny-hopping down the runway as it braked. The airframe was still bucking on its suspension when the pilot brought the plane to a swaying halt in front of the terminal building. There, done. Vasin felt a small tug of admiration for the pilot. As a ground crew in oilskins rolled a set of steps toward the aircraft and a refueling tanker pulled up, Vasin turned to descend to the arrivals hall.

As he trotted down the stairs, Vasin passed the last passengers hurrying to catch the plane on its return journey to Amsterdam. Among them was a face he half recognized—an American diplomat, evidently, with no luggage but a black briefcase embossed in gold with the spread-eagle seal of the US Department of State. The diplomatic bag was attached to the courier's wrist by a chrome chain and handcuff. The man was accompanied by a heavyset thug in a civilian suit but sporting the unmistakable buzz cut of a US Marine. Vasin thought for a moment. Of course. He'd seen the face on a *kontora* circulation list of all the suspected CIA agents under diplomatic cover in Moscow. Vasin turned to follow the fellow's retreating back. A colleague, of sorts.

Naturally Kuznetsov was one of the first passengers to clear passport control and customs. His *kontora* ID would spare him most of the formalities. Vasin spotted Kuznetsov's squat, strutting figure as soon as he emerged onto the nearly empty concourse. His face was even more deeply tanned, and the broad lapels of his capitalist's beige suit peeked immodestly out from under his heavy Moscow overcoat. Vasin advanced, his hands spread in greeting.

"Kuznetsov! Vadim! How are you doing?"

"You *have* to be kidding." Kuznetsov looked bleary-eyed after his long journey, his face puffy and his shirt crumpled. "The Ride of the Valkyries all the way down, and when I finally return to God's good earth, the first man I see is Alexander *fucking* Vasin."

"Great to see you too, Vadim. How was fraternal Cuba?"

"Maybe we crashed and I'm now in hell. Is that what this is?"

"Welcome to Moscow."

"Maybe that's the same thing. Listen—I've been on three planes in twenty hours. Thought the last one would be my last foray into the heavens. Can't whatever terrible thing you're about to share with me wait until I've had a bath and a nap?"

"Sure. Give you a lift into town? Know where you're staying?"

"Actually, no. Was planning to call in to the *kontora* and ask my boss's secretary to book me a place in the bachelor's quarters at the—"

"Rhetorical question, Vadim. Don't worry. I got you a suite at the Hotel Ukraine. Mind holding off checking in with the office for one day?"

Kuznetsov made no answer but allowed his shoulders to go slack. He raised his eyes to the roof, loosened his grip on his suitcase, and let it drop to the marble pavement.

"Fine. Whatever you say, Vasin. Resistance is useless. I know you."

Kuznetsov walked toward the exit, leaving Vasin to pick up his suitcase and follow.

3

Hotel Ukraine, Moscow
3 October 1962

Major Vadim Kuznetsov emerged from the plush oak-paneled elevators and into the lobby looking sleek, healthy, and foreign. He wore a fresh shirt and his hair and beard glistened with exotic-smelling oil, and he had changed into a suave gray check suit. Vasin peered over his copy of *Izvestia* and looked his old handler up and down.

"Feeling better? How's the plumbing in this place?"

Kuznetsov flopped down in the low armchair next to Vasin's.

"Beats the *kontora* hostel in Sagua la Grande. Weather's worse over here, though." He returned Vasin's appraising look. "And you look fucking *terrible*. I say that as a concerned colleague, by the way. What happened? It's been, what, two months since I had the pleasure of your company? You ill or something?"

Kuznetsov's tone was more concerned than mocking. Was his old comrade feeling *sorry* for him? Vasin straightened in his chair, pulled in his belly, and attempted a smile.

"Put it like this. I was all set to catch a big beast. Got some juicy bait to prime the trap. But . . . the beast never broke cover. So I'm still waiting. Every day."

"Trap? Beast? This about the spy the *kontora* has you chasing?"

"Something like that."

"You've only got yourself to blame, Vasin. Mister big-game hunter. They expect nothing but a masterly performance from Special Cases' hotshot young investigator."

Kuznetsov had folded his hands and was scrutinizing Vasin across his steepled fingers. Vasin struggled to narrow his eyes and stiffen his spine. He realized it had been a while since anyone had teased him to his face.

"You're right. Master spy catcher. That's me."

"Vasin, you're starting to worry me. When we first met, you were keen. Tight. Had a torch burning in your ass. Now you look like you're some kind of ancient apparatchik who's failed to make the cut for candidate member of the Politburo. Like a wedding cake that's been left out in the rain. I was almost looking forward to hearing your latest outrageous demand. But it seems like you're about to ask me advice on the best *kontora* sanatorium to check in to."

"You done with your charming personal critique? Not annoyed. Just curious."

"Not yet. But my next salvo will need some fuel. Which is why you're going to take me to a lavish dinner, over which you are going to quiz me about the affairs of a certain tropical island which I have recently left for a week of consultations in our great Socialist metropolis. To my great regret. Did I guess right?"

Vasin felt a genuine grin spreading across his face for the first time in weeks. Kuznetsov may have been an arrogant jerk. But he was a jerk with whom he'd been through a lot. It was almost like having a friend.

"You guessed right. I got us a table at the—"

"The National?"

"Aragvi."

"Outstanding. Lead on, Mephistopheles. I'm ready to be tempted."

The Aragvi's officious headwaiter led Vasin and Kuznetsov through the crowded tables on the restaurant floor and up to the gallery with the grave, dignified air of a high priest. Which in a sense he was. The stiff-legged old man was on nodding and even hand-shaking terms with Central Committee members, cosmonauts, and prima ballerinas. The Aragvi's maître d'hôtel wielded sufficient power to easily humiliate mere colonels and majors. But Orlov's secretary held this guy in particular thrall. Exactly how, Vasin had never asked. But at the favored Georgian restaurant of Moscow's elite, Orlov's name was sufficient to command an immediate reservation. Which was as good a measure as any—and better than most—of the real status that Special Cases held in the world.

Both officers slowed their pace as they passed booths five and six—the most central of the row of curtained-off private alcoves which over-looked the other, more humble tables. Both were occupied by boisterous groups of well-dressed bureaucrats. Vasin and Kuznetsov exchanged a glance. Both knew that these were the wired booths, the ones the *kontora* reserved for conversations meant to be recorded. Though, of course, thought Vasin as he pressed himself against the brass rail to allow a group of fur-clad young ballerinas to pass, it would be just like the *kontora* to bug every other booth instead, and just put out word. Except, as Vasin also knew, the ubiquity of *kontora* ears was an urban myth. Manning a listening station was a gruesomely labor-intensive job. Hundreds of hours of boredom, smokes, tedium in stuffy rooms heated by the humming engines of slow-turning tape recorders. They were shown to a cozy, pine-lined booth at the end of the row, decorated with carpets and Caucasian daggers on the walls.

"Just bring us everything that's good tonight, Mikheil."

The headwaiter smiled broadly, gathering the typed menus in their heavy leather cases back from the table with bowing approval. Only rubes studied the menu—on which the best dishes were in any case never listed.

"And we'll have . . . cognac?" Vasin glanced across to Kuznetsov. "And . . . some rkatsiteli for the white?"

"Mukuzani for the red," added Kuznetsov.

So it was going to be one of those evenings. Boozy. Maybe, Vasin thought, he needed it. He'd been drunk pretty often over the weeks of waiting for Morozov to break cover—but always melancholy and alone. It would be a treat to get good and pissed with someone like a confidant. But first, business. Vasin waited until the waiter had withdrawn and decorously drawn the heavy velvet curtain before he spoke.

"So. How's Cuba?"

"Cuba is more Soviet than ever. By which I mean—it's gotten very popular among Soviet tourists. Many of whom seem to be engineers on vacation. And Armed Forces members. Hard to tell, of course, when they're in their shorts on the beach. But I'm guessing."

They paused as a bottle of Armenian cognac appeared, accompanied by a tray of minced spinach and green bean *pkhali* vegetable balls. Kuznetsov poured before Vasin could object and proposed a brief toast to the Service. They clinked glasses and drank off the cognac.

"Vadim. I need you to make sense of some information. Let's do this on a clear head. So enough, for the moment."

"Guessed as much. Don't worry. Head: clear. Clearer, in fact, than before that shot. Go ahead."

Vasin fished in his jacket pocket for a sheaf of his own handwritten notes and smoothed them flat on the brilliant white tablecloth. He cleared his throat and read in a low voice.

" 'September seventeenth, 1962. Confidential Soviet Defense Ministry memorandum on progress of Operation Anadyr. First consignment of medium-range R-12 missiles safely landed on Cuba September sixth. Second consignment intermediate-range R-12s delivered September sixteenth. Missiles successfully transported to bases.'"

Vasin looked up at his companion, whose face had lost its joviality. The two men weighed each other's eyes.

"Bravo. Vasin, you are impressively well informed, as usual. And your question was—does that mean anything to me? My answer is yes, it does. Next question."

"Interesting. Well let's start with this—that information does not tally with what I have been reading in our Soviet newspapers." Vasin flipped over to another page in his notes. "Here we have *Izvestia*, dated September seventh. 'Soviet Ambassador to the United States Anatoly Dobrynin has told the United Nations that the USSR is supplying only defensive weapons to Cuba. Dobrynin categorically denies all reports of offensive weapons.' And here's another, dated September eleventh from TASS: 'The USSR officially warns Western Imperialist aggressors that a US attack either on Cuba or on Soviet ships that are carrying supplies to the island will be considered an act of war' . . . and that 'the peace-loving peoples of the USSR have no need or intention to introduce offensive nuclear missiles into Cuba.'"

"Oh my dear Vasin. Dare I tell you this awful secret? Okay. I dare. Sasha—the Soviet press doesn't always tell the truth."

"Hilarious, again. I get that. Our diplomats are denying that we are sending missiles to Cuba. But we've already delivered the nukes, apparently. That true?"

Kuznetsov made a moue, his little hands giving the sides of his beard a nervous rub as he leaned back from the table. The waiter reappeared with a steaming *khatchapuri* cheese bread, a pot of hot stewed kidney beans, a plate of white cheese in a bed of fresh tarragon and coriander leaves, and a salad of tomatoes and sliced green onions. His assistant entered with a bottle of white wine, and began to open it with due ceremony before registering his guests' frigid smiles and uncorking it quickly and retreating.

"Yes," Kuznetsov answered without preamble. "Yes. We're delivering the rockets. Good number of 'em already on the island. Forty-four, to be precise, since we're speaking among friends."

"Okay. Good start. You've seen them?"

"I have. Got stuck in a traffic jam behind one of them a few weeks back. They're kind of hard to miss. The locals were standing on the road cheering them as they went past, since you ask."

"Cheering?"

"Yeah. Mind you—they'll cheer anything, the Cubans. An exuberant lot."

"The missiles weren't concealed?"

"Well, they were covered in tarpaulins. And under heavy escort. But I think the enlightened proletariat of Cuba kind of got the idea."

"So now tell me this. What does the designation R-12 mean to you?"

"You couldn't look that one up?"

"Let's say that's what I'm doing right now."

Kuznetsov sighed and sloshed wine into both their glasses.

"R-12s are ballistic missiles. In the lingo. Come in two flavors—medium range and intermediate. That's two-thousand-kilometer and forty-five-hundred-kilometer range to you. Single-stage, road-transportable, surface-launched, storable liquid-propellant-fueled missiles. Point is—you can move them about. Cheering crowds or no."

"And the warheads?"

"Thermonuclear. Biggest they can carry is one megaton, far as I remember."

The very word *megaton* sent Vasin's mind back to his and Kuznetsov's days among the elite bomb makers of Arzamas-16. The dry vocabulary of destruction. A bomb the size of a million tons of TNT.

"Enough? Satisfied? Just please don't tell me why you're asking."

"Two shiploads delivered in September and more to come. So they've already been deployed to their launch stations in Cuba?"

"Correct."

"But did you know that the Americans know?"

Kuznetsov set his glass back down on the table and leaned toward Vasin.

"You mean all that fuss in Congress? Doesn't mean the Yankees *know*. They suspect, maybe."

"Kuznetsov—they *know*. I'm telling you. You said yourself that half the island saw the rockets being trucked to their bases. So now listen to this." Vasin found his place in his notes. "Wait . . . here it is. 'September twentieth. Confidential Defense Ministry memorandum. Notes concern about reports from numerous Soviet agents in Miami that Cuban population has remarked on passage of "very long canvas-covered cylindrical objects that could not make turns through towns without backing up and maneuvering." Many such reports passed on to US intelligence in Miami. They warn of potential security breach as defensive missiles are much shorter than R-12s.'"

Kuznetsov paused for a moment before silently spooning beans and cheese bread onto his plate. He ate hungrily for a couple of minutes before forming a response.

"So what? If the missiles are already in place right under the Americans' noses, it's too late. Point and shoot. That's the thing about R-12s. Transportable. Easily hidden. Too late for the Yankees to protest now. What are they going to do—nuke Cuba? Nuke *us*? They'll never do it. The Americans have been shitting themselves ever since that big bomb we tested last year, if you remember? So . . . they wouldn't dare."

Vasin could still see the Tupolev bomber on the tarmac at the Arctic airbase at Olenya, its silver belly cut away to accommodate the giant bulk of the most powerful nuclear bomb ever created. The RDS-220 that Professor Adamov had feared could set the earth's atmosphere ablaze. Oh yes. Vasin remembered it.

"The Defense Ministry brass thinks the big bomb makes us immune? Allows us to do whatever we like?"

"Vasin—tell me why we're discussing the finer points of Soviet military-strategic doctrine instead of tucking into our excellent Georgian dinner?"

"Let's imagine that the Americans have an agent. Here in Moscow. And that agent might be able to confirm to them the details of the R-12 missile delivery to Cuba. *Prove* that we are lying about it?"

Kuznetsov picked up a spring onion and a piece of white cheese and stuffed them into his mouth, washing them down with a large slug of wine.

"*Mean?* It means nothing. The Americans will find out for themselves soon enough. The first clear day, and the Yankee spy planes will spot them. But like I say—it's too late. The boy Kennedy's just going to have to get used to it. Just like we have to live with his Jupiter missiles in Turkey."

"*Jupiter?*"

With a theatrical movement, Kuznetsov brought his open palm to his face, placed his middle finger in the center of his brow, and grimaced as if fending off a migraine.

"Lord God, Vasin. And I thought you were up there with the cloud dwellers who know everything. Up on your special ninth floor. You don't know what R-12s are. You don't know what Jupiter is. I thought you'd been up the ass of Operation Anadyr for months. These are the bloody basics, man."

Vasin weighed a selection of sarcastic ripostes but thought better of it. Instead he picked up his glass of white wine and gulped it down.

"Jupiters are American medium-range nuclear rockets," Kuznetsov continued. "Been deployed in Izmir, Turkey, since 1959, pointing right at Soviet Ukraine. Right in our own backyard, for the last two years. So Cuba is just tit for tat. If the Americans kick up a fuss about Cuba, we just offer to withdraw as long as the Yankees pull theirs out of Turkey. It's called strategy, Vasin. Leave it to the professionals. Can we talk about women and football now?"

"Not yet. You think Kennedy plans to just sit back and do nothing about nuclear warheads being secretly deployed on his doorstep? I think you're wrong." Vasin leafed through his notes again. "Our missiles in Cuba? They're becoming the worst-kept secret in the world. Here. Listen to this: 'September twenty-second. Soviet Foreign Ministry memorandum of meeting between Cuban ambassador in Moscow and USSR foreign minister re: US Congress Joint Resolution 230. US Congress expresses resolve to prevent the creation of an externally supported military establishment in Cuba. US announces a major military exercise in the Caribbean, PHIBRIGLEX-62. Memo confirms joint public position of USSR and Cuba that US actions are a deliberate provocation and proof that the US is planning to invade Cuba.'"

Kuznetsov nodded as he munched.

"Nonsense. They're not gonna invade. Like I said—the Yankees are closing the stable door when the horse is gone. The R-12s are already in place. What's an American naval blockade gonna do about that?"

"Except we're deploying a naval force to the Caribbean, too. Here. This memo is the newest one I have. From five days ago. Ready? 'September twenty-eighth—Defense Ministry memorandum on disposition of Soviet naval forces deployed to Cuba. Four destroyers, twelve fleet auxiliaries already in position within one day's sailing of northern

Caribbean. Submarine fleet of four B-class boats reported ready for sea. Authorized to sail from Severomorsk for Cuba from October second.' Yesterday. So what do we make of that, Vadim? Their Navy deployed. Our Navy deployed. Both sides talking about acts of war."

Vasin's companion merely shrugged.

"Listen, Sasha. In politics, there are things you do for show and things you do that really matter. The R-12 deployment? That matters. Our rockets are now pointing at America's belly, just like the Americans have the Jupiter rockets pointing at ours. So it's a stalemate. One all. Which suits us just fine. And the naval stuff, on both sides? That's just for show. Like most of the Navy, actually. Pointless, if you ask me—all of it except our strategic nuclear missile submarines. They're actually good for something. As for all those surface boats? Only good for sailing up and down showing off. And that's exactly what's going to happen with this Soviet task force you're so worried about."

"Wait—we're sending *nuclear* missile submarines to Cuba?"

"No idea. You'd have to ask the boys in green. Or blue. You have some military and Navy boys on your hook, I guess?"

"Maybe I do. But what I really wanted to ask you was . . ."

Vasin looked down again at his notes—even though what he wanted to say wasn't written there.

"Was this, Vadim. I've been thinking. Sending missiles to Cuba—fine. I see the logic of that. The tit-for-tat logic, as you said. But this Soviet flotilla. The huge fleet. The submarines. It's overkill. It's . . . too much. And . . . and I can't help thinking that maybe, just maybe, someone on our side actually *wants* to start a war?"

Kuznetsov settled back onto the padded cushions of the banquette behind him.

"You were always a one for the big theory, Sasha. Give you that." Vasin felt his friend's eyes appraising him with a look that was harder than his amiably composed face. "But I'm thinking that maybe it's not just you who have been having these strange thoughts. I'm thinking—maybe you have heard this somewhere. Maybe it's something that people are saying. I mean"—Kuznetsov pointed to the ceiling—"people up there. That right, Sasha? Some little bird been whispering in your ear? You can tell me. *Who* are these people who want war? And *why*? And *who says so*?"

Both men started as the velvet curtain was abruptly jerked aside. A young waiter appeared in the opening, bearing a tray covered in steaming plates. The headwaiter followed and began to reverently unload them onto the table, along with a running commentary on the dishes: chicken with walnut sauce, lamb neck and minced meat kebabs, *khinkali* dumplings.

As the table was being filled with a feast fit for half a dozen men, Vasin in turn settled back into the broad seat. The intelligence professional in him knew that he had reached the end of Kuznetsov's cooperation. The man was starting to push back, ask questions of his own. And they were not questions that Vasin was ready to answer.

The waiters withdrew, with the air of acolytes to a sacred rite of gluttony. Vasin and Kuznetsov both sat forward once more, eyeing the indecent array of food with appreciation.

"Right. That's the official part over. Dig in, Kuznetsov. And since I'm buying, I'm going to tell you, at length, what a *fucking* pain in the ass my wife, Vera, is being."

4

Dogger Bank, North Sea
4 October 1962

Vasily Arkhipov was woken by the gentle rolling of B-59 as she rose toward the surface. He glanced at the luminous dial of the chronometer bolted to the wall. Ten minutes to eight p.m. Moscow time—close to the start of the first watch. He listened to the low whine of the electric engines spooling down, replaced by the reassuring thrum of the diesels starting up that reverberated through the whole ship. Snorkeling depth, close enough to the surface to put up a tube through which the engines sucked down air and ventilated the hull after nine hours on battery power. The motion of the boat became more pronounced with the swell. For as long as he'd been at sea, Arkhipov had always enjoyed the moment of surfacing. The submarine suddenly became a normal ship again, breathing God's good air, riding the living waves rather than silently prowling below them.

Arkhipov sat up on his narrow cot and reached over to a fitted cupboard that housed his dress uniform and wet-weather gear. His cabin measured six feet by eight—luxurious by diesel submarine standards, but still far smaller than the one he'd had on the much more spacious K-19. Below his feet were two decks entirely filled with electric batteries. That meant that everything in the middle section of the sub—the officers' and warrant officers' quarters, the command center, navigation and torpedo-targeting rooms, galley, radio and sonar rooms—were all squeezed into the steeply curving upper third of the hull. Only in the corridor that ran down the center of this upper deck could Arkhipov stand upright without stooping.

As he pulled on his oilskin trousers, Arkhipov watched the chronometer edge toward the hour. One of the officers' mess orderlies would be waiting outside his door, mugs of lemon tea in hand for the commanders, waiting for the same moment. The polite knock came on the dot of eight bells. In a few minutes, after dark, they'd surface fully and raise the radio masts.

Arkhipov sipped tea as he waited for the clatter of sailors changing shifts to die down. The central passageway was too narrow for two men to pass, causing constant traffic jams at each end of the compartment as the sailors squeezed against each other to make room for their shipmates as they made their way to their stations. On the other side of the steel bulkhead behind his head, Arkhipov could hear the hiss and suck of breaking waves that told him they were now running on the surface.

Once the thudding shift change was complete, Arkhipov slid open his door and headed aft to the control room. He had to pause outside the officers' mess as the six lieutenants who berthed there filed out to make room for the space to be transformed from living quarters into a dining room for the evening meal. Inside, a pair of orderlies were busy assembling the central collapsible table and folding down three upper bunks to form the backs of three long benches. Nine of the ship's officers could dine in the mess at a time, leaving four on duty. Arkhipov reached the round pressure hatch that led to the command center and squeezed his leg, then his body and head, through the eighty-centimeter-wide hole, ungainly in his bulky overalls.

The command center was squeezed between the curved hull wall and a series of pillar-like steel shafts that ran vertically through the center of the boat and housed the periscopes, antennas, and snorkeling gear. A man with outstretched arms could easily touch both sides of the cramped command space. Captain Savitsky, perched on the skipper's backless chair set against the bulkhead immediately beside the hatch, acknowledged Arkhipov with a curt nod.

Arkhipov returned the greeting. A vertical steel ladder right by the commander's seat led up to the periscope compartment that formed the lower part of the submarine's conning tower, and Arkhipov struggled up it in his oilskins. First Officer Manuilov was at the periscope, making a slow turn as he scanned the horizon. Above the periscope compartment was the bridge—the highest part of the boat, and the only place with access to the outside air when the sea was this choppy. Arkhipov called up through the hatchway, and a sailor nimbly clattered down the ladder to make room for him.

B-59 had been designed for Arctic waters, so the bridge was enclosed except for a row of six small windows arranged across the front. And because this upper part of the conning tower was outside the pressure hull and designed to flood while the boat was submerged, it was freezing cold. A handful of shivering sailors, one from each of the ship's seven compartments, acknowledged Arkhipov as they sucked on their cigarettes. The chilly bridge was the only part of the ship where smoking was permitted.

Arkhipov peered through the wet glass onto a dark, restless sea. Though he knew he'd probably see nothing more, Arkhipov nonetheless wanted to get out into the fresh air—at least for a few moments. A small hatch in the roof of the bridge led to a tiny, two-man lookout post at the very top of the conning tower. Arkhipov climbed up the water-slick ladder, pushing through a rubber flap that was supposed to keep out the seawater that sloshed around the tiny steel cockpit. At last, for the first time in two days, he was alone.

Up here, six meters above the level of the sea, the rolling of the boat was at its most violent. Arkhipov had to cling hard to the steel rails that surrounded the cockpit to steady himself as the boat plowed through the North Sea chop at a furious fifteen knots. The only thing visible was the whitecaps of a strong following sea. Somewhere about him, Arkhipov knew from his sonar, were the three other boats of his flotilla. And up ahead in the night, plowing through the same swell, was a fleet of fishing trawlers that would mask the submarine's passage down the British coast. With a click and an oily hiss, the long-range antenna soared into the air from its housing inside the submarine's conning tower directly in front of him, ready for the evening's comms with Moscow and the other boats. Arkhipov remained in the cockpit as the rainy night thickened around him, riding his ship through the choppy sea like a plunging whale.

Arkhipov was halfway through dinner when the senior radioman brought him a transcript of the latest fleet orders. It was in code, a meaningless sea of four-letter groups, the only intelligible part being the heading: URGENT: EYES ONLY FLOTILLA COMMANDER. There was a brief silence as the other eight officers around the mess table looked up from their macaroni with corned beef and eyed the piece of paper in Arkhipov's hand. Only Captain Savitsky studiously ignored it, spooning the food into his mouth with studied nonchalance.

"Excuse me, Comrades. Fleet HQ will be waiting for an answer."

Arkhipov walked the few steps forward to his cabin, fished out a set of keys from the chain that hung around his neck, and retrieved his personal codebook from a safe set in the bulkhead. His decryption skills were rusty, and it took him half an hour with codebook and pencil to turn the number groups into letters.

TO: FLOTILLA COMMANDER CFC VA ARKHIPOV.
EYES ONLY—FLASH
   FURTHER TO REPORTS OF HEIGHTENED US NAVY
ACTIVITY IN CARIBBEAN CONFIRMING OPERATIONAL
ORDERS FOR DEPLOYMENT OF SPECIAL WEAPONS BY
FLOTILLA SF4492/61.
   CARIBBEAN THEATER OF OPERATIONS DESIGNATED
HOSTILE/WAR FOOTING UNDER TERMS OF STANDING
ORDER 117/16. INDEPENDENT COMBAT USE OF SPECIAL
WEAPON AUTHORIZED AT DISCRETION OF SENIOR OFFICER
AND POLITICAL OFFICER OF EACH SUBMARINE IF VESSEL
DIRECTLY THREATENED BY ENEMY ACTION. FURTHER
TACTICAL FIRE AUTHORIZATION NOT RPT NOT REQUIRED
FROM FLEET HQ OR FLOTILLA COMMANDER UNTIL ORDER
RESCINDED OR FLOTILLA LEAVES CARIBBEAN THEATER.

CONFIRM MESSAGE RECEIVED AND SECURELY
COMMUNICATED TO ALL SUBMARINE COMMANDERS BY
ENCRYPTED VHF COMMS.
BY ORDER COMMANDER IN CHIEF SOVIET NAVY SG GORSHKOV.

Arkhipov looked up and saw Captain Savitsky leaning on the door-frame. Wordlessly, Arkhipov passed his decrypted notes to B-59's skipper. Savitsky grunted as he read.

"Authorization to shoot. Every man for himself. Could pot ourselves a Yankee aircraft carrier if we're lucky."

Arkhipov's face creased at the skipper's grimly belligerent tone.

"Is that what you dream of doing, Comrade Captain? Blowing an enemy ship out of the water with a nuclear warhead?"

Savitsky waited insolently long before answering.

"I was under the impression that was exactly what we all dreamed of doing, Comrade. It's what this warship was built for."

5

Pioneers' Ponds, Moscow
4 October 1962

How had Vasin's life turned into an unremitting series of defeats, a daily procession of failure? Autumn had settled over the city like a smothering gray blanket, squeezing the light from the days and pelting Vasin with rain and buffeting wind. In the corridors of the Lubyanka, Orlov barely acknowledged him. Vasin's team of watchers slouched at their posts, demoralized. A dead-end posting; a loser beat. The multiplying contagions of failure seemed to gather around everything Vasin did.

Day after day, Morozov would emerge from his apartment and embark on his daily routine. Walk, metro, office, lunch, office, metro, apartment. Occasionally dinner with friends and colleagues. As if taunting his watchers, the Colonel was looking more sprightly by the day. In summer, Morozov had taken to swimming after work at the Chaika pool near the Park Kultury metro station, often followed by a sauna. After every session he emerged looking infuriatingly fresh and ruddy with health. A rotation of watchers was quickly organized to follow him into the sports club. But instead of becoming a welcome relief from their daily routine, Vasin's beleaguered team ended up bickering over whose turn it was to spend some time in the pool.

Even the grave Schultz had abandoned them. Since his triumph in catching Morozov making his wrong-number call back in June, Schultz had departed on an extended vacation at a *kontora* sanatorium in Karelia. Vasin understood that he would return. But he had not returned. Vasin's Morozov team had become the cursed unit, staffed now only by those without the clout to bail out.

Sofia, too, seemed changed. In the days after Vasin had ordered her to hand over the Raúl Castro memos back in August, the whole team had been in a state of high, nervous alert. Vasin had seen Sofia as often as he dared—and ordered her to keep in close touch with Morozov. Yet with each passing day that Morozov was not caught red-handed, Sofia's suspicion of Vasin and his wild stories of espionage seemed to melt a little, like an ice sculpture in the sunshine. After a fortnight, with autumn setting in and still no breakthrough, Sofia's tone during her meetings with Vasin had become almost peremptory.

They continued to meet at least once a week. Sofia dutifully passed Vasin a summary of the Anadyr documents that crossed her desk—the documents that her intelligent eye had selected as being of interest to Morozov. A day or so later, once she had Vasin's approval, Sofia would pass them on to Morozov—usually over a coffee at the Shokoladnitsa or dinner at a Bulgarian greasy spoon café near Belorusskaya that he favored. The flow of information from Anadyr, via Sofia, to Morozov had become steady and constant. And still no slip. No observable contact between Morozov and the Americans.

Every morning at the tail end of summer, Vasin had woken with the same question racing through his brain: How the devil is Morozov doing it? By the time a rainy September slid into freezing, gray October, the question had become more of a dull ache in the center of Vasin's skull. Morozov was either the best spy in the business. Or . . . he wasn't a spy at all. Except that avenue of reason was not open to Vasin. Orlov has designated him an American spy. And Orlov made his own reality.

The morning after Vasin's dinner with Kuznetsov at Aragvi barely dawned at all—just a faint lightening of the sky beyond the curtains that accompanied the usual clatter and clamor of Vera and Nikita's breakfast routine. Vasin felt himself almost paralyzed with an over-whelming desire to remain in bed, to pull the sheets over his head and resign from the world. He covered his face in a pillow and groaned at the memory of the previous night. After a tsunami of food and drink at the Georgian place, Kuznetsov had dragged him to the bar at the National. And then to catch a stomping, noisy, and raucous gypsy show at the Hotel Moskva. And then to some dive bar near Kursky Station that Vasin remembered from his cop days, the haunt of black-market traders and low-rent Caucasian racketeers. Had Vasin actually been sick into the bushes as they staggered toward the taxi stand? A bilious sour-ness in the back of his mouth had seemed to confirm it.

The hands of the bedside clock that stood on the coffee table in front of Vasin's sofa bed crawled toward ten. Damn. He was due to give Sofia the all clear to pass the latest batch of documents. His fractious surveil-lance team would be expecting instructions on their precious rotations. He struggled out of bed, kicking the tangled sheets off his legs.

After that one night of drunken, convivial conversation with Kuz-netsov, Vasin felt his waking loneliness sharpen. It had been good to talk to someone. Swaying slightly in front of the kitchen telephone, he dialed Sofia's work number. Usually, he would tell her that her den-tist's appointment had been postponed until the following week—their signal to go ahead. But today Vasin felt a sudden and profound impatience with the whole charade. When Sofia came to the phone, he spoke without any code.

"Hi. It's me. Sasha. I need to see you. Lunchtime? At the metro?"

"What's happened?" Sofia's voice was immediately taut with alarm.

"Nothing. Just need to talk. One o'clock okay?"

Vasin hung up the receiver and rested his heavy head on his chest.

6

Arbatskaya Station, Moscow
4 October 1962

Waiting outside metro stations. Waiting and watching from apart-ments. Listening at microphones. Vasin felt that he had become not a man but a species of predatory shadow, forever waiting for silence and tedium to form itself into something concrete. The gloomy morning clouds had at least been blown away by a fresh autumn wind, and a few scraps of blue sky were visible high over the bare trees of the boulevard.

"What's happened? Tell me."

Sofia had appeared at Vasin's side. She, too, had discarded their customary ballet of following each other to one discreet location or another, and simply spoke to him directly. It felt, to Vasin, thrillingly illicit simply to speak to a person in the street, in plain sight.

"Hi, Sofia."

"Is he okay?"

"Which he? Morozov is okay. Your brother is okay."

"So what is this?"

"Just wanted to talk."

"What if someone from my office sees us?"

Nothing that Vasin could have done, it seemed, could unsettle Sofia more than the sudden abandonment of all their carefully rehearsed spycraft. She darted nervous glances from side to side. A stream of lunchtime commuters passed them on the way to the Arbatskaya metro station, many of them in military uniform. Vasin felt strangely light-headed.

"Sofia. I just wanted to say . . . it's okay to go ahead with this week's handover."

"Fine. And?"

"And . . . I wanted to ask you another question. About Morozov. A personal question. Not for the *kontora*. Just for me."

Sofia looked at him quizzically, as though seeing Vasin properly for the first time. Her strong, beautiful face formed into a knot of concern.

"Are you feeling all right, Colonel?"

"Forgive me. But I want you to answer a question about Morozov. From your heart. Is it truly impossible that he is betraying his country?"

Sofia's eyes narrowed and searched his face for signs of some complicated double bluff. Vasin resisted the urge to close his own, even as he felt that he was swooning into himself. He was breaking every rule of tradecraft—every technical rule, every personal rule. Rather than wait for her answer, he blundered on.

"I'm tired. And frustrated. And we have nothing, still, after all these weeks and months. And you know him, Sofia. I just need to hear it from you. Are you sure he's not a traitor, Sofia? Are you *sure*?"

To his own complete surprise, Vasin felt tears springing to his eyes. His own recklessness was as shocking to him as any line he had ever crossed before. But the adrenaline shock that swept him was as reviving as a gasp of air after an eon spent holding his breath underwater. Sofia stood absolutely still, staring. She opened her mouth to speak, but said nothing. Her eyes slid sideways, then down to look at her hands. In her hesitation, Vasin read anguish. And doubt.

"I cannot answer that question."

Sofia turned abruptly and disappeared in a moment into the crowd. Vasin leaned against the cold granite parapet and tipped his head back to gaze at a drifting patch of blue sky. He felt light-headed, somehow floating out of his own body. She had not said, "I am sure Morozov is innocent." Yet Vasin had frankly failed. How could he ever tell Orlov that he would never catch the white whale? Vasin could admit defeat to himself. But he would never, ever be able to call off Orlov's obsessive hunt.

7

Chaika Swimming Pool, Moscow
5 October 1962

Colonel Oleg Morozov squeezed his way onto the crowded B trolley-bus, leaning his hefty body against a packed press of humanity until it yielded enough centimeters for the door to clack shut behind him. The streetcar lurched into the traffic, leaving the young watcher Lyubimov among the unlucky crowd left to wait for the next trolley.

A couple of months ago, Lyubimov had been keen. But routine, the daily tedium of a fruitless surveillance routine, had ground the edge off his enthusiasm. He watched the trolleybus with his mark on board pull away almost with relief. He knew exactly where Morozov was heading. The bloody swimming baths.

Morozov disembarked at the junction of Metrostoyevskaya Street and the Garden Ring and set off at a brisk pace toward the Chaika baths. In his raincoat pocket was a packet of breath mints he had purchased at a kiosk by the Mayakovskaya metro. He used his thumbnail to ease the mints out until they all clicked loose in his pocket. The process felt obscurely satisfying.

At the entrance to the Chaika sports complex, Morozov presented his season ticket and picked up a rubber band to which a locker key was attached. He strode up the steps to the locker rooms, opened his locker, and changed into his swimming suit. The sports club had been an excellent idea, Morozov thought as he made his way to the pool. Two months he'd been a member, and now he was swimming two kilometers every visit. Everyone in the office complimented Morozov on his newly trim appearance. Friends ribbed him that he had some new mistress he was trying to impress. This was almost true.

Toweling off after his swim, Morozov could not help but glance about at his fellow health enthusiasts. Some familiar faces would crop up week to week, but that was normal in a sports club. He tugged on his clothes and, finally, his raincoat. But as he pulled it from the locker, he would leave the empty packet of mints crumpled in the back corner. With a tiny steel roll of microfilm nestled inside.

Morozov never knew who observed him at the Chaika—which made it an excellent cutout. Much better than the clumsy wrong-call system he'd used earlier that summer to signal that he was ready to make contact. But he knew, as he left, that someone'e eyes were on him. And on the empty sports locker, yawning open with its piece of insignificant trash left in the back.

8

3rd Frunze Street, Moscow
22 October 1962

The morning was once more a pall of unrelenting gray. The skies were the color of dirty drainpipes, and drizzle fell steadily over the piles of autumn leaves in Vasin's courtyard. The universe was in agreement: there was no joy to be had anywhere, for anyone.

Vasin opened his green steel mailbox in the hallway. Inside was a single piece of correspondence—a prestamped souvenir envelope with a view of the Cathedral of St. Dmitry in Vladimir. Inside, someone had typed an address: Leningradsky Prospekt 78/2, apartment 181. There was no signature.

The souvenir envelope. It had to be Tokarev.

Vasin crumpled the paper with a stab of guilt. Nearly two months that Tokarev's wife, Saida, had been in the nuthouse, and Vasin had been powerless to help her. Not that there was much that he could have done. Only Orlov had a chance to get her out—and Tokarev had gravely crossed the General. She was far beyond Vasin's helping, at least until he landed his big fish and restored his own standing in Orlov's eyes.

Vasin hurried to his car. It was three hours before he could finish his routine rounds—appointments at the office and checking in on the team at the observation station. By the time he was finally free it was almost lunchtime, and the Friday-afternoon traffic on the northbound lane of the Leningrad highway crawled from traffic light to traffic light with infuriating slowness.

Tokarev's apartment building was identical to those of his neighbors, one of a sprawl of recently built prefabricated blocks that spread across the new suburbs of northern Moscow. The young trees that had been planted along the sidewalks were spindly and bare, and the courtyard playgrounds were deserted. Vasin found the entranceway, took the elevator to the top floor, and waited, listening, on the landing. Nothing.

Could this be an elaborate trap? The GRU had not reappeared since Vasin's showdown with Zimin at Kursky Station back in August. Nonetheless, Vasin found the silence ominous. Quietly, Vasin descended two flights to apartment 181. Through the padded door he could hear the low sound of a radio and the small noises of someone moving around inside. Vasin stepped away to the landing window to check the courtyard for unusual traffic or lurking strangers. Then he pressed the bell.

"It's open!" Tokarev's voice sounded strangely strangled. Vasin pressed the handle and let himself in.

Tokarev stood at the end of the hallway. He seemed to have aged a decade in just a few weeks. His face was sunken, and his cheeks furred with gray stubble. He wore his uniform breeches over stockinged feet, with a dressing gown hanging loose over his shoulders. Tokarev straightened under Vasin's appraising gaze, squaring his shoulders.

"Good of you to come, Comrade Colonel."

Tokarev's exaggeratedly formal tone immediately put Vasin on his guard. He glanced around the apartment. The place was small and cluttered, two rooms filled with bookshelves and knickknacks. Through the open bedroom door Vasin saw an untidy pile of laundry. The place had obviously not been cleaned since Tokarev's wife had been taken away. The modest home was not much of a reward for a decorated war hero. But also not a likely place for an ambush—too cramped, nowhere for a snatch team to hide.

"You wrote to me."

"I did."

"So I came. You have something to tell me?"

"Will you have some tea?"

Vasin followed Tokarev into the tiny kitchen, where a chunky old radio with outsized dials burbled *Woman's Hour* advice from Radio Mayak. Vasin didn't dare volunteer to help the proud old cavalryman as he bustled around the kitchen. There was no lid on the kettle, or the teapot, or the tea caddy, Vasin noticed. Tokarev was so adept with his prostheses that it was almost as though he had real hands—except that he spilled tea leaves all over the counter and dropped a teacup into the sink. Once the kettle was set on the stove—an electric model which needed no matches to light it—Tokarev settled down at the kitchen table and gestured Vasin to follow suit.

"Saida's dying. They wouldn't let me see her. They kept her at the Serbsky Institute only long enough to have her certified insane. Then they took her to some KGB facility. Friend Orlov didn't want my bosses—the military brass—getting her out, of course. They wouldn't tell me where she was for a month. But an old war comrade of mine knows one of the doctors at the Serbsky. Traced her transportation orders. Made some calls. Got word to me that Saida was somewhere near Zagorsk, in some closed *kontora* psychiatric zone. Told me she was under heavy sedation. Refusing to eat. Last week they began feeding her through a tube."

Tokarev pronounced the words in a hoarse, clipped tone, as though reading an official report. Vasin swallowed hard, impressed by Tokarev's dignity. He desperately wanted to help this man.

"So, Vasin. You said I needed to find something for Orlov, to exchange for Saida. So I found you something. Now turn up the radio. And take your notebook. All this is in my head."

Obediently, Vasin did as he was told. Tokarev at least knew his basic countersurveillance—the radio made it almost impossible for microphones to follow a conversation. Vasin turned up Radio Mayak to full volume.

"And so, Comrades, today we will be talking about baking. We learned everything we need to know about baking at our mother's side—or so we think. But what are the real, scientific differences between using yeast and bicarbonate of soda? Today we have nutritionist Dr. Yulia Mitskovskaya on the program to explain . . ."

Vasin fished a pencil and pad from the pocket of his coat and joined Tokarev at the kitchen table. The Major began without preamble.

"On October second a flotilla of four submarines left Polyarniy naval base on the White Sea, bound for the Caribbean. Vessels B-36, B-130, B-4, and B-59. All Project 641–class boats. Diesel-electric, eighty-nine meters long. Long-range hunter-killers, designed for a cruise of up to thirty-seven thousand kilometers. *Not* ballistic-missile boats. Armed with torpedoes only. Got all of that?"

Vasin looked up sharply at Tokarev. He happened to know that information to be correct—it was in one of the reports that Sofia had already passed to Morozov. A fleet of surface ships and, yes, four submarines had been ordered to sea as part of the support effort for Cuba.

"Now listen very carefully. In addition to twenty-one normal torpedoes, every one of those four subs is equipped with a single special weapon. A nuclear-tipped variant of the T-5 torpedo. Which is our heaviest antiship conventional weapon. Each of these nuclear torpedoes carries a warhead of four-point-eight-kiloton capacity."

Five kilotons would make each torpedo about a quarter as powerful as the atom bomb the Yankees dropped on Hiroshima in 1945. That meant, Vasin presumed, each torpedo was capable of destroying a mere quarter of a city. Or sinking an American carrier battle group.

"Tokarev—how do you know this?"

"Knew you'd ask. An old university mate who joined up, like me, in 'forty-one became an officer in the Soviet Riverine Fleet. Ran supplies across Lake Ladoga to Leningrad during the siege, right under the noses of German artillery and dive-bombers. Three boats shot to pieces under him. He spent a night floating in the freezing water, clinging to wreckage. Paddled to shore, though his legs were full of shrapnel, then crawled along the lakeshore till he reached our front lines. Lost both feet to frostbite. So you can imagine when he and I meet. Footless, I call him. Handless, he calls me."

Tokarev pulled his face into a bitter parody of a smile.

"My mate, the much-decorated war hero Footless, now happens to be a deputy minister of river transport. Two weeks ago he was at some meeting in Moscow. All-Union Congress of Heavy Shipbuilding. Kind of thing he spends his time doing—talking to heavy shipbuilders. He runs into an old comrade who now works at the Ministry of Medium Machine Building. Heavy ships require medium machines, I guess. Anyway. A colleague of this comrade is there, too—and it turns out he makes torpedoes. The three of them get drunk at the buffet. Mr. Torpedo starts saying how excited he is that some super-weapon he's made is getting its first operational trials at sea. Super, how? asks my friend Footless. Super *nuclear,* the guy answers. Tap on the nose. *'And it's on its way to teach the Yankees a lesson in Cuba.'* That's what he says."

So far, so plausible—or so it sounded to Vasin. The boasting gossip of bosses, among their own—this kind of loose talk was one of the *kontora*'s perennial security nightmares, as everyone in Special Cases knew. Senior apparatchiks believed, almost to a man, that secrets were for the little people. Generals, too. Eavesdropping on this kind of banter had been the original basis of Morozov's espionage career. If he was indeed a spy.

"Two days after his meeting took place, I happened to call Footless. I've been in touch a lot lately with him—and all my other old mates—since Saida got taken in. Asking around for gossip, anything I can use. I can tell that Footless is dying to tell me something. We meet at the Officers' Club on Tsvetnoi Boulevard. And he tells me his gossip about the torpedoes—as I've just told you. Therefore: I know that at least one submarine has apparently put to sea, carrying a nuclear torpedo, bound for Cuba. The rest was connecting dots. You know this. All kinds of secrets hide in plain sight—if you know what you're looking for. You don't have to see the confidential fleet orders to know which four Northern Fleet boats have been provisioned and fueled for a long-range voyage out of Severomorsk."

"But how do you know that those boats are heading to Cuba?"

"Don't interrupt—listen. So I started looking at the correspondence that goes out from the office of Commander in Chief of the Soviet Navy Admiral Gorshkov. The bureaucratic protocol is this: Two copies of every operational order go to the relevant department—Northern Fleet, Pacific Fleet, and so on—where they are passed down the chain of command to officers in the field. Another copy goes into the Admiralty archive. And another goes to the General Staff headquarters. And, in the case of all confidential, top-secret and flash-priority signals, another one goes to . . . to who, Vasin?"

"To the GRU."

"Correct. To the GRU secret registry."

"Which you got into, how?"

"You don't get into the registry. You talk to people who do. Again . . . know what you are looking for, and suddenly everyone presumes you're in the magic circle. You don't ask, 'Can I access the top-secret fleet orders from Admiral Gorshkov's office?' You ask, 'Anything new come through on the Caribbean flotilla? Boats B-36, B-130, B-4, and B-59. Come across anyone's desk, girls?' And then someone pipes up, 'Oh yes. Filed something about them a few days ago.' And then you know."

"Know what?"

Tokarev was enjoying teasing out the story of his own sleuthing.

"On October second Northern Fleet headquarters signaled the flotilla, under the authority of Admiral Gorshkov. He formally ordered those four boats to sail to Cuba and take up station at Mariel Naval Base. Then, a few days later, Gorshkov formally gave the individual commanders fire control over the special weapons they are carrying. You see what I'm saying, Vasin?"

"You lost me completely. What is fire control?"

"It means that every boat's captain has the personal authority to use his nuclear torpedo in the case of enemy attack. No need to seek authorization from Fleet HQ. So there are four Soviet officers, cruising somewhere under the Atlantic right at this moment, each with personal command of a nuclear weapon. And—last and most important thing. The flotilla sailed on the same day their orders came through. October second. Their estimated sailing time to Cuba is twenty-two days."

Vasin did the arithmetic and gripped the table, suddenly giddy. It was now October twenty-second. That meant the flotilla was due in the northern Caribbean . . . in two days' time. His brain filled with a blizzard of thoughts. Who authorized this nuclear flotilla and its kamikaze orders to run the gauntlet of the American fleet? And who in hell had the authority to stop it?

"But wait. There's another thing you need to know. We have a man inside the NSA."

"The American National Security Agency?"

"Exactly. It's part of their Department of Defense. They're the listeners. The guys who monitor our radio traffic. Try to tap our embassies' phone lines. We have a spy who works there."

"How the hell do you know that?"

"The usual way. Paperwork. Guesswork. The Aquarium registry, again. I went through the logs of all the incoming agent reports. Not the reports themselves, of course. I'm not cleared for that. But where the intelligence reports go, which departments? That's all in the daily logs of the general registry. And guess what I found? Last summer, we start getting five times the usual traffic of reports going to the Aquarium department that monitors US signals intelligence. Five times more information coming from someone in the field, to that department. So I do a little digging. The files all have the same agent code. Therefore, all this is coming from a single guy. And it's originating in the GRU *rezidentura* in Washington. So I check the exact departments this man's information is being sent on to. Navy intelligence. Air Force intelligence. Our own signals intelligence people. Hardly anything at all to the political bigwigs. Nothing graded 'flash' or 'eyes-only.' Therefore, it's technical stuff, fairly low-level. But copious. And detailed. Operational stuff from across the US military—which means it's from someone with access to a wide range of American signals, across all the services. So it's probably from inside the NSA."

"Why do I need to know this?"

"Because of the Navy's map room."

"Tokarev—you've lost me again."

"There's a distribution list. Standing orders, if you like, about which departments routinely get to see the copies of every agent's product. The most boring document in the world, you might think. But no. Bureaucratic procedures can tell you a lot. The stuff our spy produces always gets copied to the Navy Staff map room, urgent priority. That's the place where our sailor boys plot all the locations of every enemy ship we know about, anywhere in the world. Which means, what?"

"That he's reporting on US naval movements?"

"Exactly! Exactly."

"So you think he'll tell us if the US Navy spots our flotilla?"

"Very possibly."

"And how do we know if he does? You said you can't read the actual content of this guy's messages."

"With the whole world on the brink of war? I reckon our Washington station would mark a signal like that 'flash-urgent.' And we'll see the Americans mobilizing their fleet to intercept our boats. That's how we will know."

"And if we want to get hold of this flash message? So we're not just guessing?"

Tokarev's face, which had been animated with an almost boyish enthusiasm as he laid out his own sleuthing, tensed back into a mask of anxiety.

"If that happens, I'll think of something. But all this information— surely it's enough to trade for Saida?"

"Yes. I mean . . . I think so."

"You *think*?"

"You know Orlov. It's not going to be easy to extract mercy from him. But . . . you're paying him in a currency he understands. And this is brilliant work. Really."

Vasin stood quickly, scooping his notes into his pocket. Tokarev stood, too, more stiffly. Vasin reached across the table and seized one of the old man's plastic hands.

"Where can I find you, Major? For updates."

"Call a pay phone number in the next-door building. I can be there every evening at five."

Vasin scribbled the number in his notebook. By force of habit, he added one to each digit for security.

"Orlov will hear of this right now. That much I can promise you."

9

Sargasso Sea
22 October 1962, 18:48 Eastern Daylight Time

Tropical rain clouds scudded low over the western horizon, piling up in angry black ziggurats over the island of Bermuda. For a few minutes just before it set, the sun broke through under the clouds in a fiery blaze and then was gone. For eight days Arkhipov's flotilla had been riding mountainous Atlantic swells, whipped up by Hurricane Ella as it spiraled up through the Gulf of Mexico, five hundred miles to the southwest. The worst blow of the Caribbean storm season, B-59's navigator reckoned, and one that had made life on board B-59 a misery.

Though B-59's five hundred tons of accumulator batteries filled most of her hull, they still needed to be charged for at least six hours a day. That meant running the diesels—and diesels needed air. Sailing a submarine on the surface, in the teeth of a tropical storm, was the maritime equivalent of climbing into a barrel and rolling down a mountain. At least a dozen of the crew lay injured, pitched violently against the thousands of levers, taps, gaskets, and pipes that protruded at every angle throughout the submarine. One young midshipman lay with a fractured arm after being hurled down the steps into the machine control room. The cook's mate had split his head open on the ventilator hood of the ship's stove, spilling a forty-liter tub of boiling soup on himself in the bargain. Even Arkhipov, with his twenty years of experience at sea, had concussed himself in the rear torpedo compartment as an unexpected roll of the ship sent him staggering against the heavy steel breech of one of the six firing tubes.

On the first day of the storm, the officers and warrant officers had abandoned eating meals in their two messes in favor of bolting bowls of food in their berths—just like the enlisted men had to do for the duration of the voyage. Arkhipov had spent most of his waking hours in his cabin, sitting with his back braced against the bulkhead and his feet against the deal table opposite, too seasick to read or even think. Every compartment of the boat reeked of vomit. Even the macho Savitsky, occupying the cabin directly opposite Arkhipov's, retched his guts out every half hour into the personal sink in his cabin. The seas had been so high that they regularly broke over the top of B-59's six-meter-tall conning tower, turning the view from the bridge windows into a gray-green screen of foam.

On the second day, they'd lost contact with B-36. On the surface, the subs could communicate using short-range VHF radio. Submerged, they relied on an underwater telephone system that picked up acoustic signals broadcast from one ship to the other via an array of stainless-steel plates along the front of the conning tower. But the electromagnetic fury of Hurricane Ella had played havoc with the radio, and the crazy currents churned up by the force of the storm scrambled the underwater signals, reducing the range of the phone from ten kilometers to less than one.

Now, on the eighth day, the sea's fury was finally beginning to abate. There had been one tactical advantage to the storm, and it was that storm weather grounded all American sub-hunting aircraft—and high waves made spotting the sub's black-painted hull all but impossible. As the swells subsided, so did B-59's invisibility to the enemy.

In the sonar room—a compartment smaller than his own cabin—Arkhipov stood nervously watching the sonarman's screen. Flanking B-59 were two green blobs, equidistant from her a couple of kilometers to the northwest and southeast and holding the same course toward Cuba. Probably B-4 and B-130. Where the fourth boat of his flotilla had disappeared to was anyone's guess.

Other than the two Soviet submarines, the area around Arkhipov's boat appeared blank, dotted only with a constellation of small, glowing specks that flickered and disappeared as the sonar's sensor turned through 360 degrees. Shoals of fish, most likely. Clumps of floating seaweed. The sea was always full of ghost noises, echoes floating up from the depths. But no large ships—at least not within the sonar's twenty-five-kilometer radius.

Reassured, Arkhipov ducked aft and made his way to the radio room. "Nothing from Moscow?"

The radio officer hooked one of his headphones behind his ear and shook his head. No word from fleet headquarters for more than a week on the long-distance radio set—not since a command to Arkhipov's flotilla to maintain radio silence. That meant that B-59 had to sail mute, listening passively for incoming long-wave radio signals from Moscow, signaling the other boats with the underwater telephone only, or by the weakest VHF short-range radio signal.

"Anything more on local radio?"

The young officer turned in his swivel seat and plugged his headphones into a different radio set that occupied the opposite wall of the cramped comms room. A powerful AM/FM radio, tuned to a local civilian station. Of course American radio was full of lies and capitalist propaganda. But for the moment—and in the absence of instructions from Moscow—snippets of radio news from the United States were all the information on the outside world that B-59 had.

Junior Lieutenant Kostev half grinned and flicked on a switch to put the AM signal on speaker. A low, roaring jumble of noise gave way to the tail end of a piece of rock-and-roll music.

"A Miami station coming through more or less okay, sir."

"Anything more about Kennedy?"

Eight hours earlier, during the previous surface run, Kostev had picked up a news bulletin trailing an important announcement by the American President. It had gone out on the airwaves while they'd been running submerged. Kostev—one of the few English-speaking officers on board—had spent the last hour sweating over his radio, hunting out a clear signal to catch up on the news.

"Two minutes to the seven p.m. evening news bulletin, Captain. Patch it through to the skipper's cabin?"

Arkhipov nodded and hurried forward to the Captain's quarters. Savitsky and Political Officer Maslennikov were waiting for him. Arkhipov squeezed in beside his two colleagues on the two-meter-long bench that doubled as the skipper's berth. Savitsky flicked on the radio speaker built into the bulkhead over his small map table. He adjusted the volume as the signal hummed in and out, before settling on a moment of silence and a series of electronic pips.

"This is WLRN, Miami, and this is the evening news at seven o'clock on Monday, October twenty-second, 1962, brought to you by Total. President Kennedy announced this evening that . . ." A burst of static obliterated the American announcer's next words. By the time the signal stabilized a few moments later a recording of Kennedy's reedy, Boston-accented voice was playing: ". . . shall be the policy of this nation to regard any nuclear missile launched from Cuba against any nation in the Western Hemisphere as an attack by the Soviet Union on the United States, requiring a full retaliatory response upon the Soviet Union."

Again the signal faded, and Savitsky gave the radio set a hefty slap as if chastising an irritating child. The announcer's voice wavered back into audibility. ". . . any Soviet ships attempting to violate the US naval quarantine of Cuba will be considered an act of war."

The three officers bowed their heads in concentration as they struggled to make out the words through the static, but the radio signal was swallowed into the magnetic swirl of the receding storm to the northwest.

"Did he stay 'a state of war'?" Arkhipov reread his scribbled notes. "Did you hear that, Maslennikov? And what the hell is a naval 'quarantine'?"

The Political Officer's Naval Staff College English was the least rusty of the three.

"An *act* of war, he said, Captain. I think. And by 'quarantine' I assume he means a naval blockade. So Kennedy's made an ultimatum. Running the blockade will be considered an act of war. That's what I heard."

Savitsky flicked off the whining speaker. The three men shared a long moment of silence. Savitsky picked a chart of the eastern Caribbean off his table. Their current position was marked on the chart's clear plastic case in blue wax pencil.

"We are roughly one thousand six hundred and sixty kilometers from Cuba. To get there we can go three ways. We can run straight in to Santiago de Cuba, as we had planned, between Haiti and the Turks and Caicos. Or we can take the northerly route, picking a way through the Bahamas. Or we can go south past Puerto Rico and skirt along the south coast of the Dominican Republic."

"Wait." Arkhipov leaned across Maslennikov to peer at the chart. "We have to assume that the Americans will be using exactly those islands as part of their blockade."

Picking up the skipper's wax pencil, Arkhipov traced a broad arc from the tip of Florida, zigzagging a little through the scattered islands of the Bahamas archipelago, then the West Indies, all the way down to the island of Hispaniola. He picked the pencil up off the plastic and resumed the line on the south coast of Hispaniola, sweeping through Jamaica and into the Caymans.

"That's the blockade, Comrades. Four hundred islands between Puerto Rico and Miami alone. Coral reefs, most of 'em. Shallow, clear water. That's where the Yankees will be waiting for us."

Savitsky, leaning close to the chart, began to mutter half to himself.

"Running on the surface at top speed for eight hours of darkness, we make two hundred seventy kilometers. Then we run for eight hours submerged, another two hundred forty. Three hours at snorkeling depth at one-third speed to recharge the batteries . . . thirty clicks more." Savitsky traced a finger across the chart. "This time tomorrow, we're here, on the nose of a thousand kilometers from Santiago. One day more and we—"

"One more day and we run directly into the American blockade," Arkhipov interrupted. "Most probably sooner."

Savitsky grimaced.

"Doubtless we will."

"Maybe you have a plan for getting through undetected by the massed sonar of the US Second Fleet, Savitsky?"

"We play the usual cat-and-mouse game. Sonar evasion. We've practiced it a thousand times."

"In open ocean, we might be able to do that. But we've practiced against just a handful of hunters. Not the entire American Atlantic Fleet."

"There are places we can go deep in the Caribbean, too. The Puerto Rico Trench, right here. We could run at a depth of a hundred meters and still have eight thousand meters under the keel. We go fast along the Hispaniola Basin at maximum depth, stick close to the steep side of the canyon . . ."

"Savitsky—are you proposing trusting our lives to our Admiralty charts? I don't personally fancy running into an underwater rock wall at fifteen knots. The Yankees know these waters. We certainly don't."

Savitsky sat back and folded his arms across his chest, fixing Arkhipov with a withering look. The tension in the cabin tightened like a stretched hawser.

"Your suggestion? We wait around here for the Americans to find us?

Head home? Did radiation poisoning rob you of your balls, Comrade Captain?"

Arkhipov blinked in shock at Savitsky's gross breach of courtesy. The skipper was a little older than Arkhipov, and they held the same rank of Captain, First Class. As flotilla commander, Arkhipov's authority exceeded Savitsky's. But B-59 was Savitsky's boat, and in this cramped steel world he was Tsar and God.

"*Chto ty skazal?* What did you say?" In his indignation Arkhipov had inadvertently slipped into the familiar form of address—which was insultingly disrespectful unless used between close friends. It was fighting talk.

Maslennikov, sitting squashed between the two captains, gave a small cough. Savitsky and Arkhipov's eyes settled on the young political officer.

"Comrade Captains. May I point out that until they are countermanded, we still have our orders? Comrade Captain Savitsky is correct. We actually have no choice but to proceed to Cuba."

There was never much love lost between sea officers and the *politruk*. But Arkhipov had taken a particular dislike to this one. Especially since the damn man was right. A half-heard news bulletin from a local Miami station wasn't enough to abandon the orders of Admiral Gorshkov himself.

"Naturally, we proceed." Arkhipov fought to keep the irritation out of his voice and addressed himself largely to Savitsky, as if the presumptuous Maslennikov had not spoken. "We keep a keen lookout. If we reestablish contact with any of the other boats tonight, we signal her by underwater phone or semaphore to confirm our course to Cuba. We do not break radio silence."

"And if we make contact with the Americans, Captains?" Maslennikov looked left and right into the stony faces of his two chiefs.

Arkhipov stood without answering. Because he had no answer.

10

Sargasso Sea
23 October 1962, 18:48 Eastern Daylight Time

All the hatches on the bridge of the US destroyer *Bache* stood open as the ship wallowed at dead slow speed through the long swells of the Sargasso Sea. The waves were still high, but the furious winds of Hurricane Ella had died down to a stiff southerly breeze that blew up hot and humid from the Dominican Republic. The tropical heat, now mercifully cooling with the dusk, had been made even more unbearable by the banks of electrical equipment that were packed at the rear of the bridge—the latest radar and sonar rigs from Lockheed Martin. The Navy Department had bought the best, and lots of it, for its newest generation of sub-hunting destroyers.

Captain Dave Billings scanned the darkening sea from the lee side of the flying bridge that formed a high balcony around the front of the ship's superstructure. Twenty-five other US Navy ships—twenty-two destroyers, two cruisers, and the aircraft carrier *Randolph*—sailed in a four-hundred-mile-long arc that stretched far beyond the horizon, all slowly sweeping the patch of ocean north and east of Hispaniola like a line of gundogs flushing out game.

A couple of days before, the US Navy had intercepted a Soviet Project 641 submarine—a Foxtrot-class, diesel-electric hunter-killer, in NATO parlance—up near the coast of Florida. She'd been wallowing on the surface, near stationary and making no attempt to hide. Her captain reported engine damage. The sub had been in international waters, so the US Navy had no right to board or sink her. So as far as Billings knew, she was still just sitting there under the watchful eye of the Coast Guard, waiting for a Soviet tender to show up and tow her home. But there was little doubt, according to the eggheads at the Office of Naval Intelligence in Suitland, Maryland, that she'd been intending to sneak past the blockade and head for Cuba. So now the whole US Second Fleet—and above all, her sub-hunters like the *Bache*—was on high alert for more subs like her.

Fucking submarines.

Billings had been in his bunk on the heavy cruiser USS *Chester* when she'd been hit amidships by a Japanese torpedo off the New Hebrides Islands. October 20, 1942—Billings's first taste of combat, twenty years ago almost to the day. He had been deep in the black, dreamless sleep of an exhausted midshipman when the torpedo exploded. The detonation made the steel hull of the nine-thousand-ton cruiser ring like a giant brass bell. The titanic shock wave had tipped him right out of his berth onto the floor, where he woke screaming in the dark, trampled by the staggering bare feet of the other midshipmen of his watch. Through the steel of the floor, Billings could swear that he'd heard the inrush of water and the creak of straining steel.

By the time Billings had pulled on his uniform pants, Mae West life jacket, and flash hood and scrambled to his battle station, the Japanese submarine was long gone. The *Chester* had lost eleven men and was holed below the waterline. But she'd managed to limp into Espiritu Santo, in Vanuatu, for repairs. Double lookouts on all stations to watch for a renewed attack as the cruiser wallowed, lopsided from two flooded compartments, across the open Pacific, her pumps running full tilt all the way. Billings remembered the heady fear-hate he'd felt during his watches. Come on, Jap assholes. Come on. Just show yourselves. And we'll kill you.

Like most surface sailors, Billings feared and hated submarines. But unlike most of his young crew, he'd actually seen what they could do to a warship with his own eyes. The Captain lowered his binoculars, tipped his cap, and wiped his brow on his sleeve. Man. Those Sovs were really getting to him.

Billings's executive officer walked onto the flying bridge, steadying himself hand over hand against the roll of the ship. Pete Kimble's salute was as close to a casual howdy as humanly possible. The two men's friendship went back all the way to their cadet days at Annapolis. Long enough for Billings to know that under Kimble's slow Carolina gentleman's manners lurked the instinct of a killer. A torpedo boat commander in his day, Kimble had a reputation for bravery. Recklessness, even. Which was maybe why it was Billings who wore a captain's scrambled egg on his cap and not Kimble. But when they'd hunted quail together outside Naval Submarine Base Kings Bay, in Georgia, Kimble had held his shotgun as though the damned birds were out to *get* him. He'd not left a single one in the sky, nearly blowing Billings's head off more than once as he'd swung through dangerous ground-hugging shots.

Kimble took the binoculars that his chief silently handed to him and made his own slow scan of the spreading Caribbean night as it darkened the eastern horizon.

"You reckon the Sov Navy's all headin' home like the President told 'em to, Captain?"

"Sure, Pete. Sounds exactly right."

"Would you tell on me if I said I sure as hell hope they don't?"

"Spoiling for a fight, Pete?"

The USS *Bache*'s executive officer didn't answer, but lowered his binoculars and smiled grimly at his old shipmate. Billings recognized the look. Kimble was in a killing mood.

11

TsSKA Stadium, Moscow
23 October 1962

Vasin trudged along the touchline of the Central Soviet Army Sports Club's soccer field. The stands were deserted; a pair of janitors in brown overalls were sweeping leaves on the far side of the muddy grass. Beyond lay a low-rise concrete oval marked TRACK AND FIELD below the red star logo of the club. A diminutive soldier in an oversize uniform stood guarding the doorway but stepped aside at the sight of Vasin's ID card. Passing through the tunnel that led to the athletic field, Vasin emerged into the arena, deserted apart from four bodyguards armed with Kalashnikovs and a lonely, squat figure plodding slowly around the gravel track.

Orlov's face was streaked with sweat and rain as he drew level with Vasin. The General spared his subordinate a single glance as he passed, then jogged on. Vasin and the guards all followed Orlov with their eyes as he made two more laborious circuits. Six men, each alone in their own way under the Moscow rain.

Orlov finally lumbered to a halt, panting, his hands on his knees. He snatched a rain-sodden towel from the railing and pointlessly wiped his wet face and neck with it. Turning to Vasin, he beckoned his subordinate toward him.

"Something urgent. I see it in your face, Sasha. But not quite urgent enough to stop for just yet." Orlov tossed Vasin the soaking towel. "Got one more circuit in me. Come."

Vasin swore under his breath and broke into a run to catch up with the retreating figure on the track.

"Sir. I wanted to say that I have received sensational intelligence . . ." Fifty yards into the run and Vasin was already out of breath.

"If you'd nailed that motherfucker Morozov you'd have a grin on your face. But you look like you're about to lay a goose egg through your asshole. So I assume you haven't."

"No, sir. But Major Tokarev came to me. It's most urgent."

They made the first turn of the track, Vasin's feet chafing against his heavy leather shoes.

"And what does Tokarev want in return for this *sensational* information of his?"

"An exchange, General. You had his wife committed to a *kontora* mental facility. Tokarev hopes that it will no longer be necessary to keep pulling the hook. He says it's critical, sir."

"Before the fisherman slackens the line, Sasha, he needs to reel in what he has caught. So what has Tokarev brought us?"

Vasin glanced over to Orlov, who stared resolutely forward as he ran.

"It's to do with Cuba, sir."

Orlov did not reply as they rounded the second turn. His breathing was heavy. Vasin pressed on.

"It's a matter of gravest national security, sir."

The third turn. Vasin was starting to fight for breath, cursing every Orbita he ever smoked.

The fourth and final turn was approaching. Vasin prayed that Orlov would not attempt another circuit. Mercifully, the General halted, panting. Doubled over, he put a hand out. It took Vasin a second to realize that he was demanding the towel which Vasin had been holding, ridiculously, all the way around. Orlov straightened, spat, and grinned.

"You know me so little, Vasin. The more you tease me, the less I believe. Answer me this. If our comrade Tokarev has already sung his song, why do we still need him? Or need to do anything for him?"

Vasin felt the blood throbbing in his temples from the unexpected exercise. He could not immediately fathom what Orlov was saying. His boss continued smoothly.

"We have administered a shock to the poor wife. I think we can assume that as a result of this shock, Tokarev is no longer our friend? No. Very much not. He provides us this information on a purely transactional basis. Which already makes it suspicious, of course."

"Comrade General . . ." Vasin scrambled to find words that could counter Orlov's logic. "I have verified key parts of his story already, it's—"

Orlov cut him off midsentence with a raised hand as he shrugged on the uniform greatcoat that one of the guards had brought.

"Important, you say?"

The General's tone was frankly mocking. Vasin nodded slowly, glancing meaningfully at the young guards that now surrounded them. Orlov tipped his head in the birdlike way he had and narrowed his eyes appraisingly. Without taking his gaze off Vasin, he half turned to the nearest bodyguard.

"Tell Khrustalev to phone the office from the car. I'll be half an hour late." And then to Vasin, "Let's go warm up."

The sauna smelled of fresh male sweat, pine soap, and detergent. The walls were decorated with mosaics of soldiers in uniform striking athletic poses. Orlov unceremoniously kicked off his wet tracksuit bottoms and underpants, revealing a plump but powerful pink body. As Vasin hurriedly stripped, a pair of young men hurried out of the steam room.

"All yours, Comrade General." The burly bath attendant looked like a cartoon bandit from the mountains of the Caucasus, all hair and muscle. "Massage?"

"No time today, Grisha."

Orlov beckoned Vasin to follow. The pine-planked Russian sauna had been heated to an infernal temperature, which Orlov made even more unbearable by scooping a wooden ladleful of water and tossing it on the iron furnace. Vasin had always hated the gruff physicality of the *banya,* the appalling heat and pouring sweat of it. Orlov settled heavily on a tiered bench, his muscular thighs spreading on the hot boards. Vasin struggled to keep his mind focused as the steam heat rose.

"Sir. Tokarev brought some alarming information. A flotilla of submarines has been dispatched from Severomorsk to Cuba. He gave me the serial numbers of the boats. The fleet has been armed with nuclear torpedoes."

Orlov grunted noncommittally.

"A few days into their cruise, the commanders were given individual authority to use their nuclear weapon if attacked."

The General said nothing. Both men were turning bright pink in the fierce steam heat. They both sat, heads down and elbows on knees, with the dripping sweat evaporating from the floorboards as fast as it fell.

"Sorry, sir, I must . . ."

Vasin stumbled out of the *banya* into the relative cool of the dressing room. The attendant pointed to a doorway that led to a large, marble-lined plunge pool. Vasin always hated this part, too. He took a breath and stepped in, the freezing water scorching his skin and rendering him numb with shock. A moment later Orlov's stocky bulk plunged in beside him, displacing a mighty wave of water. He wallowed and snorted like a walrus before clambering up the marble steps and waddling back into the sauna.

"So." Orlov spoke only when they were both settled once more, side by side on the purgatorial pine boards. "The Navy has chosen to deploy a number of nuclear-armed submarines to the Caribbean, you say. Presumably, they send such submarines all over the place, all the time. But you consider this news particularly important."

"To Cuba, sir. Right into the blockade that Kennedy just announced."

"The Yankees' declaration of a blockade means that the Soviet Armed Forces should do as they are told and stay away?"

"No, sir. But it's almost as though somebody wants to . . ."

"Start a war?"

"Exactly so, sir."

For once Vasin was grateful for Orlov's quick mind. His own was becoming dangerously muddled because of the impossible heat. This time it was Orlov who made a break for the pool first, breaking into a ridiculous skipping run-up as he plunged hungrily into the cold water. Vasin followed, more timidly.

"Enough." Orlov wiped water from his thinning hair. He strode out of another doorway into a large, thickly carpeted lounge that was lined with red leather-covered sofas. Orlov grabbed a crisp cotton towel from a stack by the door and wound it around his belly before flopping onto a sofa. An orderly in Army mess whites appeared, unbidden, with a tray of tea.

"Tell me more. Who told Tokarev about this flotilla, and its weaponry?"

"An old school friend of his. Now a deputy minister. But there's also mention of the flotilla in the documents that have been passed to Colonel Morozov. Which means it's confirmed by two sources."

"And this story about the captains being given the authority to fire at will?"

"Aquarium registry, sir. Tokarev found a copy of Admiral Gorshkov's confidential operational orders."

"And *you* have a copy of these supposed orders? Confirmation that they are authentic?"

Vasin shook his head. A pause, as Orlov eyed Vasin with frank suspicion.

"Put yourself in my shoes, Vasin. Would you believe this story yourself, if some already-compromised informant spun it to you?"

"Hundreds of personnel know about the flotilla. Hundreds more know about the special weapons. And yes—a few men know both those things. We could confirm in just a few days. But, sir . . . the flotilla must be nearly on station. Ready to run the blockade. Right now."

Orlov's heavy, balding head sank down to his chest as he paused to think, his eyes half-closed. A minute passed.

"You propose that I do what with his information, Vasin?"

"I think that you know people who would be alarmed by such a dangerous provocation, sir."

Orlov's eyes narrowed.

"People? What *people* do I know, Colonel?"

Vasin was damned if he was going to give Orlov the satisfaction of saying "Your wife Katya told me who you talk to at dinner."

"Comrade General." The numbing pain of the *banya* and of the freezing plunge pool had passed, leaving Vasin's brain clearer and more focused. Vasin's tone was suddenly harder. "Let's not beat about the bush. We both know that there are men in our military who wish to humiliate the Americans. But we do not have enough long-range missiles to hit the Yankees. Morozov is a traitor, we assume. Therefore, the Americans already know the details of our weakness. It is a badly kept secret that we have been sending intermediate-range missiles to Cuba to make up the gap in our own defenses. Half the Cuban peasantry must have seen the rockets being transported across the country. The American Congress is squawking about those missiles every day. But we don't care, now that the missiles are in place. The deception has run its course. Now we just sit out the storm of protest from weak, timid Kennedy and wait for him to get used to the new reality. That's what our generals think, isn't it?"

Vasin searched Orlov's face for a flicker of emotion, for the slightest tell, but the man's face was stone. He plunged on.

"Let's say that the Americans fold, suck it up, and accept the missiles on Cuba just like they did when we built that wall right under their noses in Berlin over the summer. Let's say our generals are right, and the Yankees are too scared of our Big Bomb—the one the Americans call the Tsar Bomb—to challenge us. Fine. But this submarine fleet with these nuclear torpedoes—that's a more dangerous thing. The missiles in Cuba are a weapon on the table. Soon enough the Yankees will prove to the world that they are there. But the nuclear torpedoes underwater—that's a hidden weapon. What happens when the flotilla is discovered trying to sneak into Cuba? If the Americans attack them, not knowing that they have special weapons? Our boats could blow an entire enemy fleet into oblivion. And that's war, General. Immediate, nuclear war."

Orlov's stare had never been more intense. Vasin felt his courage wilting under its blowtorch ferocity, painfully aware that he had been speaking continuously for far longer than was safe—or wise.

"General, I think this could be a provocation by hawks in our own military. A provocation against our Party leadership."

"A *conspiracy*, Colonel? Against the Comrade General Secretary?" Orlov's voice was dangerously calm and slow. "Is that what you are suggesting to me, Sasha?"

Vasin's heart was racing, his breath shallow. He had given himself no choice but to continue.

"I have no evidence for any such conspiracy, sir. But don't you think that this flotilla could be a kind of nuclear tripwire? A trap? Does the General Secretary know what the Navy is doing?"

"What you are asking is, who will pull the trigger on this war—the Navy or Khrushchev?" Orlov spoke almost to himself. He joined his hands into a steeple, tapping his entwined fingers on his chin in thought. An orderly approached with a plate of salami sandwiches, which Orlov ignored. It was as though the General had retreated to a remote place in his own mind. After a long silence, Orlov recovered from his reverie as abruptly as he had entered it.

"Vasin, you will take no further action and speak to nobody else about this. You will discontinue your inquiries into the flotilla, into Morozov, into anything. You will put this matter out of your mind. I will not send you away from Moscow, for the present. Nor will I enforce your silence. You have never heard me say that I trust anybody, because I do not. But I am satisfied that you have enough idea of your own self-interest, and of my powers, to obey me. You will stand by should I need you. I think I do not need to tell you that your inquiries have brought you into dangerous areas. And the thoughts of that great brain of yours have transgressed further still."

Vasin's eyes widened as though Orlov had slapped him across the face. He heard himself stammering out words.

"As you taught me, sir. You said the job of a Special Cases officer is to look into places where other security organs fear to tread."

"I did. I did say that, Sasha. You disagree with my instructions?"

"I agree and obey, sir. But, sir . . . what will you do?"

"*Do*, Sasha? I will *do* what I think fit, on both matters. And you will *do* absolutely nothing. You will hear nothing. You will see nothing. You will think nothing. You are a dumb tree stump named Alexander Vasin."

Orlov stood, and Vasin straightened to attention, absurd in his damp cotton towel. He watched his boss's retreating back as the General strode off, leaving Vasin shivering and alone in the changing room.

12

Kutuzovsky Prospekt, Moscow
23 October 1962

Vasin leaned his forehead on the chilly window glass. His eyes darted from one lane of Kutuzovsky Prospekt to the other, his pupils flicking from taillight to taillight. The cold of the glass, the scarlet spots of moving light—concentrating on concrete, meaningless things helped Vasin still his racing mind.

Embracing him from behind, Katya Orlova laid her cheek on Vasin's back.

"*Kaltgestellt.*"

"What?"

"*Kaltgestellt.* Put on ice. It's what the Germans used to call it. When you're frozen out." Katya Orlova put a comforting hand on Vasin's arm. "You know that Yury and I were posted to Germany for a while, after the war?"

He was in Orlov's apartment. For a moment, Vasin had almost forgotten. He was *in Orlov's apartment.* Vasin straightened abruptly. What had possessed him to come here, of all places? He remembered driving away from the Central Soviet Army Sports Club. Stopping to make a phone call. Traffic. Aimless driving. And here he was.

Vasin turned toward Orlov's wife, untangling himself from her arms. He looked at her with incomprehension.

"Katya, what's Germany got to do with this?"

"I'm just saying . . . the Germans have a name for it. Where you are. What Orlov did to you. Froze you out. But better frozen than dead, no?"

Thoughts came crowding back into Vasin's mind like eager shoppers charging into a richly stocked store. They clamored for his attention. For action.

"Katya. We'll all be dead if there's a nuclear war."

"Tshhhh. So dramatic, Sasha. You worry too much. My advice— worry less."

Katya released her grip on Vasin's jacket and headed unsteadily toward the liquor cabinet. Vasin heard ice clinking into glasses. It was barely late afternoon, but Katya had already been half-drunk when he'd arrived. What had Vasin hoped to hear from her? Could it be that this woman was the only person he could trust?

"You know, Sasha, when you called today, said you needed to see me urgently . . . I thought that maybe you still . . . you know . . . wanted me. Like in the old days." Katya pressed a rum-filled glass into Vasin's hand and clinked her own against it. "Not to jabber on about submarines and John Kennedy and nuclear torpedoes."

It took all the strength Vasin could summon to control his irritation.

"Katya, I wasn't jabbering. I'm terrified. *You* should be terrified. Be serious now."

Katya straightened, stiffly, into a more dignified vertical position. Her flirtatious smile faded, to be replaced with a bitter pout of petulance.

"God, Sasha. You can be such a bore sometimes. Don't you see? Orlov is releasing you. You failed to catch the spy Morozov. But he respects you too much to punish you. He will just . . . release you. Into some safe, boring job where you don't have to worry about saving the world. I've never seen it happen before."

"Katya—I promise you I would give my right arm to be in a safe, boring job. But right now we have to work out what to do."

"*We?*"

"Fine. I have to work out what to do."

"About what, darling? Your submarines?"

"About my submarines."

"What do you want them to do?"

Vasin set down his drink on a side table, untouched, and ran a hand through his hair.

"I want them to stop. Turn around."

"Try calling up the Navy."

Katya's voice was tinged with sarcasm.

"Katya, the damn Navy sent them. As I told you. So the orders have to come from the top. But only Orlov can talk to those people. And he just refused. Put me on ice, as you put it. So we're very fucked."

"Darling Sasha. Relax." Katya stepped closer to Vasin, her rum-tinged breath sweet in his face. "Everything is going to be all right. Orlov himself said so. Two nights ago. He'd just had a meeting with a Politburo someone. Came home and said, 'Well, thank the Lord that's over. They're putting an end to this Caribbean adventure.'"

"Putting an end to it—*how?*"

"Orlov said Khrushchev is ready to back down. Do what Kennedy asks. Pull the missiles out of Cuba, in exchange for the Americans pulling their missiles out from somewhere else? Didn't ask about that part. Anyway. It's decided. Everyone now just has to save face. But it's over."

Vasin closed his eyes. Suddenly Orlov's brutal indifference to Vasin's sensational news began to make a little more sense. The Politburo had folded. Stepped back from the brink. Humiliation for Khrushchev—

but peace. "An end to the Cuban madness," Orlov had told his wife. Except . . .

"Wait, Katya. Listen to me. You say Orlov believes that this is all over. Maybe Khrushchev does, too. But what if Khrushchev has no idea of this flotilla and its orders? What if this suicide mission that the submarines have been sent on is precisely *intended* to prevent the Politburo from backing down?"

Katya eyed Vasin woozily.

"Your old song. Someone, some unknown cabal of mysterious people want war? Your . . ."

"My conspiracy. Yes."

"But, Sasha, why are you always insisting that you know better than everyone else in the world?"

"Because of what you just told me. Peace is the new policy, right? Compromise? But this flotilla has orders to run the blockade and nuke any American ship that challenges them. It's been ordered to start a war. That's precisely the opposite of the policy of the Soviet government."

Katya's pouting face hardened into something angry, and hostile.

"Sasha. You're exhausting. You know what I think? I think you want to destroy yourself. You have decided that you are unhappy with your life, so you are desperate to find yourself some private Golgotha to go to your glorious martyrdom on."

Vasin stepped away from Katya. Enough. There was nothing more she could do for him.

"And you know what I think about *you*, Katya? I think you've grown so used to being a queen bee, to being a grand Party aristocrat, that your brain has stopped working. You can't conceive of any world where Orlov is not lord and master, and you are at his side to decide the lives of the little people. What I'm telling you is too big to fit inside your narrow little mind."

The two old lovers stood face-to-face, glaring furiously at each other. Both recoiled when Vasin stopped speaking. Katya's fists were clenched, and her face was a tight knot of fury.

"Sasha. If you think your information is so vital for world peace, maybe you should tell the Americans yourself."

Vasin looked around him. The Orlovs' mirrored liquor cabinet, the overstuffed furniture, the pompous landscapes and military portraits. In front of him, Katya. Overweight, overpainted, attempting to wound him with her high-handed irony. My God, Vasin thought. *These* people are the guardians of our safety. The ones who kill and imprison and terrorize in the name of keeping our children safe from harm. *These people.* Who care more about their own intrigues than the lives of the millions who trust them.

"You know what, Katya? I might do exactly that."

PART FIVE

THE HUNT FOR B-59

If they slap you on the left cheek, do not let them
slap you on the right one.

ADMIRAL VITALIY A. FOKIN, FIRST DEPUTY HEAD
OF THE SOVIET NAVY, INSTRUCTIONS TO THE CAPTAINS
OF THE OPERATION ANADYR SUBMARINE FLOTILLA,
3 OCTOBER 1962

1

Sargasso Sea
Thursday, 25 October 1962, 06:12 EDT / 13:12 Moscow Time

B-59's emergency diving klaxon sounded deafeningly in all compartments, accompanied by the noise of rushing water flooding the ballast tanks arrayed along the outside of the pressure hull. Within seconds, the boat lurched downward, sending charts and rulers skittering off the small table in the control room.

"The devil . . ." swore Savitsky as he grabbed the underside of the commander's chair to avoid being pitched forward. Arkhipov flattened himself against the periscope pillars to make room for a midshipman as he frantically worked his way along an array of taps to trim the boat's steep dive. The diesels had gone abruptly silent, their clatter replaced by the revving whine of the electric engines spooling up. A heavy clang sounded from the periscope compartment directly above the control room as the conning tower's topside hatch was hurriedly sealed. Arkhipov could feel the deep pneumatic rumble of the radio masts retracting into their mighty tubes, immediately behind his back. The depth gauge in front of him trembled before detaching and moving first to five, then ten meters. It had taken less than thirty seconds for the boat to disappear underwater.

"Plane overhead," Ivanov, the officer of the watch, called down into the control room. A moment later the young seaman who'd been on lookout in the cockpit slid down the steel ladder into the crowded control room to make his report to Savitsky, seawater streaming off his oilskins.

"Looked like American military, Comrade Captain. Turboprop, not a jet. Bearing two hundred seventy degrees. Just spotted it for a moment through a break in the clouds."

"Did they see us?"

"Don't think so, sir. Seas are still pretty high."

Savitsky leaned right and yanked the lever by his seat that controlled the main rudder toward him, putting the boat into a hard turn to port. He then cranked the three engine telegraph levers arranged above his head to dead slow. A moment later the telegraphs indicated with a ding that the engine room had acknowledged the order.

The control room crew froze in anxious silence, every man looking up to the sloping steel roof as they strained their ears to listen.

A faint sonar ping rang through the steel hull. Arkhipov turned urgently to Savitsky.

"The damn plane's dropped a sonar buoy."

Both captains knew that their best chance to escape the sonar tracking was to get into deep water, fast.

"Make our depth one twenty meters, conn," Savitsky ordered. There was no sound in the control center except the low thrum of the electric engines and the slow sloshing of water in the ballast tanks.

A second ping, fainter than the first, rang through the boat.

The indicator of the shallow depth gauge fluttered to a stop on its maximum setting—sixty meters. The deep diving gauge crept on through eighty, then a hundred meters. The midshipman at the diving controls, sweating with concentration, pulled back the forward and aft diving fins while his colleague ducked back and forth along a bewildering array of taps to even out the water in the ballast tanks. The depth indicator settled neatly on 120.

Arkhipov waited, barely breathing, his ears straining. The sonar signal had gone.

2

Sargasso Sea
Thursday, 25 October 1962, 0649 EDT / 1349 Moscow Time

Captain Billings was just finishing breakfast in the USS *Bache*'s officers' mess when his communications officer appeared in the doorway.

"Sir, recon planes have found a sub. Maybe two."

Billings snatched the message from the lieutenant's hand. An order from the admiral on the *Randolph* for the *Bache* and five other destroyers to make full speed to a position forty miles to the east.

"What have they got?"

"Sonar buoys picked up a contact, sir. Naval Air Station Patuxent River just analyzed the tapes from the reconnaissance birds. Looks like two Soviet subs. Course unknown, and no visual contact. We lost them after a few minutes."

Billings cursed softly. Hurricane Ella had stirred great bodies of cold water up from the depths of the ocean. The area where that cold water met the warmer surface water was known in the trade as a thermocline. The differing density and salinity of the two bodies of water created an underwater barrier that caused sonar signals to bounce off it like light from a mirror. The Soviet subs had dived under the thermocline, becoming invisible to the US Navy's sonar.

Still. Contact was better than no contact. And the forecast showed the weather settling. One day of calm and the seawater would mix, dissolving the invisibility cloak that masked the enemy.

"Very good. Acknowledge the message to the *Randolph*. Tell 'em we'll be on station in two hours. And get Commander Kimble to meet me up on the bridge. Tell him we're going hunting."

3

Fort George G. Meade, Maryland
Thursday, 25 October 1962, 08:50 EDT / 17:50 Moscow Time

Jack Dunlop cut the wheel of his green '59 Cadillac Coupe de Ville into a sharp right turn, making the powerful car sway on its suspension as it veered into the turnoff from Maryland Route 175. It was a glorious fall day, and the hemlock and chestnut oak woodlands that lined the freeway were a blaze of gold and red. He rolled to a halt on the rise that led to the security gates of Fort George G. Meade—a tollbooth-type building that spanned four lanes of traffic and was built to look like an old-time covered bridge, all shingle tiles and topped with a church-style spire. In front of him a huge line of cars, far more than usual, waited patiently to present their passes to the military police sentries who guarded the facility. Something was up.

Dunlop's old Army buddies had teased him about the car he'd bought shortly after leaving the service the previous year. What's a sergeant doing driving an officer's hotrod?

"Get a job as a civilian contractor like me and you could buy one your own dumb selves," he'd answered. "But you gotta grow a brain first."

Dunlop vaguely recognized the black kid who scrutinized his civilian security pass. Looked a lot like one of the grunts he'd thrown in the brig a couple of years back when he'd busted some Saturday-night beer party. The private's dirty look confirmed it.

"Y'all have a nice day now, boy," Dunlop called, jamming his foot on the accelerator and leaving the sentry in a cloud of exhaust.

The headquarters of the United States National Security Agency looked like a ten-story, concrete air-conditioning unit. The only thing that distinguished the hulking block from its neighbors—all Defense Department bureaucracies—was a row of giant white golf balls lined up on its roof. Radio and radar receivers, the most sophisticated in the world. Someday soon, talk was, there'd be another gizmo up there talking directly to satellites in space.

Dunlop cruised around the facility's gigantic parking lot looking for a space, cursing softly as he roved further and further away from the front entrance. The place was unusually full. Once he'd finally parked, he checked his tie and hair part in the rearview mirror, picked up his overcoat, and headed in to work.

Despite his smart tweed sport coat and neat buzz cut, Dunlop was only a chauffeur. True, the man he drove was the Agency's chief of staff, Major-General Thomas M. Watlington. And he was pulling down three times his old Army sergeant's salary. But basically Dunlop was a servant. And when he wasn't driving the boss back and forth into Washington in his big black Buick limo, Dunlop's job was as messenger boy to the boss. Actually, in practice, messenger boy to the boss's secretary. Mrs. Vera Lovelace—pretty name, ugly woman. Mrs. Fuckface, Dunlop called her. But only behind her back.

One of Dunlop's old Army mates had jokingly called him Stepin Fetchit a few months before, and the guys had all laughed. He'd wanted to deck the fella, but the guy was twice Dunlop's size, so he just pulled his mouth into a toothy grin and pretended to take it as a joke. Dunlop did that a lot. Grin and bear it—as well as step and fetch on a daily basis. But every time old Fuckface told him off for dawdling in the cafeteria at lunch, or sent him scurrying around the building delivering one set of files or collecting another, Dunlop would remember his own, very private, secret. And that would really make him smile.

"Morning, Mrs. L.! Some fine fall weather we're havin'." Somehow Dunlop could never resist the temptation to thicken his native accent—pure Bogalusa, Louisiana, and y'at as gumbo—whenever he spoke to her.

Fuckface looked up, her mouth as usual pursed like a dog's bottom. She hated being called Mrs. L. But something else was wrong. Her makeup was smudged, and she had dark rings of exhaustion under her eyes.

"You ever read the papers, Jack, listen to the radio news?"

"Not if I can help it, ma'am. I like to sleep good, nights."

"Well, that would account for your good cheer."

"Something I need to know about, Mrs. Lovelace?"

"Last night the President put the United States Strategic Air Command on DEFCON 2. You got any idea what that means, Jack?"

"Nothin' good?"

"We're gonna bomb Russia's what it means."

"Wow. But we gonna lick 'em, right? Had it comin' 'n' all."

An intercom light flashed on the secretary's telephone.

"You ain't got no kids, Jack."

Lovelace picked up the call, murmured an affirmative, and replaced the receiver.

"General Watlington's due at the Pentagon at twelve."

"Sure thing, ma'am."

Dunlop glanced at her out-box, which was stacked with files that had just crossed the boss's desk.

"Take those down to the typing pool for y'all? Heading that direction anyhow."

Without waiting for an answer, he gathered the stack with his cheeriest down-home smile and headed out of the office. Halfway down the carpeted corridor, Dunlop ducked confidently into a windowless room that housed the department's latest technical marvel—a miniaturized xerographic machine. The prototype Xerox 813 was impressively tiny, no bigger than a small washing machine. Dunlop waited as one of the cutest of the junior secretaries finished running off her copies and grinned shyly at her as she hurried out. She did not return his smile. Once she was gone, Dunlop began leafing through the stack of files he'd taken from General Watlington's office. He gave a low whistle as he read. Nuclear-armed B-52 heavy bombers on continuous airborne alert—twenty-three of them ordered to orbit points within striking distance of the Soviet Union. B-47 medium bombers in the vicinity of Cuba on fifteen minutes' standby, also loaded with nukes. A hundred and forty-five intercontinental ballistic missiles in silos all over the United States stood up to ready alert. Contact with a pair of Russian subs reported off the coast of Puerto Rico.

"Hot damn."

Dunlop fed the most important-looking papers into the Xerox as fast as the machine would allow.

When he'd first started his spying gig, Dunlop had been nervous as all hell. The first few times he walked out of the office with a sheaf of stolen papers tucked inside his Army tunic, he'd expected alarm bells to ring and military policemen to come running from every side. But no alarm had ever rung, and the MPs had always nodded him through. Or not noticed him at all. Dunlop was that kind of guy. Skinny and bucktoothed, he looked like one of nature's unimportant people. Sometimes General Watlington even called him Jim, not Jack. Asshole.

Dunlop soon realized that the best way to hide was in plain sight. Over the year he'd been working for Watlington, everyone had grown used to seeing him ferrying stacks of papers on his way to or from the boss's office. Pretty soon the sight of Jack diligently making photocopies had grown familiar to passing clerks, too. Becoming a civilian contractor had definitely helped. People respected you more without bars on your collar or stripes on your sleeve—they had less to go on. That was why Dunlop always dressed so smart. In a suit, you could be anyone. Almost.

His photocopying finished, Dunlop quickly gathered all the original files into the right order and slipped his copies into a manila envelope that he put at the bottom of the pile. As he entered the typing pool, he checked the clock. Less than twenty minutes had passed since he'd picked up the documents from the boss's out-box.

He slapped the files on the high desk of the typists' head clerk, waved cheerily, and continued on his way with the brown envelope in his hand. This was obviously stuff that couldn't wait.

The boss was due at the Pentagon at midday. Reckon forty-five minutes from Fort Meade to Arlington. Call it an hour, even with a police escort. The boss would likely be there until at least two p.m. That left plenty of time for a lunchtime drop.

Dunlop folded his manila envelope in half and slipped it into a wide inside pocket of his wool overcoat, which he draped over his arm. He took an elevator down to the basement garage. He had nearly an hour to put a shine on the Buick's chrome work. And to make a short personal call from the phone in the mechanics' station to a local Maryland number that was always answered by the same woman, night or day. And always on the third ring.

"Hey, honey! Wanna grab a sandwich in Arlington? Be there at lunchtime."

4

Crystal City, Virginia
Thursday, 25 October 1962, 12:00 EDT / 19:00 Moscow Time

In truth, Dunlop never could work out exactly how the Russians had found him. There'd been some smart-ass old loudmouth in a dive bar in Millersville, sounding off about how the military was the last preserve of the asshole. Dunlop had still been in the Army back then, and was figuring to maybe punch the guy out, for the honor of the colors and all. But then the guy mentioned that he was a D-Day vet from the 101st Airborne. So they got to drinking instead, and what the old-timer said about the military-industrial complex and the oppression of the working class had made some sense. Turned out Dunlop had plenty of his own to say about the assholes who populated the officer corps—and a fair bit about how the NSA was nickel-and-diming regular soldiers like himself by getting them to do clerical work for a fraction of a real salary.

They'd made a vague, drunken arrangement to catch up again the following week. But when Dunlop showed up at the bar the second time, the veteran was with a friend, name of Mickey. Heavyset, street-fighter type with a broad Boston accent. Mickey had done most of the talking, mostly about how the government was out to screw the working stiff. About how he'd found a million ways to cheat the Man, back when Mickey had been in the Navy. Stealing gas. Selling mattresses and C rations and Lord knew what else off the back of the wagon. And know what *really* sold? Paper, man. Just pieces of paper. I know guys who'll pay you ten bucks a sheet.

Two weeks later Dunlop had smuggled out the first sheaf of documents he'd grabbed randomly from his superior officer's desk. A smartly dressed older gent, trying hard to cover up a foreign accent, met Dunlop in the parking lot of the Millersville bar and gave him a hundred and twenty bucks in exchange for the documents. Mickey had been right. Ten bucks a sheet.

So that's how it had begun. Two years in, and Dunlop reckoned he'd made upward of forty grand—all in cash. Just who it was who was paying him, Dunlop didn't rightly know. Or care, really. But neither was he a complete fool. Of course it had to be the Russkies. And of course he was betraying his country. But politics bored Dunlop. The part of the gig he really enjoyed—in addition to the cash, of course—was the deep, warm glow he felt every time he drove out of Fort George G. Meade with a cache of documents in his pocket. The thrill of sticking it to every officer/manager/government jerk who'd ever humiliated him.

The Electric Diner stood at the end of a nondescript strip mall on the outskirts of Crystal City, just off Interstate 1. It was a five-minute drive from the Pentagon. Dunlop parked the showy Buick in front of a gas station next door and ducked into the mini-mart to pick up gum, cigarettes, and a newspaper. He walked to the diner and ordered lunch at the counter. Tuna melt and coffee was the least crappy menu item, as Dunlop had established after a dozen or so drop-offs. After he'd bolted his sandwich and impatiently swigged the dregs of his coffee, a nondescript, balding man in a bad suit appeared as usual at his elbow. Dunlop nodded silently at the waitress, pushed a couple of dollars across the counter, stood, and chivalrously yielded his stool to the newcomer.

"This your paper, buddy?" That's all the guy would ever say.

"Finished with it. Help yesself."

The balding man took his seat without giving Dunlop a second glance, sweeping the paper with its sheaf of documents into his raincoat pocket. When Dunlop got back to the Buick, he found the usual slim envelope containing six fifty-dollar bills slipped through the driver's-side window that he'd left open a crack.

Dunlop waited in silence for a couple of minutes before reluctantly gunning the Buick's huge engine into life to return and wait for Watlington. If there was really going to be a war, the Pentagon was about the last place on God's green earth that Jack wanted to be.

5

Soviet Embassy, Washington, DC
Friday, 26 October 1962, 15:15 EDT / 22:15 Moscow Time

Alexander Semyonovich Feklisov stood by the attic windows of the KGB *rezidentura's* office gazing past the roof of the YMCA of Metropolitan Washington to the spires of St. Matthew's Cathedral beyond. The last few days had been the most stressful of Feklisov's life—but today the KGB's Washington bureau chief felt himself physically trembling with the strain. He put down his coffee cup and forced himself to breathe slowly.

Feklisov had been bracing himself for months, of course, for the moment when the Americans found out about the missile shipments. Thank God his new boss on station, Ambassador Anatoliy Dobrynin, was smarter than the knuckleheads in the Kremlin. He'd agreed with Feklisov from the start that the Cuban missile project was madness. But Khrushchev had evidently decided that Kennedy was a weak pushover after their meeting in Vienna the previous summer. The problem was that Khrushchev didn't know America—or Americans. But Feklisov knew. He's been stationed here, on and off, since 1941. He knew perfectly well just how local their horizons were. Kennedy wouldn't start a world war over distant Berlin. But he sure as hell would over Cuba, ninety miles from his own coast.

Feklisov had always known that the shitstorm that would inevitably ensue over Cuba would be far worse than the Kremlin had bargained for. But now the crisis was upon them, and it was escalating with an unstoppable force and speed that he never imagined possible.

DEFCON 2.

He could hardly believe it. Since Kennedy's order had gone out at ten p.m. two days before, the world was officially within fifteen minutes of all-out nuclear war.

Over the preceding few days Feklisov had allowed himself to believe that the two sides were on the verge of thrashing out a face-saving compromise. His boss Dobrynin had been talking privately to Kennedy's brother Bobby throughout the crisis, feeling their way toward a diplomatic solution. And the Ambassador had also been talking to Khrushchev, practically begging the Comrade General Secretary to believe that Kennedy was serious about war.

And now, despite all that frantic backstage diplomacy, a sudden escalation. DEFCON 2 made no sense. The Kennedy brothers *knew* that Khrushchev was ready to back down. So was this a bluff to pile on the pressure? Or, God forbid, a sign that the American military was taking matters into their own hands?

"Alexander Semyonovich?" Feklisov's secretary hovered in the doorway, breaking his train of thought. "The Comrade Ambassador is back. He's waiting for you."

Dobrynin was standing behind his desk when the KGB *rezident* entered, nervously leafing through a sheaf of radiograms.

"How did it go with the journalist?"

Going to the press had been Feklisov's idea. John A. Scali of ABC News was, he knew, well connected to Kennedy's inside circle. Making a top-level offer through a reporter was certainly not the *kontora*'s usual style. But these were desperate times. The Ambassador's back channel to Bobby Kennedy was all very well. But with American bombers on patrol in the air, probably just minutes from the Soviet Union's borders, Feklisov and Dobrynin needed the world to know that the Soviets were ready to talk. Urgently.

The Ambassador had gone right over the KGB's head and sought direct approval from the Politburo. Authorization had come through that morning for Feklisov to arrange a lunch meeting with the reporter.

"It went well, Comrade Ambassador. I asked Scali to talk to his White House friends and say we're ready for a diplomatic solution. He agreed immediately. Terms as I suggested, sir—and approved by the Politburo, of course. An assurance from the Soviet Union that we will remove the weapons under UN supervision. A statement by Castro that he will not accept such weapons again. And in exchange, a public statement by the US that it would not invade Cuba. I assume Scali passed it on to the Kennedys immediately. And they know that the press knows. And Moscow?"

The Ambassador puffed his cheeks in a gesture of exasperation.

"Moscow is Moscow. They're still talking. To each other."

"Will we have a formal offer from the Comrade General Secretary to show the White House today?"

Dobrynin shrugged slowly, as though raising a gigantic weight with his shoulders.

"You know what Robert Ivanovich told me last week?" Robert, son of John—the two Russians' private name for Bobby Kennedy. "'Build your enemy a golden bridge over which to retreat,'" he said. Quoting some ancient Chinese book, apparently. But instead of a golden bridge, we have a club waved over our head. And a mire of manure to wade through, not a bridge. Damn fool Kennedys. Arrogant as ever. Worst thing they could have done now was escalate. Khrushchev doesn't like to be bullied. So—God only knows when he'll write the letter. Or if he will."

As Feklisov walked slowly up the main staircase of the grand old Embassy mansion, he paused to look out a back window over the rooftops to Thomas Circle. Since when had he, the son of a dirt-poor railway worker, become the go-between among the leaders of the world? Their guide and interpreter? Feklisov remembered the oily steam of the railway yards of the Moskva-1 depot, where he had worked before joining the *kontora,* just before the war. The unpretentious camaraderie of young working men, the easy banter. Leaning close into the warm bellies of the locomotives on cold mornings. The metallic taste of tea brewed with water drawn from the boilers. His life had been simple then—the only problem of the day a fouled steampipe or a leaky regulator valve.

Feklisov closed his eyes. When the *fuck* was that stubborn ass Khrushchev going to admit that he was beaten?

6

Frunze Embankment, Moscow
Friday, 26 October 1962

Vasin passed the evening at home in a stupefied trance. Every day after he left for work, Vera would insist on folding up the sofa bed where Vasin slept and clearing away his bedding. She also obsessively tidied his clothes away into a fitted cupboard in the corridor, along with his boots and shoes. It was as though Vera spent her days attempting to erase every trace of her husband's presence in their apartment—until his return from the *kontora* every evening to inconsiderately reassert his existence in her life. But tonight Vasin felt as though he had remained invisible. A ghost, stalking unseen through the places of his former life.

The October evening was unseasonably warm, and a dusk breeze carried the sound of children playing in the courtyard through the open *fortochka*—the small window-in-a-window that ventilated every Russian home. Vasin, slumped forward on the sofa, watched the night spread over the rooftops as though the window were a movie screen. He made no attempt to switch on the lights or close the *fortochka* against the night air. Thinking made his brain ache, like touching a bruise. So he kept very still and tried to think of nothing.

Vera bustled in, flicking on the light as though there was nothing unusual in finding her husband sitting alone in the dark. After a moment's searching, she recovered a red plastic Hula-Hoop—the latest fitness craze. She slammed the *fortochka* shut and paused for a moment as she left the room, her hand on the light switch.

"Leave this on, shall I?"

Vasin made no answer. A sentence formed in his mind, rising like a bubble in a swamp, but he didn't bother to speak it.

The apartment door opened and closed, followed by a flurry of thumping and undressing as Nikita divested himself of coat and satchel. A tousled head of dark hair appeared around the living room door, followed by a mumbled greeting. A clattering of pots and crockery came from the kitchen.

"Dad . . . you hungry?" Nikita called. Before Vasin could respond, he heard Vera answering for him, something curt and inaudible. Then the kitchen door closed. Vasin heard the radio begin to chatter. In time, there would be piano practice and homework. Nighttime ablutions. A formal good night from Nikita. Then Vera would sit and smoke by the kitchen window. Chat for an hour on the phone, maybe, with her friends. Settle into bed. Then silence would fall over the apartment, over the courtyard and the boulevard beyond, over the whole metropolis. All the silence in the world, it seemed to Vasin, had become concentrated on him.

So.

Kaltgestellt. Frozen. On ice. This was what it felt like. Life goes on, just without you in it. You can no longer speak: you are interpreted. You cannot move. No, worse: you can move, but nobody sees or hears you, even your own family. Lieutenant Colonel Vasin had, abruptly on his boss's word, become a nonperson. The sea of information in which Vasin had bobbed and dived and swum for weeks and months had swallowed him. He had drowned, weighed down with his own mad ideas. All it had taken was a gentle downward pressure from Orlov and he had sunk, just as poor Tokarev had predicted, to the dark watery realm below the whale shit.

His silent apartment felt like a place of intolerable purgatory. Vasin unfolded himself from his fetal position and stretched his cramped muscles. He felt hunger and stumbled into the kitchen in the dark. The electric clock above the refrigerator showed it was past two in the morning. On the stove he found a pan of cold stuffed cabbage leaves, which he ate with his fingers. Wiping his hands on his shirt, he reached up and retrieved the coffee tin where Vera kept her petty cash. To Vasin's surprise, it was stuffed with twenty-five-ruble notes—nearly a thousand rubles' worth, he guessed. Was hoarding her housekeeping money Vera's small revenge? And if so, why? What could she ever buy with the money? Where would she go? Had she been planning to leave him? Flee? Vasin found himself incapable of summoning any sort of emotion apart from bewilderment. He helped himself to a fistful of the cash, retrieved his best civilian suit and shoes from the cupboard, and got dressed.

Vasin had no plan. But as he closed the door—quietly, so as not to wake Nikita—he could not help feeling that he was walking away from his old life forever.

The night had turned damp. Vasin didn't bother to look around as he walked to his car. He preferred not to see the *kontora* watcher team who were surely waiting. The Moskvich revved to life with no more than the usual half-dozen false starts. Vasin nosed through the narrow archway and out onto the boulevard. The hardness of the wheel in his hands felt good. A tiny bit of control. He needed coffee. He needed to think. And maybe, to talk. Talk to . . . who? Maybe Kuznetsov?

Ignoring a red traffic light, Vasin turned left onto the Frunze Embankment and headed toward the Lubyanka.

7

KGB Headquarters, Moscow
Saturday, 27 October 1962

The *kontora*'s big basement cafeteria was open round the clock. The waitresses were bleary-eyed, but their plain black dresses and frilly aprons remained immaculate. Vasin loaded a tray with coffee, fresh white rolls, and a large cognac. He settled into a corner alcove from which he could keep an eye on both cashiers' desks. In another corner a gaggle of young female clerks in uniform giggled and gossiped in near whispers. Around the cafeteria was a scattering of solitary, middle-aged officers like himself, all in various stages of bad temper and late-night fatigue. Which of them were Vasin's minders, he wondered? Would Orlov bother keeping tabs on him inside the KGB headquarters? Or were they just watching his car, parked in the senior officers' lot directly behind the building?

A huge clock that dominated one wall gave the time as 0355. Two hours at least before the breakfast rush began. Vasin pulled a thick notebook from his briefcase. It contained his own private notes on the Morozov case. Nothing systematic—just a collection of questions, dates, his own transcripts of the key documents Sofia had passed to Morozov, interspersed with newspaper clippings and ripped-out extracts from the TASS wire. As the buzz of the hot coffee and the sweet cognac warmed him, Vasin began rereading and sorting his notes.

By a quarter to six the cafeteria began to fill with junior officers and clerks hurriedly grabbing breakfast before their early shift. Kuznetsov was not among them. A slower-moving group, stretching and yawning after the end of their night shift, showed up as the clock ticked past six. Vasin doggedly guarded his prime position in the corner against all comers, his notes and clippings spread across the table. Already all the diners around him had changed at least three times. Watchers would have lingered for hours, nursing endless coffees.

Eight a.m. brought a clutch of more senior officers—out-of-town majors and colonels gawping at the high ceilings and the extravagant piles of cakes, loading up their trays with pastries and sweets. A major-general swept in, leading a delegation of swarthy colleagues up from somewhere in the Caucasus. But there was still no sign of Kuznetsov.

Vasin swore under his breath. He remembered from their days sharing an apartment in Arzamas that Kuznetsov was never the early-rising type. The man would sooner skip breakfast than lose half an hour in bed. Or maybe he wasn't due in the office today. Or perhaps he'd already headed back to Cuba. Vasin tried to remember what Kuznetsov had told him during their drunken dinner about when he was due to return. He thought of calling up to ask his secretary to ring around the building and track Kuznetsov down. But the notion was ridiculous—Vasin had been frozen. Nobody would run errands for a nonperson.

By ten a.m. Vasin had practically memorized his entire notebook—and filled the remaining blank pages with dozens of meandering flow charts, sprinkled with question marks and crossings-out. The more Vasin thought about the problem of the submarine flotilla, the fewer options seemed open to him. He sat back, stretched, and blinked.

Something that Orlov had once told him kept running through his mind. "Facts are not truth and information is not knowledge," the wily old bastard had said, in his usual patronizing tone. But Orlov was right. Vasin had facts. He had information. But did what he knew really add up to what he thought it did? And did those facts compel Vasin to action—maybe even suicidal action?

Vasin waited out the midmorning coffee break before gathering his papers and stiffly standing up. He was unsteady on his feet and felt suddenly drunk with fatigue. But at least by now he was sure that Orlov's eyes were not on him.

The Lubyanka was like a town—a vertical town, with its main roads and its byways, its public spaces and private areas and hovels and mansions. It housed cafeterias and shooting ranges, dining rooms and elegant libraries, garrets and barracks, armories and guardrooms, *banyas* and courtyards, cinemas and torture chambers, laundries and kitchens. But unlike a normal town, an unusually large part of this secret community was underground—a full-size prison complex, vast areas of archives, a series of well-used execution chambers as well as secret bombproof bunkers. And like a giant fungus, the underground Lubyanka spread under surrounding buildings and popped up through half a dozen outposts separated from the main building at street level by roads and alleys.

Naturally the headquarters of Soviet State Security was also riddled with checkpoints, sentries, and locked doors. But for simple practical reasons, the thousands of people who worked at the Lubyanka needed free access to the communal areas—the central registry's reading room, the main cafeteria, the network of main lobbies, elevators, and corridors that linked all parts of the building. If he refrained from trying to enter any restricted area or sign out any documents from the registry, Vasin realized that he could live, sleep, eat, maybe even bathe in the Lubyanka for days, undetected. Weeks, maybe. Unless of course he bumped into Orlov himself, puffing down the corridors of the labyrinth like a hungry and furious Minotaur.

Vasin pushed his way into a crowded elevator up to the second floor. The Central Reading Room was Lubyanka Town's lavishly appointed equivalent of a public library. It spread along a whole side of the building and was entirely lined with open bookshelves full of reference books and periodicals, both Soviet and foreign. The atmosphere was one of hushed seriousness. Vasin wandered over to a table stacked with fresh magazines and newspapers. He gathered a selection of the morning's papers before pausing and picking up a periodical that was as fat as a novel. It was a proof copy of the next month's issue of the *Novy Mir* literary journal. A whole issue had been devoted to a new novella by a writer named Alexander Solzhenitsyn, *One Day in the Life of Ivan Denisovich*. Vasin had heard his *kontora* colleagues complaining about some jailbird's scribblings but had not had time to read it. If the *kontora* hated it, it was probably excellent.

8

KGB Headquarters, Moscow
Saturday, 27 October 1962, 12:57 Moscow Time / 05:57 EDT

Vasin woke with a start. He immediately looked at his watch. Nearly one p.m. He must have fallen asleep halfway through the day's newspapers. Vasin hurriedly gathered his notes and scooped the copy of *Novy Mir*—stamped DO NOT REMOVE FROM LIBRARY—into his raincoat pocket.

By now the cafeteria was packed, with a line snaking out the door into the corridor. Vasin pushed past the queue and scanned the dining room from behind a pillar. Mercifully, Vadim Kuznetsov's beard made him easy to spot in a sea of clean-shaven, balding men in uniform. He was sitting with a group of fellow officers, gesticulating with a glass of wine over one of the larger tables off to one side, reserved for large groups and celebrations. It looked like some kind of goodbye party— evidently for Kuznetsov himself.

Vasin cursed. For Kuznetsov's sake, if nothing else, he needed to catch him alone. Nothing good could come to his friend by being seen associating with Vasin, his fallen, *kaltgestellt* colleague. That thought triggered a wave of paranoia, rising in Vasin's gorge like bile. He was standing in full view of perhaps four hundred *kontora* officers—Special Cases staff very likely among them. And right now, Vasin preferred to remain invisible to Orlov's all-seeing eyes. Faking a coughing fit and covering his face with a handkerchief, Vasin retreated to the men's toilet and lingered there for half an hour. When he ventured out again, Kuznetsov's party were digging into dessert and cognac. The conversation had evidently moved on to Cuban women, judging from the cupping motions Kuznetsov was making in front of his chest.

It was well after two when Kuznetsov's jolly lunch party broke up. Kuznetsov rose unsteadily and walked to the lavatory arm in arm with a colleague, chatting animatedly as they went. Vasin, hovering by the kitchen's service doors, began to grow desperate. He trailed the group up to the northwestern corner of the third floor—the International Relations with Socialist Countries Department. Vasin watched impatiently from the lobby as Kuznetsov's mates disappeared, one by one, into their individual offices after a flurry of embraces and farewells. Only when Kuznetsov was left talking to a single colleague did Vasin dare to move closer and make eye contact over the officer's shoulder, a finger pressed to his lips.

The second Kuznetsov spotted Vasin his face fell. But he was sober enough to register Vasin's pantomime gesture of discretion and kept talking. Kuznetsov enfolded his companion in a bear hug, physically preventing him from looking round as Vasin scuttled back to the comparative safety of the nearest stairwell. His farewells completed, Kuznetsov joined him there a couple of minutes later.

"Vadim. Thank God I tracked you down. You're leaving?"

"Evening plane to Madrid. So let's start with this: no part of the heinous, hair-raising sob story you are no doubt about to tell me will keep me off that plane. You're still looking like shit, by the way. Run out of razor blades?"

"I'm living rough in the corridors of the Lubyanka. Haven't found the barbers yet."

"No? There are two. One by the north prison barracks, first basement level. And a posher one in the annex on the other side of Pervomaiskaya Street, the department that does disguises. There's a tunnel . . ."

"Thanks, Vadim, for the grooming advice."

"Let me guess. You've got yourself into deep trouble, and you need my help."

For once, Kuznetsov spoke with apparently genuine concern. Vasin could have wept with gratitude.

"Something like that. Orlov has put me on ice. Taken me off my spy case. Sent me home. Ordered me to sit still and not utter a squeak."

"And you obeyed by moving into the Lubyanka, seeking out your friends, and telling them the whole story. Got it. Go on."

"Don't have any friends at the *kontora* apart from you."

"Makes me feel so much better. So?"

"So—Khrushchev is about to back down on the Cuban missiles. It's been decided at Politburo level. He's going to fold, just like you predicted. That info comes from the top, by the way. Katya Orlova passed it on."

Kuznetsov pursed his lips for a long moment, then nodded.

"Makes sense. Guess nobody on our end expected Kennedy to

get so fucking upset. Embarrassing for Khrushchev, though. Humiliating."

"Exactly. But what Khrushchev doesn't know is that there's a flotilla of our submarines armed with nuclear torpedoes heading for Cuba with orders to run the Yankee blockade. And they are officially authorized to fire at will if they're engaged by the enemy. And they're due to arrive in the Caribbean right now."

"You're joking, right?"

"Never been more serious in my life."

"This flotilla—sent by who, exactly?"

"Exactly? No idea. Generally—by some belligerent big hats in the military who want to start a war."

"And how do you know all this?"

"From Orlov's man inside the Aquarium. He saw the official fire-order authorizations from Northern Fleet HQ. Signed by Admiral Gorshkov himself. And we knew about the flotilla already. Remember those telegrams I read to you a few weeks back? They mention the submarines. But not the nuclear torpedo part."

Kuznetsov closed his eyes as he digested the information, half turning to lean against the wall. A pair of young clerks carrying piles of files clattered down the stairs, slowing their pace respectfully as they passed the older officers.

"So you told your boss Orlov all this and he said what?"

"He told me to shut up and fuck off. Essentially."

"Okay. But no word on what he was planning to do with this information?"

"I assume that Orlov's not going to do a damn thing about it."

"Because?"

"Because he's obsessed with his own vendettas. He's gunning for Serov."

"Serov—as in, head of the GRU?"

"That Serov. And maybe he reckons Serov is involved in this somehow. So he's waiting for him to screw up."

"Screw up—how?"

"If these people succeed in turning this crisis into a war, Khrushchev will fall. The generals will take over. It'll be a coup d'état. But all Orlov cares about is ending up on the other side of this mess stronger than before . . ."

Kuznetsov put a hand on Vasin's shoulder.

"Sasha. My friend. Stop there. Are you listening to yourself? Do you have any idea how crazy you sound? Serov? Coup plots? Nuclear war?"

Vasin twisted free of his friend's grip, eyes blazing.

"Maybe it sounds crazy, but it's true. And we have to do something about it."

"We do, do we? Like what?"

An unmistakable note of mockery had crept into Kuznetsov's voice—the same sarcastic edge of contempt he'd heard in Katya's voice the night he'd been put on ice. Vasin wanted badly to shock Kuznetsov out of his complacency, force him into some kind of action. Blurt out that the only solution that Vasin could think of was to go to the Americans and warn them? That would wipe the smile off Kuznetsov's face. But—no. Vasin knew that would be unfair to Kuznetsov. The man would be obliged to do something. Either help him . . . or stop him.

Vasin forced himself to take a deep breath and remain silent. What had he wanted to hear from Kuznetsov, anyway? What advice or help could he hope for from a man like him? Kuznetsov was a survivor, not a player. One of life's detached observers.

"Listen, Sasha." Kuznetsov descended by one step toward Vasin and lowered his voice confidingly. "You're a good guy. That's your problem. You're always the cleverest. You want to fix the world."

The cleverest. Exactly what Vasin's old bosses back at the Moscow homicide squad had called him. And they hadn't meant it as a compliment.

"What you did, back in Arzamas last year?" Kuznetsov continued. "I don't pretend to know all the details. But I know that took balls. Going behind the bosses' backs. Pursuing your lead. Tracking down your spy. You're fearless, Vasin. And I admire you for that. But . . . whatever it is you're planning to do about these submarines of yours? Whatever crazy stunt you're planning? I'm begging you—don't do it. Because though you're an exasperating asshole, I actually quite like you. Think there should be more guys like you in the world. In the *kontora,* even."

Vasin's face had gone blank and hard.

"Thanks for the advice, Vadim. We might not be seeing each other again."

Kuznetsov pursed his mouth and nodded in understanding.

"Fine. Do your thing, Sasha. And . . . before you ask, I never saw you here. You can trust me on that."

The two men shook hands.

"Enjoy Cuba, Vadim."

"Sasha—that may be difficult. According to you, the island's about to be reduced to a pile of smoking, radioactive rubble."

9

KGB Headquarters, Moscow
Saturday, 27 October 1962, 16:00 Moscow Time / 09:00 EDT

Vasin had an hour to find a phone from which he could make his scheduled call to Tokarev. But finding a phone with an outside line in the Lubyanka that wasn't guarded by some secretary or desk jockey proved harder than he'd imagined. He finally located one down in the coat check near the main entrance. Evidently *kontora* wives used it to track down lost scarves and gloves—and by the platoon of coat-check clerks to organize their personal lives. One of them was halfway through a tirade against her good-for-nothing daughter when Vasin interrupted her with a flick of his ID card.

The call box number that Tokarev had left was engaged, doubtless by some spiritual twin sister of the coat-check gorgon. The call connected on his fifth attempt.

"I am listening."

Tokarev was out of breath, his voice strained.

"What's happened?"

"Our main opponent has found the submerged craft."

The "main opponent" was the KGB's officialese for the Americans.

"Shit."

A chorus of disapproving clucks came from the huddle of babushkas who were listening to Vasin's conversation with undisguised curiosity. He threw them an angry glance.

"*Motherfuckers.* You mean they've found and intercepted?"

"Just located, as of yesterday morning. Two craft spotted by electronic means. A dozen ships scrambled to hunt them down."

"Do our guys have any chance of getting away?"

"I'm not an expert. But I'd guess not much."

"So it's happening. What we feared."

"It's happening, kid. Don't know what you're planning to do about it but yes—the enemy knows. And is on the hunt."

Vasin felt the plastic of the receiver cutting into his cupped hands as his grip tightened.

"Wait—how did you get this information? You said you didn't have access to the details of these messages."

"How do you think?" Tokarev's voice had gone hoarse. "I stole them for you. For your boss."

"Brave. But fucking foolish." Vasin shot another hostile look at the old women. "I need you alive and free, old man."

"Just make sure that Orlov knows what I did for him, okay?"

"I'll be sure . . . to tell him." The lie almost stuck in Vasin's throat as he spoke it. Tokarev had no way of knowing of Vasin's new frozen status. "Same time tomorrow?"

"If God allows."

Vasin replaced the phone on its cradle and pushed his way, unseeing, through the ranks of uniform greatcoats and hats arrayed in lines like a parade of empty men.

Vasin could think of only one person in Moscow who could help him now. And she wasn't going to agree easily. But first, Vasin had to figure out how to escape from the Lubyanka without being spotted by Orlov's watchers.

10

KGB Headquarters, Moscow
Saturday, 27 October 1962, 15:15 Moscow Time / 08:15 EDT

The *kontora* annex that stood on the opposite side of Pervomaiskaya Street was sarcastically known as the Artists' Wardrobe. Vasin had never been there himself but knew that it specialized in costumes and disguises for covert surveillance. In the macho culture of the *kontora*, the employees of the Artists' Wardrobe were widely mocked as cross-dressing effeminates. So it came as a surprise to Vasin, as he emerged from the underground corridor that led to the Wardrobe, to find his way blocked by a burly native Siberian sergeant with the build of an all-in wrestler. The man sat behind a tiny desk wedged into the corner of a stairwell. He bulged around his workstation like a clown driving a miniature car.

"Department you lookin' for?" The man spoke with a heavy accent.

On the desk was a comic book, not a ledger. That made the sergeant a species of concierge rather than a security guard. Vasin flipped open his ID card nonetheless, keeping his thumb over his surname.

"Barbershop."

"Ground floor. Left down the corridor. Stinks o' perfume. Can't miss it."

Vasin nodded and sprinted up the stairs. He stood by as a heavily made-up woman steered a mobile clothes rack full of assorted clothing down the corridor. He passed open doors which revealed a seamstress's station, a fitting room—and an atelier equipped with rows of manne-quin heads, each with a wig on it. Vasin paused and peered inside. A girl in civilian clothes was laboriously brushing out a long, blond wig. She looked up, startled by Vasin's intrusion.

"Can I help you?"

"Uh. Yes." Vasin looked around the tabletops and spotted a red wig lying loose on the worktop like a particularly hairy cat. "Can I come look out of your window? Yury Gagarin is about to drive by."

"Wow! Gagarin! No way!" The young woman jumped up and ran to the window, hoisting herself up on the sill with her hands in girlish enthusiasm.

Vasin sprinted down the corridor, cramming his stolen wig on his head. The dark red nylon hair was, to Vasin's relief, only jaw-length. A minute later and he'd reached the street entrance. The duty sergeant called something after him as Vasin pushed through the doors into the fresh air of a gray Moscow afternoon and sprinted toward the sheltering anonymity of the metro.

11

B-59, Sargasso Sea
Saturday, 27 October 1962, 10:15 EDT / 17:15 Moscow Time

Arkhipov wiped sweat from his brow with a sleeve already soaked in perspiration. B-59's sixth compartment housed the boat's three monster electric engines. Running at full speed, they put out more than six thousand kilowatts of power between them, making the compartment as hot as a sauna. Arkhipov had enjoyed his weekly shower in the boat's single washroom just a day before. Now he already stank, despite the cotton-wool swabs soaked in formaldehyde that the surgeon passed around to the whole crew for nightly personal hygiene.

"Just about tapped out, sir." The engineering officer, Captain Third Class Boris Davydov, peered along the row of battery power indicators. Most stood at zero, with a few gauges hovering just above.

Arkhipov nodded. Twenty-five hours underwater, five of them at top speed. He hadn't expected the batteries to last that long, in fact. Must have been the warm Caribbean waters that allowed B-59 to extract a bit more juice from the power banks.

"Still too early to surface. Another nine hours of daylight. Can we make it that long on the crawler?"

The two men turned toward a fourth, auxiliary electric engine—one usually used as a dynamo to charge the batteries up slowly on long surface runs. But in a pinch it could turn the central of B-59's three propeller shafts at a slow three knots.

"Should be fine, if we turn off the air-conditioning and power down the galley refrigerators."

"Very good, Davydov. Make it so."

The engineer stepped aft to the controls of the main engines, each handle covered in thick rubber insulation, and cranked each magneto down to zero. The high whine of the electric motors stilled, leaving an eerie silence. At this depth there was no noise from the water that pressed in at more than ten times atmospheric pressure.

Arkhipov made his way forward through the silent diesel engine room and the warrant officers' quarters to the command center. Every few paces Arkhipov had to squeeze past other men. B-59 felt oppressively cramped compared to his old nuclear boat. At her waterline, she was just shy of ninety meters long. But inside the pressure hull there were less than sixty meters between the breeches of the torpedo tubes at the bow and stern. Seventy-nine officers and men crowded into this tiny space, sharing just two toilets and a single galley. They lived, quite literally, inside a machine, servants and acolytes to its vital functions.

Arkhipov had spent his working life on submarines, of course, and the tight conditions were second nature to him. Part of him still dearly loved the camaraderie of life on board a sub, every man a part of an efficient war machine. But more than a day underwater, with no sight of the sea or the sky, was getting to him. The one compensation for the cramped conditions on a diesel-electric boat was that it had to surface in order to breathe.

Arkhipov found Savitsky leaning over a chart in the navigator's room—a tiny cubbyhole squeezed between the periscope tubes and the port side of the hull opposite the command center. As Arkhipov ducked his head around the hatch, Savitsky stopped speaking midsentence and fixed him with a hostile stare.

"The engines have stopped." Savitsky's tone was flat.

"We're got enough power to run the crawler engine until dusk . . ."

"You ordered the engines to stop."

"I did, Valentin Grigorievitch."

"Perhaps I missed the new instructions from fleet headquarters. Are you the captain of this ship now, Vasily Alexandrovich?"

Savitsky was right. Operationally, B-59 was under Savitsky's command—the flotilla, under Arkhipov's. Exactly where the line between those authorities lay was undefined. But Arkhipov knew that he'd made a foolish error—albeit one that a less choleric captain would have ignored.

"My apologies, Captain. I should not have given the order. Shall I summon Davydov so that you can confirm it?"

"I do not confirm your order. I rescind it. We surface and recharge."

Savitsky was struggling to control the anger in his voice.

"Captain—we'll be surfacing in broad daylight."

"Thank you. I am aware. I prefer to maintain speed and get to the Puerto Rico Trench as fast as possible."

Arkhipov bit his lip.

"Comrade Popov—could you give us a moment, please?"

B-59's navigator, Lieutenant Commander Gleb Popov, stood wedged between Savitsky and the bulkhead. Obediently he shuffled between the Captain and the gyroscopic compass, then squeezed past Arkhipov and the corner of the chart table, leaving the two captains alone in the cramped space.

"You're acting in anger, Comrade Savitsky."

The Captain gripped the table with both hands, staring intently at the chart and evidently fighting down the urge to insult Arkhipov once more. After collecting himself, he stabbed a finger at the sub's position just west of the Caicos Islands.

"We are now more than six hundred kilometers away from where the Americans located us. The Puerto Rico Trench is nearly two hundred kilometers to the southeast. Sonar tells us that the thermocline has all but disappeared, so we are visible to Yankee sonar. Therefore, we make haste."

Arkhipov remained silent. The Trench was more than eight hundred kilometers long and over eight thousand meters deep, the marine equivalent of a canyon. Once they reached it, the Trench would indeed make a good refuge. But running there on the surface in daylight was a dangerous gamble. A gamble that Savitsky had only just this moment resolved to take, Arkhipov guessed, and then only in order to flex his power. Which was weak—and dangerous. Both men knew it.

"Very good, Comrade Captain. If that is your decision."

Savitsky pushed past without meeting Arkhipov's eye. The commander's post in the control center was four steps away from the navigator's compartment. The Captain flicked on all three communicators that protruded from the bulkhead over his seat, their cream-painted mouthpieces like a trio of daffodils.

"Prepare to surface!"

12

Malaya Gruzinskaya Street, Moscow
Saturday, 27 October 1962, 20:15 Moscow Time / 13:15 EDT

The chilly autumn night had already shrouded the sidewalks, turning the hurrying commuters into shadows. Vasin turned his collar up against the wind and hovered by a row of public telephone boxes. He'd spent the previous two hours riding the metro, changing stations randomly, switching back on himself, riding to the very end of the line. He was clean. And so—as far as Vasin could tell—were the environs of Sofia's house.

Despite her boxy military coat and headscarf, Sofia, as usual, was unmistakable. Vasin turned away as she passed, then followed her into the apartment building. He caught up with her between the outer street door and the inner one that opened onto a vestibule.

"You!" Sofia's voice was surprised. "What are you doing here?"

Vasin took her wrist, holding it hard.

"Come with me. It's important. Follow in half a minute."

He released Sofia's hand. Keeping his head bowed, he stepped back out onto the street and hurried to the shadows of a clump of linden trees that flanked the entranceway. For a long moment he feared that Sofia would refuse to follow him. But no. She opened the heavy street door and peered around her.

"Here!" Vasin hissed, and turned down a darkened tunnel of greenery that led away from the main road. He listened for the click of her heels as she walked twenty meters behind him. Vasin ducked into the high arch of the neighboring building's entranceway just as rain began to hiss on the thinning foliage.

"What the hell are you doing?" This time her tone was indignant. Vasin was glad he couldn't see the anger in her face in the dark, echoing archway.

"Sofia. It's an emergency. You need to listen to me for two minutes. Right now."

"They told me you'd been taken off my case."

"Did they give a reason?"

"No. And I didn't ask. They assigned me Pushkov as my new handler. That old butcher who pulled me off the street, that first time. Easier to work with him. At least he doesn't try to pretend to be my friend. Doesn't tell me lies."

"You're right, Pushkov's a butcher. But I didn't tell you any lies."

Sofia said nothing. Vasin sensed that she was summoning the courage to turn her back and walk away.

"Sofia. Everything I told you about your brother was true. I told you a lot more than I should have. Broke the rules for you. I thought you should know everything."

Sofia merely snorted and looked away. Once again Vasin was grateful for the shifting shadows cast by the lindens. He would not have been able to hold her eyes now as he scrambled for anything to say that might build some kind of trust. Vasin plowed on.

"And everything I told you about Morozov is true also. He's a traitor. He's passing the Motherland's deepest secrets to the enemy. But things have changed. I need to see him. I need him to do something for us. It's desperately urgent. That's why I needed to talk to you."

"Do something for *us*? 'Us' is who? The *kontora*?"

"For our Soviet Motherland."

"Colonel Vasin, you're ridiculous. If you want to talk to Morozov, you don't need me. Just walk into his office and talk to him. I'm sure your ID card opens all doors."

"He has to trust me."

"How are you planning to get him to do that?"

"Because you're going to vouch for me."

"Am I? Why?"

"Because of what I'm about to tell you. For your ears only. And Morozov's. Because there's something going on that even Khrushchev doesn't know about. Something unbelievably dangerous. Something that is going to cause a war. And it's happening right now."

"I think I've heard enough."

Sofia glanced around, turned on her heel, and walked quickly out into the steady rain. Vasin caught up with her halfway back to the entrance of her building. He grabbed her shoulder and spun her around.

"The Americans have located a flotilla of Soviet submarines heading to Cuba . . ."

Vasin could see Sofia's face clearly now, illuminated by a patch of street light, streaked with rain. He held her by both shoulders as she spoke, his voice low and urgent. She was nearly his own height, and strong. He could not hope to hold her if she bolted. As he spoke he felt the fight go out of her muscles. Vasin continued to hold her as she stood, silent and deflated.

"Aren't we always on the verge of war with the Americans?" Sofia's voice had become a whisper. "And anyhow—what the hell are we supposed to do about it?"

We. The first glimmer of hope. We: Did Sofia mean herself and Vasin? Or herself and Morozov?

"We have to get a message to the Americans. Warn them that the subs are carrying nuclear weapons."

"You really have gone crazy. This is treason. Let me go."

Sofia tried to wriggle free of Vasin's hands.

"No! We're saving our country from the schemes of a few madmen who want to provoke a war."

"Colonel—get yourself shot if you want. Leave me out of it. Go to that phone box and call the American Embassy yourself. Tell them about your crazy plot."

"Sofia. They need to hear it from someone they trust. From their spy."

"You mean Morozov."

"Exactly."

"And why would Morozov believe you? And why would he pass on this information just because you asked him to?"

"We would show him the documents."

Sofia stopped trying to pull out of his grasp and instead leaned closer to Vasin, her voice prickly with sarcasm.

"Oh, we would, would we? And what documents would these be? Documents someone has stolen for you, is that right, Colonel? And when you show him the documents—you, a KGB officer he has never met—he will be immediately convinced that this is not a forgery or a trap and do your bidding. Is that your plan, Colonel Vasin?"

"I will offer him a way out. I promise him my silence. In exchange, he delivers my message. His last message. Then he destroys whatever spying equipment he has, anything incriminating. And gives his word to break with the Americans forever."

"How generous you are."

A thought hatched in Vasin's mind. Could it be that there was some real affection between Morozov and Sofia?

"Sofia—listen very carefully. I am offering Morozov his life. The *kontora* has been trying to catch him red-handed for months. I've been trying. And we've found nothing. We've been waiting for him to compromise himself. Break cover. He hasn't—so far. Been too careful. Or too good for us. So he could still walk away from this. Especially with the powerful friends he has. If he stops now. Gets rid of everything. Otherwise the *kontora* will take apart his life. Search everything, until we find his camera. His codebooks. Anything. And then he will be arrested and he will die. You know that, don't you, Sofia? Your friend Morozov's life is in your hands."

A series of conflicting emotions chased one another across Sofia's face.

"What makes you think he's my friend?"

"Just a hunch."

The rain was growing steadily heavier, making a rolling drumming noise on the metal windowsills of Sofia's building.

"And why should either of us trust you?" There it was. She did care for Morozov. She wanted him to live. "You are desperate to catch him, Vasin. You said it yourself—so far, he's been too careful. Now you've cooked up a plot to set him up. Force him to break cover."

Vasin could not fault Sofia's logic. Lies could be multiplied and stretched out infinitely. Now that Vasin was telling the truth, he found his options brutally limited.

"You're right. I have no answer for you, Sofia. I'm not trained to deal with the truth. Everything in my life at the *kontora* is about lies, and their uses. But what I am saying about the submarines is true. And I can prove it. Do one thing for me. Come with me to see him."

"Tonight?"

"No. Tomorrow, first thing. And his apartment is being watched night and day by *kontora* goons. So we meet in a secure place. Just to hear me out. The three of us."

Vasin's brain was already flipping through the options, through the reams of surveillance reports of Morozov's day-to-day life that he'd plowed through over the last few months. Yes. Two weeks before, Morozov had gone for a doctor's checkup. Perfect.

"We'll get him to visit his cardiologist. At the First Kremlin Polyclinic on Sivtsev Vrazhek Street, by the Arbat. Do you know it?"

"Of course I know it."

"So will you come?"

Sofia scooped strands of wet hair from her eyes.

"And if I don't you'll do something awful to my brother? I hear what you don't say as well as what you do, Vasin."

"No, Sofia. No threats. We're not going to touch Vladimir."

She sniffed the chilly air and hugged her coat close.

"Was everything you told me about Vladimir true? That he was in danger?"

Even as Vasin was struggling to tear himself free of the thickets of lies, old tendrils nonetheless whipped out of the past to entangle him once more.

"Every word was true, Sofia. I swear it."

The lie came far too fluently to his lips for Vasin's comfort. He remembered something else that Orlov had told him—every man believes that he is right, and acts for reasons he considers good. That was true of the *kontora*'s most sadistic monsters, and it was true of Vasin. Even out in the cold, beyond Orlov's command and outside the *kontora*'s warped chain of command, Vasin still could not stop lying. He pushed the thought out of his mind and pressed on.

"We need to call from inside the clinic, or the *kontora* listeners will be suspicious. We need to reach Morozov at home before he goes out or drives to the dacha. Meet me at the clinic at seven thirty tomorrow morning?"

"You want *me* to call Morozov? He'll recognize my voice."

"That's the point. Make him realize there's an emergency."

"For God's sake . . ."

"Have you got a better plan?"

"I do. I'm going home."

Sofia turned to go, but Vasin grabbed her arm and held it.

"Sofia. If you want to save his life, you have to do this."

"And save the world, too, according to you."

"And save the world."

13

B-59, Sargasso Sea
Saturday, 27 October 1962, 14:32 EDT / 21:32 Moscow Time

Arkhipov was making his way through the deafening din of the main engine room when the diving klaxon sounded. The three 2,000-horsepower diesel engines, built at the Kolomna Locomotive Works and each powerful enough to pull a train, came to an abrupt halt. The massive fan array that filled the overhead space spooled into overdrive, ventilating the engines in the few seconds that remained before the conning tower disappeared underwater. Arkhipov made his way forward as fast as he could, hand over hand down the steeply inclined deck, and ducked through the watertight hatch between the engine room and the warrant officers' compartment just before it was slammed shut by a burly seaman.

By the time he reached the command center, the rushing of water into the ballast tanks had stilled as B-59 dropped like a stone. Savitsky was questioning the young lookout officer who stood dripping in his waterproof gear at the bottom of the ladder into the conning tower. Arkhipov squeezed close to listen in, though what had happened was obvious enough.

"Are you sure they spotted us, Lieutenant?"

"The American planes were heading right for the boat, sir. Fast and low. Below our radar. I think they must have . . ."

The unmistakable splash of a heavy object hitting the water directly above them interrupted him. The young man looked at his commander in panic.

A depth charge?

Arkhipov listened hard for a second. Savitsky answered the unspoken question.

"Sonar buoy."

As if in confirmation, a loud ping rang through the boat as though someone had struck the hull with a heavy hammer. It was followed a few seconds later by another signal from a more distant buoy. Savitsky's eyes, when they found Arkhipov's, were shining with anger and humiliation.

14

USS Beale, *Sargasso Sea*
Saturday, 27 October 1962, 14:52 EDT / 21:52 Moscow Time

Captain Billings had just walked onto the *Beale's* bridge, a cup of salty Navy coffee in hand, when the plane roared over the destroyer's bow. The Lockheed P-3 Orion—the Navy's newest sub-spotter plane—was flying at two hundred feet. The pilot dipped his wings in a triumphant signal as he circled the destroyer.

"Flyboys found something!" Billings called across to the officer of the watch. The Navy had come up with a new system for high-speed, short-range scrambled communications, which right now should be communicating with the P-3 as it made a slow circuit of the warship. The point was to avoid transmitting sensitive information long distances across open radio waves. Billings hoped to God that the damn gadget was working. "We gettin' their signal loud and clear?"

The young lieutenant commander signaled silently with a thumbs-up as he cradled a black telephone receiver to this ear, scribbling notes. After acknowledging the radio room's message he hung up, a grin on his face as wide as a watermelon slice.

"They have visual contact, Captain. Soviet submarine, looks like a Foxtrot class. Running on the surface, bold as brass. Two sonar buoys in the water. Our radio room's got the coordinates and is tuning into the buoys' signal now. The sub's maybe thirty-one miles east-northeast of us, running south. And sir—looks like we're the closest warship to them."

Billings felt the familiar, warm thrill of combat. The sonar room had been confirming clear soundings all the way down the seafloor all morning. The thermocline was gone. Once the *Beale* was on top of them, the Sovs had nowhere to hide.

"Very good. Relay the message to the *Randolph*. Plot a course to intercept. Make our speed full ahead."

15

B-59, Sargasso Sea
Saturday, 27 October 1962, 15:22 EDT / 22:22 Moscow Time

Fifty minutes into the run, Savitsky ordered the electric engines shut down. They should be some twenty-five kilometers away from the sonar buoys now. Time to pretend to be a hole in the water and listen for the hunters who would surely be flocking to the location of the sonar contact.

Submarines ran blind. At speed, the vibration of the engines and the water flowing over the sonar bulb on B-59's nose interfered with the sensitive instruments. As Arkhipov and the Captain waited for the submarine to lose forward momentum, a kitchen orderly silently handed out mugs of tea. Arkhipov winced after the first sip. The brew was hot but had a nasty chemical taste. The water had been drawn off the electric engines' cooling system. With the galley out of action to channel full battery power to the engines, the coolant heat exchanger was the only source of hot water on board.

Perhaps they had been lucky after all. Maybe the Americans had guessed that B-59 had held her course instead of veering sharply westward. The maneuver might have thrown off their pursuers, but had brought them no nearer to the safety of the Puerto Rico Trench.

Arkhipov followed the Captain forward to the sonar room. He took the Bakelite headphones off the sonarman and listened as the young midshipman scanned the dial through a full revolution. Nothing was audible but the steady, low roar that the sonic signature of deep seawater produced. Then, like the ghostly rumble of rising surf echoing through the water, he heard the distinctive pulsing throb of a ship's propellers. Arkhipov silently raised a hand. The sonarman plugged in a second set of headphones and began fine-tuning the dial. Another sound followed—just as unmistakable, even distorted by 120 meters of water over their heads. The deep pulse of a warship's powerful active sonar. The midshipman marked the contact and turned the dial further. Now there were not one but two sonar signals, one directly ahead and another fifteen degrees to the south. The sonar's ranging indicator put them at thirty kilometers' distance.

"The Yankees were waiting for us, Captain. Right in our path." Arkhipov handed the phones to Savitsky. The Captain cursed under his breath. Unbidden, Maslennikov appeared at Arkhipov's side and also leaned quizzically into the sonar room. The damn Political Officer had some kind of sixth sense for trouble.

"Wait . . ." The sonarman's face was creased in concentration. "There's something else. Cavitation noises to our northwest. Sounds like one of ours."

Cavitation: the telltale sound signature of a submarine was the tiny bubbles of vacuum produced behind the propeller as it turned underwater, a cloud that collapsed immediately under the pressure of water with a distinctive crumpling noise. It was the curse of submarines trying to hide.

Savitsky slowly removed his headphones and let them drop, swinging on their cable.

"They have us." Savitsky's voice was low and steady as he turned to face Arkhipov. "Two of our boats in the trap. So. We stand our ground. We are sufficiently well armed to meet any attack."

"Categorically not, Valentin Grigorievich. We run. Now. While we still can."

"We *run?*"

The low emergency lights half hid the expression on Savitsky's boxer's face. But Arkhipov could hear the menace in the Captain's voice.

"As we have just heard, there are two of us down here. Therefore, I am commanding a flotilla maneuver. Right, Maslennikov?"

Arkhipov glanced toward the hovering Political Officer, who nodded and half shrugged nervously in confirmation.

"You are aware that we were only able to charge the batteries to thirty-five percent capacity before we had to dive?"

"I am, Captain. So we make half speed to run for as long as the batteries can take it. Then we use the crawler engine to take us to the Trench."

"Your choice is not to fight but to run from the enemy, then crawl away—do I have that right, Vasily Alexandrovich?"

"You would prefer to stage a duel? Like in *The Hussar's Ballad?*"

When she'd sailed from Severomorsk three weeks before, B-59 had been loaded with a dozen of the latest films, specially printed by Mosfilm on space-saving sixteen-millimeter film for the submarine service.

During calm weather a screen was set up in the forward torpedo room for much-anticipated movie nights. And *The Hussar's Ballad* was a particular favorite of Savitsky's—a rollicking historical comedy with a womanizing, swashbuckling hussar officer as its hero. The Captain's expression darkened at Arkhipov's low blow, and Maslennikov let out an audible gasp.

"I shall compose a message for our companion boat and we will attempt to communicate by underwater telephone as soon as she stops running," Arkhipov continued. "For the time being, we follow her to reduce the risk of collision."

The two men held each other's eyes for a long moment. But Savitsky had no choice but to obey a flotilla order. Moodily, he pushed past Arkhipov and made his way aft to the control center.

"Propulsion!" the Captain called with unnecessary force. "Half speed ahead. Helm—course one one five."

16

First Kremlin Polyclinic, Moscow
Sunday, 28 October 1962, 07:00 Moscow Time / 00:00 EDT

It was still dark when Vasin arrived at the Kremlin Polyclinic in time for the end of the night shift at seven in the morning. The entranceway was a giant ziggurat of purple marble, crowded with nurses either exhausted from their work or on their way to their Sunday morning shift, still groggy with sleep.

Vasin had spent the night in one of the soaring marble lobbies of the Hotel Ukraine, slumbering in an armchair in the corner of the hotel's round-the-clock café. His respectable suit and expensive Yugoslavian briefcase had kept the security guards from bothering him. He'd asked a night-shift waitress to wake him at six with coffee and breakfast. All evening Vasin had struggled to remember the name of Morozov's doctor and failed. Something Caucasian.

Flashing his ID card was, as usual, enough to get him into the Kremlin Polyclinic without questions being asked. He took the elevator to the third floor and paced the near-deserted corridors of the Cardiology Department in search of a nameplate that jogged his memory. He found it without difficulty: MUSAYEV, RASSOUL IBRAGIMOVICH. The doctor's study was locked, but behind the door of an empty nurses' common room he found a white doctor's coat that fitted him. Vasin waited until the new shift of orderlies and nurses who huddled around the staff nurse's desk dispersed before approaching the matron. Another flick of the scarlet KGB card was enough to secure him a free examination room and a phone line.

All that was missing was Sofia herself. It was nearly half past seven, and a gray pall was lightening the drizzling sky. Vasin went down to wait for her in the shelter of the portico, where he could smoke. Sofia had been right, of course. There was no reason on earth that Morozov should trust him. And every reason for him to assume exactly what Sofia had—that this was an elaborate trap. What could he say to change the man's mind? That Morozov could only save his skin by incriminating himself? Vasin knew full well that his idea sounded desperate and suicidal. Morozov's every instinct—as an intelligence officer, as a spy, as a sane man—would recoil from it as from a red-hot stove.

Sofia walked alone down the empty street, her head bowed and her face gray in the pale morning light. She looked as though she had barely slept.

"You came. Thank God."

Her eyes did not meet Vasin's.

"I came. You didn't give me much choice."

"We have to hurry. We need to catch Morozov before he leaves the house." Taking Sofia's arm, Vasin pushed through the milling patients in the hallway.

They did not speak until they reached the examination room that Vasin had commandeered. Vasin picked up the phone and signaled to Sofia to sit.

"Listen carefully. You're calling from Doctor Rassoul Ibragimovich Musayev's office. Our friend came in two weeks ago and was given a medical all clear. But the doctor has reviewed his tests results and now needs to see him urgently. Today. Here. If our friend recognizes your voice, make it clear that the conversation is not private. Make sure that he comes here, at all costs, immediately. Do you understand?"

Without waiting for Sofia to agree, Vasin dialed for an outside line, then flicked the dial through the seven digits of Morozov's home number. As the phone began to ring, he handed the receiver to Sofia.

With outspread fingers he pushed a piece of paper with the doctor's name written on it toward Sofia.

"Hello? Is that Citizen Morozova? May I speak to Oleg Vladimirovich, please? This is the office of . . ." Sofia peered at the paper. "Doctor Musayev."

There was a pause as Morozov's wife went to summon her husband to the phone. Putting her hand over the receiver, Sofia began to speak, but Vasin hushed her with a finger to his lips and a shake of his head. Morozov came on the line.

"Hello. Oleg Vladimirovich? This is Doctor Musayev's office calling. Rassoul Ibragimovich has reviewed your test results from two weeks ago. He would like you to come back in and see him . . . Yes, yes, I know you saw him earlier this month. But there is a matter he would like to discuss with you urgently. Today. This morning . . . Yes, Comrade, I am aware that it's Sunday."

Vasin moved to crouch beside Sofia, half turning the receiver to his own ear so that they could both hear what Morozov was saying.

"This is very concerning. Rassoul Ibragimovich personally assured me that there was nothing to worry about."

Sofia swallowed. Her voice was becoming hoarse.

"Nonetheless. The doctor is free for the next hour if you could come and see him before he begins his usual rounds."

There was a long pause.

"*Sofia?* Is that you?"

Vasin shook his head with theatrical emphasis, mouthing "no."

"No . . . no, Oleg Vladimirovich. You have mistaken me for somebody else . . ."

Vasin jabbed at his watch and pointed urgently to the floor.

"But Doctor Musayev is waiting for you. As soon as possible, at his consulting room. Thank you. Goodbye."

Vasin reached over from his crouching position and pressed his finger down on the phone's cradle. His eyes met Sofia's, each with their own sense of shock and apprehension.

17

First Kremlin Polyclinic, Moscow
Sunday, 28 October 1962, 08:12 Moscow Time / 01:12 EDT

Vasin spotted Morozov first, bustling out of the elevator and heading
for the head nurse's station. He sprang from his vantage point by the
stairwell and fell into step with the older man. It was strange, having
spent so many months tracking Morozov's every sound and movement,
to suddenly be so close to his prey. Morozov was half a head shorter
than Vasin, balding and running to fat. He smelled strongly of Troinoi
eau de cologne.

"Oleg Vladimirovich? A moment of your time, please."

Morozov's eyes filled with instant fear, and he physically recoiled
from the hand that Vasin tried to slip under his elbow.

"Who are you? State Security?"

"We are your friends. Silence, please. Sofia is here."

Vasin prayed that Morozov would obey him as they passed the
nurses' station, followed by the curious eyes of the matron and her
assistant. There was a good chance that both would recognize their
patient Morozov, but it was a risk that Vasin had to take. He steered
the Colonel firmly down the corridor and into the room where Sofia
waited. Morozov peered left and right, glared at Sofia, and instinctively
retreated to the furthest corner of the small room as Vasin closed and
locked the door behind him.

"Where is Rassoul Ibragimovich?" Morozov's voice, naturally high,
had become even more reedy with alarm.

"Rassoul Ibragimovich has no news for you. But I do. Lieutenant
Colonel Alexander Vasin, Special Cases Department of the Committee for State Security. For eleven months I have been watching you,
because the *kontora* suspects that you are a spy for the Americans. I
know you are a spy. But right here and now I want to save your life."

Vasin had spent half the previous night rehearsing the speech. He
had intended it to be crisp and to the point, but as the words left his
mouth, he realized that his directness might be too brutal.

Morozov's face creased in fear and his complexion went purple, as though he were choking. Thank God we're in a cardiac ward, thought Vasin fleetingly.

"Whatever this young woman has told you, ignore it." Morozov gestured extravagantly to Sofia, whose eyes widened in surprise. "She is a hysteric. A fantasist. She is motivated by personal jealousy and is ready to say anything to damage me. Your suggestion is outrageous nonsense. I need to speak to my superiors immediately. This is entirely irregular!"

The last word was pronounced on a rising note, as though it were a terrible insult. Retreating half a step further back to the windowsill, Morozov repeated himself, with more emphasis.

"Entirely *irregular!*"

"Colonel. Calm yourself and listen. You are right, this is irregular. Entirely. Think about it. If the *kontora* wanted your hide, they would have hauled you into the Lubyanka. You'd be standing in a cold, solitary cell without suspenders or tie, with a soldier looking in the peephole every five minutes. Believe me, I know how it's done."

Damn. Vasin had meant to reassure the man, win his trust—and here he was threatening him with the Lubyanka cellars. He paused for a moment to regain control over himself.

"Oleg Vladimirovich. I am here entirely on my own account. Nobody knows I have come. Though the *kontora* does know that you are at the doctor's, since we have been listening to your phones. Sofia is here because I asked her to help. And before you denounce her any more, you should know that she agreed to cooperate in order to save your life."

Morozov threw a helpless look at Sofia but she had turned away, her hand to her face.

"What the hell are you—"

"Don't speak. Listen. Oleg Vladimirovich, I need you to get a message to the Americans. Urgently. Today." Morozov began to protest, but Vasin raised his voice and spoke over him. "I take your denials as read. You don't know what I am talking about. Fine. But nonetheless. On the second of this month, a flotilla of four submarines left the headquarters of the Northern Fleet at Polyarniy, bound for Cuba . . ."

As Vasin told the story, Morozov became entirely silent. It seemed to Vasin that the man was trying to escape inside himself, making his face utterly blank and staring resolutely at the floor. Only the knuckles of his hands, clutching the desk in front of him, betrayed the tension inside the man.

"So you see, Colonel Morozov, I have no choice. We cannot communicate with our own submarines. We cannot rescind the orders they have been given. And we know that the Americans have located our boats, and it is only a matter of time before they catch them. Which leaves us only one choice. To tell the Yankees. Warn them against trying to engage this flotilla. But we have to do it now. *You* have to do it now."

After a long pause, Morozov's voice came in a flat monotone, as though he were reciting from a text.

"Colonel, I have heard your insane story out because when I tried to speak you shouted me down." Morozov's eyes remained fixed on his own clenched hands, refusing to meet Vasin's. "But I must protest, in the strongest terms, that I know nothing, absolutely nothing."

"For Christ's sake, man." Vasin slammed the palms of both of his hands hard on the table. "I don't care what you did. I don't care if you betrayed our country's secrets, or why. But you must do this. Now. For your Motherland. And for America, if you care for America, too. We're talking about *imminent nuclear war*." With each of his last words, Vasin again slammed the table. He felt anger swelling in his brain like a spreading bruise but was unable to control it.

"Quiet." Sofia had stood, and put a calming hand on Vasin's shoulder. "Colonel Vasin, can you leave us alone for a moment?"

Vasin glanced at the telephone, at the window, at the intercom that stood on the examination room desk, and shook his head. But he did retreat three steps to the far corner of the room.

"Fine. Have it your way." Sofia crouched beside Morozov and took his hand. She spoke softly, as though to a stubborn child. "Oleg. I have no idea if what they say about you is true. And if it is, I cannot imagine why you did such a thing. It doesn't concern me. I admired you. You know that. Part of me always will. But Oleg, if you can help. If you can do this thing for Vasin, then you can live. Don't you see? The Chekist hasn't got to that part yet. The threats. But he will, I am sure." Sofia shot a hostile look across the room at Vasin. "Help him, and we can be free. The new life you said we could have together? The things we talked about doing, when you left your wife? Maybe not the foreign travel, the trade delegations that you promised me. Your life will be different, I understand. But I don't care about that. We can still be together."

Morozov's mouth had become slack, his eyes resolutely fixed on the table lamp, avoiding Sofia's. There was a long silence after she finished speaking. Morozov had folded his arms across his body. When he spoke, his words were precise and clipped.

"You're devilishly clever, Colonel. Trained her well. Coached her perfectly. The good angel to your evil one. Very neat."

Sofia recoiled from Morozov, withdrawing her hand and straightening her back. Her face hardened.

"Know this, Colonel Vasin," continued Morozov. "I admit nothing and never will, because what you say is not true. I will never walk into your trap, because I am not the fool you take me to be. I will not succumb to the blandishments and the lies of this woman—"

"Stop talking." Vasin's voice cut across Morozov's, an aggressive whisper. "I'll do it myself. *Me.* Do you hear? I will deliver the message myself to the Americans. Just tell me where. Give me the code. Or the camera. Or whatever it is you use."

Morozov gave a theatrical shiver, as though trying to shake off the words he was hearing. Vasin loomed over him now, his hands on the arms of the chair in which the traitor sat, his face just inches from Morozov's.

"I need you to write the message, telling them what I have told you just now. Write it without any warning words. Make sure they know this is coming from you. I'm guessing you use a camera to photograph your messages. Maybe a miniature camera. Whatever it is, you photograph the document and give the film to her. And I assume you use dead-letter drops, not brush-pasts. We've never seen you within a hundred meters of a foreigner all year. So let's say it's a dead-letter drop. You give Sofia the message, destroy whatever else you need to destroy. The camera. A codebook. Whatever evidence you need to get rid of."

Morozov was starting to twist away from the onslaught, but Vasin caught the man's chin and forcibly turned his head back to face his own.

"Make whatever signal you need to to tell them you're making an emergency drop. I don't need to know what the signal is. Wrong number phone call. Curtain code. Whatever. And you tell me where the dead-letter drop is. Plus you tell me the signals you use to flag it. Do you understand?"

Morozov's eyelids fluttered and his breathing grew labored. He shot a desperate glance toward Sofia, who refused to meet his eyes.

"In return, I go back to my routine surveillance work, which will be useless because you will never contact the Americans again. If and when the *kontora* decides to haul you in, I say we found and saw nothing in a year of listening to your snores. That's the deal."

Still Morozov said nothing. He drew his hand slowly down his gray face, and finally answered in a low whisper.

"*You* write it."

"What?"

"You write me a draft, Vasin. Of what you want me to say. In your own writing. You sign and date it. Then . . . I will see."

Vasin straightened and narrowed his eyes. Cunning son of a bitch. If Morozov was caught, he'd have a draft of the message in Vasin's own writing to prove he'd written it at Vasin's request.

"An insurance policy."

Morozov merely raised his palms and eyebrows slightly in acknowledgment. His face registered only wariness. Vasin looked out the window at the lowering October skies, but saw nothing that could help him. Sofia was perched on the corner of a table, folded into herself, refusing to look at either of them. Christ, thought Vasin. This is like a bad Gorky melodrama.

"God damn you, Morozov."

Vasin pulled out the desk drawer and rummaged through a pile of prescription forms and lab test requests. Giving up on finding a sheet of blank paper, he used the back of a form. Vasin snatched a framed medical certificate off the wall and placed the paper on it so as not to leave an impression on other papers on the desk. Force of habit. Vasin saw Morozov notice, and their eyes met for a split second of professional complicity. Vasin began to write.

"Flash—urgent. Four Project 641 diesel-electric submarines from the Soviet Northern Fleet have been ordered to run the blockade of Cuba. Each boat is armed with a nuclear torpedo and every commander has been given orders to use it if attacked without further approval from Fleet Command . . ."

When he had finished the draft, Vasin glanced up at Morozov once more. The man held him with a steady gaze, impassive but now no longer wearing a mask of feigned indignation. Vasin dared to hope that his desperation had finally convinced the traitor to cooperate. Morozov raised an eyebrow, tapping the unsigned note on the glass. Fuck you, thought Vasin. Fuck you so much.

Vasin signed and dated the paper as he'd promised, and handed it over.

"Right. We don't have much time, Oleg Vladimirovich. You need to tell me exactly when and how."

Morozov stood, tucking Vasin's note into his inner tunic pocket. He said nothing but put out his hand, which Vasin reflexively took. Morozov clenched it hard, evidently fighting for control of his emotions, risking only a brief glance into Vasin's face. Then he turned and spoke to Sofia.

"Sonyechka. Let's go to my home. I will give you everything your boss needs."

Morozov left first. As Sofia followed, Vasin caught her arm.

"Mayakovskaya metro. I'll be waiting by the concert hall. Hurry."

Sofia nodded quickly and followed Morozov out of the consulting room. Vasin watched them walk down the corridor, side by side but silent. Vasin could barely bring himself to think about what he had to do next. Morozov had walked away from the meeting with Vasin's self-written death sentence in his pocket.

Morozov and Sofia rode the empty elevator down in silence. It was only when they reached the street that she stopped and turned to confront Morozov.

"So is what the KGB man says true?"

The Colonel ran a hand over his face. His eyes, when they connected to Sofia's glare, were furtive.

"It is true that I have been in contact with the Americans. But Sofia—everything I did was on the instructions of General Serov."

"So why aren't you calling your Serov now? Why aren't we on our way to see him?"

"Because . . ."

"Don't lie to me, Oleg."

Morozov took a step backward as though propelled by the force of the woman's vehemence.

"It's complicated, Sofia. I promise I will explain it all to you. It's not what you think. But right now we need to get home and do what this man says."

"Because you want to save your life."

"That's not what you want?"

Sofia closed her eyes, hard, like a child. When she opened them, her lashes were dotted with tears. She so badly wanted to believe him. To believe in him.

"Yes, Oleg. I want you to live."

18

Pioneers' Ponds, Moscow
Sunday, 28 October 1962, 09:04 Moscow Time / 02:04 EDT

In their cigarette-smoke-filled aerie in the apartment across the Ponds, Morozov's watchers nearly missed his unexpected return home. Lyubimov was at his station by the outsized binoculars, and had been watching a pair of pretty shopgirls as they stood in the queue for ice cream when he caught a glimpse of a familiar, hurrying figure. Dropping a half-eaten doughnut on the floor, he pulled up his chair and focused hurriedly on his target.

"Incoming," called Lyubimov.

Doronin, the cameraman, was in the toilet and missed the shot of Morozov chivalrously holding the door to his apartment building open for Sofia Rafaelovna Guzman. The radioman, Gromov, was more on the ball. Within seconds he had switched his powerful set from jazz on Radio Luxembourg to the short-wave frequency that linked the station to the radio cars and put out the three beeps that meant: Alert.

"*Nichego sebe.* God damn it, he's with his girlfriend!" Like all the watcher teams, after eleven months Lyubimov knew the habits of his quarry better than those of his closest friends or neighbors. He felt almost indignant at their subject's sudden lurch into reckless vice. "Bringing her home? Lyudmila Alexandrovna just left half an hour ago! Ears—this could be good."

Gromov—"Ears"—had already switched on all four reel-to-reel tape recorders attached to the new radio microphones they had planted in Morozov's apartment. He checked the signal level on all of them, taking care to turn up the sensitivity on the bedroom mike to maximum. The sound of the front door opening came deafeningly over the speakers, followed by Morozov's unmistakable, reedy voice.

"Sofia. Please take a seat here in the sitting room. Looks like my wife Lyuda is out."

Ears silently cursed Morozov's formal tone. Didn't sound like there would be any action after all. If he hadn't turned up the microphones' volume, he might have noticed that Morozov was speaking in exaggeratedly loud voice.

"Shall I make us both some tea?"

"Good idea. I'll be as quick as I can with those papers. Excuse me, please."

The listeners heard the study door close with a firm click.

19

Soviet Embassy, Washington, DC
Sunday, 28 October 1962, 02:04 EDT / 09:04 Moscow Time

Alexander Feklisov's grandmother had been a religious woman. "It is God's will," his babushka used to murmur comfortingly in his childish ear. "Man supposes, but God disposes." As a good Communist, the KGB *rezident* was of course an atheist. But part of him envied the ignorant old woman's immovable, almost bovine, calm. Marx taught that religion was the opium of the oppressed—a belief in fate, in supernatural higher powers, invented to reconcile them to the misery of their exploited lives. But over the last twenty-four hours Feklisov had longed for his grandmother's inner peace. Because God—or whatever joker was ultimately in charge of this unending shitshow of a crisis—had chosen to play merry hell with Feklisov's world.

Late the previous night Khrushchev had finally sent his letter to Kennedy. It was a rambling, emotional document clearly penned by a leader under extreme stress. But at least it contained a clear offer to withdraw the missiles in exchange for a promise not to invade Cuba. Precisely the deal that Feklisov himself had framed. Finally, an end to the crisis. Or so Feklisov had dared to hope when he flopped, exhausted, into his bed at three that morning.

But then, just as he and the Ambassador were nervously awaiting the White House's response, fresh peril. Just after noon the news broke that an American U-2 spy plane had been shot down over Cuba, the pilot killed. The crisis had chalked up its first fatality. Possibly, if things went just a little more wrong, the first casualty of millions.

Feklisov knew, and Ambassador Dobrynin knew, that the anti-aircraft batteries set up all over Cuba to protect the missile bases were commanded and manned by Soviet troops. In all probability, Kennedy knew it, too. Nonetheless, Dobrynin had spent the afternoon fluently lying that it had been the Cubans, not the Soviets, who had blown the U-2 out of the sky. And it seemed that the White House was ready to play along with that fiction and pretend to believe them.

Again—a glimmer of hope that the Cuban Missile Crisis might end in something other than nuclear war. But then came news of these god-damned submarines.

The day before, Feklisov's agent inside the NSA had warned him that the US Navy had picked up the trail of a couple of Soviet subma-rines somewhere in the western Caribbean. Disappear, Feklisov had prayed. Sail away, far away. May the sea swallow you.

But the boats hadn't disappeared. Dobrynin sat slumped in an arm-chair in his office, sagging like a man punctured by worry. Opposite him sat the Soviet Embassy's naval attaché. Feklisov saw from their faces the moment he entered that the news was not good.

"So, Comrade Captain. The Americans have found our submarines?"

Captain First Class Dmitry Khvostov nodded grimly.

"Indeed, Ambassador. The Americans tell us they have been chasing our boats hard since noon. Fourteen hours, now."

"What kind of boats have they picked up—?" Feklisov felt his chest tighten even as he asked the question. "Not missile submarines?"

"Thank God, no. A pair of Project 641 diesel-electric subs."

"They were trying to run the blockade?"

Ambassador Dobrynin interrupted.

"Alexander Semyonovich—what does it matter now what they were doing? The problem is this." The Ambassador handed Feklisov a mem-orandum on White House letterhead and continued speaking as the *kontora* man read. "As you can see, the Americans intend to force our submarines to surface. They give us notice that they will use practice depth charges to signal the boats . . ."

Feklisov, reading from the letter, finished Dobrynin's sentence for him.

"'. . . to avoid the misinterpretation of these signals as hostile intent, we hereby notify you that the US Navy shall use the internationally recognized signal of five detonations from low-explosive depth charges at fifteen-minute intervals . . .'" Feklisov looked up at the naval attaché. "'Low-explosive'—what does that mean?"

"As you would imagine. Depth charges with one kilo of explosive in them. They make a sound wave, but do not create shrapnel or shock waves sufficient to harm a submarine."

"So what's the problem, Captain? We signal our boats immediately. Tell them that the Americans have given us fair warning. They surface, then get the hell out of there."

Captain Khvostov grimaced before answering.

"The problem, Alexander Semyonovich, is that we cannot contact them."

"What?"

"A submerged submarine has no radio contact with the outside world. We cannot warn them until they surface."

"Do the Americans know that?"

The Ambassador answered for Khvostov.

"Do you think the Americans would believe us if we told them that our submarines are beyond our control? They will think we are stalling. Maybe covering up for an attack. And if they did believe us, how does that make us look?"

"So we tell the Americans that we have passed their message on? And let them get on with dropping their depth charges?"

The Navy man shrugged.

"That is exactly what I propose. There is no point in revealing the limitations of our communications to the enemy."

"What if our submarine captains refuse? Or conclude that they are under attack? Or are we simply counting on our brave submariners to meekly obey and surface?"

Khvostov straightened, stung by Feklisov's sneer.

"Submarine warfare tactics are naturally outside the expertise of the organs of State Security, Alexander Semyonovich. I can tell you that our captains are the most courageous and best-trained in the world. But we understand that these two submarines are being closely pursued by at least half a dozen American boats. Torpedoes fired by our boats might sink or damage one or two enemy destroyers. But it would lead to the immediate retaliatory annihilation of both submarines and the total loss of their crews. Our commanders are brave—but they are not suicidal."

The three men observed various silences—Khvostov defiant, Feklisov desperate, Ambassador Dobrynin exhausted.

"So we just do nothing and assume all will be well?"

"We could pray," whispered the Ambassador.

A feeble joke? But Dobrynin's careworn face was not smiling.

20

Pioneers' Ponds, Moscow
Sunday, 28 October 1962, 09:12 Moscow Time / 02:12 EDT

Morozov worked fast. He reached for a framed photograph of the Frunze Military Academy class of 1939. He paused briefly to look at the rows of serious young faces. He allowed his eyes to scan the front row of the photograph—the senior officers who had been his teachers and mentors. They were all gone, to a man. Most of them into the NKVD's execution pits as Stalin's senseless purge of the Army's officer corps decimated their ranks on the very eve of a world war. Murdered by time-serving, cowardly *kontora* motherfuckers. Many of those who had survived fell in the first days of the war as the Germans tore through the unprepared Red Army in the first weeks of Operation Barbarossa—unprepared because of Stalin's pigheaded refusal to heed warnings that Hitler was planning a massive invasion of the USSR. Senseless slaughter, over and over.

Morozov placed a sheet of cheap writing paper on the glass and began copying out Vasin's message in block capitals. He was careful to make some additions of his own. Once he was finished, he folded Vasin's original letter and slipped it into an envelope. After a moment's reflection, he wrote a cover note and added it. Then he sealed the letter and addressed it to his wife, care of his mother-in-law's address in Leningrad. He found a stamp in an ornate brass tin he kept for the purpose and slipped the envelope into his tunic pocket. Once he posted it, Morozov's insurance policy would be safe from *kontora* hands—for the time being at least.

Next he brought down his Zenit camera from his bookshelf, a bulky old late-1940s model. Morozov unscrewed the bolt that attached the body of the camera to its leather box, then fumbled with the catch that opened the back. With his thumb he wound the sliding cloth shutter, then he held one side of it back as he pressed the release. Inside the casing a small, steel rectangle was fitted into the camera body, nestling just below the lens housing. The ingenuity of it never failed to make him smile. A camera hidden inside another camera. He eased out the miniature Minolta with a fingernail. The tiny spy camera was not much longer than his forefinger.

Morozov took a habitual glance to check that the key was turned in the lock of his study door before crossing the room. He racked the body of the tiny camera to push back the shutter spring and traverse the miniature film inside. He photographed the note he had written, three times for luck. Then he picked up a small paper knife and fitted its blade into a groove in one side of the Minolta to rewind the film. Always the trickiest part, this. He wound back the spool until he heard a flipping click from inside, cracked open the body of the camera, and tapped the tiny canister out onto his desk. Retrieving a handkerchief from his pocket, he spat on the steel tube and wiped its slimy surface clean of fingerprints before slipping it into another envelope.

Morozov looked at his hands as though they belonged to someone else. They shook, though not uncontrollably. Think. *Think.* He sat down in front of his class photograph once more, retrieved another piece of paper using his handkerchief, and began to write instructions for Vasin's dead-letter drop. "Bolshaya Sadovaya Street Twenty-Five. Courtyard. Second entrance, second floor. Trash receptacle. Packet of Kazbek." Morozov wrote slowly, making his block capitals as square and untraceable as possible. He hesitated for a long moment. Should he include the real signal that the dead-letter drop had been primed, or the warning signal? Did he actually believe that crazy bastard Vasin? Morozov looked down at the note before him, incredulous. Obviously, part of him did. Or at least he couldn't think of why a senior *kontora* officer would risk tipping him off, offering him the chance to escape with his skin whole unless he had some very good reason. Unless Vasin was playing some impenetrable game whose meaning was obscure. Some goddamned *kontora*-Aquarium political rebus, maybe. Morozov waited a moment more, then made a decision. A plague on both their houses.

"Mailbox filled signal," Morozov wrote. "A white horizontal chalk mark on drainpipe on the corner of Bolshaya Sadovaya Twenty-Five and Malaya Bronnaya."

He slipped the note, again using his handkerchief, into the envelope along with the tiny capsule. After a moment's thought he rummaged in his desk drawer, fished out a small piece of white chalk, and helpfully dropped that into the envelope, too.

The extreme danger he was in pressed on Morozov like the closing jaws of a garbage compactor. His study, once a place of security and refuge, had turned into a deadly spring trap of jeopardy. He felt himself, as though in a nightmare, suddenly spotlit on a stage, illuminated by blinding lights and scrutinized by strangers.

Belatedly, he realized that Sofia had not knocked to offer him tea. Was she waiting in the kitchen on instructions from the *kontora* for a team of armed men to burst in? All the way home, he had been too locked into his own fear to even speak to her. He allowed his mind a tiny moment to think about her. Had she betrayed him—or rescued him? Was she on his side, or theirs? Had he outrageously traduced Sofia when he insulted her in front of the snake Vasin? The possibilities reeled out of control so quickly that he physically slapped himself on the forehead to stop his spiraling train of thought.

"Fuck."

Morozov had forgotten to make the signal that would warn his controllers that an emergency dead-letter drop needed collection. He looked at his watch, desperately, as he jumped up to snatch an ugly white orchid his wife had given him for his birthday from its usual place on the left of the windowsill. He transferred it to the right corner, pulling the left-hand curtain half-closed. The emergency signal should be made before nine a.m. It was now twenty past. Exactly when the signal would be checked, or by whom, he had no idea.

The Minolta sat on his desk alongside the adapted Zenit that housed it. Impulsively, he seized the tiny spy camera and broke it in half with his hands. Wildly, he looked around for something heavy to grind it into smaller pieces. A heavy metal bust of Alexander Pushkin would do the trick. Morozov tipped the contents of his sawn-off shell case ashtray into a wastepaper basket and inverted it, making a flat brass platform where he began to quietly crush the casing into bits.

There was a soft knock on the door. Morozov froze, midmovement.

"Oleg Vladimorovich?" Sofia's voice was fearful. "Everything all right in there? Your tea is getting cold."

"Fine. Fine, just coming."

Cursing under his breath, Morozov extracted a thin tube of spare microfilm rolls from the inside of the Zenit and ground them to pieces, too. He tipped the mess of flattened metal pieces onto a sheet of paper, fished out the snaking curls of microfilm, and set fire to them in the ashtray. They burned with a fierce, acrid flame. Hurriedly, he unlocked the door and scuttled toward the toilet.

"Did you find the jam?" Morozov's voice sounded high and strangled. "There's some in the cupboard."

Locking the lavatory door behind him, he scrunched the paper containing the debris of his smashed camera and wrapped that in more toilet paper. The bundle was the size of a clenched fist. He dropped it into the basin and flushed, waited for the cistern to fill, and flushed again. For the first time in two hours, Morozov drew a deep breath.

Emerging from the toilet, he found Sofia waiting for him in the hallway. Instinctively, he put a finger to his lips, warning her of the *kontora*'s microphones. Was he really going to go through with this? Morozov felt an almost physical paralysis that prevented him from reaching inside his pocket and handing the envelope with the microfilm—the power of life and death—to Sofia.

Was this the moment to tell her that everything Vasin had said was just a crazy lie? To bluff his way out? Or could it be that what Vasin had said and written was true—about the submarines, the hawks, the nuclear torpedoes, and the captains' orders to use them if attacked? Try as he might, Morozov could not summon any shred of concern for the fortunes of the world. Only for his own skin.

But saving his own skin meant keeping his bargain. Avoiding Sofia's eyes, he gingerly drew out the envelope by one corner and handed it to her. She took it, after a moment's hesitation, and ran her fingers along the length of it. She felt the small film canister, nodded to herself, and turned into the hall to put on her coat. Sofia opened the door and walked out without another word.

21

Pioneers' Ponds, Moscow
Sunday, 28 October 1962, 09:32 Moscow Time / 02:32 EDT

"Ears, you sure the mikes are working?" Lyubimov looked up testily from his binoculars. "They've been in there for twenty minutes and barely a word from either of them. And now she's gone."

Ears fiddled with the levels on his devices and was rewarded with a deafening burst of music as Morozov turned on the kitchen radio.

"What the hell was all that?" Lyubimov sat back on his chair as Sofia passed out of sight under the golden-leaved trees of Pioneers' Ponds.

"Shostakovich's Second Violin Concerto, I think," replied Ears.

"Funny guy." Lyubimov reached for the surveillance log to record the departure of Sofia Rafaelovna Guzman from the premises. "Your turn to make us some coffee, radio-head."

22

Bolshaya Sadovaya Street, Moscow
Sunday, 28 October 1962, 09:39 Moscow Time / 02:39 EDT

At the corner of Malaya Bronnaya and the Garden Ring road, Sofia paused. Stepping into a doorway, facing away from the street, she slipped the paper out of Morozov's envelope. Her eyes widened in incomprehension as she read the instructions he had written for Vasin. So it was true. Morozov really was a traitor. A sudden, weird sense of dread washed over her. She looked up to check the address plaque on the side of the building, just above the doorway where she was standing: Bolshaya Sadovaya 25. The address in Morozov's instructions was exactly where she stood at that moment. How could he have known? She felt a moment of giddy panic before forcing herself to calm down. This was just a stupid coincidence, not witchcraft. Nothing left to do but push on with the crazy plan—to put her fate and Morozov's in Vasin's hands. She stuffed Morozov's note back inside its envelope.

Seized with a burning desire to get rid of it as soon as humanly possible, Sofia hurried toward the Mayakovskaya metro station.

Vasin spotted Sofia a hundred yards away. Her forward motion, head down as though advancing into a gale, told him all he needed to know. Morozov had given her the goods. Vasin raised his hand to attract her attention. Glancing quickly from side to side, she hurried through the cars parked outside Tchaikovsky Concert Hall.

Sofia's face was pale with tension. Her eyes, as she approached him, narrowed with suspicion. Vasin began to speak, but Sofia merely smacked the envelope into his chest and hurried away, breaking into a run as she crossed the road to the metro.

For a moment Vasin considered following Sofia, attempting to reassure her that all would be well. But he knew he had no time. If Morozov had kept his word, he'd made some kind of signal to his American handlers to collect a dead-letter drop. Vasin had no idea how soon that would be. He opened the envelope, palmed the tiny film capsule, and read Morozov's instructions.

The drop-off address was, Vasin saw immediately, just a couple of hundred meters from where he stood, and the same distance to Pioneers' Ponds. That made sense—an emergency drop site needs to be close enough for the agent to reach it in a hurry. Trash receptacle in a semi-public place. Also logical. And the chalk mark, too—standard operating procedure for spies around the world, evidently.

All he needed was a packet of Kazbek. They were old-fashioned, cheap, workers' *papirosy,* a cardboard and paper tube with an inch and a half of strong tobacco in the end. Vasin himself smoked posh Orbitas. Cursing, he pocketed the paper, wound up the window, and went in search of a tobacconist.

Yeliseyevsky Emporium, an incongruously grand pre-Revolutionary palace of a grocery shop, was on the opposite side of Gorky Street. A line of citizens stood waiting patiently for admittance. Evidently something good had just been delivered, and word had spread through the mysterious bush telegraph that connected Moscow shoppers. Vasin shouldered his way past the head of the line, his urgent confidence clearly signaling that he was not in the waiting-in-line class. There were no protests as he squeezed inside and made for the *tabak* counter.

23

USS Bache, *Sargasso Sea*
Sunday, 28 October 1962, 02:51 EDT / 09:51 Moscow Time

Somewhere under the dark sea were at least two Soviet subs, no more than a couple of miles distant. Billings knew it because his sonarmen could see the sons of bitches as clearly as burglars suddenly caught in a floodlight on a back lawn. Forty minutes earlier the second sub had slowed to a near halt some fifteen hundred yards from its companion. That meant the skipper had paused to take a look around. Run, listen, run—that was the submariners' way. And the other submarine had near as goddamned run right up his fellow Sov sub's ass. Now both Soviet commanders, listening intently on passive sonar, would have heard the screw noises of the flotilla that had been scrambled to intercept them.

But in water less than five hundred meters deep, the Sovs had no way to hide from the powerful active sonar arrays installed on the USS *Bache* and her fellow sub-hunting destroyer, the USS *Cony*. The pressure wave the deep pings made through the water traced their profiles on the sonarmen's blotchy green screens like pulsing, deadly sea ghosts. Recordings of the noise of the Sovs' propellers had been fed into some newfangled computer at Patuxent which stored all known Soviet submarine acoustic signatures. The sonar profile told Billings that the Sovs were big fuckers. And the eggheads at the naval air station had radioed a few hours before to confirm that they were Foxtrot-class subs. Oilers: the big diesel-electric boats that were the backbone of the Soviet submarine fleet. Not nuclear-powered boats, which were sleeker and faster than these guys. And not ballistic-missile subs, thank Almighty God.

The two boats Billings now had in his sights had actually been heading away from Cuba when they'd first been picked up by US Navy Orions. A feint? An attempt to evade the blockade by giving the US ships a wide berth? Or were they actually heading home? Would they still try to escape and push on toward Cuba, despite being spotted?

Billings scanned the black horizon once more. A sliver of new moon hung low over the Caicos Islands to the west. No word from the sonar team of any increase of the subs' engine noise, no blowing of tanks, no nothing. The Sovs were just . . . waiting. Which made Billings nervous.

"Pete. What you reckon?"

Kimble took his time before answering. Both men knew their orders. To force any Soviet submarine they found to surface, give it a formal warning—to be recorded on newsreel film—then make sure the fuckers headed back where they'd come from. And if they refused? Both Billings and his executive officer had been listening to the radio, too. Kennedy had been very clear. Running the blockade would be an act of war.

"Don' like it none, skip. They're just sitting there. Only one reason why an attack sub would just sit there in the water for longer than it takes to get their bearings. And that's to calculate a firing solution. Maybe these guys got orders to not be taken alive. Kamee-kadze-style. If you know what I'm talkin' about."

Billings pondered for a moment and shook his head. Soviets weren't Japs.

"Must be, what, at least fourteen hours since they could have had any comms with command, right? Probably more. If the Russki skipper wanted to take a shot, he'd already have done it. If he'd reckoned he could outrun us and get to Cuba, he'd have tried that, too. But he hasn't done either of those things. My guess—he's just sitting tight, hopin' we're just gonna give up and leave him alone. If he were on a nuke, he could go on sitting down there for weeks, makin' his own air. But Patuxent tells us we got ourselves a brace of diesels down there. Diesel subs gotta come up for air, sooner or later."

Kimble worked his tongue around the inside of his bottom lip— a habit he hadn't lost since the days of his youth when he used to dip snuff.

"We've waited just about long enough, I reckon. When do you think we'll get the green light to rattle Ivan's cage an itty bit? Focus those Russ'n gentlemen's minds a little? As in, time to come out, gals. Game's up."

As if in answer, a red light flicked on in front of the Captain's console. The radio room. Billings picked up the receiver, grunted an affirmation, then pressed the telephone into his chest for a moment as he turned to Kimble.

"It's the *Randolph*. Patching me to Admiral McKenzie. Maybe you'd better get ready to rattle those cages, Pete."

———

The afterdeck of the *Bache* was illuminated by a row of fierce white spotlights. The roll of the sea had calmed to a gentle swell, and a shower shrouded the deck in a drifting halo of mist. Billings, in a tropical rain slicker, walked out among the racks of shining black depth charges. Trolleys of practice charges, painted white with red stripes, stood by as sailors loaded them into the arrays of launchers that fanned out across the *Bache's* stern.

Billings was acutely conscious that a lot of important eyes were on his task. The signaling code—five depth charges every fifteen minutes, plus a more frequent code of max-volume sonar pings—had been cleared not only by ExComm, the White House crisis command, but by Kennedy himself. Even the damn Kremlin had been alerted. Somehow the Sovs were meant to pass that signal on to their sub commanders. Right. Good luck with that. If anyone had worked out a way to communicate with a submarine three hundred feet underwater, Billings hadn't heard of it. Sounded to Billings like Kennedy and his boys were just covering their asses.

No. Those subs were out there on their own, blind, deaf, and cornered. This was between him and the Sov commanders. Both were waiting for the other to make a wrong move. It was personal. Very.

And if the subs refused to surface? Or worse, loosed a torpedo? They would be dead. If the brass gave the order, Billings could crush the two subs as flat as stamped-on tin cans. Because the *Bache*—as well as the *Beale* and the *Cony*—were carrying special weapons of their own.

A supply of nuclear depth charges.

Only a small group of specially trained able seamen and a handful of the officers knew about the nuclear weapons. Billings himself had never seen one of the eleven-kiloton W34 bombs detonate, not even on exercises. But he did know that the things sent a shock wave through the water powerful enough to crush any submarine within a five-nautical-mile radius and raise a twelve-foot-high wave on the surface—as well as destroy most of the marine life in the visible horizon.

But it wouldn't come to that. Hopefully.

The *Bache's* weapons officer, saluting, reported that the first set of charges were ready to fire.

"Okay, boys. Let 'em go."

PART SIX

BATTLE STATIONS

If you start throwing hedgehogs under me, I shall throw
a couple of porcupines under you.

NIKITA KHRUSHCHEV, 1963

1

B-59, Sargasso Sea
Sunday, 28 October 1962, 03:01 EDT / 10:01 Moscow Time

At ninety meters' depth, the pop of the cartridges that propelled the barrel-like depth charges from the launching racks arrayed on the gunwales of the USS *Bache* were inaudible to B-59's sonar operator. But the unmistakable splash of a hundred fifty kilos of dense material being dumped rhythmically off the side of a ship certainly was. It was the noise that every submariner dreaded most—the deep, splashing gulp of a sinking barrel of high explosives. A weapon that could send a shock wave through the water powerful enough to burst his ship's steel plates like an eggshell.

Warrant Officer Sergei Komarov snatched his headphones off his ears.

"Depth charges!" Komarov's voice was an unbelieving shriek as he leapt up from his console as though it had suddenly become electric. In the command center everyone froze as Komarov's shout echoed from the intercom. Seconds passed. Then came the thud of five successive underwater explosions—muffled, but unmistakable.

Savitsky, startled, jumped up from his seat in the command station. "The attack is starting!"

Arkhipov pushed his way out of the navigator's compartment and in three steps was at the Captain's side. Both men listened intently for the deadly sounds of creaking steel that signified the boat was breaking up. But none came.

"All compartments—damage reports!" Savitsky barked into the triple intercoms behind his seat. Sounding off one by one, the seven compartment chiefs called in the all clear.

Arkhipov saw that the Captain was swaying, bleary-eyed with

exhaustion. Savitsky had refused to leave his post for more than a few minutes at a time since they had dived—even though the temperature in the command center was close to unbearable. The huge banks of accumulator batteries had been designed for the freezing waters of the North Atlantic, not the tepid Sargasso Sea. True, the temperature was even worse back in the electric engine compartment, where the chief engineer was reporting temperatures of sixty-one degrees Celsius—as hot as a *banya*. Hot enough to liquefy the heavy grease on the propeller shafts. Hot enough to shred the nerves and addle the wits of strong men.

Over the last few hours the crew had been dropping like dominoes, slumping into unconsciousness in front of their instruments. But still Savitsky sat on, his shirt drenched in sweat and his head hanging doggedly between his clenched fists. Now the dull thudding of the depth charges roused him from his torpor. He looked around the alarmed faces on the command deck which had turned to him for orders, his jaw working as he thought. Abruptly, the skipper lurched aft. Arkhipov followed a pace behind as Savitsky ducked between the periscope and snorkel tubes into the weapons control room. Political Officer Maslennikov was already there, unlocking the steel gate that closed off the compartment except during emergencies or firing drills.

The cramped space, little more than two meters square, was almost filled by the most sophisticated piece of electronics on the ship. The size of two large refrigerators, the targeting computer was capable of a mind-boggling thousand calculations per second. Back when Arkhipov had been a naval cadet, submarine captains would have to surface in order to fire their torpedoes, calculating ranges and speeds on a slide rule and aiming by eye. But that had been before the space age. Now the USSR's attack boats had the benefit of the newest technology that the Ministry of Medium Machine Building could provide. This amazing computer would calculate the B-59's speed, the sea current, the bearing and direction of the targets, and come up with a perfect firing solution for the boat's torpedoes. Junior Lieutenant Andrei Kotov, the keeper of the targeting machine's secrets, appeared at his station flustered and bleary with sleep.

"Kotov. Plot firing solutions for all the enemy vessels in the vicinity," Savitsky growled.

Arkhipov and Maslennikov exchanged glances as they squeezed aside to allow the young officer to take his place in front of the computer.

"Start with a firing solution for the special weapon. An enemy vessel at ten thousand meters' range. The bigger the better."

"Valentin Grigorievich! The special weapon? What are you thinking?"

Savitsky's lowering glare focused on Arkhipov, his voice loud and furious.

"Maybe the war has already started up there, while we are doing somersaults down here!" Savitsky roared. "Our orders are to use the special weapon when attacked. And we are under attack now!"

Arkhipov heard the unmistakable edge of hysteria in Savitsky's voice, and fought to keep his own firm and calm.

"Wait, Captain . . ."

Savitsky swiveled to the political officer.

"Tell him, Maslennikov. Comrade Arkhipov seems to have forgotten our instructions."

The younger man's eyes flicked nervously between his two superiors.

"Vasily Alexandrovich, the Captain is correct. We are required to prepare firing solutions for our weapons immediately on close contact with the enemy. That is a standing order. And I presume that to mean firing solutions for all our weapons. Including the special weapon. Sir."

A moment later another thud came through the hull, fainter and sharper than the previous ones. It was followed by four more, at roughly five-second intervals. The weapons control center had its own direct intercom link to the sonar room.

"Sonar?" Savitsky barked into the machine. A moment passed before the sonarman's voice replied.

"Not depth charges, Captain. And not from the same direction. Detonations from another American ship, sir. At this range it sounds like . . . grenades?"

Savitsky swung back to face Arkhipov.

"Satisfied now? First depth charges, now grenades. You still say this is not an attack?"

"Why would they attack us with *grenades*, Savitsky? This may be *contact* with the enemy—but it's not an attack. Read the manual, Captain."

"This ship is crewed by fighting sailors. The place for men who have swallowed a training manual is on shore. In a classroom."

229

Arkhipov held Savitsky's eye as he struggled to control himself.

"'A Soviet commander is at all times *calm, level-headed,* and resolute.'" Arkhipov was quoting from the preamble to the *Standing Instructions to Soviet Marine Officers*.

The Captain made no reply and shouldered his way out of the cubicle, pushing past Arkhipov with unnecessary force. Arkhipov and the *Politruk* exchanged a long glance before turning to watch the young lieutenant key the various coordinates of the surrounding ships into his machine.

It was a laborious process. To avoid being pinpointed, B-59 could not send out sonic pings from her active sonar, and had to rely on the indistinct rumbles and swishes that she could hear on her passive listening devices. Even with two sonarmen working as fast as they could, each contact had to be verified by three separate systems—the Feliks, Hercules, and Clarification sonars that were mounted in a bulb on B-59's bow. Moreover, to get an idea of the speed and direction of every one of their pursuers, the sonar team would have to check back on every American ship every ten minutes. And as if that were not complex enough, there was the bulk of their sister submarine—B-36—lying some five kilometers to the east and interfering with the sonar signals with the backwash of her propellers. One of Arkhipov's old instructors had joked that piloting a submarine was like trying to drive a truck up Gorky Street with the windows painted over, with only your ears to guide you. Suddenly the joke didn't seem so funny.

After half an hour of attempting to follow this complex three-dimensional chess game, Arkhipov's head was aching. But the picture that emerged on the chart where Kotov was marking off every contact was clear enough. At least five American destroyers stood off at between two thousand and five thousand meters' distance. A much larger vessel that had to be an aircraft carrier was audible roughly ten kilometers to the northeast. But the rest lay in a ragged crescent running from southwest to southeast. Directly between B-59 and the Puerto Rico Trench.

Another series of muffled explosions rumbled faintly through the water. Moments later, Arkhipov and Maslennikov both felt the slow lurch as B-59 went into a starboard turn. Savitsky had abandoned their run for the Trench.

Fed at last with all the data it needed, the weapons control computer finally began crunching the numbers. The results showed as a series of illuminated green figures on a row of displays on the green steel console. Kotov took a grease pencil and drew his first firing solution on the chart, marking the special weapon's projected course from B-59 to the American carrier in a thick blue line.

2

Gorky Street, Moscow
Sunday, 28 October 1962, 10:01 Moscow Time / 03:01 EDT

The *tabak* counter of Yeliseyevsky Emporium was closed. A canvas sheet concealed the stock, topped by a plastic TECHNICAL BREAK sign. Vasin slammed his fists on the counter in frustration, looking around for the manager. But all the shop's staff had been mobilized to the produce counter to offload a mountain of green bananas that a stream of porters were ferrying from the heavy goods entrance at the back.

Vasin stopped one of the men on his return journey.

"Comrade, do you smoke Kazbek? Swap you a packet of Orbita."

The porter, hard-faced and smelling of drink, recoiled as though Vasin had made an indecent proposal. The next man offered him a Belomorkanal—also a *papiros,* but the wrong brand. The third didn't smoke. The fourth did smoke Kazbek—but his last one was tucked behind his ear, which he offered Vasin with a comradely grin. No packet.

"Shit." Vasin pushed his way back out of the store, stopping to interrogate the shop assistant who had been deputized to guard over the line. She directed him to a tobacco store at Belorusskaya Station, a metro stop to the north. A twenty-minute round-trip, at least.

Vasin was turning to run to the metro when he had an idea. Pushing aside the shoppers, Vasin peered into the iron trash can that stood by the entrance. It was filled with ice cream wrappers, cigarette butts, and candy wrappers. Vasin began rummaging through the trash, tossing it aside in his search.

"Comrade! Have you lost your senses?" The shop assistant's shout was shrill and indignant. The people around him recoiled as though from a dangerous lunatic. But there it was. An empty packet of Kazbek, stained with the stinking oil from a discarded sardine can. But—

Kazbek. Vasin retrieved it triumphantly and sprinted heedlessly across the traffic of Gorky Street in the direction of Bolshaya Sadovaya.

3

Triumfalnaya Square, Moscow
Sunday, 28 October 1962, 10:01 Moscow Time / 03:01 EDT

Sofia half stumbled, half ran toward the swinging glass-paneled doors of the Mayakovskaya metro. The throng slowly filing through forced her to slow her pace. She willed herself to stop, take a deep breath, and think. What had she just done? Had she helped Morozov and Vasin betray their county? Had they played her for a fool?

Morozov had promised to explain. And Sofia urgently needed some answers.

She turned on her heel and stumbled back along the marble esplanade in front of Tchaikovsky Concert Hall, her pace quickening as she went. Fear that she had just made the biggest mistake of her life chased Sofia like a fury. At the bottom of the concert hall steps, she broke out into a flat-out sprint down the broad sidewalk of the Garden Ring.

She ran, heart pounding, through the Aquarium Gardens and into the maze of courtyards behind Yermolayevsky Lane. The chill air burned her lungs, and the hard leather of her work shoes cut into her ankles. But she pushed on, exulting in the pain from her feet and in her body, losing herself in the agony of it. She swerved through an archway and out onto the street, ignoring a passing government Volga and narrowly missing a woman maneuvering a stroller onto the sidewalk. Sofia sprinted on across Malaya Bronnaya, lengthening her stride to clear the slippery steel tram rails. She was dimly aware of a hulk of yellow and white metal as it slid to a screeching halt as she passed, of a stream of insults shouted by the angry woman tram driver.

Sofia was on the hard-packed gravel of the paths that surrounded Pioneers' Ponds now, moments away from Morozov's front door.

4

Pioneers' Ponds, Moscow
Sunday, 28 October 1962, 10:04 Moscow Time / 03:04 EDT

Kostas Evlogimenou cursed under his breath as a mountainous woman crushed him into the steel post against which he had been leaning. The tram was unusually crowded for midmorning. He caught some talk of a shipment of bananas to the Yeliseyevsky Emporium, whispered from neighbor to neighbor as urgent insider information. The tram braked hard as an olive-skinned young woman of foreign appearance ran, heedless, across its path. The female driver indignantly rang the tram's bell as she ran on, apparently oblivious to the world around her.

"Dumb nanny goat!" the driver shouted.

Evlogimenou's view was almost blocked by the lurching body of his fellow commuter. As the tram gathered speed, he strained to look at the windows of the apartment on Maly Patriarshy Lane 5 that for weeks and months had shown a depressingly identical combination of flower and curtain. The glimpse he caught was fleeting, but unmistakable. The white orchid had been moved, and one curtain was half-closed.

Kostas had no idea who lived in the apartment, or in any of the dozen apartments that he had to check on his circular morning rounds. A milk-round was what the British trainer who had taught him basic counter-espionage back when Kostas was a young anti-Communist guerrilla in Greece after the war had called these mundane, information-gathering circuits. What a milk-round actually meant in the nonespionage world, Kostas had no idea. But he did know that most of the details that he was asked to note would be dummies. His job was not to question but to watch, to note, to wait—on street corners, in line in bureaucratic offices. And Kostas knew he was good at his humble vocation.

Should he abort the rest of the milk-round and report the unusual signal? No. Kostas was a methodical man. He would finish the round. Five locations to go. A bus, a walk, and another tram would bring him to his place of work at the Greek Embassy on Leontyevsky Lane by noon. There, he would make his way to his janitor's den in the stable block. And before putting on his overalls, Kostas would make his thrice-weekly call to his friend Jim Delaney at the American Embassy.

When the tram reached Mayakovskaya Station, Kostas used his hip to give the woman a deliberate shove as she lined up to descend the steps. The crowd was too dense for her to fall, but she tottered forward satisfyingly.

"Russki pigs," he whispered under his breath. Kostas had grown up alongside Russian peasants in the Crimea, before the Revolution. They'd been pigs then, too. Dirty, drunk, dishonest, and lazy. The only difference between his childhood and now was that those slovenly peasants had risen up and slaughtered all the half-decent people who had kept them in line—their priests, their Tsar, and their gentlemen. Now the pigs were in charge. Kostas had been lucky to escape with his life on one of the last White Guard ships out of besieged Yalta, back in 1920 during the chaos of the civil war. And though he had nothing but contempt for what had once been his homeland, Kostas was happy to be back—doing his bit, however small, to fuck them.

5

Pioneers' Ponds, Moscow
Sunday, 28 October 1962, 10:04 Moscow Time / 03:04 EDT

Up in the watchers' apartment, it was Doronin's turn with the binoculars. He picked up the sprinting figure immediately—the streaming raincoat, the desperate speed of the running woman. But it was only when she came to a panting halt at Morozov's front door that he got a good look at her.

"It's her! Guzman is back! Looks like a scandal brewing, lads!"

Lyubimov snatched up a second pair of binoculars and peered at Sofia as she stood by the entry phone, doubled over with a stitch as she punched in an apartment number over and over.

Ears flicked on the loudspeakers. The persistent din of the entry phone rang on and on, unanswered. Morozov's radio played on. The listeners heard a series of footfalls retreating from the kitchen to the study, then silence. A light on the telephone intercept box lit up yellow, then green. A whirring of numbers, which Ears quickly recognized.

"The Aquarium. He's calling his own office."

The line connected on the first ring.

"Daria Antonovna?" Morozov's voice sounded even squeakier when relayed through the built-in microphone of the phone intercept relay. "So glad to find you on duty today. Could you pass the word to my secretary that I will not be at work tomorrow—or this coming week, in fact. I had an unexpected appointment with my cardiologist this morning. I am afraid I have been ordered to rest at home. Total bed rest. Thank you, Daria Antonovna. No, nothing, thank you. Lyudmila Alexeyevna is looking after me very well. Goodbye."

Ears scribbled a note in the log and stretched. "So the old man had some bad news from the doc. Maybe he'll drop dead and we can get on with something more interesting."

Lyubimov shot him a disapproving look.

"His girlfriend sure seems upset. Oh—she's up. There she goes. On the move again."

All three KGB men watched as Sofia straightened, rubbed the stitch in her side, and limped away from Morozov's door in the direction of the Boulevard Ring.

6

USS Bache, *Sargasso Sea*
Sunday, 28 October 1962, 03:15 EDT / 10:15 Moscow Time

Three hours before dawn, and the Caribbean night was at its darkest. To the east and west, Billings could see the running lights of the USS *Cony* and *Beale*. He glanced at his watch, counting down the seconds. The sharp bang of the depth-charge launchers came almost on the second. Billings made a crooked grin. Kimble was keeping the deck crews tight on their fifteen-minute signaling schedule.

"Captain?" The comms officer held out a printout from the new-fangled scrambler telex. "New orders from the *Randolph*, sir."

The Soviet boats had turned, just as the Admiral had intended. Now they seemed to be retracing their steps, heading almost due north, away from the pursuing destroyers and toward the carrier. Now it was time to commence the second phase of the operation. Encircle, close, and force the submarines to the surface.

And don't let the Red bastards slip away.

7

Bolshaya Sadovaya Street, Moscow
Sunday, 28 October 1962, 10:15 Moscow Time / 03:15 EDT

The courtyard of Bolshaya Sadovaya Street 25 appeared ordinary enough—oddly run-down and shoddy in contrast to the building's grand pre-Revolutionary facade. At least four doorways opened onto a main courtyard accessed through three archways, front, back, and side. Eight stories, at least four apartments per story. Vasin grunted in professional approval. A well-chosen place for a dead-letter box, busy enough with the comings and goings of the residents to make a stranger unremarkable, but at the same time not a truly public space where a drop could be swept into the trash by some overzealous cleaner or citizen.

Vasin quickly found the right entranceway. The combination door lock had long ago succumbed to metal fatigue and disintegrated. He trotted up the steps, glancing upward at every landing to check for observers. The staircase was wide enough to spot anyone coming up or down. Again, smart.

There was indeed a trash receptacle on the second landing—a hinged metal container below and an ashtray built into the iron arch above, which overflowed with crushed-out butts of cheap workers' cigarettes. The container below was almost empty, and Vasin tossed the greasy packet of Kazbek into it, taking care to crease it so that the microfilm canister would not fall out.

Vasin hesitated for a long moment. As long as he didn't move, he told himself, no doors would burst open, no stream of policemen would come stomping up the stairs. He glanced out onto the courtyard from the wide, multipaned window of the landing—damn, this was a perfect place for a dead-letter drop—and saw nothing but a shuffling elderly man and a pair of young women steering a pram.

Maybe *too* perfect?

Vasin fought back the paranoia and launched himself down the stairs two at a time. The last thing he wanted was to find himself face-to-face with some American spy coming to pick up Morozov's message. At the bottom he noticed a service door tucked behind the elevator shaft which led into the next-door courtyard.

Vasin was alone, and somehow still free. At least until Orlov tracked him down.

8

Pioneers' Ponds, Moscow
Sunday, 28 October 1962, 10:15 Moscow Time / 03:15 EDT

The chill of the cooling sweat on her body brought Sofia clarity as she walked aimlessly through the backstreets behind Pioneers' Ponds. For the last fourteen hours, Vasin's and Morozov's words had seemed to scroll in front of her brain like the subtitles of a foreign film—clear enough in their meaning, but their real significance hidden from her. All through her silent, tense trolleybus ride from the clinic alongside Morozov and during the minutes she had sat mute in his kitchen while he banged about in his study, her mind had been a blank white balloon. She hadn't even dared to move her head too suddenly lest it burst. Don't move, don't speak, don't think. Maybe this will all disappear.

But it hadn't disappeared. Instead, it was the Morozov she thought she knew so well who had vanished. The dashing and amusing man, the persistent and persuasive officer whom she had once admired— whom she had considered taking to her bed—was gone. His face and body seemed the same, but they were inhabited by a different being. His stammering excuses, his promise to explain sometime later. This was a frightened, floundering man she no longer recognized. It had been like seeing a loved one dead.

Sofia had walked to the rendezvous with Vasin like a clockwork doll, nearly paralyzed by nerves. Why had she stopped to open the envelope? Its eerie message—the exact place she had been standing—was like some kind of evil juju let out of its confinement, infecting her. Now the cathartic exhaustion of her desperate run, the biting pain in her ankles, had burst the balloon in her head. She inhaled deeply, head back, watching the scudding autumn clouds.

What had she wanted to say to Morozov? Demand his promised

explanation, then try to believe it? Denounce him as a traitor to the Motherland—or assure him that he was now saved, the bargain with Vasin complete? To slap the man's face, or embrace him?

All of those things.

But the fucking coward hadn't even opened the door. She'd helped save his worthless, liar's hide and he hadn't even let her in. Just as Morozov had suddenly seemed a stranger to her, Sofia abruptly failed to recognize her previous self. The girl who fancied a life with a globe-trotting older man. The girl who'd enjoyed flirting with a colonel who knew important people, important secrets. But more, she found herself baffled as to why she had allowed herself to get dragged into this whole dirty game. Stealing papers for Morozov. Showing the papers to Vasin. She hated all the men who had charmed, cajoled, or threatened her into doing this thing or that thing.

Sofia felt a powerful need to cleanse herself, an almost physical desire to rid herself of all the filth and the lies and deceit. And she needed to know the truth about Morozov from the only man who could confirm or deny his story about working as a double agent for the good of the Motherland. She walked another block, turning an idea over in her mind. The more she considered it, the more firm became her belief that there was only one thing she could do. On Tverskoi Boulevard, she found a pay phone and dialed a number from memory. As the call connected, Sofia closed her eyes. If she'd been a believer, what she was doing would be called praying. Praying for clarity, and absolution. Above all, praying to have the world that had flown so suddenly into a million shards put back together again for her.

"Hello? Put me through to the office of Director Serov, please."

9

Nikitskiye Vorota, Moscow
Sunday, 28 October 1962, 10:32 Moscow Time / 03:32 EDT

The green Army UAZ jeep pulled up at the street corner where Sofia was waiting a little more than fifteen minutes after she had made her call. Sofia had allowed numbness and shock to deepen and envelop her in a soft, anesthetic cloud. The passing cars and trolleybuses blurred into a moving kaleidoscope of muted urban color. As if in a dream, she crossed the road and stood by the statue of the mathematician Klimint Timiryazev at the head of Tverskoi Boulevard. The trigonometric diagrams that illustrated the plinth were as completely, comfortingly incomprehensible to her as hieroglyphs. She was returned to reality only by the soft touch of a hand on her arm. Startled, she pulled away—but relaxed when she saw a green camouflage uniform with a major-general's star on the lapels, red staff officer tabs, and General Alexei Zimin's ruggedly handsome, familiar face.

"Sofia Rafaelovna? Come with us, please."

"Is Morozov a spy?" was all she could think to say. And when that elicited no response, she said it again. "You don't understand? Oleg Morozov—could he be a *spy* . . ."

Unresisting, she allowed herself to be led to the jeep, which unceremoniously pulled a wide U-turn across the intersection of Nikitskiye Vorota and sped toward Bolshoi Znamensky Lane.

10

Greek Embassy, Moscow
Sunday, 28 October 1962, 11:32 Moscow Time / 04:32 EDT

Kostas Evlogimenou ambled along the sidewalk to the Greek Embassy on Leontyevsky Lane, nodding at the policeman who guarded the double gates of the stable block as he fumbled with the key to the gate. Inside the courtyard he hesitated. Maria, the Ambassador's plump cook, had spotted him from the back window and was gesturing at Kostas to come inside for their customary cup of midmorning tea. Perhaps she'd made some sweets for him. Kostas could think of no reasonable way to refuse, and turned toward the back door of the mansion that led to the kitchens.

It was only forty minutes later that Kostas, fortified by tea and a plateful of *khvorost* sugar-dusted pastries, made it to his den. It was a small, well-heated space which had once served as the pre-Revolutionary mansion's tack room, now hung with fan belts and the triangular decals of Greek football teams. Picking up the prewar, nonsecure phone that hung on the wall, he dialed a Moscow number.

11

US Embassy, Moscow
Sunday, 28 October 1962, 12:12 Moscow Time / 05:12 EDT

In his office above the garage block of the American Embassy on Novinsky Boulevard, Jim Delaney had just decided that he'd had about enough of Kostas Evlogimenou's bullshit. Unlike Kostas's cozy tack room, Delaney's workstation was a drafty shed of a place thrown together by a gang of drunken bricklayers sometime in the late '20s. The slapdash beige-painted brickwork annoyed him several times an hour—as did the shoddy iron-framed windows and the coughing, leaky radiators. From downstairs came the sound of the in-house mechanics trying to revive the carburetor on one of the Embassy Buicks—a confident roar on starting up, followed by three or four choking revs, then a spluttering into silence. The smell of the exhaust from the crappy Moscow gasoline that had probably gummed the carburetor in the first place drifted up the stairs into Delaney's office.

That's my cue, thought Delaney, glancing at the battered wood-cased prewar Chicago-made clock that had been handed down from office to office until its final exile in the Embassy's garages. Late is late. He stood, gathering the daily reports from three other CIA gofers—mostly, like Kostas, technical employees of other Western Embassies—who had managed to phone in their reports on time. The boys over in the Chancery would be getting impatient for lunch, too. Pulling on his coat and gloves, Delaney wondered if the Soviet cooks in the canteen would manage to ever finally produce a Philly cheese steak worth the name.

As he hauled the door closed, Delaney's phone rang. He hesitated, half closing his eyes in exasperation. Cursing, he returned to his desk and snatched up the receiver.

"Delaney? Kostas, your friend and ally here." No point in concealing their identities on an open line. Just one Embassy garage manager calling another. "Listen. Was just over at State Garage Number Six—guys there said they'd got hold of some spare Volga parts. Interested? They have one left wing mirror, and a right headlight. Something you guys need?"

Delaney scribbled down the coded message. Garage Number 6. The location on Pioneers' Ponds the bosses had been asking about. The one with zero reported activity for all the months Delaney had been on station. And though Delaney didn't know—didn't want to know—the exact meaning of the code, he'd been on the job long enough to guess that "headlight" meant emergency.

"Sure. Thanks, Kostas. Let me check with the boys in blue downstairs. Right back atcha—gimme maybe a coupla hours."

Delaney hurried across the rain-slicked garage forecourt to the squat bulk of the main Embassy building.

12

US Embassy, Moscow
Sunday, 28 October 1962, 12:22 Moscow Time / 05:22 EDT

"Sir—I think you need to see this."

The officer who hovered in the doorway of Moscow CIA station chief Wallace Baker's office was Richard Jacob, the new boy.

"Something urgent, Jacob?"

"We picked up an emergency drop signal this morning, sir. Response marked for your immediate attention."

Baker swiveled his banker's chair upright and snatched the scrap of paper from the junior officer's hand. Garage Number 6 was HERO's apartment. HERO had never given any emergency signal—at least not on Baker's watch. Could be a false alarm, of course. Happened often enough with the window codes. But false alarm or not, the dead-letter box needed to be serviced, immediately. And that would be damned hard. The Sovs had been keeping close tabs on his men for months, sticking to every American diplomat who ventured into town like shit to a blanket.

"Goddamn. Operational officers' meeting. In the Bubble. Fifteen minutes."

Of Baker's CIA staff, only he and his deputy station chief had been cleared to handle HERO intelligence. Too risky to send anyone who actually knew the importance of HERO—much less his identity—into town to clear a dead-letter box. Not counting the analysts in the back room or the small army of outside helpers like Kostas, that left just eight staff CIA officers available for operations. Baker knew that not one of them could truly pass for a Soviet citizen without a good deal of luck.

Baker surveyed the faces around the table in the basement conference room. The walls were lined with sound-baffling foam surrounded by a steel mesh designed to block all listening devices. Or so Baker fervently hoped.

"We're going to pull a rush, gentlemen. Too bad it's been a while since we practiced it. But you still remember the drill. You're all heading out of the Embassy within a ten-minute window. Six of you in two cars. First team, head toward Smolenskaya, then U-turn to Mayakovskaya. Team two, head toward Barrikadnaya and pull a U-turn at the zoo. I want you all dropped off at separate metros. The other two, just walk. I want all of you dry-cleaning your asses off for two hours. You head out between 1255 and 1305. Maybe we'll catch the goons changing shifts. Soon as you pick up a tail, keep 'em busy even if you can't shake 'em. Act suspicious as all hell. Ask passersby the time. Drop cigarette packets and matchboxes. Newspapers. Buy stuff. Leave it on park benches. Chat up girls at the bus stop. Whatever it takes to get maximum manpower scrambled to work out what the hell you're doing. I need anyone who thinks they're clean to call in by 1500. Pay phone call to the garage. Usual code word. Memorize the drop address, the drop signal, and the danger signals."

Baker passed around a card with the details written on it in pencil. Soundlessly, the station chief pointed out the spot on a map of central Moscow that lay under glass on the conference table.

In the event, Jacob was the only CIA man who succeeded in shaking the *kontora*'s surveillance. He made his call a couple minutes after three. Delaney and Baker had been sitting, smoking nervously, by the garage phone. Two rings, hang up, then two more, hang up again. Jacob's voice sounded slurred as he asked for Maya—the name that after much trial and error had been chosen as the easiest for an officer to pronounce within earshot of Russians without sounding too foreign. Someone else was likely waiting impatiently to use the pay phone.

"Mayi net" was Baker's equally gruff response. He repeated it for

emphasis. Which meant, "You're up, kid." As he replaced the receiver, Baker offered a silent prayer. Jacob. The most conspicuously Yankee-looking of all his staff, the one who still had to be reminded that his goofy, all-American grin gave him away on a Moscow street as surely as a Stars and Stripes lapel badge. Pale and lanky, Jacob hadn't made Skull and Bones at Yale for some reason, if Baker recalled correctly. Nonetheless the Agency had taken the kid on. Probably because his father was some state senator from Connecticut. He had some Russian-language skills, at least. And no conspicuously dumb ideas in his head that Baker knew of. Please God, prayed Baker. Make everyone Jacob meets on his way to the drop behave like a true Muscovite asshole and wipe that grin off the kid's face.

13

B-59, Sargasso Sea
Sunday, 28 October 1962, 05:22 EDT / 12:22 Moscow Time

For the last hour, the ghostly noise had existed on the edge of Arkhipov's consciousness, both heard and unheard. Now a sudden swirl of the deep-water currents brought the sound loud and clear. Not a small metallic ding like the noise of the sonar buoys, nor a rolling explosive rumble from the depth charges, but a deep, ringing impact like the tolling of a vast underwater bell. Every officer on board knew the sound from their training. The active sonar of a warship, transmitted at full blast at short range and tightly focused on their submarine.

The B-59's sonar room had been plotting the American destroyers closing in on them for seventeen hours, their zigzag paths converging inexorably on the boat as she crept northward. The noise of the depth charges had also grown perceptibly louder. Now three of the Yankee warships were within two thousand meters, all lashing the B-59 with their sonar and the nerve-shredding explosions that came like clockwork every quarter hour.

As Arkhipov entered the control center, Savitsky was barking savagely into the intercoms.

"Comrade Chief Engineer—what's our battery power?"

The officer's answer came as a flat monotone.

"Just under eight percent, sir."

They'd been forced to dive with the batteries only 35 percent charged. They'd dashed at half-power for the first hour, running the batteries down by another 10 percent. Ever since, the boat had been crawling along at just three knots, eking out every watt. In theory, they could continue like this for maybe a day more, creeping back and forth under the intense sonar gaze of their pursuers. But Arkhipov knew—and Savitsky knew—that escape was no longer an option.

The Captain straightened, ignoring the anxious stares of the command center crew. He seemed to withdraw into himself, his eyes glazed. Then he flicked on the intercoms once more.

"Blinov. Maslennikov. Report to my cabin immediately."

Senior Lieutenant Georgy Blinov: "the Nursemaid," as the junior officers had nicknamed him. Blinov was the weapons officer whose sole responsibility was the nuclear T-5 torpedo. Nothing else. He even slept alongside the thing in the relative silence of the forward torpedo compartment, the most spacious and quietest part of the ship.

"Captain—what are you doing?"

Savitsky ignored Arkhipov and ducked into the hatchway that led to the second compartment. Arkhipov followed him forward along the narrow central corridor that led past the radio room, the officers' mess, and the sonar room. When they reached the Captain's cabin, Blinov was already waiting. The young officer was flushed with the heat and he swayed a little, but his face shone with a sense of occasion. Blinov saluted the commander smartly. Savitsky returned the salute, slid open the door, and waited for the pudgy Maslennikov to make his way forward.

Arkhipov, the Political Officer, and the Weapons Officer crammed side by side into the Captain's bunk. Savitsky himself remained standing, sliding the door closed behind him. He addressed them like schoolboys.

"We will assemble and arm the special weapon." Savitsky stilled Arkhipov's objection with an imperious hand. "Which is an operational order in line with our orders to prepare the ship for full battle readiness in the event of hostile engagement with the enemy. I quote the exact wording of our battle orders for your benefit, Captain Arkhipov. And Comrade Maslennikov will confirm I am acting correctly. He and I reread the instructions together."

Arkhipov turned to the Political Officer. Maslennikov looked sheepishly down at his hands and nodded in confirmation.

"So—Blinov," continued the skipper. "You will commence assembly and report to me when we are ready to arm."

Savitsky stooped to unlock his personal safe, retrieved a heavy, waterproof-canvas document case, and broke its wax seal. Slapping it on the table, he slipped out a manila envelope containing a freshly printed stack of small cardboard folders. They contained the combinations to the weapons lockers that housed the separate components of the special weapon's warhead. Wordlessly, he handed the folders to Blinov. The kid's face was ashen. But he stood to accept the codes, saluted, and squeezed out of the tiny cabin, leaving the three senior officers alone. Arkhipov waited until the door slid shut before speaking.

"Valentin Grigorievitch—this is madness."

Savitsky's face convulsed in a tic before he answered.

" 'If they slap you on the left cheek, do not let them slap you on the right one.' Do you remember those words, Comrade?"

Arkhipov's answer was a grudging whisper.

"I do."

"Our young comrade was not present at the commanders' briefing." The Captain turned to the Political Officer. "Those, Maslennikov, were the instructions of Admiral Vitaliy Fokin, first deputy head of the Soviet Navy, the day before our flotilla sailed. October second, 1962, should you wish to record that in your own logbook. And may I add another quote? 'I suggest to you, commanders, that you use the nuclear weapons first, and then you will figure out what to do after that.' That was Vice Admiral Rassokha, chief of staff of the Northern Fleet, at the same briefing. Am I telling lies, Vasily Alexandrovich? Making things up? Did I misunderstand something about our orders?"

Savitsky was leaning forward over the table now, the heels of his hands dug into the beveled wooden edge and his face insolently close to Arkhipov's.

"You misunderstood one thing, Captain. And that is that if the Americans had wanted us dead, we'd have been at the bottom of the sea right now. They are *not attacking*."

"Are they not? Dropping depth charges is not an attack?"

"At this range and depth? Come on, Valentin Grigorievitch. We both know the tolerances of this boat. A fully armed American depth charge is deadly to a thousand-meter range. Dangerous at two thousand. And they've dropped, what, sixty so far? And yet we live."

Savitsky straightened, closed his eyes, and took a couple of deep breaths.

"I see, Comrade Captain. We wait until the Americans are right on top of us, until our hull cracks and the boat fills with high-pressure water and we all take our last, desperate lungful of air. *That* is the moment we know we are under attack?"

Maslennikov cleared his throat, softly.

"Comrade Captains? I believe that Blinov should be ready for us now."

Savitsky turned, opened the sliding door with a savage swipe, and strode forward in the direction of the main torpedo compartment with Maslennikov in tow. Arkhipov lingered a moment before ducking into his own cabin, directly opposite the Captain's. He opened his personal locker. Inside hung his number one uniform, his leather service belt, and his Makarov automatic in its leather holster. Arkhipov looked at it for a long moment, then fought down his crazy thought. The pressure hull of B-59 was twenty-four millimeters thick. A stray nine-millimeter pistol round could not, of course, punch through it. But the pressure of ten atmospheres would concentrate on the weak spot and . . . Arkhipov shook his whole body at the insanity of the idea of taking his pistol. The heat, the detonations, and the inexorable sonar lashing were playing tricks with his mind. He followed the Captain into the torpedo room.

14

KGB Headquarters, Moscow
Sunday, 28 October 1962, 12:25 Moscow Time / 05:25 EDT

Vasin eased his tinny Moskvich into first gear and nosed out of the crowded Lubyanka parking lot. The attendant would doubtless call in his departure to Orlov's office. But Vasin needed to be mobile. His plan was executed—at least all that depended on him. What the Americans would do next was out of his hands. Now he had an overwhelming urge to be alone, and to get away from this cursed city. From the *kontora* and all its works. And if it came to it, away from incoming American ballistic missiles.

At the end of Pervomaiskaya Street, he pushed the accelerator all the way to the floor. The engine whined in protest as the little car gathered speed in the fast lane of the Garden Ring. On the downslope of the Crimean Bridge, his speedometer hit sixty kilometers an hour. He had to swerve to avoid the rear of a wide-swinging trolleybus as he sped toward Paveletsky Station, and at Taganskaya he raced a red light, squealing onto the intersection right under the nose of a Kamaz truck. The speed concentrated his mind and banished all other thoughts as he flew onward. It was only when he was forced to stop at the junction of Tsvetnoi Boulevard that he released his grip on the steering wheel and forced himself to breathe slowly and deeply. In a couple of blocks he would be back at Mayakovskaya. His illusion of flight had brought him right back to where he had begun.

Think, Vasin.

He shifted down into first gear and moved off with the traffic. In a moment he would pass Bolshaya Sadovaya 25. Slowing to a crawl and moving into the right-hand lane, Vasin stole a glance at the non-descript building. What was he hoping to see? Or afraid to see? Traffic and pedestrians were passing by as normal. Vasin felt his urge to flee subside, only to be replaced with a swell of clamoring questions and jeopardies that rose like tidewater.

First—Sofia. The agitation in her eyes as she'd flung Morozov's envelope was worrying. What would she do next? Run to Morozov? Or someone else?

Vasin bumped the Moskvich into a sidewalk parking spot by the Barrikadnaya metro station, just opposite one of the largest banks of public telephones in central Moscow. He found an empty booth immediately, and dialed the dormitory block where Sofia lived. The shared phone on Sofia's landing rang out. Vasin dialed and redialed. An elderly man who had been waiting for the phone booth began to admonish him by tapping with a coin on the window, but Vasin ignored him.

Another call to the building's concierge got him through to some evil matron who told him to mind his own business. Vasin threw down the receiver with a loud curse. It was still four and a half hours until his appointed call to Tokarev, and he did not dare call the man at home.

Vasin pushed his way out through the sprung door of the phone booth. He slammed the car door behind him and forced himself to think through his options. For a moment he considered parking near the dead-letter drop and watching for a pickup, but quickly dismissed it as too risky. The Americans would doubtless case the area before collection, and a man sitting in a stationary car watching the building could scare them off. And in any case the place had too many entrances to be surveilled by a single watcher.

Easier to tick off the things Vasin couldn't do until he knew that his plan had worked. Go home. Go to the office. See anyone who knew him.

That left only Sofia to deal with. The woman was loose in Moscow. If her fear had turned to fury at Morozov's betrayal, the danger to his plan would be clear and present. Vasin had seen her anger before, the visceral spitting rage. He had to find her, talk the edge off her nerves. Stop her from doing something stupid—like going to her bosses. Or the KGB. Unless, Vasin realized with cold, dawning fear, she'd done that already.

15

B-59, Sargasso Sea
Sunday, 28 October 1962, 05:32 EDT / 12:32 Moscow Time

The forward torpedo compartment in B-59's nose was, after the diesel engine room, the largest space on the submarine. It had to be, in order to accommodate the racks of six-meter-long T-5 torpedoes arranged on both sides of a narrow passageway between the weapons, six torpedoes on each side. At the front of the compartment were two vertical rows of three torpedo tubes, each steel breech door decorated with a large red star. Each tube was big enough for a man to crawl inside. Five were already loaded with conventional torpedoes. One—the middle port tube—remained empty to allow the unhindered loading of the special weapon.

At first glance the nuclear T-5 looked like the other torpedoes—except that its nose was painted in distinctive yellow and black checkerboard squares. Like the rest, most of the weapon's length was given over to tanks of compressed oxygen and kerosene, the propellant that would drive its twin oppositional propellers for up to ten kilometers toward its target. But the front portion, a meter and a half long, lay open. Arkhipov approached as if the thing were some kind of sacred object. He'd never seen the inside of an atomic bomb.

The warhead itself was surprisingly tiny: a half-meter-wide steel sphere nestled in the nose of the torpedo. Arkhipov knew from his briefings in Moscow that the thing contained a hollow ball of highly enriched uranium surrounded by shaped TNT charges. As Arkhipov, Maslennikov, and the Captain approached, Blinov was concentrating on attaching a series of wires to the warhead, tapping each one to a polished steel knob on the rack that held the torpedo before he pressed it home. The Lieutenant turned to his superiors as he worked.

"Got to ground these cables to make sure there's no residual charge in the wires!" Blinov chirped, composing his face respectfully. "Or else there could be unpleasantness."

Holy Jesus, Arkhipov thought. The boy is arming a nuclear warhead as though he's assembling a tractor engine.

"And now—the detonator battery. Comrade Maslennikov—a hand?"

With difficulty, Blinov and the Political Officer hoisted a heavy, half-meter-long battery array into the final remaining space in the torpedo. The apparatus clanged painfully several times against the steel housing before they got it in. With exaggerated caution, Binov wiped off the four connectors on his overalls and grounded them against the racks one by one before attaching them to the detonator control. As soon as the last was connected, a green light blinked on. Satisfied, Blinov produced a voltmeter from his pocket and carefully checked that every circuit was at zero before declaring his work done.

"Comrade Commanders. Reporting: special weapon ready to deploy once armed. The firing circuits are ready for testing."

Wordlessly, Savitsky stepped forward and put his left hand on the T-5's casing. With his right, he reached inside his undershirt and pulled out a steel key.

"Your arming key, Maslennikov."

The Political Officer and Arkhipov exchanged a glance before Maslennikov obeyed, pulling the chain from around his neck and handing his own key to the Captain. Savitsky took the two halves and fitted them together to make a complete key, then slipped it into a slot on the detonator. He paused a moment to shoot a withering look at Arkhipov, then turned the arming mechanism. The indicator light on the detonator turned from green to red. Involuntarily, all three men stepped back from the weapon as though it were electric.

"Firing circuit functional. Thank you, Captain." Blinov's voice trembled a little with excitement. Savitsky leaned forward gingerly, as though putting his hand into a briar bush, then carefully turned and removed the arming key. The indicator flicked back to green. The Captain stepped back and raised his arms to put both key chains over his head.

"Sir? My key?" Maslennikov extended a hand. Savitsky waited a beat before nodding curtly, untangling the chains, and reluctantly handing one of the keys back to the Political Officer.

"Permission to complete final assembly, sir?" Blinov stood at attention, one of the casing plates under his arm. The Captain nodded. Slowly, almost tenderly, Blinov began to carefully screw the casings home.

Arkhipov and Maslennikov stood aside as the Captain stomped out of the torpedo compartment. While the special weapon was being armed, Arkhipov and the seven torpedo-room hands who bunked at the rear of the compartment had watched the process as though bearing witness to some very terrible sacrament. All except Blinov, who had spent years of his life around the special weapon and seemed to treat the machine like a friend, or a lover. The lad seemed unfazed that this was the first time he had ever actually armed a nuclear T-5 for real.

As Blinov worked, Arkhipov fought hard to make himself calm. His mind raced, forcing himself to retrace his training exercises.

A torpedo on the rack is not a torpedo in the tube, he told himself. As a junior officer, Arkhipov had done the loading maneuver so many times that he performed it in his dreams. First, the smooth traverse of well-greased ceiling-mounted gantries into position directly over the weapon. The rumble of the chain loops that led to the overhead winches—every link encased in a ball of rubber to reduce noise as they ran. The slow lowering of the winch hooks to the steel eyes set into the bodies of the torpedoes, then another rumble to hoist them clear of their racks. Five centimeters' clearance, and they should be perfectly aligned with the tubes. A seaman standing by with the meter-long detachable wrench that opened the breech. It took a hard, full-body haul to move the locking mechanism, and another haul to swing open the heavy steel door of the torpedo tube. Then, guiding the torpedo's nose into the breech by hand—an officer's job, because of the risk of crushed fingers. A fiddly business connecting the nose to the protruding thumb of the loading slide, followed by several minutes of hard winching to feed the torpedo into its tube all the way until the loading thumb turned downward at the forward extremity of its chain. Close breech. Flood tube. Trim the boat to compensate for the extra weight of water. Open outer torpedo hatch. And then—finally—the weapons officer's hand would go to the red-painted handle on the starboard side that released compressed air into the tube to eject the torpedo into the water. Arkhipov's own hand had made that hard, backward jerk a hundred times. Suddenly, his thoughts scrolled back a beat.

He had it.

The last bolt fastened, Blinov allowed himself an affectionate pat of his weapon, smoothing the painted steel skin like that of a prize animal. As at every moment of his waking life on board, Arkhipov felt the eyes of other men on him.

"Good job, Lieutenant." Arkhipov clapped Blinov on the shoulder, paused, and turned confidingly to Maslennikov. "You didn't see the film, did you, Ivan?"

Maslennikov's eyes went wide at being addressed informally by his first name.

"Er, no, Comrade Captain. Which film?"

"They showed all the commanders a classified reel of the tests of the special weapon. You neither, I guess, Blinov?"

Both of Arkhipov's subordinates were standing at attention now, their faces frozen into exaggerated seriousness by his alarmingly personal tone.

"See, Lieutenant, I was on K-19 when we had the reactor accident. You've probably heard that. There are no secrets on a submarine. Comrade Maslennikov here has heard all my war stories. How the radiation poisoning made the skin of my comrades' hands come off like rubber gloves. How we had to listen to them as they screamed, begging to die—"

"Captain Arkhipov?" interrupted Maslennikov, his voice high with alarm. "Sir, perhaps we could discuss this elsewhere?"

Arkhipov swung his eyes over Maslennikov's shoulder to the torpedo room crew sitting silent and bowed on their bunks, pretending not to listen.

"Terrifying thing, radiation. Invisible. Tasteless. Odorless. Burns a man up from inside. See, Maslennikov, I'm the only man on board this ship that has actually seen what this thing can do to men."

Arkhipov placed a palm on the warm steel casing of the special weapon. He felt the concentrated death inside it emanating like radiating heat.

"Undoubtedly, Captain, the weapons that our scientists have created to defend the Motherland are very terrifying." The Political Officer dropped his voice to a hiss and moved closer to Arkhipov. "Sir! Not in front of the men."

Arkhipov ignored him and switched to his loudest instructor's voice to reach the back of the compartment clearly.

"Well, this weapon, for one, will have to wait for another day to defend the Motherland. Not on this cruise. Sorry, Blinov, if you were waiting to see what she could do. Can you tell me why, Lieutenant?"

"Sir?" The young Weapons Officer sounded disappointed.

"It is too late to fire this torpedo. See, Blinov, there are five enemy destroyers within two thousand meters' range. They have been listening in to our every fart for a day now. And the minute we turn this . . ." Arkhipov took two paces toward the torpedo tube breeches and put his hand on the cock that flooded the tube. "Our American adversaries will hear it. And when we turn this . . ."

Arkhipov shifted his grip to a five-centimeter square knob at the end of a rod that ran the length of the tube to a worm gear that operated the outer torpedo hatches. On a more modern boat like the K-19, all these mechanisms were electric or hydraulic. But apart from the sonar and the newfangled targeting computer, everything on B-59 was still worked the old way—by hand.

"When we turn this they'll definitely hear it. So, well before we get to aim and fire, the Yankees would send us to the bottom of the ocean. Understand? Remember from fleet exercises—we always go in for attacks with the tubes already open. Or we wait with open tubes for our enemy to cross our path. This is the reason why. Noise. Remember that from your tactical training, Blinov?"

"Yes, sir. I remember," stammered the young weapons officer.

"Very good." Arkhipov looked down the length of the compartment. By now all the torpedo room crew were unabashedly staring at him. "Men—don't be alarmed. The weapon has been armed as a precaution only. Captain Savitsky and I will get you all home to your wives and sweethearts safely, all with commendations for your brave service. I promise you that. Glory to the USSR! Glory!"

"Glory! Glory!" The sailors' automatic call-and-response was ragged and uneasy.

"Very good. Carry on, Blinov."

Arkhipov waited until Maslennikov had followed him through the hatch into the central corridor of the officers' quarters before catching the Political Officer's arm and propelling him into his cabin. As Arkhipov slid the door closed behind him, Maslennikov began speaking, his face pale with indignation.

"Vasily Alexandrovich, how could you say such things in front of the enlisted men? I answer for the morale and political consciousness of the crew and I have to tell you that your words . . ."

"Is it not obvious to you, Ivan Semyonovich? I spoke because I do not wish the special weapon to be fired."

"I see that, sir. But you are encouraging sailors to disobey their orders."

"They will not have to disobey orders. That weapon will never be fired. Now give me your arming key."

"Comrade Captain, you know I am forbidden to do that. The senior Party representative on board always has the second arming key. To prevent the special weapon being used contrary to the instructions of the Party."

"You heard me back there. Any attempt to fire a torpedo will result in the total loss of this vessel, as well as our sister ship."

"Sir, with respect, our operational orders give the Captain authority to use the weapon at his discretion."

"Not if an attempt to use it results in our destruction. We do not have orders to commit suicide. Nor to start a nuclear war. Do you want to die, Maslennikov?"

Maslennikov, his uniform shirt soaked in sweat, slumped down on Arkhipov's bunk, his hands wrung together.

"I am ready to die for my country, sir," he replied weakly.

"Commander, this is not a test of your political convictions. We are both loyal Soviet military men. I mean, die senselessly?"

"I do not, sir." The Political Officer's voice was barely a whisper.

"So give me the key. That is an order."

Maslennikov shook his head doggedly, his eyes fixed on his hands.

"I cannot. Sir, only the senior Party representative of the Red Banner Northern Fleet is authorized . . ."

"Oh, for God's sake."

Arkhipov saw that he'd pushed the man far enough. Any more, and Maslennikov would run blabbing to the Captain. Maybe he would do that anyway. Arkhipov sat down on the bunk beside the Political Officer and ran a hand over his perspiring face.

"Of course you are correct, Comrade Commander. Forgive me. We will do everything by the book. Everything. Agreed?"

"Agreed, sir."

"Glory to the Motherland!"

Maslennikov merely nodded. Both men were exhausted. Arkhipov struggled to his feet and made his way aft toward the control center. As he walked, the now-familiar rumble of muffled depth-charge detonations resonated through B-59, followed by the merciless deep gong of the American sonar.

16

GRU Headquarters, Moscow
Sunday, 28 October 1962, 14:30 Moscow Time / 07:30 EDT

"So, to recap, Morozov said nothing to you when he gave you the envelope? Not another word?"

Sofia shook her head. Her eyes were red with tears, and her face flushed with the stuffiness of the overheated office. Opposite her, on the other side of a wide oak desk, Zimin nodded and added a final line to his notes.

"You opened the envelope. It contained a metal canister which you believe to have been microfilm. And a note in Morozov's writing with instructions for a dead-letter drop. Which you passed to this Lieutenant Colonel Vasin."

"That's correct, Comrade General. But sir—you still have not told me whether it's true, what Morozov said. That this was all for you. That all his contacts with the Americans were on General Serov's orders. Please. I have to know."

Zimin pursed his lips and looked closely at Sofia. The woman was clearly no idiot. So how had that fat oaf Morozov ever sweet-talked her into his confidence—maybe even into his bed? Zimin had always taken Morozov for a mediocre yes-man, one of many such toadies that surrounded his boss Serov. But clearly he had underestimated the traitor's powers of persuasion. The Morozov case would be something for the spy manuals one day—the gray man whose carapace of ordinariness hides his malice and skill. It was just a pity that the traitor had chosen such a charming creature for his unwitting victim. Perhaps Zimin might even be able to save her from the wrath of the system. But she would first have to learn the virtue of silence. And she would have to work hard to earn his favor, of course. He curled his thin lips into a regretful smile.

"I am afraid that is classified information, Sofia Rafaelovna."

She looked around the sparsely furnished room. A framed portrait of Lenin hung on one wall above a set of plain Soviet bookshelves stocked with uniform red volumes interspersed with zinc models of tanks and aircraft. The world of high military bureaucracy. Sofia's world, turned suddenly cold. Outside the window, the light was already draining from the day. Silently, a grave young orderly sergeant entered bearing two fresh cups of lemon tea. He leaned confidentially to whisper a message in Zimin's ear, after which the General nodded and stood.

"Lieutenant Guzman. You did well to come to us . . ."

The door opened abruptly as an older man in the uniform of a colonel general of the Soviet Army barged into the room. He was of medium build, a little thick around the belly, and he immediately fixed Sofia with a cold, appraising stare. She knew the face immediately, of course, from the official photographs that hung in her own office. General Ivan Serov was no less stern in real life, and his glare was as hard as a statue's. Sofia stood and snapped into a salute, eyes front.

"At ease, Lieutenant."

Serov's voice was a tossed shovelful of gravel. Zimin silently handed his boss his sheaf of notes. As he read, Serov's whole body seemed, to Sofia, to loosen in his immaculate uniform. When Serov's eyes sought out hers again he seemed suddenly hostile, as though she were his enemy.

"Why did you not come to us immediately when Vasin first approached you?"

Zimin's tone, for the past hour, had been full of encouragement as she had breathlessly spilled her story. Sofia looked in alarm from one man to the other, but found no succor from Zimin in the face of Serov's abrupt anger.

"Sir, I . . ."

The relief that Sofia had felt as she had told her story—most of her story—to the understanding ear of Zimin suddenly twisted into a knot of alarm. How could she tell these men about her brother in Miami? A tangle of unsayable words jammed in her mouth. Only one phrase came out.

"I was scared, sir."

Serov grunted contemptuously. But as he turned to his deputy, Sofia noticed that a muscle in Serov's jaw trembled. As he addressed Zimin, his voice was quavering.

"You think what she says is true?"

Zimin nodded grimly. Serov puffed his cheeks and took a long moment to stare out the window, as though he were performing some complex calculation in his head—or seeking some inspiration in the darkening Moscow sky.

"Devil take that *fucking* man."

Sofia lowered her eyes to the red carpet. It seemed that both men had momentarily forgotten her presence.

"Okay. Looks like we have no choice," Serov continued. "I want them all rounded up. That damn film. Morozov, that fucking *snake*."

Sofia closed her eyes and felt her world lurch into a maelstrom of rushing shapes. Morozov, the snake. Morozov, the traitor.

"And Vasin?" Zimin said the name as though it were sour on his lips.

"*Vasin*." Serov's face contorted into a grimace. "We know who *he* works for. Who's behind this shitshow." He paused and addressed Sofia. "Your man Vasin ever mention a General *Orlov* to you, Lieutenant?"

But Sofia did not answer. Slowly, as though she were about to perform a deep curtsy, she sank to her knees, then crumpled, unconscious, onto the carpet.

17

Malaya Bronnaya Street, Moscow
Sunday, 28 October 1962, 15:44 Moscow Time / 08:44 EDT

When Jacob finally found his way onto Malaya Bronnaya from the maze of backstreets and courtyards behind Herzen Street, he felt almost giddy with relief. He'd been weaving his way across half of Moscow, navigating by intuition, coming up against locked courtyards and dead ends. The crappy Soviet shoes he was wearing rubbed his feet and his cheap rabbit-skin hat was damp with sweat. At least he was sure—pretty sure—that he'd shaken off his tails with a neat dry-clean run through GUM, the cavernous department store on Red Square.

"Mayi net." That told Jacob he had been the only Agency guy to have come out clean—otherwise Baker would have said *"Net Mayi,"* meaning he'd entrusted the job to someone else. Someone more experienced. Jacob was grateful for the gathering late-afternoon twilight. It was the spies' hour before the streetlights went on, and he could relax a little about being spotted—"made" as a foreigner by a staring child or the vigilant eye of some babushka. He was about five minutes from the address, Jacob calculated, and quickened his pace toward Pioneers' Ponds.

A line of shoppers spilled from the door of the butcher shop near the corner of Spirodonovsky Lane, so Jacob tried to cross the street to avoid them. But as he stepped from the sidewalk, a careering military Kamaz truck roared past him, followed by another. As they passed, Jacob noted they were all filled with armed soldiers. The trucks trundled in formation down the side of the Ponds and continued on to the Garden Ring. Jacob hurried on. Only two blocks to go.

18

Garden Ring, Moscow
Sunday, 28 October 1962, 15:44 Moscow Time / 08:44 EDT

Zimin sat in grim silence in the back of his sleek black staff car as it accelerated down the central lane of the Garden Ring, forcing cross-town traffic to a skidding halt. Roaring past the yellow and white bulk of the American Embassy on Novinsky Boulevard, they passed a convoy of three Army trucks bearing the marking of the Tambov Division, all full of young soldiers. They passed the boxy green buildings of the Tunisian Embassy, surrounded by a high wall and topped with radio masts. Zimin remembered that the mansion had once been the residence of Lavrenty Pavlovich Beria, Stalin's last and most ruthless secret police chief.

Beria. The last time that the Soviet Army had meddled in politics had been to remove the monster Beria before he could murder his way to power in the wake of Stalin's death back in '53. It had been Marshal Georgy Zhukov, the Soviet Union's greatest wartime commander, who'd taken action. The story was a whispered legend in the corridors of the General Staff. Zhukov and his most trusted officers had smuggled automatic rifles into the Kremlin under their greatcoats. They surprised Beria in the middle of a Politburo meeting, slapped handcuffs on him, and bundled him down a back staircase. Kidnapped the chief of Soviet State Security, in short. Zhukov had posted soldiers from his personal bodyguard—trusted men who had fought under his command from Stalingrad to Berlin—around the Kremlin palace. They had orders to shoot any of Beria's NKVD men who resisted. Luckily it hadn't come to that. Nearly, but not quite. In a shootout in the corridors of the Kremlin, Zhukov's tiny team would have been quickly outgunned by the secret police who controlled the place.

They'd gagged Beria, bundled him into a car, and covered him in a coat. With Zhukov himself in the front passenger seat, they'd driven out of the Kremlin right under the noses of Beria's own NKVD guards. Drove him to the Tambov Division's headquarters, twelve kilometers outside Moscow. For days they'd actually stood the division on combat alert in expectation of a physical attack by the NKVD's troops.

The only reason a shooting war—Soviet soldier versus Soviet secret policeman—hadn't broken out was that Beria had left no deputy or challenger alive inside his own organization who could have organized a rescue.

Zhukov had pulled off a coup, pure and simple. Sure, he had the backing of most of the key members of the Politburo, Khrushchev among them. And only a man of Zhukov's invincible reputation and energy could have done it.

Within a few days Beria had been quickly tried and shot. In time Khrushchev came to power, because the Army had put him there. And ever since Zhukov's coup, the Army and the KGB had hated each other. No branch more so than the Army's own secret intelligence service, the GRU.

And Serov? Serov had been, as always, on the right side of history. Khrushchev had made him KGB chief in Beria's place—then soon after appointed him across the divide to head the GRU, precisely to tame and subdue the military's spooks.

So what the fuck was Serov playing at now? Zimin was leading a company of Soviet soldiers into a military operation in central Moscow. Their only authority was Serov's spoken order. And their mission? To recover a dead-letter drop that was the only evidence against a traitor to the Motherland. Colonel Oleg Morozov.

Why?

Was Serov protecting his friend Morozov out of loyalty? Fat chance. Zimin knew Serov for a ruthless and unsentimental son of a bitch. To save the GRU the embarrassment of having a traitor in its ranks uncovered by the KGB? Unlikely. Serov couldn't care less about the GRU and its reputation—he was, after all, a lifelong KGB man. To cover his own backside after having unwisely tried to protect Morozov for too long? Now *that* felt closer to the truth.

Zimin had been sent to destroy evidence in a major espionage case in order that his boss could escape punishment for having befriended, then sheltered, a traitor. The next order, Zimin was sure, would be to arrange for Morozov to have a discreet accident. There were GRU labs that specialized in that kind of thing, Zimin knew. Heart attack pills. Seizure-inducing nasal sprays. Serov would want something discreet. Something, naturally, that wouldn't reflect badly on the career of Ivan Serov.

Zimin's car had pulled up on the corner of Malaya Bronnaya and Bolshaya Sadovaya Street. He peered out the window and saw the fresh horizontal chalk mark on the drainpipe of number 25, just as Sofia had described. Five Kamaz trucks were parked by the side of the road up ahead of him, the three subalterns in command standing in a huddle awaiting orders.

Zimin's personal driver looked over his shoulder, expecting an instruction. The General ignored him. The evidence of Morozov's treachery would be destroyed. Then Morozov himself. But what of the three other people who knew? Sofia. The nosy asshole Colonel Vasin. And . . . Zimin himself? Would they all soon also meet with nasty accidents? Zimin knew Serov well enough to imagine how he'd apportion the appropriate death sentences. Sofia—suicide by overdose, leaving a grief-stricken note about being unable to live without her dead lover, Morozov. Vasin, the automobile enthusiast? Crushed by a runaway ZiL truck full of concrete blocks. And General Zimin? Would Serov leave his loyal subordinate alive in gratitude for his discretion and silence? Promote him, perhaps, to the directorship of the Frunze Academy? Or command of an agreeable Soviet military district like the Caucasus?

Serov—grateful? Like hell. Serov would soon find a grave for Zimin, too.

Zimin reached for the door handle, stepped out onto the sidewalk, and summoned the two lieutenants and a captain with an imperious wave. Within a minute 112 soldiers were dismounting from the trucks, shouldering their Kalashnikovs and streaming into the courtyard of Bolshaya Sadovaya Street 25.

19

Bolshaya Sadovaya Street, Moscow
Sunday, 28 October 1962, 15:49 Moscow Time / 08:49 EDT

Jacob checked the rear entrance of the building that opened onto Yermolayevsky Lane. Clear. He crossed the road once more and approached the corner of the Garden Ring. The chalk mark was right there on the drainpipe closest to the street corner. Just ahead he could see a row of military trucks and a huddle of officers conferring. He turned on his heel to avoid attracting attention. Quickening his pace as discreetly as he dared, Jacob hurriedly retraced his steps and entered the archway that led into the back courtyard.

The place was dingy and deserted. A single bare bulb illuminated the doorway of entrance number 2—and indeed, as promised, the combination door lock was broken. Casting a final glance behind him, Jacob slipped inside and began mounting the stairs.

Second floor. Garbage can. Packet of Kazbek cigarettes. Jacob could see it, half-buried in the trash. Before pocketing it, he stopped once more to listen. The usual noises of a Soviet apartment building—discordant music from rival radios, raised voices calling children, a halting piano arpeggio. But then came another, much more alarming noise. The thunder of dozens of pairs of pigskin boots in the courtyard. Shouted orders. The slam as the entranceway door was flung open and a section of soldiers thundered up the concrete stairs.

Jacob had missed the Korean War. Moscow was his first foreign posting. Except for a few rib-cracking forays onto a high school football field, he'd never been in any kind of physical danger before. The imminent prospect of violence seemed too outlandish to fit into his brain. Jacob didn't flee upstairs or dive into the elevator. He simply stood rooted to the spot, watching with fast-diminishing disbelief as a crowd of armed, green-uniformed figures appeared on the stairs. The leading soldier, an athletic young man with officer's stars on his greatcoat, didn't even seem surprised to see him. In a quick, unhesitating movement he crossed the stairwell and slammed Jacob backward, one hand to his throat and the other pinning his right hand to the wall.

"Sergeant! Get the Comrade General here, now!"

20

Bolshaya Sadovaya Street, Moscow
Sunday, 28 October 1962, 15:56 Moscow Time / 08:56 EDT

Zimin mounted the stairs two at a time, pushing past the soldiers who flattened themselves against the walls to allow him space. A single glance at the pale, skinny man who remained pinioned in the grip of a hulking young officer, openmouthed, confirmed Zimin's worst fears.

Despite his shabby Soviet clothes, the man looked wrong. He took a step closer. The suspect smelled foreign. Quite literally. An odor of alien shaving soap, exotic cologne.

An American intelligence officer caught in the act of collecting Morozov's dead-letter drop.

Shit.

Zimin's mind raced. He knew that he could be moments from a career-destroying disaster. What was a team of Soviet infantrymen doing apprehending an American citizen in downtown Moscow? If the man was a CIA spy, he'd most likely be a diplomat. The US Consul would show up. Followed by the KGB, of course, in force. They'd find whatever was in the drop. Question him about how he knew about it . . . A train wreck of truly epic proportions would unfold.

"Stand easy, Lieutenant. Release this citizen. Leave us. All of you."

Zimin kept his eyes on the detained man, fixing him with a furious stare and raising a single finger into their shared line of sight. A silent admonition. Keep your mouth shut, foreigner. Just keep it *shut*.

They stood in silence as the young subaltern led his troops back downstairs.

"*Chto proizkhodit?*" What is going on? The first words out of the spy's mouth told Zimin everything he needed to know. The foreign twang was immediately obvious.

"*Molchat!*" he answered. "Shut up."

Warily keeping half an eye on the American, Zimin glanced into the trash. A packet of Kazbek, again as Sofia had described. He reached in and pulled out the fish oil–stained cardboard packet, rattled it, and rolled a tiny microfilm tube out onto his gloved palm.

Both Jacob and Zimin stared at it. The CIA man began to speak, but Zimin shushed him. So it was real. Zimin held the evidence of Morozov's treachery in his hand. Serov had ordered that the dead-letter drop, and its contents, disappear. Immediately.

But what to do with the American? Jacob's face was blank with incomprehension. Zimin scanned the agent's weak, soft face with contempt, then turned on his heel and descended the now-empty stairwell.

21

Bolshaya Sadovaya Street, Moscow
Sunday, 28 October 1962, 15:59 Moscow Time / 08:59 EDT

By the time Zimin reached the courtyard, the soldiers were meekly filing out of the main archway and lining up to mount their trucks. The three officers hurried them on, evidently keen to get their men off the street. Zimin saw in their eyes that they were nervous, sensing something going on beyond their pay grade. The General called them aside and gave each of them a grave, confiding look.

"You've fulfilled your instructions precisely. I can confide in you that today's operation concerned a matter of the gravest military security. None of you are to mention what occurred here to anyone."

The three young subalterns nodded obediently. Zimin shook their hands, weighing each of them with his eyes. The young lieutenant who had grabbed the spy held the General's hand a fraction longer than strictly appropriate. And was that a spark of complicity in the kid's eye? Of familiarity? Nope. That one was not to be trusted.

"Your names, Comrades?"

A pity, thought Zimin as he walked back to his staff car. They seemed like good lads. But by next week they'd find themselves urgently posted to somewhere very, very distant. Spitzbergen. Norilsk. Chukokta. He hovered on the sidewalk, watching the Army trucks depart. General Zimin caught the eye of his personal driver, who was doubtless reporting on his movements to the boss. In his overcoat pocket, he fingered the tiny tube of metal.

Serov would be expecting a report in person. And the evidence in his hand, as soon as he knew that there was evidence. But at that moment only two people in the world knew what had really just happened on that staircase. Zimin himself. And the American spy.

The dilemma formed itself with diamond clarity in his mind. Give Serov the canister—and set in motion Serov's clean-up operation that would in time doubtless consume him, too? Or . . . he could use the American spy and canister to throw Morozov to the wolves. And with him . . . Serov?

The thought was so electrifyingly dangerous that Zimin shuddered with the enormity of it. But as he turned tail and began to walk back to the building the clarity spread. It was him or Serov. And while there was no way he could take down Serov himself, he knew who could—and would.

The KGB could. Orlov could.

Zimin guessed that the American spy would take the back entrance, just as soon as he'd watched the soldiers departing the courtyard. Rounding the corner of Yermolayevsky Lane, the General broke into a trot. The young American's unmistakable figure was hurrying down the street in the direction of the metro.

"*Stoi!*" Zimin shouted. Wait!

The kid hesitated for a moment, and seemed about to break into a sprint. But the sight of a muscular Soviet general officer jogging down the sidewalk toward him shocked the Yank into immobility. As soon as Zimin caught up with him, he grabbed the kid's coat sleeve.

"Citizen. Wait."

Jacob looked around in panic. At Langley they'd trained him to make as much noise as possible if any attempt was made to kidnap him in a public place. Scream, they'd told him. Shout "AMERIKANSKY DIPLOMAT!" at the top of your voice.

"Come with me, Citizen." Zimin tugged Jacob by the sleeve, but the American refused to budge. Jacob began to croak some words of Russian, but Zimin spun him round and slammed him against the roof of a car. Twisting one arm behind Jacob's back, he grabbed him firmly by the collar of his coat. It had been a while since Zimin had done this kind of thing, but the knack returned quickly. Hustling captured German officers into captivity, somewhere near Breslau back in '44, maybe '45. He kneed Jacob, hard, in the back of the leg to push him off balance and get him walking. As the American boy buckled, Zimin forced him forward, his head deeply bowed and his torso pressed up against the older man's through the force of his twisted arm.

"Let's go," hissed Zimin. "Just walk."

Staggering slightly as he went, Zimin half pushed, half dragged the young American in the direction of Pioneers' Ponds. Jacob was trying to shout "AMERIKANETS!" but Zimin twisted his collar tight in his left fist to strangle the words. The clarity of fear for himself had turned into a kind of adrenaline-fueled recklessness that propelled Zimin forward toward the street corner. His plan, if he could call it that, was desperate. But he needed to get the KGB's attention, and fast. And if the *kontora* had their eye on Morozov, they'd have someone on Pioneers' Ponds watching the bastard's apartment. Zimin had even been to Morozov's place in person. They'd picked Morozov up from Maly Patriarshy Lane 5 often enough for lifts to Serov's dacha. Dropped him off, drunk, after official dinners.

All Zimin needed to do was put himself under the watchers' eyes, draw their attention. Dragging a screaming American diplomat through a public park should do the trick and bring the KGB running. Or so the General fervently hoped.

A startled pair of women shrank out of Zimin's way as he frog-marched his prisoner across the intersection to the entrance of the park that surrounded the Ponds. A policeman stopped in his tracks and called after him, but Zimin silenced the man with a furious glare. The large general's stars on the epaulettes of his overcoat were justification enough—for the moment at least—for his bizarre behavior.

Halfway down the gravel track that ran around the small lake, Jacob stumbled and fell to his knees, nearly taking Zimin with him. The General momentarily loosened his grip on the man's collar, allowing him to holler freely for the first time.

"AMERIKANSKY DIPLOMAT! AMERIKANSKY DIPLOMAT!"

A wide circle of gawkers had formed now around the spectacle. The policeman had plucked up the courage to approach. Zimin hauled his captive to his feet and clamped his gloved hand across Jacob's mouth. But it was clear that the American would not be frog-marched a step further as he deliberately buckled his legs, forcing Zimin to support his full weight.

"Comrade General! Allow me to assist you . . ." The constable put a hand under Jacob's arm—at the same time moving to body-block Zimin's progress toward Morozov's front door. He was just a hundred meters from his target. "What has happened, Comrade General? What has this man done?"

Zimin was about to answer when Jacob bit his hand, hard, so instead he swore furiously. The policeman's face hardened and he reached into his left breast pocket for the police whistle that hung there on a steel chain.

"No! Comrade Constable. Do not . . ."

There was a sudden movement to their right and left. From both ends of the park, two pairs of heavyset men came at them at a run. They wore good civilian clothes, but the authority on their faces was as distinctive as a uniform.

"State Security?" yelled Zimin, releasing Jacob into a collapsing heap and nursing his injured hand. "What the hell took you so long?"

22

US Embassy, Moscow
Sunday, 28 October 1962, 18:30 Moscow Time / 11:30 EDT

"You *lost* a goddam officer?"

Ambassador Foy Kohler's voice was a low, hoarse midwestern drawl. Ignoring the standing instructions against smoking in the Embassy's unventilated Bubble, Kohler lit up a filterless Camel.

"Correct, sir. Agent Dick Jacob was sent to clear an emergency dead-letter drop at three p.m. Never reported back."

Wallace Baker wished his old boss were here, not his son-of-a-bitch replacement. Ambassador Llewellyn Thompson was a gentleman, an old-school State Department professional. But Thompson was in Washington, one of the wise men summoned by Kennedy to guide him though the Cuban storm. The new ambassador, by contrast, was the most undiplomatic diplomat Baker had ever had the misfortune to serve. Kohler was minor Ohio gentry who'd polished his manners interrogating Japanese officers after the war. A dedicated Commie hunter in his time, a McCarthy man to his bones. Kohler seemed to regard career diplomats as sissies—and CIA officers as sneaks.

"This about what I think it's about?" Kohler gestured around the empty room, eyebrows raised.

"Sir?"

"We're alone, here, Baker. You sent your brain trust of kids outta the room. So got to be some eyes-only stuff."

"Yes, Ambassador. It's about Agent HERO."

Just five weeks before, the CIA station chief had briefed Kohler about the agent code-named HERO, immediately after Thompson's departure for Washington. Baker, Kohler, and Baker's deputy were the only three men in the Embassy who knew that HERO existed.

"'The most important and senior Soviet source we have ever had.' Wasn't that what you told me, Baker? 'The intelligence product that offers a vital insight into the inner workings of Soviet military thinking.' *That* guy? Whose spy work is so good that even you don't get to see it? Or me, for that matter. And you don't even know who he really is?"

"Correct, sir. Nobody in-station knows HERO's real identity. We have special protocols for communicating with him, designed by my predecessor. An emergency drop signal was observed at HERO's home this morning. We mobilized every officer . . ."

"Skip the details. Is he blown?"

"Jacob? Yes, I'm assuming at this time that he was caught servicing the dead-letter box."

"Not your goddam kid—he'll show up. I'm talking about HERO."

Kohler fixed his subordinate with a flat stare and took a long drag on his Camel.

"We can't tell, sir."

"You don't know where your officer is. You don't know if your star agent is blown. You know your ass from a hole in the ground, son?"

Baker guessed that the pompous jerk Kohler was no more than ten years his senior. But at least the acting ambassador hadn't called him "boy."

"Sure, I know an asshole when I see one. Sir."

The Ambassador's eyes narrowed dangerously before he cracked a crooked smile. So Kohler was a man who liked to be stood up to. Baker breathed a little easier. But at the same time there was no way that Kohler was going to carry the can for the loss of the best agent the CIA had ever had. Baker would have to weather that shitstorm on his own. He pictured the secure telex in his office, four stories above their heads, frenziedly chattering to life as the word of the disaster spread through the upper levels of CIA headquarters in Langley, Virginia.

"We're gonna need to know how this is playing with the Sovs—if they really do have this HERO guy. Are we looking at a diplomatic showdown? Are they putting Jacob on trial? They likely to put HERO on TV saying how we made him spy on the goddamn Motherland? Or they just gonna hush the whole thing up? Traitor in the top of their defense establishment too embarrassing for the Sovs to go public with?"

The boss might be abrasive, but Baker had to admit that the Ambassador had his brain screwed in right. He'd summarized the options in seconds.

"Too soon to tell, sir. My guess is that they'll keep it quiet. But there's something that worries me more right now."

"Like what the hell was HERO trying to tell us so damn urgently?"

PART SEVEN

THE SOLITARY TRUTH

Only the solitary seek the truth, and they break with
all those who don't love it sufficiently.

BORIS PASTERNAK

1

General Orlov leaned forward in his chair, placed his fingers delicately on his temples, and stared at the tiny steel microfilm canister on the desk blotter in front of him. A stack of enlarged photographic blowups of Morozov's message lay beside it.

On the other side of the desk sat General Zimin, his hands clasped in his lap and his face tight. In two hours' conversation, Orlov hadn't been able to sniff any hint of a trap. Before him sat a man afraid for his life. A man motivated by fear—and hatred for his boss. These were things Orlov could understand. Oh yes. Zimin was well and truly on the *kontora's* hook. And the beauty of it was that this angry, frightened man with his trove of deadly secrets had been led to where he was by Serov's own actions.

"Any word from the Americans?" Zimin's voice was low and hoarse.

Zimin's driver would have called in his boss's absence to his superiors within half an hour. From Orlov's office, Zimin had phoned in a message to Serov's secretary—a confused excuse that the dead-letter drop was empty, but that he was following up an important lead. Even the secretary sounded like she didn't believe a word of it. By now Serov would have worked out that Zimin was off and running. And Serov would guess easily enough to whom Zimin had run.

Zimin had made his choice. His life was Orlov's now.

"We have heard nothing from the Americans through official channels. My guess is that the Embassy began to panic"—Orlov checked his steel commander's watch—"about an hour ago. Now they're working out what to do. First thing they'll do is call the Foreign Ministry. Our people will say they're looking into it. Calling police stations, hospitals, morgues, all the usual nonsense. Once the Americans get really agitated—tomorrow morning—we will tell them that a citizen answering the description of their missing diplomat was detained for breaching the peace. And Mister Jacob will be released with no hard feelings."

Orlov picked up the cardboard Foreign Ministry accreditation card that identified Richard C. Jacob III, born in Hartford, Connecticut, on 2 April 1933, as a second secretary (cultural) at the US Embassy, Moscow.

"It seems our friend dropped his ID in the scuffle. Took our guardians of public order a night to positively identify him."

Zimin nodded sagely.

"Has Jacob identified Morozov yet?"

Orlov didn't answer. The two general officers had, for the last few minutes, been speaking almost as if they were equals, talking through operational details. Sometimes Orlov enjoyed slackening the line a little, letting the hooked fish swim freely. But this soldier Zimin was evidently even stupider than he looked. A useful idiot, but nonetheless an idiot. Of course Jacob wouldn't talk. As an accredited diplomat, he knew he'd be back at the Embassy within hours—a day at the very outside. Especially in the current febrile atmosphere of crisis over that piece of nonsense in the Caribbean. And Jacob knew that he would be on a plane to New York a day or two after that. And what were the chances that a junior American CIA officer knew the real identity of a top-ranking spy inside the Soviet establishment? Zero, if the Americans had the first clue about spycraft. Which, Orlov had to admit, they clearly did, given that they'd been able to run Morozov undetected for so long.

Not that that mattered, of course. Orlov had already conceived a contingency plan. Not one he felt the need to share with the GRU general who sat opposite him.

Zimin was a man not used to having his questions ignored. Orlov's silence deepened his humiliation and his sense of powerlessness. But he pressed on.

"Do you have Morozov safely in custody?" Zimin leaned forward confidentially. "You know—Serov has friends everywhere. You never know what he might do. To stop Morozov talking about, you know—"

Orlov stood abruptly, cutting off Zimin midsentence, and began gathering the evidence into a box file.

Oh yes. Morozov was safe. Orlov had made very sure of that. No normal booking and fingerprinting procedure for Morozov. The traitor was, at that moment, cooling his heels in the Lubyanka's most remote and private prison wing. Two trusted Special Cases officers sat in his cell to watch him—and each other. Two more armed men guarded the prison door. For good measure, Orlov had chosen a cell with a solid steel fitting for a padlock, installed for the most special and personal prisoners of the late and unlamented boss, Lavrenty Pavlovich Beria. Only Orlov had the key. But again—that wasn't something this fool Zimin needed to know.

"And what about Sofia Guzman? And your man? This Vasin character?"

Really, thought Orlov irritably, Zimin was too much. "This Vasin character"—the man whom Zimin had abducted and interrogated? Did this moron really imagine that Orlov didn't know? Men should know when they're on someone else's hook, and summon the sense to shut up. Orlov pondered whether it was worth bothering with a cutting response. Ever cautious, he chose icy courtesy.

"I imagine that Comrade General Serov is keeping Sofia Rafaelonva close. Certainly, we have not been able to find her at home or at work. So we can assume that she's"—Orlov pulled a taut little smile as he searched for the appropriate word—"she's become cannon fodder. The dross of history, you might say. She need no longer concern us. She knows too much for Serov's comfort. Therefore, she is gone. For all practical purposes."

"And Vasin?"

Here Orlov's smile snapped shut, like a trap.

Vasin.

Now Vasin was definitely Orlov's personal problem.

2

B-59, Sargasso Sea
Sunday, 28 October 1962, 12:30 EDT / 19:30 Moscow Time

As Arkhipov swung through the hatch to B-59's rear torpedo compartment, he immediately had to steady himself against the bulkhead and take a deep breath. The air was fetid, humid, and hot—and clearly dangerously low on oxygen. Fifty-two enlisted men lived in a space not much longer than a Moscow bus, cramming by turns into twenty-six bunks arranged in stacks of four along the length of the compartment. Some men slept. Others lay on their bunks, playing checkers on cardboard boards or flipping listlessly through well-thumbed magazines. A few were finishing the remains of their evening meal—crackers and tinned corned beef, washed down with tepid tea and spoonfuls of jam. It had been a day since the men had eaten hot food, since no electricity could be spared to power the galley's stoves. For the same reason the air-conditioning fans ran for only a few minutes every hour to ventilate the crew's quarters. The place was eerily quiet. The usual droning thrum of the three propeller shafts that ran under the steel floor was reduced to a slow-turning whine from just one. And there was none of the usual chatter from the crew.

"At ease, men!"

The petty officer who served as compartment chief was halfway down the space handing out fresh underpants and cotton shirts to the men while a seaman followed him collecting armfuls of dirty linen, wet as dishrags, into a canvas bag which would be jettisoned into the sea. There was no laundry on a Soviet submarine. The chief straightened and saluted.

"Sir!"

"All well?"

"Morale and battle readiness excellent, Comrade Captain!"

The formulaic response told Arkhipov nothing. But the men's eyes did. They followed him as he moved down the compartment like iron filings drawn to a magnet. Scattered among the bunks, Arkhipov saw the distinctive green wrappers of Clumsy Bears candy from the Political Officer's personal supply—evidently Maslennikov's attempt to cheer the crew. Many lay uneaten, dribbling molten chocolate on the sheets. A bad sign, when the men ignored prized treats.

It had been nearly seven hours since Arkhipov's doom-laden lecture in the forward torpedo room about how close they were to destruction. But news had obviously traveled the intervening sixty meters into the ship's tail—carried by the crew changing watches and by orderlies who ferried their messmates' rations in large, stacking aluminum tins back and forth from the galley. In the men's nervous stares, he felt the questions they dared not ask.

There are no secrets on a submarine.

When he reached the end of the compartment, Arkhipov faced the four rear torpedo tubes. His back to the crowd of sailors, his thoughts returned to K-19. The awful hours of waiting as the doomed, desperate engineering crew worked to fix the reactor leak. The panic that flickered and flared up and down the ship like an electric circuit burning up. The fear of how quickly discipline could dissolve that had made K-19's captain order all the weapons on board collected and thrown overboard, keeping only a few for himself and the senior officers.

Maslennikov was right. It had been reckless for Arkhipov to speak of a submarine being sent to the bottom in front of the crew. He had jeopardized the only things that kept order among seventy-eight men packed in a sixty-meter space—rigid hierarchy and faith in their commanders. But what choice did Arkhipov have? If it came to a showdown with Savitsky, he needed the crew on his side.

Arkhipov turned back to face the compartment. He felt himself almost swooning in the sticky heat. Over the last day, the enlisted men and warrant officers had all been maintaining their rotation of four-hour watches—sleep, duty, rest and cleaning, duty. But Arkhipov and the other senior officers had been up since they had been forced to dive at noon the previous day—more than twenty-four hours ago. Did he dare catch some shut-eye?

"Let's get those air-conditioning fans switched on for you, lads."

Stumbling as he went, Arkhipov made his way forward to the electric engine room, where the single crawler motor chugged along steadily. Most of the battery indicator dials were on zero, with just half a dozen of the forty cells showing some juice. Maybe half a day's more power left. He continued through the silent diesel room, the engine control room, the warrant officers' quarters, and entered the command center. The six crewmen in the space stood hushed. At the forward end, Savitsky was slumped back on his commander's chair, his head leaning on the steel bulkhead. He was unshaven and his uniform overalls stained with grime. And he was snoring loudly.

Arkhipov ducked between the steel columns of the periscope and snorkel tubes into the weapons control center and examined the fire-control chart that the exhausted Kotov updated every ten minutes. Just as for the previous ten hours, the formation of American ships continued to plod behind them at three knots—little more than a fast walking pace—keeping their wary distance of one to two thousand meters. And their incessant, dismal booming. No change to spook Savitsky into panic.

Arkhipov picked his way carefully past the sleeping Captain and made his way to his cabin. He had to get his head down. He left the door open in case there was a sudden rush of men to the forward torpedo compartment. And as soon as his head hit the bunk, he was fast asleep.

3

Bolshaya Gruzinskaya, Moscow
Sunday, 28 October 1962, 19:40 Moscow Time / 12:40 EDT

Vasin shifted in the fiendishly uncomfortable seat of his car, stretching a leg that had been cramping on and off for three hours. Night had spread like spilled ink across the street outside Sofia's apartment, starting in the shadows of the archways and spilling onto the shaded areas under the lindens. Lights flicked on all over the building as a stream of trolleybuses disgorged their loads of tired, homebound citizens. Small groups of young men and women in uniform arrived at the Defense Ministry housing block in chatty gaggles. He checked his watch. Past seven thirty. How long could he maintain his hungry, coffee-less vigil outside her front door?

Vasin cursed himself for letting Sofia go. She was the weak link, the most imminent threat to his whole scheme. A scheme that seemed more insane the more Vasin thought about it. How could he know that Morozov hadn't given the Americans a danger signal rather than the all clear? What had Morozov really photographed on the microfilm roll? And while Morozov's instinct for self-preservation would probably hold, what was Sofia's motive for keeping her mouth shut? Patriotism? That could land either way.

Most of all, Vasin was tortured by the constant thought that maybe, just maybe, his mad gamble had worked. He tried to imagine the CIA men in the American Embassy developing and reading the message he had written out for Morozov. The coded telexes flashing across the Atlantic. The Yankee generals and admirals debating the warning around conference tables. Even President Kennedy, his careworn but intelligent young face crumpling in concern as he read the message that he—Vasin—had sent. The message that would avert war . . .

Christ, Vasin. He tipped his head until it rested on the back of his steel-framed car seat and closed his eyes. You believed that this would actually *work*?

He could not wait for Sofia any longer. For all he knew, she and Morozov could be holed up in some hotel room having a romantic reconciliation. Or could both be under arrest. Vasin had no idea. And he needed a plan. If his idea of warning the Americans had failed, he would need to escape, somehow. If it had worked, perhaps he could talk Orlov into forgiveness. Somehow.

To make a plan he had to find out what the hell had really happened. And Vasin knew who could tell him. His old surveillance team, stewing in their stuffy apartment with their eyes constantly on Morozov's apartment.

4

KGB Headquarters, Moscow
Sunday, 28 October 1962, 20:03 Moscow Time / 13:03 EDT

Famously, no man had ever visited every corner of the vast Lubyanka complex. Certainly, very few people had ever found their way to Special Repository 9/84. The small suite of rooms was, unlike all the other prison spaces of the Lubyanka, actually on the ninth floor. As he rode one of the building's many elevators upward, Orlov had a fleeting memory of leafing through the memoirs of Casanova. Must have been back when he was a theology student in the seminary, and his interest in the dead Italian's rakish stories had been frankly masturbatory. But he recalled Casanova's account of his incarceration under the baking-hot roofs of the Doge's Palace in Venice. A stinking hellhole of a prison, perched high above the heads of the great and the good who went about their business down below.

Orlov reached the suite of secure rooms via a series of corridors and vigilant sentries who checked his papers rather than wave him through, though he had appointed all of them personally. There were heavy bars on the windows that overlooked the Lubyanka's internal courtyard, but otherwise the Special Repository had more the air of a secure archive than of a prison. And in fact an archive was exactly what it had once been, before some discreet transformations commissioned by Beria himself.

In the anteroom of the innermost part of the suite sat two of Orlov's trusted personal bodyguards. Two more were inside the cell itself. The young sentries jumped to their feet, saluting in silence. Nothing to report. Good. Orlov opened the heavy padlock and hauled open the steel door of the windowless archive room. The sour, heavy stink of the latrine bucket, mixed with the smell of sweaty uniforms, assaulted his senses. Morozov sat on a camp bed, his left hand shackled to a steel bookshelf that was bolted to the wall. Two sergeants sprang to attention, tipping over their folding chairs as they hurriedly stood.

"At ease, boys. Go get a cup of tea. Take the piss pot with you."

Orlov stood aside as the pair filed out with grateful salutes. The General waited until they were gone before addressing Morozov. The man, forced by his cuffed wrist to sit on the low bed, looked like a punctured balloon. His Sunday sports jacket was crumpled and his hair lay plastered to his forehead with sweat.

"I have no time to hear out your denials, Comrade Morozov. I'll be sending some other people to do that for me. You can waste their time, but not mine. I'm here to talk—" Morozov began to speak over Orlov, a high-pitched whine of indignation which the General cut short with a backhanded slap across his face. "No! I talk, you listen. Understood? So listen very carefully. We have Sofia. We have Vasin. We have your microfilm. And . . . we have your American contact. Caught red-handed emptying your dead-letter drop. Oh, and I almost forgot. Your wife and daughter are also in custody. Is there any part of that you didn't understand?"

Morozov spread his uncuffed arm in a gesture of desperate pleading, and once again began speaking. Again, Orlov cut him off with a slap. The stinging impact felt sweet on Orlov's knuckles.

"One. Word. Do you confess?"

This time Morozov merely shook his head.

"Have it your way. I'll be back later. The American will talk."

Orlov stalked out of the cell, motioning the next two bodyguards to take their places guarding the prisoner—along with a young lieutenant from Special Cases who waited with a sheaf of papers ready to record Morozov's frightened babbling. He locked them all in once more with his personal padlock.

Oh, that was good, Orlov told himself as he stalked back toward his own suite of offices. Very nice. Leave the poor bastard Morozov with the hope. If the American doesn't talk, I'll be fine, the traitor would be thinking. They have nothing to pin on me. Just the word of the crazy renegade KGB officer, Vasin. Yes—Morozov would be lying his head off for the next few hours, trying to save his hide. Orlov even allowed himself a quick, barking laugh as he returned to his private study, startling his secretary.

Of course the American spy would never talk. But it didn't matter.

There was no way that Jacob could know what Morozov looked like. It followed logically that Morozov didn't know what Jacob looked like either. The real Jacob could never identify Morozov in a lineup, Orlov felt sure, even if he wanted to. So the answer was simple—he would conjure another Jacob. Any pale, jug-eared Baltic-born *kontora* officer could play the part, as long as he was half-smart. Make him look a little roughed-up, coach him on exaggerating his non-Russian accent. Put him in a room with Morozov, and after a suitable pause for protests and denials—maybe accompanied by a few punches to the head—have the kid eventually point an accusing finger. Positive identification by an American CIA officer. Then the film canister. The blowup of the crazy message with its bizarre warnings of nuclear torpedoes and secret submarine flotillas.

Orlov was holding a full house. He knew he'd have Morozov's confession by morning.

Then he'd deal with Vasin. Just as soon as he could find the traitorous bastard.

5

B-59, Sargasso Sea
Sunday, 28 October 1962, 14:03 EDT / 21:03 Moscow Time

Arkhipov breathed deep. The metallic odor of the new instruments reminded him of hot solder. The polymer sealant that surrounded the banks of electronic indicators gave off a reassuring antiseptic tang. And underneath it the familiar, human submarine stink—the smell of unwashed men and strong tobacco, the taste of sweet Navy tea in his mouth. At the furthest edge of his consciousness, Arkhipov heard muttering voices and the reassuring exchange of orders. In his mind's eye he saw the second hand of the electric clock purring forward, and his bladder tightened in anxiety. He knew that in a moment he would see the instrument panel of K-19 blossom with red warning lights.

His eyes snapped open. Arkhipov focused on the clock—his own bedside clock, not the command center clock of the doomed K-19. Through the bulkhead a few centimeters from his head he heard the distinctive noise of compressed air hissing into the ballast tanks arrayed on the outside of the pressure hull. B-59 was rising.

Arkhipov was upright in a second. He made a step toward the corridor, then paused. After a second's hesitation, he opened his wardrobe and eased his service Makarov out of its leather holster, followed by the ammunition clip, which he pressed home into the butt. He tucked the gun into the back of his trousers, covered it with his uniform shirt, and ran aft.

The command center was crowded and buzzed with palpable tension. Savitsky was on his feet, his eyes locked on the diving controls as the ship rose.

"What's going on?" Arkhipov called.

The Captain merely thrust his unshaven chin toward Maslennikov, delegating the answer to the Political Officer.

"Two American destroyers have overtaken us," hissed Maslennikov, his pudgy face streaked with sweat. "Just heard them charging past, five thousand meters to our port and starboard, at thirty knots. They're trying to flank us. Cut us off."

Kotov, the computer master, appeared at the Captain's side holding a scrap of paper scribbled with coordinates.

"The latest firing solution for the American carrier, Comrade Captain. Good for another ten minutes."

Savitsky took the paper, peered at it, and sat down. He reached for the main rudder control lever that protruded to the right of the commander's seat and pulled it toward himself.

"Making our course . . . two seventy-three. Level the dive at firing position. Ten meters' depth."

Arkhipov stepped forward, directly in the Captain's sight line.

"You really want to do it, don't you, Valentin Grigorievich? Take a shot at the American carrier?"

Savitsky ignored him once more and turned instead to the Political Officer.

"Come, Maslennikov. We need to arm the special weapon."

6

USS Bache, *Sargasso Sea*
Sunday, 28 October 1962, 14:03 EDT / 21:03 Moscow Time

After more than a day, irritation at this interminable slow-motion chase was beginning to get to Billings. Usually ice cool, the *Bache's* commander found himself pacing the bridge like a tethered animal. The sonar reports came through with a regularity that was becoming monotonous. No change in the Soviets' crawling speed or course.

Kimble, implacable, had remained on the rain-swept deck supervising the depth-charging, watch on watch. They'd used up all their practice depth charges hours before, and Kimble had set the armory chief to unpacking the high explosives from the real depth charges to leave only their detonators in place. Thank God they had hundreds of the things in the magazine.

"Captain—closest Sov boat's rising." The officer of the watch's voice was triumphant as he stood, phone receiver to the sonar room tucked under his ear.

Glory fucking hallelujah, thought Billings. The assholes have finally run out of power. They heard our destroyers closing the circle around them. They're giving up.

"And they're changing course. Setting on . . . two seventy-three."

Billings's grin turned into a frown. He crossed the bridge to the sea chart and squinted at the smudged plastic sheet on which the duty navigator had kept track of the movements of the whole American flotilla—in blue—and the two Soviet submarines, marked in red.

Why the hell would the Soviet skipper turn?

Then he saw it. The USS *Randolph* stood at a bearing of 273 to the Soviet boat, five nautical miles distant. Just about the maximum range of the Soviets' torpedoes.

"Holy God. The bastard's lining up to fire."

Billings turned to the officer of the watch.

"Reload all launchers with high-explosive depth charges. Tell sonar to listen hard for torpedo door noises. Engine room on standby to increase speed. And get Kimble up here. Now."

At the first whisper of a torpedo tube flooding, Billings could hit the gas and have his destroyer right over the Soviet sub in under two minutes. Then he'd finally crush the sucker like a roach.

7

Pioneers' Ponds, Moscow
Sunday, 28 October 1962, 21:04 Moscow Time / 14:04 EDT

Vasin made two slow circuits of Pioneers' Ponds before parking right below Morozov's windows. The lights were on, and somebody was moving around inside the apartment. Reassuring . . . maybe. A gray Volga stood on the opposite corner, its lights out, with two men inside he didn't recognize. It had the look of a *kontora* radio car. Also reassuring. If a *kontora* team was still surveilling the place it might mean that Morozov hadn't been arrested.

The night was damp and chilly and the Ponds were deserted apart from a heavily muffled teenage boy who was dragging a reluctant puppy on a circuit of the park. Vasin turned up the collar of his coat and hurried through the shadows to the entranceway of the *kontora* watchers' apartment, directly opposite Morozov's on the far side of the park. He punched in the door code, took the elevator to the seventh floor, and stood outside the familiar padded door, listening. Nothing.

Orlov had never thought to demand that Vasin return the key to the surveillance post. Vasin turned the lock as quietly as he could and opened the door slowly. Silence didn't necessarily mean there was nobody there. Vasin prayed that he would find Ears sitting at his listening post, his headphones plugged into Radio Moscow. Or young Lyubimov, sitting quietly by the window reading the latest edition of *Science and Life*. Or even just an anonymous *kontora* goon, slumped in inscrutable silence over a cooling cup of tea. But there was nobody in the kitchen or sitting room. A glance at Ears's listening equipment told Vasin all he needed to know. The table was piled with coiled-up rolls of telephone cord and cables. An open wooden case stood half-packed with a disassembled recording machine. The *kontora's* expensive long-range photographic equipment was gone. Only a standard-issue pair of military binoculars remained—the ones with a crooked eyepiece that Lyubimov had trodden on months before.

Vasin picked them up now and looked across the tops of the wind-stirred trees to Morozov's apartment. Through a half-open curtain he caught a glimpse of several figures in uniform. One paused to pick up a pile of books or files. The man's breeches were not military green but KGB blue.

So it was over. Morozov was blown. And Vasin's message? Almost certainly blown, too.

From the door came a fumbling of a key in the already-open lock. The hallway light flicked on.

"Anyone home?"

It was the voice of Lyubimov. Before Vasin could answer, the kid had put his head around the door of the unlit living room and looked in to see him, standing by the window in the dark. The cheer drained from the young officer's voice as he flicked on the light and saw his old chief's face.

"Boss! Gave me a start. All okay? Thought you'd been . . ."

"Morozov?" was the only word Vasin could summon.

Lyubimov's face creased in wariness.

"Yeah . . . so Colonel Pushkov told us not to, um. Say anything."

"About what?" Vasin's voice was barely above a husky whisper, like an alcoholic's.

Lyubimov did not reply but looked warily around the room as though checking for accomplices. His hand slid down the inside of his coat.

"Well, sir. About Morozov's arrest and all. But, sir, I'm sorry, but I've been ordered to . . ."

Vasin looked down at the floor. So it really was over. He had failed. When he raised his eyes again, he saw that the young officer had drawn a gun. Slowly and deliberately, Vasin put down the broken binoculars on the windowsill and smoothed his hair. He assembled a smile and aimed it at Lyubimov.

"So we got him at last? Good job, kid."

Vasin crossed the room, his eyes on his young protégé's and not on the Makarov he held in his hand. As he drew level, he put a friendly hand on Luybimov's shoulder.

"You know, I always had faith in you, Misha."

"Sir . . . stop! We have orders to . . ."

Vasin blinked in reassurance, turned, and walked calmly out the front door. The second he was out of the apartment, he began sprinting down the stairway as fast as he could.

8

B-59, Sargasso Sea
Sunday, 28 October 1962, 14:10 EDT / 21:10 Moscow Time

"You will *not* load the special weapon." Arkhipov's voice was tight with tension. "I do not authorize it."

Savitsky paused, then continued to move toward the hatch as though the flotilla commander had not spoken. Maslennikov made no move to follow him.

"Did you hear me, Captain?" Arkhipov raised his voice to a shout. "Have you taken leave of your senses?"

The whole command station crew had frozen in mute horror. Arkhipov no longer cared.

"Savitsky, get back here. Maslennikov—remind the Captain of our instructions."

The Captain straightened, his back to Arkhipov, and addressed the Political Officer.

"I gave you an order, Commander Maslennikov. We are going to arm the special weapon. I command it."

"Sir. Comrade Captains." There was a stammer in Maslennikov's voice as he faced his two superiors. "Our orders are that we may retaliate if attacked."

Arkhipov took a step closer toward the trembling man.

"And that the decision to fire is at whose discretion, Maslennikov?" Savitsky answered for him.

"The boat's commanding officer. And its political officer. Now let us get on with the attack."

"No, Captain." Arkhipov struggled to keep his voice steady. "The boat's *senior* officer. That's what it says, in black on white. On this boat, you command. But the senior officer of the flotilla is *me*. Is that not correct, Maslennikov? We do things by the book, remember?"

Quaking, the Political Officer met Savitsky's fiery stare.

"Actually—Comrade Arkhipov is right, Captain. The decision is the senior officer's. And that is the flotilla commander."

"Correct. The decision is mine." Arkhipov pushed in between Savitsky and the hatchway. "And my order is that we *do not fire*. We are not under attack."

"We're being chased around the Sargasso Sea by an American fleet!" Red spots of anger were kindling in Savitsky's already flushed face.

"I tell you again that we are *not* under attack, Valentin Grigorievich."

"You prefer that they sink us before we have a chance to use the special weapon, Comrade Captain?" The natural imperiousness of Savitsky's voice had become husky. "I would rather die than become the shame of the fleet."

Arkhipov placed his hand, palm flat, on the steel bulkhead behind Savitsky's head.

"I, as chief of staff of the flotilla and senior officer on board this boat, will be the judge of what shame is to be apportioned."

The Captain's voice sank to a vicious, urgent hiss.

"The crew will obey me, not you, Arkhipov."

Tension snapped between the two men like an electric charge. Barratry. That was the sea-law term for what Savitsky was suggesting.

Mutiny was an uprising by the enlisted men. Barratry was a revolt of the officers against their commander. Except in this case there were two commanders—B-59's own and the outsider, Arkhipov. Which would the crew choose, if it came to it—loyalty to their skipper, or their lives?

"You want us to continue to circle like goldfish until the batteries run out, then surface and surrender?" Savitsky continued, implacable. "You wish to hand over the Red Banner Northern Fleet attack submarine B-59 to the enemy without a fight? Are you a *traitor,* Vasily Alexandrovich? Or just a coward?"

Arkhipov felt tension throbbing in his sweating temples. He would have liked to have a man-to-man shouting match with the truculent Captain. But he fought to keep his voice low to match Savitsky's hiss. The two men's faces were centimeters apart.

"Surrendering is not my order, Captain. And no—the men will *not* obey you. Opening the torpedo tube doors with the enemy this close will be suicide. They all know it. They will not do it. And the second you step through that hatch, I will make an announcement on this intercom here that our mission is aborted and we are returning home. Try getting them to follow your order then."

Arkhipov's hand had crept along the bulkhead and rested next to the bank of three intercoms over the commander's seat. All he had to do was flick a switch and the whole boat would be able to hear their conversation. Savitsky's eye flicked from Arkhipov's face to the intercoms. The Captain could easily reach up himself and shout his own order. But he hesitated a second. And a second more. Finally Savitsky took a deep, ragged breath, as though it were the first he'd taken for minutes, and hung his head.

"Good. Enough of this." Arkhipov flicked on the intercom to the communications room. "Radio? Contact our comrades on B-36 on the underwater telephone. Flotilla ordered to surface and recharge batteries. No independent radio contact with the enemy."

Maslennikov spoke up, indignant.

"Sir—what about radio silence?"

Arkhipov ignored him and addressed the control room crew.

"Raise periscope and snorkel. Blow tanks and surface."

The petty officer who sat at the diving-plane controls looked from Arkhipov to Savitsky and back again. His hands did not move.

"Captain, give the order. This is a flotilla maneuver under my authority."

Savitsky, sitting in his commander's seat, remained motionless. His voice, when it came, trembled with anger.

"I will not allow you to surrender my boat."

"Fine. Have it your way."

Arkhipov reached over the Captain's head to the three engine-room telegraphs and quickly racked the levers from Full Stop to Stand By. A couple of seconds later, the chief engineer responded, the three dials acknowledging the order with a trio of loud mechanical dings. Arkhipov sprinted four steps aft to the bank of taps that controlled the supply of compressed air to the ballast tanks. Before the able seaman who stood at the post could react, Arkhipov twisted one tap, then another and another. The distinctive rumble of displaced water came from all sides of the command center. The main diving gauge immediately began to sink toward zero. From a depth of ten meters it would take B-59 less than a minute to surface.

Savitsky gave a cry and lunged for the diving fin controls just a couple of meters from his post—a desperate way of forcing the sub deeper under the power of its engines, even as its sudden buoyancy propelled it toward the surface.

"No, Captain!"

Arkhipov's hand closed around the handle of the Makarov tucked in the back of his trousers.

9

USS Bache, *Sargasso Sea*
Sunday, 28 October 1962, 14:12 EDT / 21:12 Moscow Time

From his post on the flying bridge, Billings saw the creaming, narrow wake of B-59's periscope break the ocean's surface, followed by the thicker column of the snorkel pipe. Was the Sov commander going to try to recharge his batteries by ventilating his engines through the snorkel? That would be as dumb as a little kid trying to hide behind his own hands.

But no. A wider wake of spreading white foam appeared, followed by the black steel profile of the submarine's conning tower. A billow of thick, black smoke erupted from the vents at the top of the sail as the sub's diesels rumbled into motion. Following the column of exhaust as it traveled across the water like an unfurling flag, Billings spotted the distinctive black sail of another surfacing sub a couple of thousand yards distant. Red stars were painted on the sides of both boats' conning towers. After two decades of hunting and evading Soviet submarines, these were the first Billings had ever actually seen as anything but menacing shadows on a sonar screen.

"Well I'll be goddammed."

Billings pressed the intercom on the far extremity of the bridge.

"Scramble those deck teams, double quick. Sov submarines on the surface."

10

B-59, Sargasso Sea
Sunday, 28 October 1962, 14:12 EDT / 21:12 Moscow Time

Arkhipov felt the weight of the pistol in his hand, but he did not draw it. If he pulled the gun, Arkhipov knew that he would immediately put himself in the wrong. And that someone would die. Maybe him. And that all survivors would end up in a court-martial—and then, most likely, the Gulag.

As the rumble of the starting engines vibrated through the boat, the intercom on the bulkhead crackled to life.

"Comrade Captain?" The sonar operator's voice was timid, but the alarm in his tone commanded the immediate attention of everyone on the command station. "Something strange is happening."

Arkhipov, Savitsky, and Maslennikov all froze. The Captain turned to bark irritably into the machine.

"What?"

"It's . . . music, sir. From the American destroyer. I can hear music."

The three senior officers looked at one another in incomprehension.

"Put it on the speakers."

There was a crackle as the young sonarman fiddled to place his headphones over his own intercom. The noise that came through the speaker was muffled but unmistakable. A band was playing . . . *jazz.*

Every man on the bridge stood transfixed by the bizarre, tinny noise of jaunty music spilling from the public address system. Arkhipov's mind, pounding with adrenaline, at first refused to process what was happening. But at that moment cool, fresh air pumped by the powerful engine-room fans began to blow from the air-conditioning vents. The air cleared the confused fog in Arkhipov's mind like an opened window in a smoky room.

"They're playing us up. Savitsky! The Americans are welcoming us. There is no damn war."

Savitsky stood, wide-eyed, like a man stunned. His bloodshot eyes met Arkhipov's.

"There's *no war,* do you understand?" Arkhipov repeated. "We're in international waters. No need to surrender."

Arkhipov took another lungful of sweet, fresh air and closed his eyes. He would have offered a prayer, if he'd known how.

11

KGB Headquarters, Moscow
Sunday, 28 October 1962, 21:32 Moscow Time / 14:32 EDT

The arrangements were far from perfect, Orlov knew. But then again, what was ever perfect in the Lubyanka? In life? He was constrained by time and space. The necessity to keep his prisoner a very close secret. Two men may speak in private, the founder of the Soviet secret police, Felix Dzerzhinsky, had once said—as long as one of them falls into a deep hole immediately afterward. By this point, five hours after he had detained Morozov, some dozen people—his entire personal staff—knew. At least they knew that a secret prisoner was their private guest in the classified archive on the ninth floor. And by necessity, that number now included the lanky, pale Estonian misfit that Orlov was waiting, with mounting impatience, to brief in the anteroom before seeing Morozov.

The boy was a senior sergeant, hauled up from the anti-dissident section of the *kontora* and hastily dressed in foreign clothes borrowed from the Actors' Wardrobe. The idea of the Lubyanka in the role of a giant opera house, equipped with a casting department and even a costume store, gave Orlov half a second of amusement. Dressed in a slightly baggy suit of old-fashioned American cut, his unruly red hair peremptorily Brylcreemed into submission, the kid almost looked the part of an American spy.

"Sven Arvovich?" The boy stood to attention, his already pale face washed chalk white with apprehension. Orlov handed him a memorandum, hastily handwritten in the General's own hand. No need to share his secrets with a typist. "This is an account of what you did over the last twenty-four hours. You have fifteen minutes to memorize it. At that point you will be brought back here, an apparent prisoner. A man will be waiting in this room. The two of you will undergo a formal judicial confrontation, before witnesses. I will question you. You will speak in bad Russian. Your heaviest foreign accent. You will answer to the name of Richard Jacob, an American diplomat, which I will read from an identity card."

Orlov fervently hoped that his secretary was up to the job of substituting this young man's photograph on Jacob's Embassy ID, and inking in the Soviet Foreign Ministry stamp on a corner of the image. Orlov had no wish to involve the professionals on the fourth floor.

"You will protest that you must speak to your colleagues at the American Embassy. I will tell you that you are under arrest for an assault on a Soviet officer. And for espionage. Both criminal acts and violations of the new Vienna Convention on the proper conduct of diplomats. We will not go into details, but I shall show you a microfilm canister with which you were caught red-handed. I will tell you that you may be released if you answer our questions concerning the man before you. You will demur. I may hit you. I may hit you hard. But when I press you, the second or third time but not before, you will positively identify this suspect as an agent whose photograph you have seen at the CIA station at the Embassy. Your place of work. You will answer no to my questions only once—when I ask you whether you know the man's name. To that you will answer that it was a secret. Now repeat my instructions back to me. In your accent. Go."

The young Estonian, by now in a state of quaking shock, managed to stammer through a close enough recall of his orders. Frightened was good. Orlov surveyed the kid one last time before his brief, but vital, appearance in the little show that Orlov was staging. Something was wrong, though it took the General a minute to work out what it was. The kid smelled. The familiar semiwashed tang of a Soviet young adult. Pleased by his own perspicacity, Orlov sent an orderly to fetch the bottle of French eau de cologne that he kept in his office drawer for his own private purposes.

"Now—read. Memorize. And remember—the security of the Motherland depends on your performance, Sergeant."

12

Pioneers' Ponds, Moscow
Sunday, 28 October 1962, 21:52 Moscow Time / 14:52 EDT

There was a man in a children's storybook Vasin used to read to his son, Nikita. A carpenter. The man had no wife and was lonely, so he made himself a toy child out of wood. He fashioned pegged joints for the doll's knees and elbows so that he could move almost like a real boy. As he walked back to his car, Vasin's legs stiffened and his entire body seemed to turn rigid and woody. He felt an urgent need to urinate. He had become like the wooden boy: not really alive. An inanimate thing, inexplicably walking, jerking into life propelled by nothing but the power of loneliness.

What Vasin wanted to do most—almost more than he'd wanted to do anything in his life—was to drive home. Let himself into his own apartment and kneel down by his sleeping son. They'd never said much to each other, especially when alone. Vasin had always thought of quiet as his gift to the child, eternally harassed by a demanding world which bombarded him with a constant onslaught of demands. Nikita was a taciturn kid, thoughtful, obliging, not spoiled or cocky like the other children who played in the courtyard of the elite apartment block where they had moved the previous year.

He'd like to kneel down by his son, watch his no-longer-childish face sleeping for a little while. And if the boy woke, he'd suggest a game of chess. And a cup of tea, sipped in companionable silence in the still of the night.

Vasin realized that he'd been standing, stock-still and keys in hand, in front of his car. The street was deserted. Slowly, he gripped the cold steel of the handle and got in. He did not turn the ignition.

He had failed. He had risked his life to save the Motherland, to avert war, and his plan has misfired spectacularly. Betrayed by Sofia? He had to assume so.

Where could he go where Orlov couldn't find him? What was the point of running, except to die tired? What was the point of fleeing, if nuclear war was about to break out and destroy his family?

13

B-59, Sargasso Sea
Sunday, 28 October 1962, 14:52 EDT / 21:52 Moscow Time

The taste of the tropical sea air as Arkhipov climbed through the hatch onto the top of B-59's conning tower was inexpressibly sweet. The tiny cockpit was already crowded with two lookouts, but they instinctively made space for Arkhipov as he made his tour of the small steel oval.

Three destroyers lay within a half-kilometer circle around B-59, crews on deck gawping at the Soviet submarines. The Americans had already identified themselves by radio and semaphore as USS *Cony, Beale,* and *Lowry*. Arkhipov had ordered only the briefest of acknowledgments.

A few hundred meters to the north he saw their sister boat, B-36. The two disgraced Soviet ships had exchanged only curt messages, knowing that the Yankees would be listening in to their radio comms.

A band on the deck of the USS *Beale* doggedly played on. New Orleans jazz. Songs by Louis Armstrong, according to one of the kids from B-59's radio room. The sailor evidently spent too much time listening to American radio stations.

Arkhipov looked up. The sky was overcast, and a turning wind blew the diesel exhaust that billowed from the vents into the cockpit. But he was alive. His crew, the American musicians, the crew of B-36—they were all alive. Right now, that felt good enough.

In just over four hours, B-59's batteries would be charged once more. And they'd maybe be able to finally reestablish comms with Moscow. Contact with the enemy was listed as an authorized reason for breaking radio silence. Already the radio room was busy sending out Arkhipov's coded report to fleet headquarters. Trapped by enemy boats, forced to surface. Requesting further mission instructions.

Not a good message for any flotilla commander to have to send.

Arkhipov guessed what his new orders would be: Abandon mission, return to base. And there, in all probability, disgrace. He'd put even money on Savitsky denouncing him for cowardice, in cahoots with Maslennikov, during their inevitable debriefing by military intelligence. It would be their word against his. At the very least, Arkhkipov knew that this would be his last operational command.

He gripped the chilly steel rail of the cockpit and felt the roll of his boat in the long Atlantic swell. Christ, Captain Arkhipov thought. It's good to breathe air.

14

KGB Headquarters, Moscow
Monday, 29 October 1962, 07:25 Moscow Time / 00:25 EDT

Morozov broke just before dawn. To the prisoner, it was always the hour of despair. Some old-school NKVD bruiser who specialized in extracting confessions had once advised Orlov to bring the accused out into the yard at daybreak to look at the sky. The colder and bleaker the morning, the better. As he walked down the corridor to his office, Morozov's signed confession in his hand, Orlov wondered why that trick worked so reliably. Perhaps something to do with the prisoner's realization that his nightmare was seamlessly about to become a daymare. Maybe it was that a glimpse of the world from which he had been so violently removed was heartbreaking. Or perhaps some trick of the sleepless mind—the dawning of day confirming that there would be no rest, no slumber until the accused did what was demanded of him.

Orlov had never been much of a confessions man back in the bloody days of the '30s, when the *kontora* had moved into the business of mass murder. He'd spent that dangerous time attached to the headquarters of the Far Eastern Military District. A kind of in-house spy, reporting on the senior Army and Air Force officers—but steering clear of the interrogation rooms and the Gulag death factories that sprang up around the region like mushrooms.

The rest of the *kontora* though . . . Orlov shook his head at the memory. At the height of the Purges, the whole NKVD seemed suddenly transformed into a giant collective of radio-drama authors, every investigator penning his own sprawling tale of conspiracy, sabotage, and espionage in order to send more and more people to the execution pits. Murder by quota. Orlov had seen the lists, signed by his former bosses Yezhov and Yagoda and handed down the chain of command: "Adzharia, 1,500; Arkhangelsk Province, 1,250; Astrakhan Province, 2,300." And so on down the alphabet. The month's stipulated number of enemies of the people to be rounded up, terrorized into confession as efficiently as the *kontora* could devise, then quickly tried and shot.

The paperwork! A dozen documents were required to arrest, charge, interrogate, and condemn even the lowliest worker. For a senior Party member, maybe ninety pieces of paper were needed—not just confessions but cross-referenced confessions from other suspects, all interlocking, all correctly collated. And woe betide the *kontora* officer who got his suspects confused, his plots twisted, his accusers muddled with his accused. Such mistakes could even lead to something as horrific and unthinkable as an acquittal. That did happen. Not, of course, because the accused was any more or less innocent than the next man or woman. But because the NKVD investigator had screwed up.

Those unfortunate, bumbling *kontora* men were themselves quickly fed into the shredder, hurriedly charged with anti-Soviet activity, or sabotage, or even falsification of evidence. Yes—making up evidence had been both officially a crime and, unofficially, a job description. But everyone knew that these officers' real crime had been to slow down the machine of terror, and the price was to substitute themselves for the people they'd failed to convict. The statistics, after all, didn't care.

The *kontora*'s bosses, of course, had set the pace. Some men, in those heroic prewar days, had built the Revolution in bricks and mortar, constructing factories and cities in record time. The *kontora*'s equally passionate leaders built their personal revolution out of the bodies of the enemies of the state. The more bodies, the safer the state. And who could fault their logic? Orlov had certainly never dared—not at the time, anyway.

Orlov strode into his office, a bleary-eyed orderly holding open the door for him. He walked over to the window, surveying the spread of the bleak, gray morning light over Lubyanka Square. He read over the one-page summary confession that Morozov had signed just minutes before. Anti-Soviet feelings triggered by execution of comrades and friends before the war. Disillusionment with Communism after the suppression of the counterrevolutionary bourgeois uprising in Budapest in '56. Anger at the warmongering political line of the Party. A voluntary approach made to British diplomats in Moscow, back in '60. Contact made by the CIA during a business trip to Paris in '61. Documents solicited under false pretenses from inside Operation Anadyr . . . and so on.

At Orlov's prompting, there was plenty on Morozov's long-standing friendship with Colonel General Ivan Serov. How the senior man had promised to protect his protégé; how Serov had dismissed the *kontora's* suspicions as nonsense. Oh yes—Serov had been amply and thoroughly implicated from Morozov's mouth. Not implicated in Morozov's treason, of course. But in turning a blind eye to treason, definitely. And that would be more than enough for Orlov's purposes.

Only one thing was missing from the confession. Morozov had said nothing about the American spy that Vasin had shot in Arzamas-16 the previous year. By the time Orlov had raised the question, the terrified suspect had been in full confessional flow, almost tripping over himself to spill whatever details could possibly keep him alive. But not a peep about the traitor Colonel Pavel Korin, not even a hint of a connection. It hadn't sounded to Orlov like Morozov was holding back. And what would be easier for the flailing man than to confess to a connection with an agent who was safely dead?

But that was just a detail. Orlov shook his head and replaced his notes in their folder. Amazing how the world turned, he thought. A generation ago, thousands had suffered and died on just such far-fetched charges of treachery and espionage. And almost none of them had been true. And now, for once, Orlov had caught a genuine spy. A real, bona fide Yankee agent. And one at the very heart of the Caribbean crisis.

Orlov knew that what he held in his hands was dynamite. And therefore dangerous. It was poison for the old bastard Serov, of course. He would never survive the scandal of his friendship with a traitor.

But that wasn't the dangerous part. The real high explosive was Morozov's final signal. The letter that Vasin had dictated. Who had ordered the submarines to run the blockade? Clearly, military brass unhappy at the prospect of Khrushchev backing down. Which brass? Would they win? Could Orlov bring them down by revealing their plans? And if so, why would he wish to? What would Orlov's silence be worth to them? Conversely, how much would Khrushchev's allies trade for his information? Or could he help the hawkish generals bring Khrushchev down?

Orlov's mind flicked through months and years of conversations, handshakes, whispered confidences, secret memoranda. He'd been playing this game long enough to know that there was no such thing as principles in politics—only a constantly shifting kaleidoscope of individual men, facts, interests, power, information. The latter two, of course, being the same thing. Friends, enemies? These, too, were abstractions. If you played the game right, the powerful were your friends. And the about-to-be powerful were your even better friends.

The traffic was approaching its rush-hour peak on the roundabout that circled the elongated iron figure of Felix Dzerzhinsky on his plinth in the middle of Lubyanka Square. The stern, metal eyes of the Soviet secret police's founder looked across the sea of red, white, and blue car tops into a Revolutionary future.

A future that was now in Orlov's hands.

15

KGB Headquarters, Moscow
Monday, 29 October 1962, 07:31 Moscow Time / 00:31 EDT

Orlov's secretary interrupted his reverie.

"Comrade General? I have Lieutenant Colonel Vasin on the line."

"*Ah.* Put him through."

Orlov put down the files he had been cradling and moved toward the telephone extension nearest to the window. He was mildly surprised. He'd half expected Vasin to try to run. There were ways one could escape from the USSR. A few people every year even managed it. On foot through the Karelian forests to Finland. By boat from some small Estonian fishing port. A long hike through the Hindu Kush. Stowing away on a ship from Leningrad or Odessa. Stamina and luck were all it took. Having a private car and a *kontora* ID were inestimably useful.

Orlov would have put Vasin's chances at maybe 20 percent. Part of him would even be rooting for the crazy young fool.

Orlov was always expecting people to do stupid things, and they usually did. But Vasin was not stupid. The man would now try to plead for his life. Orlov would be interested to hear how he'd try to do it. But again, he'd give the boy no more than the same 20 percent chance of survival.

On the tenth ring, Orlov finally picked up the phone but said nothing.

"Comrade General?"

Orlov merely tutted in answer. There was a long silence on the line.

"General. I need fifteen minutes of your time. Face-to-face. Neutral ground."

A reasonable opening move, Orlov had to admit. A dumber man than Vasin would have asked for an hour, even a lone minute—please, sir, I beg you. Or, worse, begun pleading then and there on the phone.

"Fine, Vasin. I agree."

"Very good. Today at noon? By Iron Felix. In the little park opposite the Polytechnical Museum. Do I have your word that we will be alone?"

Orlov stifled a chuckle.

"Of course."

The General replaced the receiver in its cradle and turned back to the window to consider the problem of Vasin. His first instinct had been to just bury the insubordinate little fucker. But, Orlov knew, that was simply irritation at being defied. Acting in anger was weak.

Orlov lowered his eyes to the iron statue of Derzhinsky that dominated Lubyanka Square and savored his triumph. For the moment—a sweet, long moment—there was nothing more to do but wait. He held all the cards. If Vasin was right and one of the Navy boys in the Caribbean set off his nuclear firecracker at some American ship, it would be war soon enough. That would be one set of outcomes. If not, then no war. Another set of outcomes. Serov could fall—or Serov and his friends could rise. Either way, the man was firmly on Orlov's hook. Drown his enemy; save his enemy. The choice would be his. Orlov felt himself unconsciously clenching and unclenching his fists. Power felt good.

Orlov flicked on his intercom and instructed his secretary to keep a close watch on the American news wires for any information about armed confrontation in Cuba. And instructed her to put the word out to his little birds in the Aquarium and General Staff to stay alert for any naval news from the Caribbean. Otherwise, he was not to be disturbed.

The General, with the files with Morozov's confession cradled in his arms, flopped onto his leather sofa and sank into sleep.

16

Lubyanka Square, Moscow
Monday, 29 October 1962, 12:00 Moscow Time / 05:00 EDT

Orlov rarely walked on Moscow sidewalks. A few yards from his car to the theater, occasionally. But to walk, almost alone, along a deserted city sidewalk was a novelty he hadn't experienced for years. Two of his bodyguards followed on foot at a discreet distance, of course. And a single car containing two more armed men trailed him. Close enough to being alone. As Orlov entered the newly built underpass from the Lubyanka to the traffic island opposite the Polytechnical Museum, he wondered if Vasin would actually dare to keep him waiting. He was enjoying this. It had been so long since Orlov had gone into an interrogation without knowing exactly what he wanted, or what he would do.

A light drizzle began as Orlov emerged from the underpass. The small park was deserted. The spot was well chosen—for symbolic reasons if nothing else. It was dominated by the illuminated statue of Iron Felix, clad in a drifting halo of misty autumn rain.

The insistent, squeaky quack of a Moskvich's horn sounded from the opposite side of the traffic island. Oh, that was good. Vasin had pulled up in such a way that Orlov's own car would have to circle the whole square before following. The General checked left and right for his guards, then approached the car. The passenger-side window was already wound down. Tentatively, as if putting his head in a bear trap, Orlov leaned over and peered inside. Vasin flicked on the interior light against the dimness of the day and held up his hands.

"Comrade General. I'm alone. Unarmed. Come for a ride with me?"

Orlov hesitated. How much smarter than most of his adversaries was Vasin, calculating that Orlov's vanity and sense of invulnerability would propel him into the car. And by God, the man would be right. Making a slight gesture to his guards to follow in the chase car, Orlov opened the door and got into the tiny Moskvich, his bulk making the vehicle sag on its weak springs. Vasin switched off the light, put the car into gear, and nosed into the empty expanse of Marx Prospekt.

"So, Vasin. You heard the news?"

Orlov half turned in his cramped seat—as much as his muscular bulk would allow—and examined Vasin. The man clearly hadn't shaved. His car also smelled funky, as though someone had slept in it.

"What news would that be?"

Vasin kept his eyes stubbornly on the light traffic ahead as they passed the Hotel Metropol. It was somehow so much easier to talk to Orlov when he didn't have to look at him.

"The news about nuclear war. Or rather . . . the lack of nuclear war. Unless it was somewhere low in the radio bulletin and I missed it. Anyway. It's over. Your submarine game. Those boats you were so worried about were intercepted by the US Navy yesterday, somewhere in the eastern Caribbean. Intercepted without incident. Turns out the lead boat was commanded by some level-headed fellow. Not one of the Navy's usual blockhead cowboys. The Captain was a survivor of some reactor accident, they say. He didn't feel like sending a nuke up the backside of the US Second Fleet. Anyway, our subs surfaced, waved at the Americans in a comradely manner, turned for home. Thank God Almighty."

"Are you serious? It's *over*?"

"It's over, Sasha. You failed to get your message to the Americans. But it came out okay in the end."

Vasin felt his hands relax involuntarily on the wheel. In front of him the traffic light at the intersection with Gorky Street turned red and Vasin rolled to an obedient halt in the middle lane, the goon car filling his rearview mirror.

"You got Morozov, I see."

"We did. No thanks to you."

"That's ungracious, sir. You could say I finally flushed the traitor out for you."

"Ah. 'The traitor.' Yes. Good word. Let's talk about treason."

Vasin ignored Orlov's ironic tone.

"And did the traitor Morozov sing?"

"Sasha. You know me. Of course he sang. Like a canary. First dawn after his arrest. Quite an amazing song he sang, too. This time next month he will have sung his way to a bullet in the back of the head."

"And Sofia? You have her as well?"

Orlov gave a low chuckle.

"Always *cherchez la femme* with you, eh, Sasha? But no, in fact. I don't have her. She went to the priest of a different parish to make her confession, as it happens."

Vasin furrowed his brow in incomprehension, risking a glance at Orlov. The old devil was smirking in self-satisfaction.

"And Tokarev?"

"Same story, I'm afraid. I am reliably informed that our friends in green have arrested him. Court-martial pending. Divulging state secrets, apparently. I'm sure you know more about it than I do. Maybe you'll tell me all about it one day. *Doprygalsya, nash bezruky tovarishch.* Our handless comrade has jumped his way into trouble."

Orlov gave a throaty chuckle. Vasin felt an uncontrollable urge to wipe the smile off the fucker's face. The traffic light changed to yellow, and Vasin put the car slowly into gear. A postal truck to his right revved slowly and moved off with the rest of the column of traffic. Without warning, Vasin cut the wheel right and swerved behind the truck and across another two lanes to make a hard right turn onto Gorky Street. He left Orlov's escort car trapped momentarily between streams of moving traffic, beeping furiously.

Vasin accelerated as fast as he could up the hill toward the Central Telegraph Office. Once he was over the crest of the first rise between the Kremlin and Pushkin Square, Vasin braked abruptly and pulled over to the curb without signaling. He slipped into an empty parking space in front of a Kamaz truck and quickly killed the engine. Orlov looked over his shoulder in alarm. A moment later, both saw the Volga containing Orlov's bodyguards charging past them, oblivious.

Before Orlov could react, Vasin restarted the car and swerved into a side street by the Hotel Tsentralnaya.

"Sorry, General. Precautions."

Orlov said nothing for a long moment. Vasin could feel the older man's fury at his sudden, wholly unfamiliar vulnerability. Vasin turned right again at the Institute of Marxist-Leninism and headed back toward Lubyanka Square.

"No problem at all. I'm enjoying the ride." Orlov's jollity was obviously forced.

"You promised me fifteen minutes. So I want to tell you a few things. About what I did. And why."

"If I recall, you already told me why. In so many words. You had a bee in your bonnet about those submarines. Wanted me to call Khrushchev at home, get him out of bed to warn him of deadly danger, if I remember correctly . . ."

Vasin turned to glare at his chief, almost driving into a traffic light at the bottom of Pushkin Street.

"Whoa there, Sasha." Orlov gripped the plastic loop above the door to steady himself as Vasin swerved. "Eyes on the road. I'm not mocking you."

"You called me a traitor. But I'm no traitor, General."

"Are you not? Are you not? Well. I'm so glad to hear that, Sasha. I'd hate to have been wrong about you when I picked you out for Special Cases. Had you down as a bit of a patriot, if anything. Man of principle. One of the things I never quite trusted about you, to be honest. But, just between friends, would you share with me one thing? How will you explain to the State Prosecutor that you made contact with a suspected Yankee spy, encouraged him to compose a message betraying the deepest operational secrets of the Motherland, and then took that message to the spy's dead-letter drop and delivered it personally to the Americans for collection? Maybe I have it all wrong, of course."

Kuznetsky Most brought them back onto Lubyanka Square. The sinister form of the statue under which they'd met a few minutes before was now shrouded in a gathering rainstorm. Another red light loomed ahead. Vasin wondered whether Orlov would bolt if he stopped. He calculated probably not. Orlov enjoyed mind games. Vasin's only chance of survival was to somehow get his boss to understand why he'd acted as he had. Right now, he was talking for his life.

"Sir. Think about it this way. What would Iron Felix have done if he had discovered a clique of mad warmongers trying to undermine his boss, Lenin? What was it my history teacher used to drill into us? . . . 'The world Socialist Revolution was in its cradle. Bolshevism had to be defended at all costs.' And Felix did what needed to be done. He made

301

deals with the imperialists, with capitalism itself. But did that make him less of a patriot?"

The light changed and Vasin pulled out onto Lubyanka Square once more. Checking his mirror, he saw a rare thoughtful look flicker across the General's face.

"An angry Pole is what Felix Edmundovich was. An aristocrat to his bones . . . and a Revolutionary hooligan." Orlov's voice was confiding. "But always, resolutely, a Soviet patriot. A Soviet imperialist, to be precise. Felix knew that the new empire had to be defended with all possible measures. Yes. That's true."

"So would Felix, on uncovering a conspiracy to draw his country into a war with its most powerful enemy, simply stand by and watch—"

"I got it, Sasha." Orlov cut him off with his habitual imperious irritability. "I understand your defense. You are saying that Felix would have acted to avert an unwinnable war. Done whatever was necessary to save the USSR from humiliation, to ensure its survival. He would have acted, in fact, just like you have done. Put country before personal interest. Even if that meant passing a warning to the USSR's most implacable foe. Do I have it right?"

"Exactly. And—"

"Wait. So does that make you an idealist or a pragmatist, Sasha? What is your diagnosis of yourself, please?"

Vasin accelerated down Old Square, past the Central Committee offices and toward the Moscow River. He felt like a man suddenly stranded in an infinite minefield, every path in Orlov's verbal labyrinth strewn with deadly danger.

"Sir. You're a feared man. You're a hard man. But I know you always strive to keep your reason clear and your judgment fair."

"Are you trying to flatter me, Sasha?"

"No, General. But I want you to consider admitting one truth to yourself: I did what I did to save our country from war. And I want you to consider that you left me no choice."

"Yes. I can see that. 'Comrade Prosecutor—my boss, General Orlov, made me contact the American spy, it was all his fault . . .'"

"Mockery, sir? Usually what people resort to when they have no better answer."

Vasin turned sharply onto the Kremlin Embankment, heading westward, pushing Orlov hard against the door as they swerved around the corner.

"Slower, please. Fine. You're right. I already said it. You're an idealist. Man of principle. A rebel—I've said that before about you, too, remember? Ach, Sasha. The spirit in you! No sense of proportion, of course. Superiority complex, which won't do at all. Always the cleverest. But balls . . . my word, yes." Orlov had been speaking half to himself, as though thinking out loud. But as they took another right at the Great Stone Bridge, he turned back to Vasin. "There is one thing more. Something that Morozov didn't say. Nothing about your American spy in Arzamas-Sixteen. That Colonel Pavel Korin, whom you shot dead. Not a word, though the traitor Morozov was certainly frightened. Babbling frightened. Poor fool still thinks he can save his life. So why no mention? Obviously we can stitch some stuff about Korin into his confession during our later conversations. But I'm interested—why nothing about the agent we thought he controlled? You know I hate mysteries, Sasha . . . Take a left here, please, and you can run me home. Join me for lunch with Katya."

Obediently, momentarily lost for words, Vasin changed lanes and merged into a stream of cars turning toward the Central Military Department Store and Kutuzovsky Prospekt. His mind was racing . . . Could there be any way to turn the Korin story to his advantage?

"You hate mysteries, sir? Is that why you gave up the priesthood?"

Orlov responded with one of his rare, explosive laughs.

"Oh, very good, Sasha. Droll. Next you're going to say that I chose playing God over serving him? Maybe you would be right. But: Korin, your dead American spy. Tell me."

"He must have had another controller. Someone who wasn't Morozov?"

"Interesting. Logical. Maybe your next assignment will be to find Korin's real controller. You'd like that, wouldn't you, Sasha? You'd be terribly well qualified."

A tiny, naïve part of Vasin leaped in jubilation at the chance of mercy. But of course it wasn't a chance at all. Vasin sneaked a glance across at Orlov and saw his usual mocking, sadistic grin.

"Ha! Oh, Sasha. No fooling you, I see. Damn, I'm going to miss you."

"You don't have to miss me. You can spare me. You should."

"Could I? Should I? Please tell me why."

"Because if you accept that I am not a traitor . . ."

"Sasha—may I finish your part for you? You have told me that your intentions were pure. That your motives were patriotic. You betrayed your country because you had no other choice. But there's something else you didn't say, I think. Please—don't be afraid. Say it."

Vasin hated Orlov most when the man was pretending to be reasonable.

"You're right, General. I wanted to . . ."

"You wanted to tell me that I am an opportunistic monster? That the security of our country is not safe in my hands? That you are the real defender of our Motherland, not men like me? Or words to that effect?"

"Something like that."

The fucking man had taken the words from his mouth. What had Vasin wanted from Orlov? Expected him to say? Certainly, despite his bravado, Vasin could see no real plan or path to clemency. He just wanted . . . to kill Orlov. Yes. With sudden, blinding clarity, Vasin realized that was what he wanted. This man, dead. If only to surprise the maddening asshole. Just to see the look on his face.

They were coming off the Kalinin Bridge past the soaring bulk of the Hotel Ukraine. Vasin floored the accelerator. The motor, revving flat out, pushed the heavily laden car to nearly fifty kilometers an hour. At the rise to the Victory Arch, Vasin made no attempt to take the U-turn that would have brought them to Orlov's front door. On the downward slope toward Poklonnaya Hill, they nudged sixty, then seventy, then eighty. The eight-lane road ahead of them was nearly empty.

A single traffic light remained until the final straight stretch of Kutuzovsky Prospekt. The light was turning red. Vasin could not risk Orlov hopping out, so he accelerated straight through the empty junction and kept his foot on the gas.

"*Ah*. I see."

The realization had begun to dawn in Orlov's mind that his life was in Vasin's hands. In the distance a convoy of ZiL trucks came into view. Ten-ton trucks. All Vasin had to do was swerve into them at top speed and his tinny car would be crushed flat. Vasin glanced across at his passenger, and was rewarded by the sight of his boss's face crumpling in fear.

"Such a pity about your son. Nikita, was it?"

Orlov was making an effort to keep his voice level.

"What the devil do you mean?"

Vasin's throat constricted in panic. The trucks were about three hundred yards away now, the distance closing fast.

"You didn't speak to your wife?" Orlov's voice was steadier now, though he spoke quickly. "Poor child. We took him in for a psychological assessment this morning. *Kontora* people. Excellent pediatric psychiatrists we have. But you know, with the boy's family history. His aunt, Klara. Terrible business. Even the sunniest children can suddenly crack."

A hundred yards now. Vasin's face was set in a rictus. Orlov had to be lying.

"You're bluffing."

"You think I would let you take me for a ride without taking any precautions? I thought you knew me, Sasha."

Nikita. In a psychiatric hospital. The thought of it paralyzed Vasin. Klara, his poor crazy sister, on her urine-soaked sheets, her eyes filled with pure fear.

He released the accelerator. The little car swung in the draft from the passing column of trucks as it lost speed. When he spoke, Vasin found his voice had shrunk to a humble squeak.

"Sorry, Comrade General. We seem to have missed your turn."

Orlov remained silent for a long moment.

"That's fine, Sasha. You can turn at the next light. Oh. I didn't tell you. Katya and I were discussing your next posting. You know she's very fond of you. She insisted I think of somewhere nice for you to go. I promised her I would."

So Katya had pleaded for his life.

"Yes," Orlov continued smoothly. "I thought maybe you should get away from the bustle of the big city, Sasha?"

Vasin rolled to a halt by the traffic light and switched his indicator for a left turn. The two men looked at each other. Vasin could find no words to speak to the man who was about to tear his life apart.

"You know, we are not so different, you and I."

Vasin shuddered.

"We both do think that we are right. We both think that we are cleverer than the men around us. And we are probably right. But you really want to know what the difference between you and Dzerzhinsky is? Felix had the entire apparatus of Soviet State Security to back his choices. And so do I. Whereas you have only your good intentions. Understand?"

Vasin nodded mutely, put the car into gear, and made a slow turn toward Orlov's apartment building.

"Sasha. This is my decision. I just want you to . . . *be*. You interest me. Not many people have ever dared challenge me. Perhaps one day you will be useful to me again, once you have learned a little humility. After all, who knows the way the world will turn? So I have decided to give you a promotion. To full colonel. A commander, Sasha."

The mockery in Orlov's voice was unmistakable. Vasin did not dare to take his eyes off the asphalt that rolled toward him.

"The commander of a penal colony. In Siberia. It's that—or the other thing."

Vasin gripped the wheel, silent, and pressed the accelerator.

AUTHOR'S NOTE

At dawn on October 2, 1962, a flotilla of four Project 641 diesel-electric submarines set out from the Soviet Arctic naval base of Sveromorsk. Their sealed orders, to be opened by the captains only when the boats reached open water, were to proceed to a new station at Mariel, Cuba. In addition to its complement of twenty-one conventional T-5 torpedoes, each boat was armed with a single nuclear-tipped torpedo known as the "special weapon." Each RDS-9 nuclear warhead was a steel ball just fifty-three centimeters wide, but it packed an explosive power equal to nearly five thousand tons of high explosives—about a quarter of the power of the atom bomb that destroyed Hiroshima. The flotilla's chief of staff was Captain First Class Vasily Arkhipov, who shipped on B-59. The previous summer, Arkhipov had survived a reactor accident on K-19, the USSR's first nuclear ballistic-missile submarine, which killed seventeen of his shipmates.

At ten to two on the afternoon of Monday, October 22, 1962, a team of KGB officers arrested Colonel Oleg Penkovsky of Soviet military intelligence as he walked down Gorky Street in central Moscow. He was charged with espionage for the Americans and the British. The arrest sent shock waves through the Soviet security establishment. Penkovsky had been a former Soviet military attaché in Ankara and had worked at the Soviet Committee for Scientific Research. He was also a personal friend of GRU head Colonel General Ivan Serov. Penkovsky—code-named Agent HERO by his CIA and MI6 handlers—was the most senior Soviet officer known to have worked for Western intelligence.

The information HERO provided on Operation Anadyr and on the Soviets' real nuclear capabilities in the run-up to the Cuban missile crisis played a key role in President John F. Kennedy's decision making.

Red Traitor is based on these two true stories. Though it is a work of fiction, many details are closely based on eyewitness accounts. The memoirs of Penkovsky himself and his MI6 handler, Greville Wynne, are the basis for the Moscow-based spy story; the memoirs of KGB Washington *rezident* Alexander Feklisov, for events in Washington. For the submarine drama, I have drawn on the memoirs of Captain Alexei Dubivko, commander of B-36; the diaries of Captain Third Class Anatoly Andreyev, deputy commander of B-36; video interviews with Captain First Class Rurik Ketov, commander of B-4; Senior Lieutenant Vadim Orlov, radio officer of B-59; Lieutenant Viktor Mikhailov, junior navigator of B-59; Lieutenant Gary Slaughter, communications officer of the USS *Cony;* and Lieutenant Andrew Bradick, antisubmarine warfare officer of the USS *Cony.*

Many of the characters in this book bear the names of real people. I have tried to be fair to their memory.

Vasily Arkhipov was, in the words of his widow, Olga, "a kind and calm person, a real human being." His fellow captain and friend Rurik Ketov of B-4 described him as "cool and level-headed. A true submariner." Though Arkhipov rarely spoke of his experiences during the reactor accident on K-19, his wife knew that it had affected him deeply. "He saw with his own eyes what radiation did to people—he saw them carried out of the reactor," Olga Arkhipova told a Russian documentary team in 2011. "That tragedy was the reason he said no to nuclear war."

Valentin Savitsky was a "hot-headed man," according to Ketov. During the tense hours when his submarine was suffering the impact of depth charges and sonar from half a dozen pursuing American ships, Savitsky became "furious" and "agitated," according to B-59's radio officer, Vadim Orlov. He "screamed" at his subordinates and ordered the assembly of the special weapon before being overruled by Arkhipov.

Ambassador Andrei Dobrynin and KGB *rezident* Alexander Feklisov deserve, alongside John and Robert Kennedy, the lion's share of credit for defusing the Cuban crisis. Dobrynin, a career diplomat with long experience in America, argued against the Kremlin's hubristic view that Kennedy was weak and would fold in the face of the news that Russian missiles had already been secretly deployed in Cuba. Feklisov, a worker's son from Moscow whose first job was at a locomotive factory before the war, worked his way up through the foreign intelligence department of the NKVD. He had been posted to the United States almost continually from 1941, and he had a far better feel for American politics than his masters in the Lubyanka. It fell to Feklisov, with his keen sense of what was politically possible for Kennedy, to draw up a face-saving deal that would allow Khrushchev to withdraw the missiles in exchange for a US promise not to invade Cuba. Feklisov's private lunch meeting with John A. Scali of ABC News at the Occidental Restaurant, two blocks from the White House, on October 26, 1962, to communicate the Soviet willingness to compromise was a crucial turning point in the crisis.

The Kennedys, for their part, also stood up to the combined voices of the US Joint Chiefs of Staff, who advised the President that the only way to resolve the crisis would be to invade Cuba or even launch a preemptive nuclear attack against Soviet missile bases there. Robert Kennedy kept in close touch with Dobrynin in the run-up to the crisis—the back channel that helped the Kennedys communicate a more conciliatory line than their public tough talk suggested. President Kennedy was also exceptionally careful to avoid an accidental slide into war, especially when it came to plans for the US Navy to intercept Soviet submarines bound for Cuba.

I have changed the names of three characters who are based on real people—my fictional traitors Oleg Morozov and Jack Dunlop, and the handless Major Tokarev.

The real Oleg Penkovsky offered to work for the CIA, and later the British MI6, because he feared that Soviet aggression and recklessness could lead the world to an accidental war. He was also disgusted by the force that Khrushchev had used to crush a reformist Communist movement in Hungary in 1956. By his own fragmentary account, published posthumously as *The Penkovsky Papers,* he was sick of the brutality and oppression of the Soviet state. Between June 1961 and his arrest the following October, Penkovsky photographed hundreds of pages of documents detailing the tiny true number of ballistic missiles in the Soviet nuclear arsenal, as well as on the secret Soviet deployment of R-12 missiles to Cuba. Elaborate security procedures were developed by the CIA and MI6 to protect HERO's identity, and his intelligence product was hand-couriered to the West via diplomatic bag.

The CIA station chief in Moscow, Wallace Baker, only realized that its top agent had been blown on November 2, 1962, two weeks after Penkovsky's actual arrest, when CIA officer Richard C. Jacob was detained while collecting a dead-letter drop. The real address was 5/6 Pushkin Street, not 25 Bolshaya Sadovaya Street, as in my story. Until the building was reconstructed in the late 1990s, the cast-iron radiator on the first-floor landing behind which Penkovsky would hide his microfilms was still intact. The drop that netted Jacob was a trap set by the KGB. Penkovsky had confessed that he signaled to his CIA handlers that a message was ready for collection via two wrong-number phone calls and a mark on a lamppost. HERO's handler, Greville Wynne, had been arrested in Budapest just before the Pushkin Street sting, en route to meeting his agent in Moscow. Jacob, as an accredited diplomat, was released. Wynne was sentenced to eight years' imprisonment but was released in a spy swap in April 1964.

According to Alexander Zagvozdin, chief KGB interrogator for the investigation, Penkovsky was questioned more than a hundred times before being convicted of treason by a three-man military court. He was shot on May 16, 1963. Later defector accounts that Penkovsky was cremated while still alive are unsupported by evidence.

The reasons why a man chooses to betray his country are complex. As my fictional General Orlov observes, every man justifies his actions by telling himself that he is serving a greater good. Penkovsky was, to his handler Wynne at least, a brave man who died for the cause of peace. My fictional Morozov is a much less sympathetic character, driven in part by anger at the Soviet regime's murder of his colleagues during Stalin's purges but mostly by vanity and a sense of personal affront. He is a cynic and a manipulator. Morozov is not Penkovsky. He is his dark twin.

———

The KGB had evidence of Penkovsky's treachery as early as October 1961. Their source was a Soviet spy in the US National Security Agency, a lowly former sergeant named Jack Dunlap who worked as an NSA civilian contractor. The technique used by my fictional Dunlop to steal documents is based on the Carroll Report into Dunlap's espionage. As personal chauffeur to NSA chief of staff Major-General Thomas M. Watlington, Dunlap had top-secret clearance and "no inspection" status. He would regularly collect papers from the General's desk and photocopy them en route to the typing pool and mailroom.

The real Dunlap was, according to US military investigators, a drunk who agreed to work for the KGB for money, not due to conviction. The KGB, for its part, was concerned that arresting Penkovsky immediately could jeopardize their well-placed agent in the NSA. There was also initially some question in the KGB whether Penkovsky was in fact working as a deliberate double agent, or "dangle," at the behest of his friend and boss Ivan Serov. The KGB therefore spent nearly a year building a "discovery case" against Penkovsky, hoping to catch him red-handed in order not to throw suspicion on their mole (or by some accounts, moles) in the NSA and, possibly, MI6.

Dunlap was never caught. He committed suicide by carbon monoxide poisoning in his car on July 23, 1963, a day after taking an FBI polygraph test. Because he died with a clean record, Dunlap is buried alongside other Army veterans at Arlington National Cemetery in Virginia. Like Morozov, my fictional Dunlop—the greedy Louisiana braggart who spies for money—is an unsympathetic character. To give the real man the benefit of the doubt, I have changed his name, albeit by a single letter.

Major Tokarev is based on a real-life war veteran named Vitaly Kabatov. Like Tokarev, Kabatov was a cavalry officer who lost both hands to a grenade near Smolensk. He married Saida, a university friend of my mother's, and wore heavy plastic prostheses. Remarkably, Vitaly was able to live a more or less normal life. On one memorable occasion I even saw him remove his plastic hands and play the piano, a little clumsily, with his stumps. He always said that he was better off than many of his comrades who had lost their lives.

Several veterans of the Cuban submarine flotilla outlived the USSR and the vow of secrecy that they had made to the Soviet Navy. Many told their stories after the fall of Communism in the form of memoirs and interviews with the newly free Russian press.

Captain Rurik Ketov of B-4 recalled the instructions on the use of the special weapon that Vice Admiral Rassokha gave just before they sailed for Cuba: " 'Write down when you should use these,' " Rassokha told the flotilla commanders. " 'In three cases. First, if you get a hole under the water. A hole in your hull. Second, a hole above the water. If you have to come to the surface, and they shoot at you, and you get a hole in your hull. And the third case—when Moscow orders you to use these weapons.' These were our instructions. And then he added, 'I suggest to you, commanders, that you use the nuclear weapons first, and then you will figure out what to do after that.' "

Captain Nikolai Shumkov, commander of B-130, recalled being told by Admiral Vitaliy A. Fokin, first deputy head of the Soviet Navy, "If they slap you on the left cheek, do not let them slap you on the right one."

It was clear to all the flotilla's skippers, Ketov recalled, that "for the first time in history, a commander had a nuclear weapon and the power to use it."

The Americans had no idea that the Soviet submarines were carrying nuclear weapons—just as the Soviets had no idea that the antisubmarine destroyers USS *Bache* and *Cony* were carrying nuclear depth charges. In my fiction, the Soviet flotilla is dispatched by hawks in the military in order to provoke a nuclear confrontation with the United States in case Khrushchev's nerve failed during the coming standoff. The truth is less dramatic, but in many ways more surprising. It seems that in the stress and chaos of the unfolding crisis, the Soviet high command and the Kremlin simply forgot about the existence of the Anadyr flotilla and their fatal weapons. Indeed, it emerged during the later inquiry that the chiefs of the Defense Ministry believed, absurdly, that the flotilla had been composed of nuclear-powered ballistic-missile submarines with their strict command-and-control procedures rather than a group of diesel-electric boats, each with its own nuclear weapon under the operational control of the commander.

The day after Kennedy announced his blockade—or "quarantine," as he phrased it, since a blockade is technically an act of war—of Cuba on October 22, 1962, the Soviet naval command ordered the four submarines to abort their progress toward Mariel and remain on station in the Sargasso Sea. And then, silence.

On board the Soviet submarines, the commanders and crew were all expecting nuclear war to break out imminently—and to be ordered to use their special weapons to attack the nearest American ships. B-36's captain, Alexei Dubivko, wrote that "the success of being the first to use our weapons depended on the timely reception of the signal to start combat operations . . . We were expecting such a signal from one hour to the next."

In the absence of any orders from Moscow, in high seas whipped up by Hurricane Ella, all four boats tuned into local US radio stations for news. On B-36, Captain Dubivko heard on Miami public radio that "President Kennedy [had] announced a blockade of the island of Cuba, and warned his people about a possibility of a thermonuclear conflict with the Soviet Union on the all-American radio; the Americans are preparing a powerful landing on Cuba; our missiles with nuclear warheads and service personnel are already in Cuba; special camps are being prepared on the Florida peninsula for Russian prisoners of war." On B-4, Ketov recalled that "everything I knew and everything I did was from listening to Kennedy."

The White House ExComm, a group of top advisors assembled by Kennedy to deal with the crisis, was aware that the Soviets might attempt to use submarines to run the US blockade. A force of more than a hundred ships—including vessels from allied South and Central American nations—was scrambled to intercept Soviet ships and hunt for submarines. As soon as weather permitted, medium-range P-3 Orion planes were also dispatched from Maryland to drop hundreds of sonar buoys across the sea-lanes to Cuba.

A transcript of the ExComm meeting on October 24 shows how worried Kennedy was that intercepting Soviet submarines could trigger a shooting war. "If he doesn't surface or if he takes some action—takes some action to assist the merchant ship, are we just going to attack him anyway?" Kennedy asked Secretary of Defense Robert McNamara. "At what point are we going to attack him? I think we ought to wait on that today. We don't want to have the first thing we attack as a Soviet submarine."

"The plan is . . . to send antisubmarine helicopters out to harass the submarine," McNamara replied. "And they have weapons and devices that can damage the submarine. And the plan, therefore, is to put pressure on the submarine, move it out of the area by that pressure, by the pressure of potential destruction, and then make the intercept. But this is only a plan and there are many, many uncertainties." According to Robert Kennedy, the discussion of how to force the Soviet submarines to the surface was "the time of greatest worry for the President. His hand went up to his face and covered his mouth and he closed his fist. His eyes were tense, almost gray, and we just stared at each other across the table."

McNamara and the chief of the Navy Staff came up with a system of nonlethal signals using practice depth charges. On October 25, the White House sent a "Notice to Mariners" message to the Soviet Embassy in Washington detailing the US Navy's procedures for intercepting vessels suspected of breaking the "quarantine" of Cuba. Under the section on "Submarine Surfacing and Identification Procedures," the US Navy warned that its ships would drop four or five harmless low-explosive sound devices accompanied by an international sonar code signal to "rise to surface." The notice contained an assurance that all signaling devices were harmless. The Soviet Embassy never acknowledged the message. In any case, there was no way for Moscow to signal submarines that were submerged.

As the Sargasso Sea calmed and the underwater thermocline under which the Soviet boats could hide from sonar detection disappeared, US destroyers first located B-36 and began bombarding her with the agreed-upon depth charge and sonar signals. "Our sonar could effectively be used as an offensive weapon," recalled Lieutenant Gary Slaughter, communications officer of the USS *Cony*. "It's like you have five strong men pounding on a barrel. It's gotta drive them crazy . . . There were so many weapons, so many sonars—he was like a rabbit inside a small cage with fifteen hounds outside the cage and fifteen hawks above the cage. That rabbit was dead."

According to the USS *Cony*'s antisubmarine warfare officer, Lieutenant Andrew Bradick, their orders were to "hunt [the subs] to exhaustion. You would keep contact with the submarine and he could have to surface because his batteries were going flat." The US ships kept close to the Soviet submarines, never letting up. "We knew that they had been under great strain for a long time," said Slaughter. "It was hot, it was miserable. So what we were trying to apply was basically passive torture."

B-36's deputy commander, Captain Third Rank Anatoly Andreyev, described the ordeal of the sonar lashing in a journal he kept in the form of a letter to his wife. "For the last four days, they didn't even let us come up to the periscope depth. My head is bursting from the stuffy air . . . Today three sailors fainted from overheating again . . . We are sailing with a risk of dropping down to six thousand meters. This is how much we have under [our boat]. The regeneration of air works poorly, the carbon dioxide content is rising, and the electric power reserves are dropping. Those who are free from their shifts, are sitting immobile, staring at one spot . . . Temperature in the sections is above 50. In the diesel [sic—he meant the electric engine room]—61 degrees."

At nine in the morning of October 27, 1962, as the US fleet was chasing B-36 across the Sargasso Sea, a CIA U-2F spy plane piloted by USAF major Rudolf Anderson took off from McCoy Air Force Base near Orlando, Florida. Just over three hours into his flight over Russian installations in Cuba, Anderson's aircraft was shot down by an S-75 Dvina surface-to-air missile over the northeastern town of Banes. When Kennedy was told about the crisis's first fatality, he went quiet and said, "Blood has been shed." The order to fire had been given by a Soviet officer acting on his own authority.

Khrushchev, terrified that events on the ground were about to spin out of control, ordered the Soviet commander in Cuba, General Issa Pliyev, to instruct all his batteries not to fire on any more US planes. Kennedy, for his part, wisely chose not to react. But his brother sent a harsh personal message to Soviet ambassador Dobrynin to signal that the White House's patience was nearly at an end. The crisis was in its critical stage. "You have drawn first blood," Robert Kennedy wrote. "The president has decided against advice . . . not to respond militarily to that attack, but he [Dobrynin] should know that if another plane was shot at . . . we would take out all the SAMs and antiaircraft . . . And that would almost surely be followed by an invasion."

Just minutes after the wreckage of Rudolf Anderson's U-2F had tumbled to earth over eastern Cuba, the USS *Bache* made its first contact with a second Soviet submarine off the northern coast of the Dominican Republic—B-59. The destroyers USS *Bache, Beale, Cony, Eaton,* and *Murray,* backed by the aircraft carrier USS *Randolph,* closed in on B-59 and began the same sonar and depth-charge lashing they had been meting out to B-36 for days.

Captain Alexei Dubivko of B-36 had suffered the American sonic bombardment without considering the use of the special weapon. But B-59's captain, Valentin Savitsky, was a man of a different temperament. Savitsky decided that the detonations were an attack, not an aggressive form of signaling. "There is a specific signal that we have and that is three explosions you have to surface," recalled B-59's junior navigator, Viktor Mikhailov. "The American signal was not three."

B-59's radio officer, Vadim Orlov, remembered that "the Americans hit us with something stronger than the grenades—apparently with a practice depth bomb. We thought—that's it—the end. After this attack, the totally exhausted Savitsky, who in addition to everything was not able to establish connection with the General Staff, got furious. He summoned the officer who was assigned to the nuclear torpedo, and ordered him to assemble it to battle readiness. 'Maybe the war has already started up there, while we are doing somersaults here'— screamed agitated Valentin Grigorievich, justifying his order. 'We're gonna blast them now! We will die, but we will sink them all—we will not become the shame of the fleet.'"

Savitsky ordered the weapons officer whose sole responsibility was to look after the special weapon to assemble and arm it, and demanded Maslennikov's half of the arming key in order to do so. But he did not give orders to load the weapon or to flood the torpedo tube.

Exactly what happened next lies between the lines of the survivors' testimony. Radio officer Orlov would not have been personally present in B-59's tiny command center during the tense confrontation between Captain Savitsky and flotilla chief of staff Arkhipov—but his recollection is the closest we can get to an eyewitness account to the standoff. "We did not fire the nuclear torpedo—Savitsky was able to rein in his wrath," Orlov recalled. "After consulting with Second Captain Vasily Alexandrovich Arkhipov and his deputy political officer, Ivan Semenovich Maslennikov, he made the decision to come to the surface." Olga Arkhipova said that her husband told her that he "knew it was madness to fire a torpedo with a nuclear warhead . . . [and] didn't hesitate to say no."

What Orlov tactfully described as Savitsky's "consultation" with Arkhipov must have in reality been a tense clash of authority. Savitsky commanded the boat. As Ketov put it, "On board a submarine, the captain is next to God." The second missile key was, as per regulations, held by the senior Communist Party representative on board—Political Officer Maslennikov. Arkhipov, as flotilla chief of staff, had no official executive role in B-59's chain of command. But though Savitsky and Arkhipov held equal rank, Arkhipov had higher authority—and formally he would have to consent to the firing of the special weapon. On two of the flotilla's boats—B-36 and B-130—the captain and political officer alone could have fired their nuclear torpedo. On B-59 and B-4, which carried Brigade Commander Vitaliy Agafonov, the decision effectively needed the consent of three officers. The fact that the hotheaded Savitsky's belligerence was matched and overruled by Arkhipov's trauma-inspired horror of nuclear weapons was pure chance. A coincidence that saved the world from nuclear war.

As Arkhipov and Savitsky argued, dusk was falling over Washington. "'The sun is setting. It could be the last sunset we ever see,'" McNamara said to Secretary of State Dean Rusk, recalled White House advisor John Stoessinger. "And that's when I got scared."

With the Soviets given a final warning after the downing of the U-2 earlier that day, the Cuban missile crisis was just one more violent incident away from spiraling out of both Kennedy's and Khrushchev's control. A nuclear attack by a Soviet submarine on a US carrier battle group on the evening of October 27, 1962, would, without a shadow of a doubt, have resulted in a full-scale retaliation by Kennedy.

Astronomical twilight in the Sargasso Sea fell at 18:18. Just over an hour and a half later, B-59 and B-36 finally surfaced. They found themselves in a pool of floodlights from the *Beale*, *Bache*, and *Cony*. A Navy band on the deck of the *Bache* played jazz to emphasize the US ships' peaceful intent. The submarines did not respond to signals, but the crew were allowed on deck in groups to breathe fresh air. Around four hours later, when the batteries would have been half-charged, the submarines dived once more and turned east toward home.

Arkhipov's role in averting nuclear catastrophe did him little good when the flotilla returned to Sveromorsk. The submarines had been discovered and forced to surface, which the command of the Red Banner Northern Fleet considered as little better than surrender. Each captain was required to present a report of events during the mission to the Soviet deputy minister of defense, Marshal Andrei Grechko. Grechko was infuriated by the commanders' failure to follow strict radio silence after they had been forced to surface by the Americans. Grechko "removed his glasses and hit them against the table in fury, breaking them into small pieces and abruptly leaving the room after that," recalled one of the officers present.

" 'It would have been better if we had all been drowned,' " Arkhipov's wife recalled him saying. "That's why he didn't like talking about it. They didn't appreciate what he had gone through."

Though Arkhipov never again had an operational command, he rose to the rank of vice admiral and retired honorably in 1985. He died on August 19, 1998, at the age of seventy-two. Recalling the Cuban missile crisis in 2002, Robert McNamara said that the world had "come very close" to nuclear war, "closer than we knew at the time." Kennedy advisor Arthur M. Schlesinger Jr. said the October standoff was "not only the most dangerous moment of the Cold War. It was the most dangerous moment in human history." A room in the CIA's headquarters at Langley, Virginia, is named for Arkhipov. It seems a scant memorial to the man whose level-headedness saved the world from nuclear war. This book is dedicated to his memory.

—OM
Wytham Abbey, Oxfordshire, August 13, 2020

FURTHER READING

OLEG PENKOVSKY

Jeremy Duns, *Dead Drop: The True Story of Oleg Penkovsky and the Cold War's Most Dangerous Operation* (London: Simon and Schuster, 2013).

Oleg Penkovsky, *The Penkovsky Papers* (London: Collins, 1965).

Greville Wynne, *The Man from Moscow: The Story of Wynne and Penkovsky* (London: Hutchinson, 1967).

THE CUBAN MISSILE CRISIS

Graham Allyson and Philip Zelikow, *Essence of Decision: Explaining the Cuban Missile Crisis,* 2nd ed. (New York: Longman, 1999).

James Blight, *The Shattered Crystal Ball: Fear and Learning in the Cuban Missile Crisis* (Savage, MD: Rowman and Littlefield, 1990).

Alexander Fursenko and Timothy Naftali, *One Hell of a Gamble: Khrushchev, Castro and Kennedy, 1958–1964* (New York: W. W. Norton, 1997).

Raymond Garthoff, "New Evidence on the Cuban Missile Crisis: Khrushchev, Nuclear Weapons, and the Cuban Missile Crisis," in *Cold War International History Bulletin* 11 (Winter 1998).

Anatoly Gribkov and William Smith, *Operation Anadyr: U.S. and Soviet Generals Recount the Cuban Missile Crisis* (Edition Q, 1994).

Peter Huchthausen, *October Fury* (Hoboken, NJ: John Wiley, 2002).

THE CUBAN SUBMARINE FLOTILLA

Captain Third Class Anatoly Andreyev's diary, in Nikolai Cherkashin, *Povsednevnaya Zhizn' Rossiiskikh Podvodnikov* [Daily Life of Russian Submariners] (Moscow: Molodaya Gvardiya, 2000).

Thomas S. Blanton and William Burr, "The Submarines of October: U.S. and Soviet Naval Encounters During the Cuban Missile Crisis," *National*

FURTHER READING

Security Archive Electronic Briefing Book 75 (October 31, 2002), https://nsarchive2.gwu.edu/NSAEBB/NSAEBB75/.

Alexi Dubivko, "In the Depths of the Sargasso Seas," in *On the Edge of the Nuclear Precipice* (Moscow: Gregory Page, 1988).

Alexander Mozgovoi, *Kubinskaya Samba Kvarteta Foxtrotov* [The Cuban Samba of the Foxtrot Quartet] (Moscow: Voennyi Parad, 2002).

Svetlana V. Savranskaya, "New Sources on the Role of Soviet Submarines in the Cuban Missile Crisis," *Journal of Strategic Studies* (2005) 28:2.

ACKNOWLEDGMENTS

Many people helped this book in its journey onto the page—first and foremost my dedicated and brilliant editor, Robert Bloom at Doubleday, who worked tirelessly above and beyond the call of duty to shape and polish *Red Traitor*. Without my agent Toby Mundy I would never have hooked up with Rob, or thought to make Alexander Vasin the hero of a trilogy. And without the encouragement of my friends I would never have imagined writing my first thriller in the first place. Particular thanks to Lisa Hilton, Jonny Dymond, Andrew Jeffreys, and Charles Cumming for all their help and support while the book was being written. And to Xenia, Nikita, and Teddy for putting up with a writer in the house, which is no easy fate. Finally, a bow to the real Alexander Vasin, my late uncle, who as a young Soviet tank commander lost a leg outside Smolensk in 1944 but despite his disability rose to be the USSR's deputy minister of justice and a wise and loving husband to my aunt Lenina.

ABOUT THE AUTHOR

Owen Matthews reported on conflicts in Bosnia, Lebanon, Afghanistan, Chechnya, Iraq and Ukraine and was *Newsweek* magazine's bureau chief in Moscow from 2006 to 2016. He is the author of *Black Sun*, the first book in a series of political thrillers featuring KGB officer Alexander Vasin, and several non-fiction books, including *Stalin's Children*, *Glorious Misadventures* and *An Impeccable Spy*. He lives in Moscow and Oxford.

You can follow him on Twitter: @owenmatth